THE
SINGULARITY
PROJECT

THE
SINGULARITY PROJECT

F. M. Busby

A TOM DOHERTY ASSOCIATES BOOK

NEW YORK

THE SINGULARITY PROJECT

Copyright © 1993 by F. M. BUSBY

This book is printed on acid-free paper.

A Tor Book
Published by Tom Doherty Associates, Inc.
175 Fifth Avenue
New York, N.Y. 10010

Edited by David G. Hartwell.

Tor® is a registered trademark of Tom Doherty Associates, Inc.

Library of Congress Cataloging-in-Publication Data

Busby, F. M.
        The singularity project / F. M. Busby.
                p.   cm.
        "A Tom Doherty Associates book."
        ISBN 0-312-85443-9
        I. Title.
     PS3552.U79S56   1993
     813'.54—dc20   92-42575
                                                                CIP

First edition: February 1993

Printed in the United States of America

0 9 8 7 6 5 4 3 2 1

To Wrai and Carol Ballard

THE
SINGULARITY
PROJECT

CHAPTER ONE

Until the fat man yelled, I didn't see the knife. "Tixo!" and then a string of syllables that made no sense—but the little Indian, standing his ground in front of me, put the knife away. On the haft I caught a glimpse of jewels.

All five feet of him stayed put. My own five-four must have loomed, but Tixo's economical, dried-up face gave no sign. The black eyes reflected no more shine than a stone. He wasn't going to let me into Coogan's office, and that was that.

I turned to face fat Borg. Slaty blue eyes, sunk into hummocky flesh: I didn't expect I'd ever come to like Coogan's front man. He said, "You'd better leave, Banning. Tixo is extremely—and single-mindedly—loyal."

No argument; nodding, I agreed. "I noticed. Thanks, Borg." Not looking toward Tixo at all now, I walked past Borg to the outer door. The intelligent move was to pass through that door while I still could. So I did. But before closing it, I looked back and said, "Tell Coogan I'll see him later."

I didn't wait to see Borg's reaction. Or Tixo's.

Looking at major components of the Seattle skyline while I waited for the elevator, and then riding down from the Trosper Building's twenty-third floor, gave me time to think. Not that any of it managed to make a great deal of sense . . .

* * *

Dauna brought the idea home; someone phoned it to her at work. She's Associate Editor at *Westside Weekly*, and as long as the magazine stays afloat, she likes the job.

She's good, too, and not only with writing: you ought to see her do on-screen graphics from verbal description.

The magazine, though, has policy problems. Its Chief Editor wants to expand area coverage, while the publisher's after concentrating on increased local circulation. Dauna's not sure which one has the answer, so she stays out of the hassle and pays attention to her own work. She may be a young scrawny beautiful bean pole, but the love of my life is no dummy.

It was after dinner when she told me. She'd washed her hair and was blow-drying the length of its light-brown mass; something more than two feet, it had to be. She ran out of Chablis so I brought a refill. She thanked me, then said, "Oh, Mitch: something I forgot, from work today. There may be a story in it, for one of us."

I sat to listen. "So tell." With me, writing's a sideline; I'm a freelance of sorts, but my lance tilts toward designing communications systems, giving the customer the cheapest setup that will do the job. The phone company doesn't like me much.

But I do write articles, science-popularizations and sheer speculation, for any market that will pay. It's good side money, though irregular; nothing that resembles steady income. So if Dauna had a subject, I wanted to hear it.

After a few more seconds she shut the dryer off. "Somebody named Elihu Coogan is trying to sell Aladdin's lamp to Howard Hughes, junior. The asking price has two commas in it."

Translation from the Daunish: this Coogan, whoever he was, was working on George Detweiler's fascination with weird gadgets, and trying to snocker at least a million out of the deal.

I thought about it. The Howard Hughes joke stretched fact quite a bit, but for a local entrepreneur, George was making his mark. When the old man—Arnold Detweiler, who built the business—had his stroke, George quit being a playboy and took over; within two years Detweiler, Ltd. was on the Big Board—and George was only beginning. He'd tackle any idea, no matter how far-out it might seem. And a surprising number of his guesses paid off.

As his holdings grew, George did take on a certain aura of eccentricity. Maybe the Howard Hughes bit wasn't so far off, at that.

I'd known George, in a way; at prep school he was three years ahead of me. Somebody once asked me what he'd been like in his teens. I didn't have to think. "A prick with ears."

Now Dauna shrugged. "That's all I know; my tipster wouldn't give his name. What he said was that Coogan's trying to promote himself a real package, and that the bait is right down Detweiler's alley." Brows raised. "Mitch? What do you think?"

My turn to shrug. "Where's the story?" I sipped from my own glass. "For me, that is; yours I can see. But—"

She swung her hair forward in front of her shoulders and began smoothing the two falls down across her petite breasts; another thing I could see was that this conversation might not last much longer. She said, "I'm not sure I have a story. Farringen was interested, but then he talked with Charles Wilford and now he isn't." Ned Farringen's the Chief Editor; Wilford wears the publisher hat.

"Uh-huh. Afraid of losing the Detweiler ads?"

She nodded. "Probably. I didn't get a flat no, but—"

"Sure. Well, that's the game." Lousy, sometimes. "Now, tell me where *I* come in. I'm no reporter; my markets don't go after financial shenanigans."

Dauna leaned forward. "Coogan's gadget; what else?" She shook her head; I liked the effect. "I don't know what it is, at all. But you've done nutty inventor stories before. Why not again?"

I surely had. One of them paid our way to Hawaii once, when the weather stank and we needed a change. On the Boeing SST, strictly primo class. All right. "Where can I find this Coogan? You have any idea?"

"Sure I do." On someone else her smile might be a little toothy, but for her it's just right. "The frail, courageous girl, braving all odds, ravaged the secret files of the implacable enemy and obtained the vital data."

That one I couldn't translate; I waited.

"Coogan's in the new phone book. Offices in the Trosper Building."

I got up and so did she. Even barefoot she stood four inches the taller. But if it didn't bother Dauna, it didn't bother me, either.

She and I had been together, by then, about a year and a half; we met a few months after my divorce. I'd been married long enough, before things came apart, to have two kids walking and talking but not in school yet. Liliane remarried and moved to Hilo; Dauna and I visited the new family briefly when we were over there, but our welcome lasted about an hour so we left.

Child support strapped me sometimes, which was why the writing money came in so handy. I wouldn't have minded, really, if I could have seen Pat and Nicky more than once in a while.

That's one reason Dauna and I avoided the subject of marriage: financially I wasn't my own man, and wouldn't be for maybe fifteen years. Dauna, now, wasn't sure she wanted kids at all. But if she ever should, sometime—well, I guessed, though she'd never said any such thing, that she wouldn't be wanting *short* kids. I could see it.

The way we got together was really funny. But that's one story I don't tell around; it's too precious for sharing. The important thing was that once we got past the absurdity of the situation, everything clicked. And eighteen months later, give or take some, still worked. If ever it didn't, I'd know.

As I knew, we looked odd together. I don't think I look so bad per se. Okay, I'm short, and my squarish face is outsized, with a permanent blush. Dark curly hair suits me but the temples are heading for ebb tide and my crown-cowlick is the advance marker for someday's bald spot. I'm built wide for my size: big bones, and I've worked at the muscles. Liliane used to call me Teddy Bear and I liked it.

But alongside Dauna? Tall, slim, with that hair and the wide-slanted grey-green eyes? Wide mouth, too, and cheekbones to break a sculptor's heart. Hell, I know what everybody saw. Two people trying out for parts in *The Tempest*. Guess which.

The age thing was okay. I was born the day of Kennedy's nomination; Dauna was a week old when Camelot ended.

Her real name is Gudrun, not Dauna; the paper where she once worked thought Dauna made a better by-line, and later she kept it for reader familiarity. That was before she tried her hand at TV news, but gave up because all she caught were the scut jobs.

Her last name, Haig, is for real. Like the rest of her.

Next morning after Dauna left for work I called Joey Aguilar, down at the *Times*. Elihu Coogan he'd never heard of. And anything he might know about George Detweiler, he couldn't say. Howard Hughes, Jr.? Maybe so, at that.

The Trosper Building's management office referred me to a rental agency. Teal-Hennings, I gathered, handled quite a string of properties, both downtown and suburban. A woman there gave me my first solid info: two months ago, Elihu Coogan had leased Suite 2310-14. Which was to say, he'd moved in then; the deal had been signed somewhat earlier. Sure; that's how he made it into the new phone book.

So what did I have? Not much—except in my real job, some work to do on a system layout, suggested by the telephone company rep, that was overdesigned for my client's needs. Part of the answer was that the phone moguls were peddling more message capacity than Pentco Fabrications would need for maybe five years. Even then they'd likely stay in plain old teletype, not a computer net. Among other differences, such as costs, TTY systems never have virus problems.

I called Steve Chang, my liaison at Pentco; after greetings I told him, "What I missed is that you don't need eight-level capability and the channels to carry it. Five-level, and narrow band telegraph links, can handle your load just fine.''

He cleared his throat. ''When we inquired about that, the phone company wasn't encouraging. Do you think—?''

''I think they're high-grading you. The older stuff's still in their ratebook; they have to provide it if you ask. And another thing we can kick around . . .''

Not much later, I hung up feeling good. I like coming up with answers that let me feel I'm earning my pay.

Having skipped breakfast I was hungry, so I lunched on night-before-last leftovers. It's a mistake, I feel, to eat the same thing two meals in a row.

Then I realized I had the whole day, what was left of it, all to myself. Why not look in on Elihu Coogan?

I didn't call ahead for an appointment.

I'd like to meet the man who designed that house of ours. It sits on a bluff, far above the street where the garage is. Somebody was a bug for comfort and convenience; the garage stairway's in a tunnel. Every time I used it, I felt like a kid in a *secret* tunnel. I suppose costs were a lot lower when the place was built.

Dauna had taken her Vee-Dub Jetta. My Volvo lacked the zoomie I remembered from my dad's great old 144S (when we hadn't begun to worry about pollution, OPEC was only a shadow on the horizon, and fuel had some real octane to it): considerably fewer horses, and cost maybe eight times as much. Handled like an angel, though; I guess progress is whatever you want to call it. The computerized works gave a quick start; I left for downtown. Light traffic; sooner than I expected, I reached the waterfront and parked under the viaduct. The unprepossessing Trosper Building was three steep blocks uphill; I was glad the morning's rain had stopped.

Without too much stop-and-go the elevator got me to the twenty-third. Suite 2310-14 was to my left; along the corridor I walked on thick fibrous carpet between walls of tinted glass, further shielded by dark Mylar shades. The decor might or might not have had class, but I'm sure it cost a bundle.

The door of 2310 read "Progress, Inc.: Transportation Specialists." The *g* in "Progress" was on crooked; dependable help is hard to find. I went in anyway.

The light in the reception area was dimmer than I expected. It took me two blinks and a shift of mental gears to accept the fat man behind the desk as a receptionist. He looked no more pleased than I felt. "You want something?"

The desk nameplate read "Ansel Borg, Liaison." I paused for a good look at him: pale and paunchy, with a blond crew-cut going thin on top, and hardly any eyebrows. He wore a grey suit; the label should have credited Omar. I said, "I'm Mitch Banning. My business, Mr. Borg, is with Elihu Coogan. Can you help me?"

His eyes hid under lowered ridges. "With what?"

Not promising. I said, "With checking me in to see Mr. Coogan, for starters. Wouldn't you think? A little talk . . ."

Two men came in the same door I'd used. One was taller than most people who don't play basketball for a living—six-six, maybe—but crowding fifty, when even Harlem Globetrotters tend to retire. Thin and erect, he walked fast; I registered an unpruned bush of red hair going a bit grey, large deep-set brown eyes straddling a big beak nose, whiskers trimmed down to mustache and goatee. Not stopping, the man said, "Anything new, Borg?"

"Nothing important, Mr. Coogan," and the tall man walked on, into a farther office. I turned toward its closing door and found the other newcomer in my way. A very small man, but looking solid where he stood.

I had no idea of his origins: Filipino, maybe, or Malay. But he was one of those people whose faces give nothing away. I turned back to Ansel Borg. "Can I see Mr. Coogan now, do you suppose?"

"No." I waited for more data; Borg said, "Mr. Coogan initiates his own appointments."

I glanced again toward the small man, small even to me. Jerking my attention back to himself, Ansel Borg said, "Don't bother trying to influence Tixo. He comes from the Amazon Valley; Mr. Coogan and I are probably the only persons in North America who speak his language. He understands no other."

The big man made it all sound as if he'd just proved something. I couldn't figure what he meant; I had no intention of arguing with the help. I turned to have a better look at Tixo, standing rooted in front of Coogan's door.

That's when Borg yelled, and Tixo put away the knife I hadn't seen him take to hand, and I got my confused butt out of there.

CHAPTER TWO

Outside, rain again—a halfhearted drizzle that would take some time to wet anyone down very much. Walking to my car, missing each light and having to wait for it to change, I thought about Elihu Coogan. He rang no bells; he wasn't anyone I would have seen before—but somehow he seemed familiar. And whatever he was doing here, I'd lay odds it had a shady side.

I drove home and garaged the Volvo. Before climbing the tunnel stairway I checked the mailbox. Junk mail, mostly; it burns me, having first-class postage subsidize all that nuisance stuff.

People sometimes kid me about being behind the times, doing business by mail and phone. Unfortunately, the alternatives have their own drawbacks.

I tried fax for a while, but there's junk there, too. A more virulent kind: not only does it print out on your own paper, but it ties up your line when a customer might be using it. Oh, they've tried passing restrictive laws, but the junkers simply move operations to another jurisdiction. I suppose regulation will win eventually, but meanwhile I don't need the hassle.

I gave the computer net idea a whirl, too, figuring the new and improved virus traps should make things safe enough. That part did work out fairly well; I lost some job estimate files once, but the customers were patient about it. What eventually screwed me up was the introduction of Gigabyte Power ("Up your RAM!") to commercial espionage, for real-time code breaking. The outfits I dealt with dropped off the regular networks and invested in dedicated fiber optics links. Fine for them, but too rich for my blood.

Oh, I still kept my computer; I *love* those crazy voodoo boxes. But strictly for home use, on the principle of avoiding crowds during flu season. For outside communication requiring hard copy, it was back to the Post Awful.

In this day's batch I found one envelope from Seaboard Ventures; upstairs I roundfiled the rest and took that one, along with a cup of coffee, to my office area. Then I opened it.

Well, good. In a way, at least: Seaboard liked the system I'd roughed out, but now they wanted to add four stations. Which complicated matters. When I'd specified the limitations, their spokesman assured me the problem wouldn't arise. I got on the horn to Arnie Kreghler, their Chief Engineer, and put the question again.

"It's all right, Mitch," he said. "This latest change is final; consider it solid."

"That's what they said the last time. Could you check again, Arnie? One more expansion would require adding a whole new module; the redesign and extra gear would cost half again what we agreed. Just be sure they understand the problem; right? And I'll fire in a memo, confirming." Always make sure these things are on record. At both ends . . .

A half hour later he called back; yes, the plans were now firm. I promised him the necessary modifications in tomorrow's mail. In point of fact the work took me less than an

hour, not counting a snack break. I took the revised estimate, plus cover memo, down to the mailbox. The drizzle
had stopped.

Back upstairs I put a CD in the stereo. A potpourri of old
stuff, not loud; sounds to relax with. I am, admittedly, your
basic unreconstructed midcentury nostalgia buff: music,
comic books, movies, the whole loop. Why, my *Casablanca* disk is the decolorized version.

I leaned back, to enjoy. Seaboard was off my mind now,
and Pentco also. Elihu Coogan wasn't, though—nor
George Detweiler.

On the stereo it was 1970: Tony Orlando wanted Dawn to
rap three times on the ceiling; then he was telling Candida
that according to the gypsy, he and she could make it
together. Eyes closed, halfway dozing, I was being ten years
old again. Like the time I met my dad for lunch downtown,
at the little café across from the courthouse, and the juke-
box was noodling, and—

Wide-awake, I sat up. *What the hell was Elihu Coogan
doing there?*

Only it wasn't quite Coogan. The disk came to its end;
my memory picture faded. I reset the CD to run again; the
trigger was there, if I could find it. After a time, into 1969
with Paul letting it be, Dauna hollered "Hi, Mitch!"

I stopped play, and stood. She started to talk, but I cut
in. "Just kiss hello for now; all right? I'm onto something,
have to concentrate." Her startled frown went away; she
came over for greeting, squeezed my shoulder, and headed
for the kitchen.

I hit Play again, and couldn't quite remember who it was,
asking Ma to look what they'd done to her song. Once
more I sat back, eyes closed.

Not even the passage in French did it for me. Then the
sequence cut to '67, with Peter Noone wanting no milk
today, while I thought of the little beanery, and my dad
talking about the trial he was working on for the prosecu-
tor's staff, and—

—and there was Coogan again! Now the recall came clear.

Not the same, no. He'd been balding early; the bushy red hair, now, had to be a wig. He no longer wore the thick glasses, and the mustache and goatee were new. But through Peter's plaint came memory of my dad's voice. "There he is, Mitch! Emil the Stork, himself!"

I cut the sound, and stood. Dauna looked at me. "Emil Storchesson," I said. "Emil the Stork. Walking out from lunch, he towered over his lawyer." Of course Dauna had no idea what I meant. "The man tried the biggest scam that ever hit Miami, and almost made it work. My dad helped prosecute, which is why I was interested at age ten, and Emil's trial made two weeks of headlines. I wonder how long he's been out."

Dauna's eyes went wider than usual. "Mitch—what in the world are you talking about?"

"Elihu Coogan." So I told her about Ansel Borg, and Tixo the little Indian, and Tixo's knife. "Maybe I should try to have a word with George Detweiler."

Eyes narrowed now, she shook her head. "Mitch. This Stork person: you're talking something that happened more than twenty years ago. Even if it *is* the same man, if you tell Detweiler that Coogan's a crook and it turns out that this time he isn't—"

Dauna can talk straight English when she wants to. Yes. If the Stork *had* gone honest, and I went to Detweiler and ruined whatever deal there was, I wouldn't like myself much. And Storchesson—Coogan—could likely sue my ass off.

I stood. "All right. After dinner I'm going down to the library. Maybe they have microfilm of old Miami papers."

"What for?"

"I need a way to get in and see Coogan."

The Main Library is downtown; on a Friday evening, parking's a bitch. The employees' lot was only half full so I took a chance. Inside, at the filmed-journals section, getting access to a viewer didn't take long.

I found the trial, all right. No point in looking later; the Stork's release from prison, whenever, wouldn't make news. I made prints of the better news-spreads—three with pics—and paid for them.

My car hadn't been towed, which does happen there sometimes, so I went home and showed Dauna what I had. She said, "Do you think this will get you a look at Aladdin's lamp?"

"Who knows? Maybe the Stork will even let me rub it."

Given a choice, I come awake slowly and rise late. The next morning, waking and dozing and following my uncopyrighted exercise program of turning over every time I do wake, I thought a lot. Why did I want to get involved—with Elihu Coogan, Stork or no Stork—or for that matter, with George Detweiler? Just to do an offbeat article that might net me a few hundred?

Or because Borg and Tixo had put a kink in my pride? That was silly. Silly or not, when I finally got out of bed, I found my half-awake mind had decided to go ahead. Full steam.

Still less than bright-eyed I did all the alliterative morning chores, of which several are shave, shine, shower, and shampoo. I used to have a beard, but alongside Dauna I looked like one of the Seven Dwarves so I gave it up. Even though I hate shaving.

My cooking is an adventure in the classic sense—meaning, there's no knowing how things will go. The eggs came out well; I felt heartened to the day's challenge. Until I stopped to think about it clearly—which, washing up the dishes including last night's, I tried to do.

All right. First step, call Coogan's office. Borg answered. He didn't give his name, just "Progress, Incorporated." But I recognized the voice.

"Good morning, Mr. Borg. Mitchell Banning here. I did promise, you'll recall, to get back to Mr. Coogan as soon as possible."

Wishing I could see Borg's face I sat through silence until

he said, "I told you, Mr. Coogan initiates his own appointments. He hasn't indicated any desire to see you."

Ah, so. "Tell him I want to discuss storks. If not with him, then with a number of other people." Including George Detweiler, but it never pays to put all your chips on the first roll. Borg asked me to hold, so I did.

After nearly five minutes he came on again. "Mr. Coogan will see you at one-thirty. Be here on time."

I assured him I would. Thanks didn't seem necessary.

The Trosper Building was its usual featureless, boxy self; for years, so-called architects filled our cities with oversized cornflakes containers and got paid for it. I envy them the money but not the grade of self-respect.

Crossing the lobby I saw a group leaving an elevator and recognized one: Tixo, the wee warrior. He wasn't looking in my direction. Stepping into an already crowded car I punched for twenty-three, then held the door for a wheel-chaired woman; before we headed up, several more folks jammed in. The woman wheeled out at six; when I got off, after a frustrating number of slow, delaying stops, only one man had outlasted me.

Neither the corridor nor 2310-14 had changed. Nor, at the desk, had Ansel Borg, who gave me a quick up-glance while pretending not to. A good thirty seconds later he looked up openly. "Banning, huh? You used to box, didn't you?"

Of all the things I didn't expect. Sure I used to box; back in high school I was even good. Until I filled out, so that everyone in my weight class had the reach on me. I stuck with it through frosh year at college, when the coach told me, "The skinny ones will beat your head in, Mitch. Try wrestling; for that, you've got the leverage." I did try, and learned a little, too. But I was coming in late, which seldom works well.

Before that, though, a fast lanky southpaw did a job on my nose. Nothing personal; he got to it once too often, was all. And I supposed that was what Borg clued in on.

So I said, "Yes, I used to box. Now I write articles."

I waited; he said, "Mr. Coogan has nothing to say for publication. Your appointment is cancelled."

"Why don't you ask Coogan first? He might like a vote."

If I'd had any silly idea that Borg liked me, I'd have dropped it right there. Friends, we weren't going to be. Rasp-voiced, he said, "What are you trying to push, Banning?"

That was more like it. "If you don't know, Coogan does. Ask." So, lifting the phone, Borg talked too softly for me to hear, then hung up and pointed toward the office Coogan had entered the day before. I hadn't sat so I didn't have to rise; I turned and walked to the door. As I gripped the doorknob, at the edge of vision I saw Tixo come in. I looked at my watch and wondered how he got up here so fast. An express elevator?

The building wasn't my concern. I went in.

Behind the fancy desk sat Elihu Coogan. My recalls flashed again from when I was ten years old, and there before me was Emil the Stork: The wig new, and perhaps contact lenses, but not much sign of aging.

He was doing a half-smile, maybe dentures and maybe not; no matter. Looking, I waited for him to speak first.

Under the circumstances, he did. "What is it you want?"

"A story. George Detweiler's always news; you must know that."

I'd said it wrong; he shook his head. "Absolutely not."

I pawed the air a little. "Wait a minute, Mr. Coogan. I know Detweiler hates any publicity he can't dictate. I promise you, nothing will appear in print until your deal is solid." For the moment he was listening; I followed through. "That's my colleague's beat, anyway. I'm a science writer, part-time; what I want to hear about—and again, the lid's on until you give your okay—is the gadget you're peddling."

His bushy eyebrows took on a pronounced dihedral angle. On a clock they'd have read ten minutes to two. "You're out of your mind—Banning, is it?"

He hadn't offered the use of a chair; I pulled one over and

sat facing him. Not as close as I'd have liked; it was a big desk. "All right, then, Coogan. Let's talk about storks."

"Get out of here!"

"And go talk to George Detweiler about storks?" I didn't bother to pretend I was walking out; I waited.

"I don't know what you're talking about. You're trespassing, and—"

"Oh, cut the crap! You're Emil the Stork with a wig and beard and contact lenses. So let's work something out, here."

"Blackmail? You must know my answer to that."

I knew one answer, all right; quickly I showed him my Miami news prints. "Xerox comes cheap; naturally these aren't my only copies. Guess where the others are—and where they're going if you cause me any trouble." An afterthought: "You, *or* Tixo."

He closed his eyes; for a moment he knuckled at them. Then, "Who are you, Banning? Why are you here? What is it you want?"

I tried to phrase it right. "Not money—except for what I can get for the article. I'm no leech, Coogan. I—what I want is the data for that article. And to know if you're on the level this time." I sat back. "Convince me."

He shrugged; he spread his hands and looked sincere. I was sure he was good at it. "What can I say?" Now he leaned forward, elbows on the desk and hands clasping. "I'm still a promoter, Banning; the great Stork has no other talents. But no longer a con artist. By necessity: after the publicity at Miami, I decided that my physical appearance makes me too conspicuous for that line of work." He smiled. "So I've gone legit."

"Like how?"

At ease now, he leaned back and made a wide gesture. "I'm managing an inventive genius—a real genius, attacking the frontiers of physics—who, on his own, couldn't dicker his way out of a pay toilet. And George Detweiler is possibly the only financial source who would even look at my client's latest discovery."

Coogan frowned. "The government, you realize, must

get no word of this. They'd confiscate it, under cover of national security. My client and I would go begging."

"Client, you say. Genius, too. Anybody I know?"

"Have you heard of Dr. Olin Pedicord?"

"The guy who claimed to build black holes in his basement?"

Coogan snorted. "An oversimplification. As always, in the press. The professor stated an analogy; it was printed as a purported factual claim. The *real* fact is that Dr. Pedicord posits a means of instantaneous transportation."

"A teleport?" Sure, I read those stories; they're fun. "You get in a phone booth in L.A. and dial a number and step out in New York?" He nodded.

So, the big question. "Does it work? For real?"

First came a pause; the Stork had to be thinking fast. Then he said, "With our limited resources to date, only marginally. But given George Detweiler's backing, we could prove out a practical working model."

The matter took some thought. Not that I was at all convinced; if I had been, I'd also have been thrilled and elated at the awesome possibilities of such a doodad. The puzzling question was, what did I want out of this situation? And how could I get it?

I saw Coogan's impatience; I said, "I'll need to talk to Pedicord. Not for publication—well, not until your deal with Detweiler is either solid or down the spout. And if you do make the deal, I want to be unofficial recording secretary for the entire project. A complete scoop, Coogan, for my colleague and myself." His face told nothing; I said, "Do we have a bargain?"

Not right away, we didn't. Coogan needed promises and safeguards, and I thought of a few of those on my own account, and Dauna's. When we finally shook hands and I turned to leave, there Tixo stood. I hadn't heard him come in. He was sliding his thumb back and forth along the edge of his knife. He looked up at me just once, stony eyes blank, then slid the blade back into its sheath.

I turned my gaze back to Coogan; he didn't say anything and neither did I. I just walked into and through the other room—Borg's desk was vacant—and went my way out of the building.

And, fuming more than somewhat, drove home.

It's not that I make a habit of macho games. But *twice* now, that little dried-up piece of whang leather had flashed a knife on me and got away with it. Not a good precedent.

I tried to think of what I might have done, and came up with nothing better than maybe pulling a bluff. But without doodly to back it with: in Unarmed Combat training during my Army hitch I'd been no good at all against a knife. Flunked that part, in fact. So I'd better've had a very *good* bluff. If at all . . .

I got home needing a change of mood. I looked for just the right CD. First I tried my "Midnight Villa" tetrad: Baron Heron doing the Mendoza arrangement. Something on the essential side.

Even so, it didn't do the job. I looked further and came up with a collection of favorite oldies; when Dauna came in I was singing right along, helping Johnny Cash walk the line. Not as deeply, of course.

I waved, and cut the sound. It was announcement time. "Dauna, I think we have us a *big* one."

CHAPTER THREE

Talking the situation over, by the time we got to after-dinner coffee we had it about straight. Dauna no more believed in Aladdin's lamp than I did—nor in the Stork's new halo. Still, though: ". . . benefit of the doubt," she said. "Until the lamp is actually rubbed, we can't be sure the genie's from Central Casting."

Translation clear; I nodded. "But the odds say he is; right? Union card and all."

One slim shoulder moved. "Until you know more, let Detweiler worry about that. Mitch—what do *you* do next?"

She'd accepted, without my saying so, that for now she wouldn't be likely to get any kind of news interview. I said, "First I have to meet Pedicord, the Stork's tame genius. After that, I get to be one of the courtiers when Coogan deals with George Detweiler. A barrel of laughs."

Her quick smile. "And the tycoon won't climb a rope and disappear, on being faced with this mysterious figure out of his past?"

"Me?" I shook my head. "Nah. Detweiler won't recognize me." Back in prep I'd been skinny, scraggly, and mostly three years below the level of the young big-shot's notice. "And if he does, so what? There's no law against people going to the same lousy school."

I'd hoped to meet Dr. Olin Pedicord in his working digs—a lab Coogan had hinted was well into operation. But Borg set the appointment for Suite 2310-14, and I had to go along with it.

On the way into Coogan's office, one thing happened. I found Borg sitting behind his desk while Tixo stood alongside. And once more the incomprehensible little bastard gave me his stony glance, pulled his knife partway, and slid it back to rest.

I made up my mind. Stepping past Tixo I put a hand out to give Ansel Borg the big handshake; after a moment he met me halfway. So I grinned at Tixo, nodded to both men, pulled my hand loose and offered Tixo the handshake. When he took it, I reached out southpaw and stole his knife.

Tixo's face turned a darker shade of slate; he had no idea what to do. I didn't give him time to decide. I smiled, freed my left hand by tucking his knife under my belt at the back, and made a slow ceremony of extending that hand, third and index fingers, to touch his forehead.

He hesitated; I spoke to Borg. "Tell Tixo this: that he and

I are now friends, and that friends only display their knives to each other if they wish to make gifts of them."

Borg scowled. "Why should I say any of that?"

"Because if anything should hit the fan, you're in this room, too—and a long way from the door."

So he turned to Tixo. "*Su vay—!*" I didn't understand any of the rest, either. But after a while Tixo nodded, and looked at me with those dull stony eyes, like a child waiting for a reward.

So I gave it to him. I gave him his knife back.

For the first time in my experience, Tixo smiled. His teeth showed solid brown; I don't know what they chew, down where he came from, but it has to be potent. And with the first and third fingers of his left hand, he reached out and touched my forehead.

That's probably the best bluff I ever ran in my whole life.

In Coogan's office, Dr. Olin Pedicord disappointed me. Gaunt except for a potbelly, he stood with an awkward, shambling sort of posture. He mumbled, not very clearly; I thought he might be on something but had no idea what. His early incoherence could have been sheer nervousness, though; after a time he did come clearer.

I'm being unfair. The man had more going for him than that. Basically his features were good—though they twitched at times, and somehow looked as though they'd melted and run a little, like wax. His steel-wool hair topped off an exceptionally high forehead but seemed to be holding fairly well. The voice, though, didn't hold worth doodly.

Coogan—he was there too, though not getting my prime attention—hit the buzzer and ordered coffee in. It struck me the Stork was behaving more affably than I had any reason to expect. I doubted that he'd dropped his resentment, but he covered well.

Tixo brought the pot, and probably I wasn't supposed to notice Coogan dropping a little something into Pedicord's cup. Whatever it was, pretty soon when I asked questions my ears worked better. Or else his head did.

It went along. "Black holes?" the man said. "Of course

not. What I told that reporter—" He shrugged. "—but you know how they are. I do *not* postulate creating and collapsing a neutron star; how could I?" A coughing spell interrupted; then he went on. "But black holes aren't the only source of singularities, or even what might be called, in a pragmatic sense, event horizons." He scowled. "Mr. Banning. Do you have any idea what I'm talking about?"

I half nodded. "Assume I'm catching on. Keep telling me."

More at himself than at me, perhaps, he frowned. "Toy with such parameters, Mr. Banning, and anything may happen. Literally anything. An object, even a person, may disappear from point A and appear at point B. Or even from *time* A to time B. Though I see no practical way to accomplish the latter. Would the former satisfy you?"

I guessed so and said so. "You can do that?"

"In theory. My experiments—" He shook his head. "I've had results, of a kind—dealing with particles only, to date. Since it's not possible to tag a given proton for identification, I cannot *prove* it is the same one, transported. But my mathematics indicate as much—and also, there is the fact that no known particle interaction could produce the same result."

"From particles to persons," I said. "That's quite a jump."

"Energy. Power. Those are the limitations. For a one-way device the power requirement varies directly with mass, and with the square of the distance. My present equipment—well, roughly speaking, its limit is transportation of an alpha particle over a distance of approximately ten meters."

Alpha particle. Sure, a helium nucleus, massing about as much as four protons, I thought. "That's quite a few orders of magnitude, wouldn't you say?—to send a person any distance at all." Something else caught my attention. "One-way device, you said. Why?"

Before Pedicord could answer, Coogan did. "If we could build two-way terminals—transceivers, in communications terms—we could simply *exchange* positions of objects, including people, weighing about the same. Which would be a much more economical process, energy-wise. Isn't that right, doctor?" Pedicord nodded. "But we simply can't afford to duplicate everything; when Detweiler saw that estimate, he went thumbs-down. So we're stuck with several times the power requirement of a two-way system."

My coffee had cooled; I sipped it anyway. "How much power are we talking about?" Pedicord named a figure; after I translated it, I shook my head. "You'll never get it. Not in this area, anyway. What with industrial *and* residential growth, Bonneville's talking about rationing. So how do you think they'll feel about adding this kind of load?"

"But that's *operating* power," Pedicord said. "It's used only during the tests themselves. Standby load, keeping the equipment on-line and ready for use, is approximately two percent of peak demand."

"And that," said Coogan, "is another major reason for dealing with George Detweiler." I showed him raised eyebrows; he said, "Our test requirements are roughly the same as the operating load at Detweiler's Riverside plant, which currently is working only two shifts. All he has to do, any day we're testing, is start the plant up a few minutes late, or close down a little early. Because it's *his* kilowatts, bought and paid for, that we'll be using."

That answer impressed me; I tried not to let it show. Before I got my next question together, Coogan said, "I have to make some calls. Stay here; I'll use Borg's desk." He went out.

Without my asking, Pedicord began explaining the basic physics underlying his project. He lost me on the first curve; my engineering math isn't too rusty, but the physics people go a long way past it. I tried to keep track of the hardware: the synchronized particle accelerators, the superconducting helices, the shielding. "It wouldn't do, you realize, to irradiate passengers with fast particles."

"No. Of course not." I wished I knew whether I was getting a grand, glorious snow job—but the man *sounded* enthusiastic.

Pedicord drew rough sketches of his overall installations;

I began to get some idea of their physical layout. And size: big, but not exactly the Eighth Wonder of the World.

What caught my eye, though, was something that *wasn't* on the drawings. "Telemetry," I said. "You're going to need a lot of it." While I was saying that, Coogan came back in.

He said, "It's included in our estimates."

I grinned. "I'm sure it is. What I was getting to, though: telemetry's part of my specialty, in my main line of work. When you get around to that part, I'd like a chance to bid on the design job."

After beginning a scowl, Coogan smiled. "Why not? That would give you a reason, in case Detweiler wondered, to be around the project."

And maybe tie me to it a little more strongly, with a contract? All right; if Coogan thought that would give him leverage, I didn't mind. This thing was a big story *either* way, and I wasn't even close to broke. Well, not very . . .

For another half hour I listened to Pedicord talk without understanding much of what he said. I took notes anyway; maybe library research would make sense of it. When he seemed to start running down I looked at my watch and invented an appointment to get me out of there.

We all shook hands. Coogan said he'd call me before the meeting with Detweiler, and Pedicord would draw up preliminary data on the telemetry requirements. I gathered I had that job without bidding.

Going out through Borg's office I got a big grin from Tixo. The aberration wasn't catching; Borg kept his usual granite expression.

Waiting for an elevator, mentally I scanned through the session. All the details, the side planning, made this thing sound real to me.

Then I shrugged. Emil the Stork had always done his homework.

I was home and comfortably settled before I remembered it was my turn to cook—and I'd forgotten, that morning, to put the pot roast in the crock pot. Well, I'd have to fake it. Making a guess on the heat level and timing, I used the micro instead.

I left the tiled kitchen, with its almost-hospital austerity, and again plunked down in the living room. I found its plywood paneling more comfortable, though it had darkened quite a bit since the previous owner installed it.

I'd brought the paper up with me; now I unfolded it and scanned the front page. At the lower right I saw that the Creighton-Ogsberth bill, designed to outlaw all cash transactions over one hundred dollars, was being logrolled out of committee to the Senate floor. Not exactly a new idea: Bush had proposed it first, back when Reagan's chair had hardly cooled. The excuse was to get a handle on all those suitcases full of drug money.

That was a laugh; the druglords would convert their takings outside U.S. jurisdiction and be home free. The real point was to curb the Cash Economy, to put all significant private exchange of goods into the computer net where every level of government could grab a slice.

As usual in modern times, the pretext was the curbing of Big Corruption but the impact would be on the guy who didn't know the loopholes and couldn't afford them anyway: Reagan-Bush policies *lived*. Little Joe the Wrangler had been elected from the other side of the political fence, but the grass there was *not* greener. Though I'd voted for this compromise candidate, the dark horse fresh from Wyoming, with no real hope of significant change, a surprise would have been nice.

The story jumped to page seven, but I'd seen enough; on the comics page I was pleased to see Hod Neill's *Thom Tumb* taking a crack at "Cretin-Hogsbreath." Not exactly Walt Kelly or Gary Trudeau, still Neill got some good licks in. This time Thom was telling Berlinda, his German girlfriend, "You got to admire them legislooters; they never gives up their principals."

Skipping the more lamebrained strips, I settled down to tackle the crossword and Jumble puzzles. But just as I was

getting relaxed—it's a law of nature, I think—the phone
rang.

"Mitchell Banning?" I acknowledged the fact. "What did
Pedicord tell you? That thieving bastard!"

Not the most informative conversation I ever had. The
man—well, the voice seemed too deep for a woman's,
though the varying huskiness might have been faked—gave
neither a name nor any reason for calling Pedicord nasty
ones. So I put out no info, either. Not that I would have,
anyway. On general principles.

Eventually my caller got down to impractical instructions for self-fertilization, and wound up by saying, "Act
smartass all you want, Banning. You won't get away with it,
any of you!" Anticipating slamdown at the other end, I had
the phone well away from my ear.

I still had phone in hand, maybe all of five seconds later,
when Dauna came in. I hung up and went to greet her. She
looked pooped, and for the first time in a month or so,
carried a briefcase that had to be full of work.

So I sat her down and took her shoes off and brought her
a drink. With one foot she nudged the briefcase away; then
she asked how events had befallen at the Trosper Building.
I told her, and then about the phone call.

"Enter Second Ruffian," she said, "from left field. What
do you make of it?"

"So far, not much. But at least it's not boring me." She
laughed. We kicked the entire mess around some more,
but no new answers came out.

Next morning, roughing out the five-level setup for Pentco,
I discovered a possible worst-case situation that could grid-
lock the whole system. I didn't want to use the cop-out of
a manual restart, so I began to rethink the sequence.

I was about halfway through it when Coogan called. The
meeting with Detweiler was set up for three days from now.
Fine; I had to go out of town first, but by then I'd be back.
I asked when Pedicord could give me his telemetry Wish
List. "A preliminary idea, to start on?" Possibly at our next

meeting, Coogan said—or, on the other hand, maybe the following week. All right?

What choice? I guessed so. Pausing a moment, thinking in alternatives, I told of the abusive phone call. "Somebody's pretty mad, Coogan. You have any idea who? Or why?"

After a time he answered, "I can't think of anyone. Dr. Pedicord's hypotheses are controversial, of course, but what you describe doesn't sound like academic disagreement." Silence, then; I could imagine him shaking his head. "A crank, I would suppose."

Which was no answer at all. Our talk ended; I went back to Pentco's problem. The break had sparked my subconscious; almost immediately I saw how to fail-safe my signal codes. My first try wouldn't fit, right away, but the modifications took less than an hour. I knocked off then, to fix myself an early lunch.

That afternoon I was due in L.A. to check modifications on an interface setup I'd done for Ettlin, Ltd. I drove out to a rental agency parking lot, and their shuttle got me to Sea-Tac in plenty of time to catch the flight. It was one of the old 727s, the few that hadn't been retired yet. I've always liked that design because its thrust is centered at the tail. So if you're in the john and hit turbulence, it doesn't bounce you off the ceiling.

No matter how often I sit down at LAX, I wonder if we're really going to clear Sepulveda Boulevard. We always do, though; promptly at four-thirty-eight the tin goose touched down.

The job's details wouldn't much interest anyone but my creditors. It took longer than I'd expected so I stayed over. And next morning caught a puddle-jumper that put me back at Sea-Tac about an hour ahead of the earliest nonstop.

Getting home is always nice. I checked for messages and found one in Dauna's distinctive, ornamental script:

Wendsdy five-thirty-eight pip emma: the Stork says he has a bundle for you. If it's a baby I plead Not Guilty.

So I called Coogan. I'd hoped his bundle would be Pedicord's telemetry plans, but he said, "At ten tomorrow morning I meet with Detweiler. I trust you still wish to attend?"

"Wouldn't miss it for the world. Where?"

"His new office complex. Do you know where that is?"

"Sure." Well, roughly. One of the many new glass boxes polluting the horizon of Bellevue across the lake; I'd seen it from I-405, the Eastside freeway. I could find it.

"Well, I don't," he said. "Could you drive us?"

Us? "How many?"

"Borg, Pedicord, and myself. We'll be here, at the Trosper Building."

"All right." I thought about it. Half an hour should be plenty for the run. "I'll pick you up at nine-thirty. Be out in front, would you? Parking's tough around there."

"And, in the circumstances, a waste of time. Certainly. Nine-thirty at the front entrance. And thank you, Banning."

"Any time, Coogan. See you then."

So much for that. I leafed through the mail; nothing looked urgent. A couple of checks were welcome, especially the one that was more than a little overdue. I endorsed both, made out a deposit slip, and put the lot into a bank-by-mail envelope. My bank still used postpaid ones, but I knew that couldn't last much longer. I trotted down the tunnel to the mailbox, but walked up more slowly.

I still had a lot of afternoon on my hands and not much that needed doing. I changed to shorts, picked up a book and a blanket. Outside in the sun—not baking, like L.A.'s, but warm and pleasant—I soaked up mild heat and diffused ultraviolet, and read into the book.

It was about a man who had a weapon that could destroy the world. Rather, he was the villain; well, how else? The hero learned of the menace by way of a gross coincidence I didn't believe for a minute, but nobody took his warnings seriously. And why should they? Instead of dealing his few facts off the top of the deck, the man came on like a raving maniac. Then he sought the assistance of a mystic guru. . . .

I must have dozed off. Emil the Stork was going to destroy the world and no one would pay any attention. Dauna said, "Fine; tear it down, and build it *right* this time." All around me, things were falling over and shattering. . . .

I woke up—and after a minute, laughed.

CHAPTER FOUR

Haze clouded the western sky; feeling chilly, I took my accessories indoors. My skin had the iodine smell of dried sun-sweat, quite different from the juices of effort or emotion. I took a quick shower; drying off, I looked at my watch on the counter. Dauna would be home soon.

When she did arrive, I caught her up to date.

She'd brought more work home. After dinner she sat down with it, but within five minutes she put it aside. "No way."

So we listened to a CD, then watched teevy a while. We hadn't had the high-definition flat set very long; the novelty still made up for the banal quality of much of the product.

As often happens, I'd bought the thing without any real idea of how I wanted to use it, having held off from HDTV until a fully compatible system was offered, and then springing for the fancy flat-screen model. So, lo and behold, here I had a wall model, and no convenient wall to hang it on. What I wound up using was a sort of easel-frame on casters, with the power cord and cable feed coming off reels mounted in a ceiling box.

Probably the only wall-model portable in town.

After a little while we began relieving the dullness by talking back to the commercials. "Coming to a theater near me? Not if I can help it!" "Less taste! More calories!" Some guy I'd never heard of announced, "I'm Walter Barbers" and we chorused *"We're* not!" Silly horseplay, but we enjoy it.

We went to bed early. After all, I'd been out of town. They say you can't ever catch up, but it's fun trying.

Next morning came with grey overcast and "misting." I arrived at the Trosper Building's marked loading zone maybe two minutes early, and my party was on the spot. Nobody saying much, they got in.

The newer Mercer Island floating bridge made the shortest route, so I headed the Volvo for it, through the Mount Baker tunnel. Crossing the bridge itself, to our right I saw workers putting some final touches to the newly built replacement for the one that sank a few years ago when the pavement repair contractor pumped its pontoons full of wastewater.

The island's own tricky express lanes were blocked off eastbound because morning commuter traffic goes the other way, but eventually we reached the I-405 junction and started north.

Approaching Bellevue I kept a lookout for Detweiler's new showplace; when I spotted it, I took the next exit. One too soon, actually, putting us into arterial traffic for longer than I liked, which would have been effectively zero. Bellevue drivers have this peculiarity: they won't let you change lanes if they can help it, even if it would get you out of town.

But with a little yelling and downright bluff, pretending I didn't *care* about my fenders, by nine-fifty-five we were parked in Detweiler's acre-sized lot. One end, I noticed, was all peewee stalls for Detweiler Commutes, the small electric cars he was starting to promote by selling them to his employees at big discounts, just to get them out there providing some exposure.

Lot and building alike bore absolutely no signs to iden-tify the place as Detweiler's stronghold; if you didn't know already, you'd have no idea whose it was.

Going toward the building I led the way; once inside, I shuffled my feet until Coogan was in front. Apparently he had directions; he passed the information desk and led us up some wide, carpeted stairs to a mezzanine balcony. On that level the outer walls were largely tinted glass; I looked out and saw that on the south side, at least, Detweiler had left the trees alone. One point for his side. Until he needed more parking lot . . .

On this floor the office section was straight ahead east, and sure enough, the door read "George Detweiler, Execu-tive President." Why not, I wondered, "Executive Presi-dent in Charge of Everything?" If you're going to be redundant, why fool around with half-measures?

When Coogan was a few feet short of that door, it opened. A woman came out, turning back in obvious pro-test, with George Detweiler gripping her upper arm. She was tall and strongly built, with red hair falling straight to curl at the shoulders. Her black dress showed a lot of cleavage—not all that deep, though. Her face was so taut with rage that she could have been anything from beauty to bag.

Detweiler shook her. "The answer's no, Ronnie, and that's that. I've told you before: do *not* bother me here during working hours. You—"

She shook her head; I was close enough to see her center parting, more dark than red. "It's my own money, George. That's all I'm asking for—my own money!"

He snickered. "In trust, and I'm trustee. You're getting your living expenses, Ronnie. Be thankful for that."

Twisting, she broke free and took a step away, bumping into Coogan but moving free of him as she shouted, "You horse's fistula! The old man's stroke was the best break you ever got in your life, wasn't it? Just because he couldn't talk

up at the hearing, you had him declared incompetent—
when he's still smarter than you'll ever be! Some day,
George—*some* day—" She turned and walked past us, away
and down the stairs.

With nobody saying anything, I had time to look at
George Detweiler. He hadn't changed much: still the big,
swarthy jock, his black hair longer now but not so greasy
looking. He was beefier, yes; no potbelly yet, but thick all
the way down and starting to bulge. Oddly, the extra face
fat gave his habitual upstage sneer a milder look.

After a moment he shook his head, apparently decided
we were the people he'd been expecting, and invited us in,
introducing himself and shaking hands all around. "Mr.
Coogan," "Mr. Borg," "Dr. Pedicord," and finally, "Mr.
Banning; don't I know you?"

"Not really. One year we were both at prep; that's a long
time ago." He blinked; then his lips twitched and I saw him
remember.

For years I hadn't thought about it: the day he and three of
his hangers-on cornered me in the john at prep and he had
them pants me. I was fourteen, a greenhorn freshman
uprooted clear across the country when my dad died;
George was a senior. When I tried to fight, none of them
even bothered to hit me. Detweiler stalked out with my
pants and came back without them; I don't know how I
could have forgotten his carrion-eating grin when he said,
"If you want your pants, Banning, ask Sheila." That was
Sheila Lanford, his number-one jock groupie. "She put 'em
in the trash can," said big George. "In the girls' toity."

Then he laughed, and so did the others, and they went
out and left me there.

The last to leave, Detweiler turned back. "You know
better than to make trouble, don't you, Banning? Next
time, *all* your clothes. And maybe a little workout, just to
keep in shape."

There was absolutely nothing I could do; while my
classes went on without me, I hid in a stall with the door
locked. Twice I heard teachers talking—but if I asked their

help, they'd want the full story. When classes finally ended I waited until I thought everyone would be gone; then I came out and sneaked down the hall to the girls' john.

Going in was the worst part. But I found my pants; that far, Detweiler had played fair. Putting them on, I felt half-way human again.

A janitor caught me coming out the door. It was a bad five minutes, but finally he believed my story—I named no names—and laughed, and let me go.

How could I have forgotten that day? Because I had to, I guess. Now I looked at George Detweiler and rethought a few things. Such as, if the Stork ripped Detweiler's ass off, both cheeks down to the bone, it wouldn't bother me one bit.

Not that I'd promote an outright swindle, or help cover one. But for damn sure and certain, I wouldn't look too hard.

George had a big office, a big desk, a thick blue-green carpet and chartreuse walls and an off-white ceiling and amber cove lighting. If he was trying to show he had taste, you couldn't prove it by me. When we were all seated, with two chairs left over, he set a flunkie to mixing drinks for us. The man was so self-effacing, I have no idea what he looked like.

Ten in the morning isn't my usual drinking time, but I saw the label on the gin and asked for a double Martini, just to sample the brand at Detweiler's expense. When I saw the size of the glass I had second thoughts: a goldfish could get lonesome.

After George reeled off some small talk—what do you think of the Mariners' chances, as if these out-of-towners would give a hoot—he got down to cases. He also quit sounding like a recorded message. I decided I preferred the recording.

Mostly he queried Pedicord, not Coogan; the doctor gave much the same spiel I'd already heard. Sipping at my half-pint of expensive gin, I paid good heed anyway. Then it got better.

After Pedicord explained the energy and mass and dis-

tance things, Detweiler asked, "Exactly what kind of demonstrations do you plan to make? What installations am I
expected to finance?"

Two, it turned out. One fairly long-distance for small
objects, and one short-haul but big enough to handle a
human being. "Together," said Olin Pedicord, "the two
should amply prove that my theories can revolutionize
transportation."

After a few more questions, Detweiler started giving answers. For the larger setup he had a place in mind; up in
Snohomish County the Navy had abandoned a high-powered radio transmitter site and George had an option on it,
complete with existing power lines, support buildings, and
some heavy concrete foundations where the transmitters
used to be. Pedicord looked to Coogan; the Stork nodded.
Funny; I'd've expected that exchange to be the other way
around. Oh, well . . .

After a bit more talk, Detweiler made his offer; the
amount surprised me. Well into six figures for just the
preliminary work, and Coogan/Pedicord had a free hand
with it. "Just show me the invoices and receipts every
month. Later, on the major construction, give me the estimates and I'll authorize payment."

With a few handshakes the session wound up fast.
George hadn't thought to ask what I was doing there, and
I didn't volunteer anything. Coogan looked bemused, and
that's exactly how *I* felt. If this were a grift, with the old
Stork still winging it, he'd just been handed a check for
over two hundred big ones, that he could walk away with
if he timed things right.

Or could he? Detweiler wouldn't be that simple; there'd
be safeguards, watchdogs of some sort, whether he said so
or not. And if I could suspect that, so could Emil the Stork,
and probably faster. So if he had a con going, it had to be
smoother than grab-and-run.

On the way back to town everyone was quiet again; I had
time to think. It wasn't, I decided, necessarily a pleasant
situation I was involved in. But sure as hell, it didn't look
to be boring.

* * *

At the Trosper Building I dropped them off. Coogan thanked me and said he'd be in touch; I pointed the Volvo homeward. Once out of downtown traffic I could relax.

What with driving and all, I'd left most of Detweiler's gin in the glass, but the sample gave me a yen for a bit more of that premium brand. Well, at home we were out of gin, so why not? And right now there was a liquor store only a couple of blocks off my course; I made the turn and went there.

I bought my gin, plus two bottles of wine marked down for closeout, and started out of the place. Just outside I came faceup to the woman I'd seen earlier: Ronnie, whom George Detweiler had thrown out of his office.

Starting to move past, she halted. "Are you following me?"

I shook my head, then had another thought. "But if I were, would you talk with me? There's a bar down the block."

Not the greatest invitation I've ever made, but after a time she nodded. "All right. But I ask the questions."

The place was nearly empty, dim-lit shoddy in worn plastic and tarnished chrome. We got our drinks fast: gin-and-tonic for her, and on second thought I settled for coffee. Well, decaf . . .

We sipped; I looked at her and said, "What we have in common, I think, is that George Detweiler isn't our favorite person."

She said, "You came out of that store with bottles; I was going in. So you weren't following me. What did you go see George about?"

All right. "I'm a technical fella. One thing I'm working on is a project George may finance. The people I was with, it's their project, and on it I'm *not* an expert. Who are you?"

The change of pace threw her a little. "Don't you know?"

"If I did, I wouldn't waste time asking." I waited.

"I'm Veronica Detweiler." The name rang no bells; I

shook my head, which gave no jingle either. I'd never kept track of Detweilers, but they did hit the papers sometimes, usually in a civic sort of way. And I didn't remember any Veronica.

She smiled. "I used to be George's half-brother. Ronald."

Ronald-Ronnie-Veronica: a sex change! I could guess how George the jock liked *that* development. I said so. Looking pained, Ronnie shrugged. Trying to remember what Ronald looked like, I couldn't; he'd been a lot younger than me. I asked. Nine years behind George, which put six between me and Ronnie. To a kid, six years is practically a generation.

Embarrassed and not wanting to be, I said, "I've never met anyone before who—" What to say? "I won't ask questions. I'm curious as hell, I admit it. But I won't, anyway."

Ronnie said, "I haven't had the operations yet. That's what the fight was about, the money for them."

I looked. Smooth face—and the bust, though not deep, was real. "Then you're still male?"

"Not functionally." Gesture. "I've been cross-dressing for nearly two years, but physically, so far it's just hormone shots and electrolysis." Shrug. "I've not had an erection—or been capable of it, or wanted to be—for over a year. I'm in limbo, you might say. And George thinks if he can keep me there long enough, I'll give up."

Curiosity trampled tact. *"Why?"*

Not a very clear question, but she answered. "Because I'm driven to be what I really am, inside, not what my body carries as a biological accident. Can you understand that?"

I thought about what this person wanted done to her—his?—body. "No. No, I don't think I can. But I respect your right to your own needs; is that good enough?"

Again Ronnie smiled. "If I were already fully a woman, would you feel differently?"

"Fully?"

"Oh, I'll never menstruate or conceive—but does a hysterectomy unsex a female? Think about it."

I looked, trying to figure whether I was seeing a man in drag or a woman stuck in a physical, more permanent disguise. I'd heard or read enough on the subject, here and there, to know most of the arguments. Finally I said, "And in your own mind, what are you now?" It wasn't a putdown; I really wanted to know.

Not a smile now, more of a grin. "A woman with an unwanted chastity belt growing on her body. How does that grab you?"

"Well, after all, you could . . ."

"Oh no. Not with a man. I've *been* raped, on a camping trip when I was twelve; one of George's friends got drunk. Those acts repel me thoroughly. Oh, I've flirted around the edge of the lesbian bit once or twice. But with men I'll be a real woman or not at all."

Flushed and rigid, her face dared me to disagree. I said, "I see. Well, if it were up to me, I guess I'd say go ahead."

She leaned forward. "Then get me a job, on the project."

Doing *what?* Just like that? I asked, and Ronnie said, "Data processing. I'm good at it, and if your setup doesn't have a slot I can fill, I'd be surprised."

"I don't get it; why me? I mean, we live in a big town."

"Because George put out a blacklist on me, with every company he could find that uses my specialties." She spread her hands. "I need a job; I need money. And if George is financing this setup, it may be the one place he'd forget to look."

"He'll see the payroll; you can bet on it."

Her shoulders slumped. "I guess so. Well, I'll just have to think of something else."

"Yeah. Good luck at it."

"Sure." Suddenly, she brightened. "You could still do me a favor." I sighed, and she said, "Not for me. A friend of mine, fairly new in town, *not* in George's bad books. Needs a job, too." She made a shrug. "Nothing urgent. But Eddie—Eddie Machell, his name is—he's an electronic tech. So if he hits you up, would you give him a chance?"

"I'll give anyone a chance, who's qualified."

"That's good enough." She killed her drink, and stood; my coffee was long gone. "Thanks. I'll see you around."

I rose also. "Could you use a ride?"

"My apartment's only a couple of blocks from here; I'll walk. But thanks anyway."

I took my bottles to the car and drove home.

Somehow the morning's doings had pooped me; I found nothing urgent in the mail, and fixed myself a late lunch. Then I took my book and blanket outdoors again, to see how Dauna's new sunblock would hold up under bona fide sunshine. What happened was that I went to sleep—but woke often enough to turn over and avoid too much exposure on any one side.

When Dauna came home I was back inside, wondering whether or not my casserole would pass muster. At table I thought it was passable but not much better. Dauna spoke very carefully; she didn't say it was good, but not that it was lousy, either.

So it was lousy. I came to cooking late, was all.

Then passed considerable time when everything happened pretty much the same. Day by day, week to week, I worked at home and went down to the Trosper Building to put together Pedicord's telemetry package—or rather, to convince him that I *was* putting it together—while I polished off some other current jobs and picked up a couple of new ones. All told, I did keep busy.

At one point, for two weeks I saw nothing of Borg or Tixo. Coogan said they were out of town, but not where. The first day they were back, I gave them a cheery wave and hello. I neither expected nor got any return cheer from Borg, but ever since I'd done my trick with Tixo's knife, the little Indian had been a regular Smiley-boy. Not this time, though; stone-faced he backed away, and put his hand to the knife. Just like old times.

I looked over to Borg. "What's with Tixo? Short memory?"

Looking startled, Borg rattled off a string of jabber I couldn't follow. Tixo shook his head. Borg repeated himself, near as I could tell, only louder—and Tixo nodded. He didn't exactly put his heart into what passed as a smile, but moved up and handed me the knife. I smiled back, nodded, and did the business of two fingers to his forehead. Then, as before, I gave the knife back.

Borg said something else; Tixo reached out and returned the forehead touch. Then he put the knife away and resumed his usual station.

I looked at Borg again; his expression told me nothing. I shrugged, and went on in to talk with Coogan.

About six weeks later, Coogan and Pedicord began lining up a crew. By this time, most of the preliminary work was contracted out; Detweiler had picked the winning bidders. I had no need to be in any of that; in fact, I hadn't yet had a chance to see the transmitter site. The only direct hiring, by Coogan, had been a couple of young draftsmen. But now things were moving; the real job was due to start, and it needed people, fast.

Seeing a bottleneck in process, I volunteered to screen applicants. Coogan was pleased; Borg wasn't; Pedicord didn't seem to care. For some jobs, Coogan or Pedicord did the final interviews; for others, my own choice governed.

Ronnie Detweiler thought of something else, all right. One morning I was interviewing a young fellow named Steve Broyles, and couldn't figure why he grinned so much. His appearance wasn't outstanding in any way: unremarkable features, a mustache that wasn't very assertive, light brown hair worn semi-mod with sideburns; he had on a loose sports jacket and light tan slacks.

When we were done I told him to wait; the job was one that needed Coogan's okay. He said, "Thanks, Mr. Banning."

But now the voice was different; I did a double take and looked again. I suppose the sideburns were glued on, and

certainly the mustache had to be. The eyebrows had grown,
maybe aided by a little makeup. Until this minute, the
voice *hadn't* been Veronica's, and the loose jacket gave no
hint of unmasculine contours. Hormones or no hormones.

Very briefly, I grinned back. "Stay in character, huh?"

"Sure."

When Steve came out from seeing Coogan he nodded to
me.

"Everything's fine. Thanks again." Two or three days
later, Ronnie's friend Eddie Machell also got Coogan's
okay—and then Pedicord's, too, because Machell's job was
highly technical and also out of my field.

Well, if George Detweiler found out about Ronnie and
raised hell, at least Coogan had managed to spread the
blame around!

Later it was Steve—I had trouble remembering to think of
Ronnie by that name—who tipped me off about something
that had puzzled me a lot. Dr. Pedicord was having one of
his weird days when he didn't seem to make much sense.
Then Coogan called him in for a conference, and a few
minutes later he came out chipper, all shaped up. I was
standing by Steve's desk, giving him some raw data to
punch into the system, when the doc walked past. I suppose my puzzlement showed; Steve said, "Haven't you
figured it out?" I shook my head; he said, "Buy me a drink
after work, and I'll clue you."

A couple of hours later, in the building's penthouse bar,
I said, "So give."

Steve laughed—unaware, maybe, of relaxing enough to
let a little of Ronnie into that laugh. "The eminent Dr.
Pedicord is a junkie." I stared. "Oh, I know the signs; a
friend of mine went that route. Until a couple of years ago,
when he OD'd."

"On what? Heroin, you mean? That Pedicord's using?"

"Looks like it. Maybe something else, but that's my best
guess. And the estimable Coogan is his fairy godfather who
keeps him maintained."

"And on the string. I'd wondered how the Stork—"

"What?"

"Nothing. Slip of the tongue." I sipped the last of my mild, "Happy Hour" drink. "Thanks, Ron—uh, Steve. I don't know how this fits in, but thanks anyway."

Real or not, Steve's brows raised. "Fits into what?"

"I don't know yet. When I do—"

"When you do, then what?"

"Then if I can, I'll tell you."

Something else itched my curiosity; I gestured toward Steve and said, "ID. It has to check out solid. Where'd you get it?"

Discomfiting me, for a moment the smile was pure Ronnie; then the face resumed character. "It's real. Name and all. From a fellow I knew at the Gender Identity Clinic. With a little help"—she touched the mustache—"our physical stats aren't that far off. He's gone; that is, it's Stephanie now. But she's making the legal name change in California; it won't show in local records. At least, not for a long time."

"Do tell." I nodded. "Well, whatever works."

And we left.

CHAPTER FIVE

Firming up the project's circuit needs—communications, control, and monitoring telemetry—Pedicord took his own sweet time. Working through Coogan I got Detweiler to round up a set of the old Navy installation drawings. The equipment itself was gone, of course, but most of the power and signal cabling had been left in place. If I could use some of it, if it would handle our needs, we'd be time and money ahead.

Offhand, prospects looked good. Obviously I'd have to

go out there and do some testing; drawings don't tell you about deterioration.

Eventually I squeezed out of Pedicord a tentative needs package: his guess as to how many channels, in what ranges of bandwidths, would handle all the functions he required.

On a job that size, I like to check my own thinking against the standard reference material. I dug out my Handbook disk and put it into the CD-ROM drive I use for research. It's a sweet toy; if I wanted to, I could have the *Brittanica* on one of those CD disks. Or the Oxford Unabridged.

I pulled up the relevant tables and found that my own layout needed no major changes, but *could* be made just a bit neater. Not being new in the game I left plenty of room for expansion.

To wrap things up, I made out a list of the necessary equipment and gave it to Coogan.

I thought the hard part was over, but I reckoned without George Detweiler; he took over the ordering and shopped for bargains. Knowing nothing about comm gear, he bought items that didn't interface well. Such as some Mil-Spec channel terminal gear the Army was surplusing; naturally the military has its voltages bassackwards from commercial practice, but George wouldn't know that.

I could have rewired the units, but I didn't *want* to spend three weeks on that kind of scutwork. It was Detweiler's doing; let him hire the job done. I sent a memo and hoped for the best.

Finally Pedicord gave me a detailed list of circuit requirements. Of course he kept changing it; I expected as much and had made allowances, so his foibles didn't necessitate any additional procurement. All they meant was that I wouldn't have had time to clean up Detweiler's mess, anyway.

I was working long hours. Too long, because when Dauna brought her Office Flu home, my resistance was down and I caught it. Her case was light; mine put me in bed for a week. I never met a virus that respected deadlines.

When I went back to work, still a little shaky, Coogan was snappish. You'd think I invented the flu bug myself. I waited until he simmered down and began to make constructive sense.

I was overdue, it seemed, to visit Range A, his code name for the transmitter site. Before authorizing the start of construction, Detweiler wanted the cable systems checked out. "To avoid having to lay any new runs into a working construction area," Coogan said. "You understand what he means, Banning?"

Oh, sure; I nodded. The coordination didn't strike me as all that difficult; still, it was Detweiler's money and Coogan's project, so my place was probably to humor them both.

I looked at the Stork. "Is tomorrow soon enough?"

After a brief frown, he said, "Yes; that might be best. Detweiler will be out there around noon, and maybe we can all settle a lot of things in a hurry."

Now that Coogan had decided something, he felt good: on top of things, moving briskly. "Don't bother coming down here. Borg and Tixo will pick you up at nine. All right?"

Why not? I agreed, and went to my desk. Paperwork wasn't stacked nearly as bad as I'd expected; I had it cleared by midafternoon and left early. As soon as I got home I packed the drawings and test gear I'd be wanting. No point in having to hurry anything, next morning.

After dinner, Dauna and I ran into an old movie on cable. *2001*, it was. She watched it; I kept going to sleep. That film certainly takes a long time to do not much of anything.

Pretty, though . . .

With my stuff ready to go, I had plenty of time to dawdle over breakfast and other morning chores—and still hauled my kit down to the street ten minutes early. My ride was five minutes late, giving me time to appreciate the neighbors' flower beds, passing cars, and the more scenic aspects of pedestrian traffic.

The car was a red Toyota five-speed. Tixo drove, while I shared the back seat with Borg, who navigated. Except for his occasional directions, understandable to Tixo but not to me, little was said. The diminutive Indian had the gears and such down pat, but not smoothly; he did everything twice as forcefully as need be, gunning and braking as though our placid arterial were Le Mans. Once on the freeway he relaxed more, staying in the left lane and holding at about eight miles over limit.

Which is, as a matter of fact, my own system. I'm not sure why it works, but except in heavy traffic it generally leaves me all alone most of the time, with a bunch of cars ahead that will sort themselves out before I catch up, and another bunch behind that will eventually send a few to pass me.

Tixo did one thing different, though; for the fast ones I pull over, then back again. He stayed in place; anybody wanted to pass him, go around on the right or forget it.

After less than an hour on I-5 we turned off through a small town—Tixo was back to nervous, now—and took a road into the Cascade foothills. Not much later he found a side road. Maybe two miles along it, after passing a few houses, we came to a sign: PROJECT AREA. KEEP OUT. The sign was new; the posts weren't. I figured the original sign had been the Navy's. And now the road wasn't exactly maintained. Overgrown at the edges, and a number of potholes which didn't bother the Toyota too much.

After zigzagging up a ravine, this trail came over into a valley. Below, I saw Range A, and tried to fit the view to the drawings I'd seen. All right; the big, bare set of foundations had held the transmitter building itself. The smaller one puzzled me; then I decided it had to be the generator shed, for standby power. Several prefab buildings had been left in place, which was probably cheaper than clearing them away.

I looked to the hills flanking the valley and saw the bare towers that had supported the great catenary of the low-frequency antenna. That transmitter had been a real moose!

I wondered what the Navy was using now, instead. Proba-bly something Classified.

Power lines still stood as advertised, along with most of a quite respectable junior-grade transformer farm. Power still ran to most of the prefabs, including the large one off to the right, where Detweiler's contractor had set up shop. Tixo drove us into the weed-grown parking area and stopped in front of a smaller building. "Used to be the detachment commander's office," Borg said. "Ours now."

We got out of the Toyota; Borg led us into the prefab. Inside we found dimness; not much light came through the dirty windows. Borg reached for a pull-chain switch, and everything blew up.

Not everything, really—but that's how it seemed. The lights did, and something over to my right, and Borg—well, Borg sprouted an aura of sparks as he convulsed and fell. Tixo started toward him. I grabbed the little man; snarling, he tried to break away. I shook my head, yelling "No!" until I could half-pull, half-throw him out the door.

Outside I yanked it shut, and waited. Tixo came toward me; then, as he looked past, into a window, his eyes wid-ened. I looked too, and saw smoke in there, with a hint of flame.

I beckoned to Tixo and started running back along the power lead, looking to see exactly where it originated. If he followed me, fine. If he went back into the building—well, I'd tried.

I found the transformer and reached for the high-voltage disconnect. I expected the handle to work stiffly if at all, even with the extra leverage of the insulating extensor, but it moved with only normal resistance. The breaking circuit arced across briefly, with its characteristic crashing noise. At the disconnect's pivot pin I saw fresh graphite.

The building would be safe now; out of breath from run-ning back to it, I opened the door. Smoke puffed out, but the flames from charred wiring hadn't spread much. A few whiffs from a dusty old CO_2 extinguisher took care of the fire problem.

Borg had no more problems at all. One look at his charred hand, still gripping the cord he'd pulled down when he fell, told me that resuscitation was a vain hope. A touch confirmed the opinion: too much of him was, quite literally, cooked. Even though I'd never liked the man, I shuddered. And turned away.

I looked around; the unidentified explosion had been an electric clock sitting on a filing cabinet. The lights were blown, of course, and so was the building's wiring. My guess was, Coogan needed to pick a new field office.

Now some of the contractor's crew came up, badges reading "Associated Electronics." Traditionally we expect the women to suffer meltdown at gruesome scenes, but on seeing Borg, the only one who upchucked was a fortyish guy who could typecast as a movie heavy. Lucky he got outside first.

Briefly I wondered why I wasn't affected the same way. Maybe I was in shock; if so, I'd settle for it.

Larry Des Palmos, the crew chief, was a self-important young fellow in wire-rim glasses. Naturally he wanted to know what happened. Actually he put it a lot more forcefully, but I only said, "When I find out, you'll be the first to know," and headed back up toward the transformers.

I had several questions. The transformer, when I took the cover off its strapping field, answered the first one. "What happened" was that somebody had changed some straps. The transformer was one of several single-phase feeds to various buildings. It was, on the face of things, a special job, with quite a layout of strapping options to adjust voltages. Now the way it's supposed to work, the high- and low-voltage windings are each grounded at one end. But someone had disconnected both from the ground and connected them together instead. So that what the building got was thirteen thousand volts fed through both windings in series, which didn't slow it down a whole lot.

Putting it back to normal would have been easy, except that in some kind of delayed reaction my hands kept trembling. But eventually I had the thing safe again, and resealed it.

All of which took care of my first question. The others, for which I had no answers, were: "Who did it?" and "Why?"

When Coogan arrived, he didn't like it much. Well, who did? Things had moved too fast for me to really notice how I felt, but once I'd solved the transformer bit and explained it to Des Palmos and others, I had plenty of time to think on what it meant. And wonder whether my stomach would let my breakfast stay put, after all—let alone give clearance for lunch, later.

All I could tell Coogan was what I knew; it took him three run-throughs to get that point. "But who would do such a thing?" His voice was pitched high, rough at the edges.

I spread my hands. "How do I know who might be after you? Or Borg, or maybe Pedicord."

"How about someone gunning for *you*?" From the look of him, he meant the question seriously.

I shrugged, then had an idea. "How long since anyone was in the building, that you know of? Someone who'd have had the lights on."

He took his time answering. "Four or five days. Why?"

"Was there a schedule? Would anyone know when someone would come here next. Or who?"

"I don't see how anyone could know. We didn't decide until yesterday that *you'd* be here today."

So the transformer was a broadside shot, not a sniper's act. I said so, and then, "That phone call I had, early on. The fella—I *think* it was a man—who cussed Pedicord out so much." The Stork looked at me; I said, "Well, that's the only clue *I* know of, that you've got a hostile out there running loose."

He nodded. "I wish you had recorded that call."

In a way, I wanted to laugh. "Recorded? Coogan, I don't record calls; I don't even have the equipment." Oh, I could haywire something out of my junk box, but telling that to the Stork would only confuse matters. So I didn't.

Coogan was still grumpy, nursing his obvious jitters, when George Detweiler swooped down the valley in his oversized black Continental. By talking instead of listening, beefy George managed to take longer than Coogan had, to absorb the basic information. I knew he wasn't stupid in the usual sense, but his ego got in his own way too much.

Once he had the picture, he said, "Has anyone called the sheriff's office?" I shook my head; Des Palmos followed suit. "Then don't." The crew chief began a protest; Detweiler said, "We can't have publicity at this stage. Or a herd of deputies underfoot, either. So it's an accident: old equipment, not maintained recently. Something shorted out, or whatever it does. But it won't happen again, because Banning's going to check everything."

He stared at Larry Des Palmos. "Do you understand your instructions?" The man nodded. "Then have someone drive the body in to the coroner's office. You go along, too, and do the talking." Des Palmos motioned to another man, and they went into the smoke-smelling building.

Detweiler turned away; Coogan and I followed him. He said, "Pick another prefab; I'll start getting things moved out from town." He looked at me. "How's the cable system?"

"I haven't exactly had time to inspect it. The first thing Borg did when we got here was pull that light switch."

"Well, get on it. And on those transformers, too; I wasn't kidding about that. You make sure—"

I waved him off. "I can make sure they're all right *now*. That doesn't mean somebody can't gimmick another one tonight."

First scowling, then he grinned. "Anyone who tries it could catch a load of buckshot. I'll lay on a guard watch."

I thought about it. "You may have to, at that; there are lots of ways a determined saboteur could operate. But for the transformers themselves, to prevent any repeat of what happened, just lock up the disconnect extensor handles."

"Maybe so," Coogan said, "but I like the guard idea, too. At least until next week, when the night crew starts."

Around the clock, they planned to work this job? News to me. I decided these people meant business, all right.

The two talked job some more; neither said a word about Borg, except for the inconvenience his death was causing. I excused myself and went to look over the other transformers. The chore went quickly; only two were carrying any load, so far, and I checked with Des Palmos's assistant before cutting their juice. These pivots hadn't been lubed; even with the extensors I had to throw some weight on them to get movement.

Actually I could have cleared the whole installation by eyeball without ever touching a screwdriver; the covers and their retaining screws were dusty, and obviously hadn't been opened for a long time. But it never hurts to go through the motions.

Then I got to the main job: sorting out the signal cables. Some of the cable heads were intact, the terminal boxes sealed. Others had been pulled out, leaving messy sprays of varicolored wires; on those, I had to separate the twisted clumps, make sure none of the ends were shorted. Then I began testing, and jotting down pair-by-pair lists of conditions at each terminal.

It wasn't bad at all; always a few dead pairs, but considering the age of the installation, not too many. The job would have gone faster if I'd had a helper to work the far ends with me; as it was, I did a lot of walking back and forth, and noticed after a while that I didn't really have all my strength back from the recent flu bout. But the work wasn't strenuous; I took my time, using the effort-saving system that solo testers developed a long while back. Eventually I wrapped it up, all the routes between terminals Pedicord might plan to use.

I went to Coogan's new choice of HQ building and found him and Detweiler relaxing with matching drinks. Bourbon over ice, it looked like. It looked good, too. Without saying

anything I made a point of gazing at their table. Nobody
noticed, so the hell with it; I sat and reported.

Detweiler was pleased; now he could get on with construction. I said, "When anyone's going to do any digging
or bulldozing, have him check with me first. Some of those
cables probably aren't dug in too deep." I saw him make a
note.

I heard a car approach, then stop; in a minute or so,
Larry Des Palmos came in. Detweiler asked questions; the
report was, Borg's death was listed as accidental. "They
said something, Mr. Detweiler, about having an expert
come up and inspect the transformer."

George flushed dark red. "Who the hell told you to say
anything about a transformer? I—"

I cut in. "It's no problem, Nobody else saw that strapping panel, just me. I can tell it as an accident, convincingly.
Don't worry."

Detweiler wanted more details; I gave them. I don't think
he understood much of what I said, but he nodded. I resisted the temptation to throw in some double-talk; Des
Palmos might have called me on it. Then I went to fake the
props for my story.

Strapping links aren't just bars with a hole at each end;
they're side-slotted, so you don't have to take the screws all
the way out to move one. What I did, after killing the high
juice and uncovering the transformer strapping panel again,
was to loosen some mounting screws and nudge one strap
down to touch another. If such a thing had happened by
accident—vibration, for instance—the vagaries of high-
voltage arcing *could* have juiced the prefab and killed Borg.
Or might have done something else entirely—which was
why I didn't depend on hotting up the circuit. Instead I
faked the melting and splattering with a welding torch, not
forgetting the inside of the cover panel.

When I was done, I almost believed it myself.

I took the fused, eroded straps—my "evidence"—out of
the panel housing and set them down. In the bottom of the
housing, spares lay dusty. I wiped two clean and installed

them, thinking how long it must have been since any of these units had normal maintenance. I was reaching for the cover, to reseal the panel, when I heard someone behind me. I looked around.

It was Ronnie Detweiler's friend, Eddie Machell. I'd met the man only twice and wasn't sure I liked him. A couple of inches taller than I am, still to most people he was short, and seemed to have the overcompensating feistiness some shorties use a lot. I got rid of that, or hope I did, about halfway through college. So I can't really sympathize too much.

Now, though, he smiled friendly enough. A blondish guy with a chubby face, though not too pudgy in the bod, he looked about six years younger than the thirty that showed on his job application.

He looked at my doctored circuit straps and quit smiling. "Banning, I heard about it. What *happened?*"

Well, I could use a dress rehearsal. Making full use of my slagged-up visual aids, I ran through my story. At the end of it he said, "I thought power circuitry was more foolproof than that. Not that I know a great deal about it . . ."

I shrugged. "It is, usually. On most rigs you won't find strapping options on the low end. I guess the Navy must have had some reason for this special setup, but I can't think what. But it was damned bad luck for Ansel Borg—and could have been for any of us who pulled that switch."

"Yes." Scowling, Machell looked away. He saw my welding torch and pointed to it. "What's that for? Here, I mean."

Banning, you stupid ass! I hoped nothing showed in my face. I picked up one of my weld-treated straps and turned it over. "Right here, it was melted stuck to the frame." Yes, there was a spot I'd made; I indicated it. "If I'd tried to pry it loose, I might have broken the terminal, so—" He nodded, but I wasn't sure he'd bought the story.

Well, supposing he hadn't; what could he do about it? At any rate he was kind enough to carry my welding rig, walking back, so that I had only my other gear to tote.

If Detweiler and Coogan were pleased to see Machell with me, they didn't show it. I said, "I salvaged some melted-up junk that confirms my guess, how the high-voltage shorted through." I set the twisted metal down on the table in front of Detweiler. "The arcing splashed around quite a bit, inside the panel enclosure. Made a mess."

Detweiler nodded. For a second I thought he might smile, but he caught himself and didn't. Coogan's eyes narrowed a trifle; otherwise he showed no reaction. He said, "It's been a tough day; let's be done with it. If you're ready to go, Banning, Tixo will drive you home."

Since the moment I left Tixo outside the lethal prefab and ran to discover the transformer sabotaged, I hadn't thought of him at all; I had no idea where he'd been. Nor did I ask; he was in the Toyota when I went to it, and he did drive me home.

On the way I did some thinking. Why had I agreed—volunteered was more like it—to cover up sabotage that had killed a man? I wasn't sure I understood my motives, and the lack bothered me. Finally I decided I didn't *have* a good reason, except that I wanted to see whether the Stork's project could really fly. And police interference, along with the inevitable publicity, would surely abort the entire fabulous possibility.

I couldn't really accept that answer. But for the time being, it was the only one I had.

Except that whoever had killed Ansel Borg, I didn't want the sonofabitch to win by it.

CHAPTER SIX

Twilight had hit a lovely stage when Tixo left me off. I climbed up through the tunnel and found Dauna unclothed. Nothing on for dinner, either—and by then my stomach had forgiven the day; I hungered.

Dauna, though, had other ideas; dinner would have to wait. Any time she gives signals of that strength, Dauna is extremely orgasmic; we had fun. And when I eventually cooked up some leftovers, that part worked out all right, too.

On teevy we found a sitcom with all adult characters, no obligatory herd of cute kiddies mouthing double-entendre lines. By the program's end, Dauna had cooled out and could focus. So I told her about my day: Borg's death and the whole package. Not the kindly thing to do, but I needed some feedback.

The grue didn't seem to upset her much; she could track. "Somebody did it on purpose, Mitch?"

"How else?" She didn't know beans about circuits so I left that part out. "It was a hands-on job, Dauna; take my word."

Hands—she put hers forward and grabbed mine. "Get out of it, Mitch! You don't need the money. And there's crazy people in this. Has to be; don't you see that? Mitch—" She shook her head, the long hair rippling along its length.

I had no answer. I reached for my tall lady and hugged her. Then we got to kissing, to the point that I wished I had a faster recovery time. But she was worn out herself; time for sleepy-bye. So I didn't really have to feel bad about not being Superman.

*   *   *

After a while I got up and put a robe on. Curled into her favorite sleeping position, Dauna was set for all night, but I wasn't. I went out and cleared up from dinner, leafed through the paper, then turned the TV back on. The prize picks were three cop shows and a docudrama on teenage prostitution. The phone rescued me.

"I warned you, Banning." The husky voice still sounded faked. "One down; too bad it wasn't Pedicord." The man—now I was sure the caller was male—laughed.

My hunch said that trying to probe was the wrong way to play it. I tried a long shot. "What are you talking about?" How much he knew might point to who he was.

"The late Ansel Borg. Don't act stupid."

All right. "You're trying to take credit—or blame—for a freak accident? I inspected the faulty transformer myself."

I heard him suck in breath. "So that's the line you're taking." His tone showed no surprise. A little silence; then he said, "That's fine; that's just fine. Go ahead, Banning. Cover up all you want; that just gives me more room to work in. Until pretty soon I'll pile the crap so high you *can't* cover it. Have fun trying."

Before he could hang up I said, "Tell me something, friend."

"Such as?"

"Why me? Why deal through me? I'm only the hired help."

"Because you're not Pedicord, or Coogan. Or even Detweiler."

"I'm not the queen of Romania, either. Make sense to me."

Instead, he made a snort. "Pedicord's a thief, Coogan's his fence, and Detweiler's a willing customer for stolen goods. You, though—I had the idea you might be reasonably honest."

I wished I had a beer, but wishing didn't make it so. "I generally try to be."

"But you're covering up for Detweiler." So this man knew who'd ordered the lid put on. Interesting . . .

And maybe a handle, too? "If there was a cover-up—if there was anything to cover—what makes you think Detweiler isn't on the receiving end?"

"Don't hand me garbage!" He was angry now, mad as hell. "I heard it. Through my sources, I mean." He hung up, and the pause between sentences had been just about right for a fast thinker doing a little covering on his own account.

I went for that beer I needed, and sat to think some more about the whole mess.

It was late, but I decided to call Coogan's apartment. Why? I wasn't sure. The Stork was mostly an unknown quantity, but in my book he was no killer. Nor even a bully, after the style of George Detweiler. So I phoned him, and reported my previous call as near verbatim as I could manage. "It has to be someone with access to Range A," I concluded, "not a sneak-in intruder. And with a heavy grudge against you and Pedicord. Any ideas?"

I waited, until he said, "The grudge. There was a man— but he's dead now." Before I could ask, he said, "Natural causes. Cancer; the doctors found it too late. And Allert was paranoid; his accusations against Dr. Pedicord were ridiculous."

He stopped; I asked, "Any more ridiculous than my menacing caller? Or Borg's frying himself on a light switch?"

I could almost hear a shudder as Coogan said, "I'll think about it. There can't be any connection, but—well, thanks for the information, Banning."

Before I was three steps away from the phone, it sounded. I got it on the first ring. "Banning? It's me again. The Green Hornet. I guess you've been talking to Coogan. Or was it Detweiler?"

Green Hornet, huh? Could the guy have a sense of humor, or did he really identify with an oldtime comic-book hero? I said, "What makes you think so? Either way?"

"I gave it a little time, then dialed you and got a busy signal. So—"

The hell with this; I yawned, loudly. "You ever try to order a pizza this time of night?"

The sound of the voice evoked a taut face with narrowed eyes. "Don't give me garbage, I said! Especially since I have something for you. To pass on to Coogan, I mean."

"Briefly, I hope." Might as well push it . . .

"Half. Is that brief enough for you? If he and Pedicord want me to let them go through with this deal, I get half."

Well, now. Things began to make sense. Not much, but a little. So get on it: "Sure. Assuming they agree, how would you like the check made out?"

"Funny, fun-*nee*. Quit playing Sherlock, Banning, and stick to your—uh—soldering iron. Just pass the word to Coogan."

I hung up first. I know a punchline when I hear one.

I didn't call Coogan; I saved the Green Hornet's demands for next day at the Stork's office. I won't say I missed Borg's personality—as I came through his area I saw a young black man sitting in Borg's chair and talking on his phone—but the feeling of his *permanent* absence was not at all pleasant.

On the other hand, Tixo was having one of his friendly days, being the one to initiate our knife-passing, forehead-touching ritual. Sometimes that little Indian struck me as having a split personality.

In the back office he brought Coogan and me some coffee, then went out again. I related my late-night call. Coogan looked puzzled; I could hardly blame him. "He calls himself the Green Hornet? Why, I wonder?"

I shrugged. "Maybe it's a joke, maybe he believes it. Either way, does it matter? Half, the man wants. Gross or net, he didn't say. Meanwhile he's already cut your payroll expenses." I'm not really that callous about human life, but it seemed time to shake Coogan up a little.

Possibly it worked; he said, "Just like that. How *could* he?"

I didn't feel up to a philosophical discussion on why

some people can add deaths and dollars in the same col-
umn. "That's not the question, Coogan." I banged my
empty cup down harder than I meant to. "Look. This is
none of my business, really. I'm supposed to be gathering
material for an article and designing a digital-data system
for pay. But the question isn't what this weirdo can do, or
why. It's what you intend to do about it."

He shook his head. "I won't pay a nickel. Not to a
damned terrorist."

I stood. "That's your last word?" He looked startled, and
I realized how it sounded. "Your ultimatum, I mean?"

When he wanted to, the Stork had a mean stare. "Are
you in on this? Or perhaps—are *you* the Green Hornet?"

"Yesterday was my first time at Range A; you know
that."

He relaxed. "Yes, of course. But—" He shook his head.
"All right; if the man calls again, try to get him to talk with
me directly. If he won't—well, see what you can find out."

"Sure." We were done with it for now, so I went to my
own work area and repackaged some more circuits to fit
Pedicord's latest change list.

Maybe someday he'd make up his mind.

The next few days passed with no word from the Hornet;
at Range A I accomplished quite a bit. Detweiler's people
wasted no time installing my terminal equipment mount-
ings in the newly constructed buildings, and the MilSpec
modules came back from his shops, rewired so I could use
them.

This was by no means my first job with several different
activities going on at once, so I knew about working around
other people's schedules. Things go better when folks don't
get in each others' way. Finally I had all my carrier gear and
terminal repeaters in place—with spare channels in each
speed range, to allow for Pedicord's whimsies.

I couldn't do my testing yet, because at that point the
juice shut down for installation of new, more flexible
power panels at both terminals of the experiment. So I took
a few days off, caught up on tag ends of other work, then

skipped town with Dauna for a seaside weekend. Saturday was fine but Sunday came up rain, so we returned home early.

When we climbed up the tunnel and entered the house, we found we'd had company.

Someone had made a real mess: no destruction, just objects strewn all over the floor. Dauna can cuss a blue streak when she feels like it, and I said a few things myself. Then we began putting the place into some kind of order.

After an hour or so we took a break. Near as we could tell, nothing was missing. "Looking for something," Dauna said. "Would this be a sting from your Hornet? We need a flyswatter."

"First we have to figure who to swat. I think I'll call Coogan."

He wasn't home. I tried his office; he didn't answer until the eighth ring. "Who the hell's that?"

"Mitch Banning. Is anything wrong?"

"It—never mind. What do you want?"

I explained what had happened. As a cusser, Coogan couldn't rate in Dauna's league, but he did try. Then, "Someone's been a busy little bastard. Broke in here and tried to open my safe, jammed the lock. I've had to call in an expert. At double time. If I ever get my hands—"

"Sure," I said. "Me too. Except we don't know *who*." I paused a moment, thinking. "Any other buzzing from the Hornet?"

When Coogan answered, his voice sounded careful. "I received a package in the mail." My first thought was explosives, but he said, "A phonograph record. One of those little ones."

"A forty-five?"

"What? Yes, I suppose so. Did you know there was a rock group called Green Hornet?"

I hadn't, but in recent years I don't follow such things much. Dauna does; I asked her. She'd never heard of it. I told Coogan so, then asked, "Is that all? To the story, I mean?"

"Not exactly. The song titles . . ."

He told it. One side read "Fifty-fifty All the Way;" the flipover was "Baby, You'll Never Lose Me."

I almost laughed. But it wasn't really funny. "Music-wise, how do you rate the record? Is it Top Forty material?"

He gave me a snort. "I don't own a record player. Do you think—?"

"I don't know. But it might be a good idea to play the little sucker. Just a hunch."

All right. In about an hour he'd bring the disc over to the house. I thought there might be an old disc player down in the garage in a carton, and I was right.

Dusted off, the thing worked. Good enough; when he did arrive, a little later than predicted, Dauna and I had finished most of the tidying and were having coffee.

Elihu Coogan—or Emil the Stork, take your pick—deigned to have a cup. Cream, no sugar. Then he showed us the record. I couldn't tell much by it; Dauna said, "Rubber Dubber?"

We looked at her; she laughed. "You could catch flies, with your mouths open. I meant, the label's a cheap printing job, like one of the old-time pirate recording outfits. Let's see if the contents are, too." She went over to the turntable and found one of those little insert-goojies (the Hornet hadn't supplied one) and put it in, and set the record to play.

It was a 1967 Beatles single. "Penny Lane" we heard all the way through, to make sure there was no hidden message, then "Strawberry Fields." I rather enjoyed being reminded of '67—it had been a good year in my childhood—but otherwise we weren't getting much of anywhere.

I shook my head. "It's all in the label, Coogan. Nothing more."

His frown looked more puzzled than angry. "But what does it mean? What's the point?" He waved a hand. "Oh, certainly. The titles, reiterating his extortionate demands. But why this way?"

I shrugged. "Maybe he does have a sense of humor. I'd wondered about that."

There wasn't much more to it. Coogan finished his second cup, retrieved his record, and left. Dauna and I went ahead with the last of our work, putting the place back together, and polished off the rest of the coffee, too.

It was dinnertime but we were off sked. The TV was on its news hour, but we weren't in the mood; after seeing that Senate opposition to Cretin-Hogsbreath was still fighting a rearguard action, I shut the set off. I was coffeed-out, but made a pot for Dauna who can drink the stuff all day. As she began on it I poured myself a little claret and walked over to look out the front window: down the darkening hillside and along the valley.

From an apartment house across the street a few doors away, I saw a quick flare of light. Directly in front of me, glass shattered; an angry bee whined past to make a splatting crash behind.

I suppose that's when I dropped the wine.

CHAPTER SEVEN

Flat on the floor, where I found myself without noticing how I got there, I reached up and pulled the cord to close the drapes. Still on the deck, I wriggled back to cut the lights. Then I stood; by the glow from the hallway, I looked around.

Dauna hadn't budged; she hadn't even spilled her coffee. Of course she wasn't in the line of fire, either. Draining her cup, she made a face. "Mitch? Get *out* of this."

Some might have said a lot more; Dauna made her point and stopped. I shook my head and she shrugged; we'd have to talk this out, but now wasn't the time. I turned up some light, and went over to look at the wall and see what the splat had done.

A wide, shallow crater with no depth. That fit with the *wheeee*-snarl of the passing bullet: something in a small caliber, very lightweight and very high velocity. Just hitting you around the edges, that stuff can kill by hydrostatic shock. But those light slugs are no good at plowing through interference; anything at all deflects them.

In the cratered plaster I saw only flecks of metal, nothing to interest a ballistics lab. No point in calling the police. When Dauna said "Why not?" I realized I'd said it out loud, and explained.

With both hands she pushed her hair back. "You're *not* getting out, are you?" I guess my silence was answer enough; she said, "Then I'm getting in." I looked at her; she meant it, all right.

She gave a quick laugh. "I'm supposed to be writing an article myself. So get me George Detweiler, for an interview."

Well, sure. Next morning I called and set it up. Before, I couldn't have done that; George would have stonewalled. But being co-conspirators now, in the matter of the late Ansel Borg, I figured I had more leverage. And I was right.

We met at Range A. Waiting for Detweiler I showed Dauna around the construction-in-progress at Pedicord's sending and receiving terminals, where the Navy's transmitter and auxiliary power station, respectively, had been. If she was impressed, she didn't show it. But then, Dauna wasn't much given to looking overawed.

After the inspection tour we walked around and enjoyed the scenery. The valley, with its surviving trees and more recent growth of flowering bushes, was worth seeing on its own account.

When Detweiler was nearly an hour overdue, a county car pulled in over the hill and came to rest at the far side of the parking lot. I didn't pay much attention, until Coogan brought a tall, fiftyish man over and introduced him. "Deputy Capcek, Mitchell Banning."

We shook hands, and Capcek told me what he wanted; he was the expert sent to look at the transformer. So we stopped by Coogan's HQ prefab, where I showed off the strapping I'd gimmicked; we then walked up to the transformer farm. Dauna tagged along; I could see she was enjoying herself and hoped it would last.

When I got the cover off the first strapping panel, Capcek frowned. "Bad engineering, leaving the chance for an open at the low end." He was right, of course.

I told him so. "But keep in mind, this was designed for a military installation. Were you in the service?"

"Yes. Tail end of 'Nam, just before the evac. You'd be still a kid then; right?"

I nodded. "I did put in a hitch, fresh out of high school. In Alaska, mostly." I'd done it for the GI college money, but didn't exactly regret the experience, either.

That wasn't the point, though. I said, "So we both know that sometimes the brass gets its ego up, and outvotes the working troops who know their business. Five gets you ten, that's what happened to this transformer design."

I watched him think about it. "You could be right. But there's no reason it has to stay that way." I waited. "Get yourself a welding torch." My breath caught; had this man guessed what I'd done? But then, "You don't need ground-end options at all. So weld those straps down solid; make the whole setup standard-commercial from the safety standpoint. And then I'll be done here. With the entire mess."

All right; I got the torch and did what the man said. Matter of fact I felt silly for not thinking of that answer myself. Reluctance, maybe, to clobber someone else's property.

At any rate, I finished the job. Whereupon Deputy Capcek gave me a handshake and his thanks, and drove away.

Somewhere along the line, Dauna had left our inspection team. Looking for her I noticed Detweiler's Continental had arrived, so I went to his contractor's office. There I found Dauna interviewing Howard Hughes, jr.

"So if your venture succeeds, Mr. Detweiler, what do you have in mind to *do* with such a revolutionary device? So many, many possible applications . . ."

Detweiler laughed. "You'd think it was easy, wouldn't you? Something you can put an object into—or a person—add X number of kilowatts and transfer the subject to a distant location. Unlimited possibilities; right?" Another laugh. "Wrong."

Hanging on the great man's every word, Dauna waited; she does a beautiful act when it suits her. Detweiler aimed a forefinger. "Cost effectiveness, that's your answer. Pedicord's invention is limited to cases where time and distance are worth the *money*." George was enjoying himself. "In short, it'll never replace the Postal Service."

"Too bad," I said. "Something should." I caught a glare that told me to quit stepping on Detweiler's lines.

"I've studied the doctor's power estimates," he said, "and made a tentative list of profitable uses. For instance, if we could assemble a working two-way terminal on the moon, a lunar research station or even a full-fledged colony would begin to pay off in less than three years. Compared to present NASA costs, operating expenses would amount to practically a free ride." He spread his hands. "Then think of Mars: how does *that* idea strike you?"

It struck me that Congress might approve it if someone else paid the tab, but I kept my mouth shut. Detweiler was thinking wide-track; no point in derailing him. Now he said, "Here on Earth, the applications are largely confined to government and major business enterprises. Instant travel for heads of state and comparable VIPs. Secure transport for eyes-only reports, objects of great value, and so forth. That's the sort of thing I have in mind."

He paused long enough that it didn't seem rude to put in a question; Dauna beat me to it. "Instant travel, you said. *How* instant? Does the speed of light enter into it?"

Every time I'd tried to ask about such matters, Coogan or Pedicord had sidestepped. I listened as Detweiler said, "Light? Not directly. Of course the telemetry and control circuits have that kind of limitation." I hadn't known he cared. "As I understand it, though, there is some kind of time-constant—rather small—that's linked to distance but not one-for-one."

Which was more than I'd known. Apparently George was using the purse strings to draw out information I certainly hadn't been able to get. Whether he understood it, or not.

But he'd said it all now, and was beginning to repeat himself. I quit listening and pondered. In the physics I'd studied, such a constant had no place. If Pedicord had actually discovered something totally new . . .

I came out of my own thinking to hear Dauna ask, "—the risk, to a human being, if the signal garbles in transit?"

George shook his head. "That's just it; there is no signal. Two spaces momentarily become the same space, and the transfer occurs. Or doesn't; *that's* the only risk."

For a moment I almost heard the Stork talking. Detweiler had to be quoting him directly; Pedicord would never have been so coherent. Then Dauna asked about schedules: construction and eventual testing of the gadget. I'd seen all that on paper, knew how tentative it was at this point. So I drifted outside and over to the former generator site, where the new building was filling up with components for the device's receiving end. Not much new: a little more than yesterday, was all. I walked up the valley, looked at scenery a while, and came back again. I was less than sixty yards from the prefab when Dauna and George came out. They had taken maybe a dozen steps when I heard the bullet's spiteful whine, then the sharp crack of the rifle.

Beside Detweiler a bush shuddered and sprayed leaves. The man didn't move; he stood, looking around, as Dauna tried to pull him back toward the building. I stared uphill, where the report had come from: a tangle of underbrush near the hillside's crest. I saw no one, and the gun didn't sound again. I started running down to where the others stood, then slowed to a walk. There didn't seem to be much need to hurry.

Detweiler acted more surprised than scared. "I don't understand." Well, neither did I. I looked at the bush, then back up the hillside. George said, "What was that for?"

I shrugged. "Either to kill you or scare you; I'm not sure which." Two items. The bush wasn't straight in line between the rifle and where George had stood; I was sure of that. And I'd have given odds it was the same gun that shot near me the night before. Answer: someone was either a consistently lousy shot, or was aiming to miss. Question: tell George, or not? I flipped a mental coin and told him all of it.

For at least a minute he didn't speak. Then, "Why? What's the point?"

"To scare us off the project." Detweiler scowled; I went on. "It wasn't a bad move," I said. "Or wouldn't have been, if the Hornet trusted his ballistics. If he'd shot straight at you through that bush, those little twigs would have deflected the bullet. But he didn't want to take the chance. At least, that's how I'm guessing it."

Again he paused. Then he shrugged his big shoulders. "Either way, it doesn't matter. There's a billion dollars waiting for me to grab it, and no creep with a popgun is going to stop me." He looked up at the hillside, and squinted. "Armed men, say fifty of them. Clean sweep operation and then a perimeter guard, on shifts; nobody comes in without a pass. I—"

Dauna was shaking her head; George stopped talking. She said, "*After* the fact, you safety everything. Mitch fixed the transformers; you'll set guards against the rifle. But how do you know what *else* this Hornet may sting with?"

Detweiler didn't like her attitude. He broke off the talk, rounded up his sidemen, and booted out in the Continental. Watching dust settle in the car's wake, Dauna grinned. "Well, I got my article—though it can't run until the Stork's gidgie either spits people out or doesn't. But when the test results do prove up, one way or the other, George's signature says I have an exclusive." As the big car topped the ridge and vanished behind it, she said, "Actually,

Mitch—if I never see that man again, the sight would be welcome.''

Others had heard the shot, of course; by now, several were outside and looking around. Larry Des Palmos came over to ask if we knew anything. Figuring it was no secret, I told him. In detail, adding, "What puzzles me is the way Detweiler took it."

Des Palmos wasn't a bad guy when you got to know him. Now he made a brief half-smile. "A lot of people don't like George Detweiler. But for guts you have to hand it to him."

I looked a question; Larry said, "Two years ago, in that Teamster hassle, he got some death threats. The way I heard it, he just went ahead anyway."

Back at prep I didn't remember George as any iron man; I said so. Des Palmos answered, "There's a story about him; I heard it one time before, when I worked on a job for him. He was a little drunk, so maybe I don't have all the details straight. It happened in Army training; somebody went to throw a grenade and it slipped out of his hand. Detweiler fell on it, covered it. He didn't want to, didn't intend to—but his training took over and he did it. And then the damned thing didn't go off."

I blinked. "I don't get it."

"He said it felt like hours, waiting, while he kicked himself for throwing his life away. Then when it was certain the thing was a dud, he got up. A different man, he says. Before, he'd been scared of bad risks, like everybody is. But now he figures that if he ever dies, it's just that lousy grenade finally catching up to him."

After a bit, I nodded. "If you don't look at it too close, I guess it makes sense."

Dauna said it better. "If it works for him, then what the rest of us think doesn't really matter, does it?"

For this day, Dauna had her story—what there was of it, so far—and my own work was caught up to waiting for other people to clear me some space. I checked with Coogan, who had been in a basement area during the shooting and needed a news transfusion, and got his okay to leave early.

On the way home, Dauna and I stopped for groceries. At the house I checked the mailbox and we carried things upstairs. I had one check, a job-estimate response, and a lot of junk mail—plus one heavy legal-sized envelope with an impressive, unfamiliar return imprint. Verdesting, Ltd., with a Chicago address—but a local postmark. I opened the envelope.

Inside was a sheet of thick, clear, unmarked plastic and a brief note, typed all in caps.

> MITCHELL BANNING: THIS IS NOT A LETTER BOMB,
> SO YOU ARE STILL ALIVE. IT COULD HAVE BEEN,
> THOUGH, AND THEN YOU WOULD BE DEAD. IS THAT
> CLEAR ENOUGH? GET YOURSELF OUT OF THE
> THIEVING SCHEMES OF PEDICORD AND COOGAN.

No signature: only a crude drawing, in green ink, of some kind of wasplike insect.

I looked at the envelope again. Verdesting? All right; verde means green, and sting was obvious. Not exactly a scholarly job of word-coining, but I'm no world-class scholar myself. Saying as much, I showed the thing to Dauna.

She said, "You know something, Mitch? Killing doesn't take much scholarship."

I had to agree. But, "Except for his wild swing with the transformer, which happened to get Borg instead of somebody else or maybe no one at all, the Hornet hasn't really tried to kill anyone."

Frowning, Dauna said, "You talk like a man with an eighty-proof IQ. What makes you think your Green Hornet runs on tracks?"

She was right, of course. And took the idea further. If our sniping friend needed me to dicker, to get him half the anticipated loot, why did he keep pushing to get me out of the game? It's easy enough to dismiss inconsistencies by saying somebody's shooting craps with blank dice, but it doesn't really get you anywhere.

So, as we agreed over dinner a time later, all that made sense was to wait for the next move.

For a week or so I had little to do with the project. Heavy equipment was arriving, and my best place was out from underfoot while Pedicord supervised placement, installation, and assembly. How I reached that conclusion was that one day the eminent physicist invited me to get my ass the hell out.

I don't have to have a house fall on me; a small shed does the job nicely. I stayed home and caught up on some business correspondence, crossword puzzles, and my suntan. Then came two days' rain; I decided nuts to Pedicord and went back to Range A.

As a matter of fact, the unpredictable doctor was glad to see me. His particle accelerators at sending and receiving ends needed, he said, to be perfectly synchronized. For the big units, the passenger model with both ends at Range A, he'd managed to make the adjustments himself. But the smaller, long-distance version was giving him trouble. For that one, the receiving end was being set up in the security room of Coogan's downtown office suite; running a special power feed up through the Trosper Building was costing a fair bundle. At any rate, compensating for signal delays in the control and telemetry circuits was giving Pedicord a case of the fits.

As it turned out, the answer was easy enough; sometimes these theory boys are close to helpless with the hardware aspects and this was one of those times. Dr. Pedicord was adding one set of delays in the wrong direction, was all.

I didn't tell him that. To save his face and inflate my own prestige I set up an impressive but unnecessary CRT display, then quietly reversed the phase where he had it wrong, and talked him through the consequent adjustments.

He thanked me; further, he offered me a tour of the Holy of Holies: the transporter apparatus room itself. The crew working there, Coogan had hired personally; neither Detweiler nor I had had anything to do with it.

Well, except for one man. Borg was to have been straw boss, sitting in for Coogan and Pedicord. As his replacement Coogan had picked Eddie Machell.

Who met us at the door. Authority agreed with Eddie; his smile, when Pedicord okayed me for entrance, spelled welcome. Leading us over to the transmitter chamber housing—we were at the sending end—his walk had a healthy bounce to it.

The chamber itself wasn't installed yet; it sat over to one side. But the big helices were in place, with some of the shielding, and Machell pointed to the complicated spiral supports that would pivot the chamber to center stage. "They're shaped for minimum interference with the particle fields."

Pedicord cut in. "Particle *flows*, Machell. Or streams, if you like. There are fields involved also, but they are not composed of particles. And there will be no accelerated particles traversing this space." He sniffed. "I hope your direction of this installation is better than your nomenclature."

Eddie Machell's face reddened. "Mr. Banning isn't a physicist. I was giving it to him in layman's terms."

"Sure," I said. "And thanks." Whatever was cooking between those two, I didn't want to be in the middle. Pedicord grumped a little more and then got off his crew chief's back. Machell went on explaining things; I couldn't tell how accurately, but it didn't matter. Either the thing would work or it wouldn't.

And that's what *my* story would be about.

One thing bothered me, but I wasn't going to ask Machell about it—or, for that matter, Pedicord. After a while the tour ended. The doc and I walked back to Coogan's field HQ. When Pedicord went into a back room to do whatever he might do there, I put my query to Emil the Stork.

"That transmission chamber. On the small side, isn't it?"

"As small as we can make do with. I've told you how the power requirements increase with size."

"But with the amount of shielding Pedicord indicated, how are you going to get a man inside that thing?"

Then Tixo walked past the door, and I knew the answer; I thumbed in his direction and raised my eyebrows. Coogan said, "That's right. We designed the chamber to Tixo's measurements. Once we have positive results, you realize, money will be no object—nor energy, for that matter. And the chamber itself is all that will need replacing, to accommodate larger persons." He paused. "Well, the supports must be modified, of course."

Something didn't fit, and it wasn't Tixo. "What if our little friend doesn't like the idea? Or gets run over by a skateboard?"

I wasn't sure what I was fishing for, but whatever it was, Coogan didn't like it. "Tixo's devoted to me. I saved his life, you know." I hadn't; maybe I still didn't. Coogan went on, "There are other small people. You yourself could probably get into the chamber. Not comfortably, but I think you could do it."

His stare wasn't comfortable, either: a lot too intense for my taste. I shrugged. "No, thanks." His expression changed, in a way I couldn't interpret, to something more relaxed. Switching subjects, I told him that Pedicord's signal delay problems were solved (though not how). For a few more minutes we talked shop, to very little point except to assure him that for the time being I was pretty well abreast of the job.

Time to leave. If anyone wanted me, they had my phone number.

Out in the parking lot, the Volvo had a flat. The tire had a nail in it. The nail was in the sidewall, not the tread.

Somebody was trying to tell me something. Unfortunately, I already knew what it was.

CHAPTER EIGHT

When I got home, Dauna was pacing up a storm. Nothing to do with me, it turned out: what she said was, "How do you think you'll like living with a Welfare Mother?"

This one looked to take some sorting out. "Depends. Who did you have in mind?"

I got a laugh, which was all I was after at that point. "I'm not giving you to anybody. I think Wilford canned me."

The publisher of *Westside Weekly?* "I thought Ned Farringen controlled hire-and-fire."

"They two had themselves a fight together. A biggie. I think Ned used something concerning me as a point on his side, and Chuck Wilford shot me down for overkill."

Tense, trembling a little, she was really hurting. I went to hug her. "Honey, we're not in trouble. You're good enough to work on any sheet in the area and we both know it. Meanwhile—" I shrugged. "We're loose for money just now; you know that, too. It stretches fine, what we have on tap."

She said, "I know. It's just that I feel like used food."

Something . . . "What was that mother bit all about? Did I miss a point?"

Now she laughed again. "No. It's merely that when one gets screwed over the way I did today, it's hard to avoid feeling a little bit pregnant."

In a way, I was surprised to find, I was disappointed.

We were free and clear. Dauna wasn't going near the magazine until someone called and asked her, including an apology. I wasn't needed on the Stork's caper, whatever that might turn out to be, until further notice. I was up-to-date

with Pentco and Ettlin and so forth. In short, there was no
need to hang around.

We flew to San Fran, then to L.A. and on to Albuquerque, where we rented a car and drove up to Santa
Fe. There at seven thousand feet we found the place where
we wanted to stay for a few days. A motel is a hacienda if
you like it well enough.

I enjoyed the break a lot, and when Coogan finally called
the number I'd phoned in when we arrived, I was sorry to
leave. If it hadn't been for credit cards, though, we'd never
have got away with all the silver-and-turquoise jewelry
Dauna discovered. Beautiful stuff, mind you. But preparing
for takeoff at Albuquerque, I wondered (aloud, of course)
whether our 787 would really get it all upstairs safely.

We picked up the Volvo at the Rent-a-Heap lot and I drove
us home. What greeted us first was a blackened, exploded
mailbox. I didn't have to Guess Who. We went up the
tunnel fast; the house was all right. I got on the phone to
Coogan.

He'd had his own share of harassments: stink bomb
under his car's hood, smoke bomb on button twenty-three
of one of the Trosper Building elevators. Either, obviously,
could have been lethally explosive if the Green Hornet so
chose, and of course that's what the obnoxious insect was
pointing out.

What really got to the Stork, though, was something
quite different. For two days, now, he'd been peeing blue.
That's an old joke; I think the chemical in question, quite
harmless, is called methylene blue. But someone had
slipped the stuff into something he ate or drank, and he had
no idea how it was done. Or where, or when.

"Dr. Pedicord's scared, too," he said. "He won't say
what happened. But he's acting very strangely."

I wanted to ask Coogan how he could tell the difference,
but I didn't. Instead, "No clues to the Hornet, I gather?"

"Nothing at all. Only his threats and sabotage. Not a
comfortable situation."

I guessed it wasn't, and added, "How about Detweiler? Has he been bothered?"

"I don't know. For all his brave talk he hasn't been near Range A since the shooting incident. But he's made no mention of any further threats or demonstrations."

"That's something. Well, then; what comes next?"

"We go ahead, of course; I'll see you tomorrow at Range A."

No sooner did I hang up than the phone chimed at me. Ned Farringen. When Dauna consented to take the call, I left the room. Puttered in the kitchen, visited the bathroom. But when I ran out of places to go, she was still on the wire.

"I don't know, Ned." From several feet away I could hear Farringen talking loud and fast. Dauna laughed. "Maybe so, maybe not. You may tell *Mister* Wilford that suddenly the carpet in my office doesn't suit me." While he talked some more, Dauna winked at me. Then, "Well, red would be nice, don't you think?"

I grinned. No physical carpet; it was the treatment she meant. Farringen took longer to catch on; several more exchanges passed before Dauna said, "Now you have it, Ned. Yes. Oh, any time in the next two or three days."

Something he said, then, made her frown. "No. After that, I won't be available. All right, Ned; thanks for calling. I appreciate it."

As she killed the phone and came over to me, Dauna smiled. "Chuckie's hoping I'll forgive and forget. But I won't. He's going to have to kiss it and make it well, or next week I go downtown and see about rejoining the newspaper business. The *Times*, I think."

"Want me to ask Joey Aguilar about prospects?"

She shook her head. "Thanks, but I'd rather wing it."

Next morning, for a change I got up early. For one thing, we needed a mailbox. After a quick breakfast I drove to the nearest shopping center with anything resembling a hardware store, and picked out the biggest box I could find, along with bolts and brackets for mounting it. Back home the job didn't take long, except for getting the wreckage of the old box off the wall. The blast had melted one screw to some hanging shreds; a little heavy pry-work took care of it.

Not much later than usual, I left for Range A.

Detweiler had his guard system in operation, all right. By now he'd cut it to eight men, well placed for strategic coverage. Men *and* women, rather; the gate guard was female. My name was on her list; she made a quick thing of the ID check and waved me in.

At the side of the parking lot nearest the buildings I saw several of the small Detweiler Commute cars; a closer look showed that charging posts for them had been installed. That need, of course, was the main obstacle to marketing the little electrics in quantity.

Detweiler had taken a realistic approach to this enterprise; Preston Tucker, he wasn't. Nor even Henry Kaiser, who with a much more viable capital base had given the Big Three a good run, I understand, for five or six years before they froze him out.

No, George was building from a local strong-point and hoping to spread out gradually. He used body, chassis, and running gear manufactured by Suzuki for the Ford Parva, ordering them in hundred-unit lots and adding his own battery-motors setup.

The batteries were a special lightweight item that he got surplus from a cut-back military program; I don't pretend to know which esoteric alloys gave them such a mass-to-energy advantage.

But batteries need recharging, and on that angle, Detweiler's people had come up with a cute wrinkle: charging posts installed just like parking meters. When you plugged in, your unit sent its ID number to a central computer for billing. At home, of course, you were on your own meter so who cared?

All in all, a good effort; I wondered how far George would get with it.

* * *

As I left the Volvo I noticed a group outside Coogan's building, so I walked over there. The star attraction was Eddie Machell, explaining why he had his arm in a sling.

"Just the one shot," he was saying. "It broke my car window and threw glass around, but luckily it only nicked me." .

Apparently he'd been through the story a few times, but obliged me with a rerun. Yesterday evening, still mostly daylight, he'd gone out to his car—parked curbside—and got in. He was reaching to fasten his shoulder harness when the shot came: noise, glass splinters, and a sting in the forearm.

With not a witness to be found. Eddie shrugged. "I guess it's true, people don't want to get involved."

I asked what the shot sounded like. He described more or less the same high-velocity small-caliber whine of the rifle the Hornet had used with me and with George Detweiler. And the doctor who checked the wound had also guessed that a small, grazing bullet caused it. But that didn't fit. . . .

I said, "Have you talked to the police?"

"Yes. I didn't say anything about the project, though, or the attack on Mr. Detweiler. I knew he wouldn't want that."

Some latecomers arrived; the same questions began again. Having, probably, all the useful info I was going to get, I left the group.

On a hunch I went looking for Machell's car. I didn't know what kind it was, but found a green Hyundai with a jagged hole in the driver's window and crazed glass all around.

Looking inside I tried to visualize where Eddie's arm would have been, reaching up and back. I shook my head.

Two things were wrong. At that angle the high-fps pellet was more likely to blow up and spatter than to break through. And if the thing had hit Machell, more than a skin-graze that wouldn't need a doctor at all, it should have blown out a piece of meat fit to feed a medium-sized dog.

So Machell was a phony.

*   *   *

Or was he? Talking to him, the police would have looked at the car, too—and seen exactly what I saw. I looked more closely: inside, for signs of bullet damage.

Anywhere the slug could have hit, everything was intact. Squinting through the hole I saw glass splinters, nothing more. No holes, no splattered metal.

It took some thinking. I know it's fashionable to badrate the cops: they take forever to catch the motiveless likes of Ted Bundy or the Green River Killer, if they ever do get them. And the drug gangs, with their crack and crank and crush, own areas of most cities in fee simple. But our own municipal force impresses me favorably; consistently they come up with pretty good work. So maybe I was overlooking something.

While I eyeballed the car further, I thought through Eddie's story. If the Hornet used a less powerful gun, or even a lighter load—but the window said high velocity loud and clear, so cancel that guess. Maybe . . .

Then I saw another answer. I had to check it; I went to Des Palmos's office and used a spare phone there. Nine-one-one put me on hold twice; both times I hung up and tried again. On the third go I talked my way through several layers of bureaucracy until I was on with a Sergeant Corey, who had the file on the Machell shooting.

My song-and-dance wasn't especially cute: I was calling for Mr. George Detweiler, Mr. Machell's employer. Machell's account of the incident hadn't been too clear in places, so perhaps, for our insurance forms . . .

Details got in the way, but after a time the punchline came. "He didn't get hit with any bullet; not in that car, he didn't. The slug probably shattered and bounced, so what got Machell was most likely a piece of glass. We didn't see the wound; it was already bandaged. But the rest of the evidence supports that conclusion."

"Thanks, Sergeant. I think that takes care of it." Well. I was happy to have thought of the idea independently first. And especially pleased that now I could quit worrying about Eddie Machell being some kind of ringer.

I headed down toward "Origin"—the new name for the old transmitter site, what with Pedicord's sending terminals now going in there—and found Coogan.

Pedicord wasn't with him; Coogan said the doc was staying downtown that day. We didn't need him, anyway; Machell was running some system tests, and my job was to refine—rebalance—time delays in the signal channels. No big problem: what with installation people going in and out so much, we had a little thermal drift. When things were complete, it would stabilize.

Eddie Machell surprised me. If getting shot improved his bossy disposition this much, I was inclined to hire a part-time sniper to wing him about twice a week. He didn't push, didn't crowd, or even do the little toe-bounce that emphasized his small height advantage. I said, "For a guy who nearly got signed off, you're pretty happy."

He grinned, not ruffled at all. "Close calls, Banning, remind you how nice it is to be alive and healthy."

"Or how easy it could be, to get dead?" There was no excuse for saying that; I must have a mean streak.

Machell didn't answer. I checked my log-sheets for the day's work, initialed them, and went home.

The new mailbox held nothing of major interest. Upstairs I found a note from Dauna:

> *Out to dinner with Chuck Wilford. Fancy and expensive, as a peace offering should be.*

Okay. Chuckling a little, I looked in the fridge and found nothing worth cooking up to eat solo. Going back down to the car I tried to think of somewhere I'd really *like* to eat. Finally I shrugged and headed for the nearest spot that served edible food and had bar service. It was a short drive; twenty minutes later I had a table, a menu, and a Martini.

I ordered the stir-fry chicken-and-veg plate and was sipping on the Mart, spacing it with ice water, when someone sat down across the table. Smiling, Ronnie Detweiler said, "Hi."

Not Steve Broyles; Ronnie. Auburn wig and no fake whiskers, a pair of dark shades hiding the untweezed eyebrows. I said, "This is a surprise; hi, yourself. I thought—"

"I can't just disappear and be Steve *all* the time. George might wonder. Now and then I show up as me; it irritates him."

"I'll bet."

Ronnie leaned forward. "You knew George back in school, didn't you?" I nodded. "What did you think of him? What kind of relationship did you have?"

The waiter came by; Ronnie ordered a vodka gimlet and a chef's salad. The business gave me time to think. I said, "There were three years between us. He was a big gun. We didn't have much contact." No point in telling the pantsing incident, so I didn't.

My voice must have held an edge; she said, "You resented him? Maybe you still do?"

"I don't even resent the past three presidents of the United States. I can't afford to waste my time on old turns."

"But you don't like George."

How did I get into this? "I do not hate George, nor despise him, nor thirst for his blood." I raised a forefinger. "Neither do I wish every healthy child to grow up in his image. I—"

"You don't like George."

Why argue? "I don't like George."

That ended it. We shifted gears and talked project, Ronnie dishing me up some innocuous gossip from the office end.

All in all, I enjoyed our meal together.

Ronnie had come to the place in a cab; this time she let me drive her home. And invited me in. "You could use another drink, couldn't you?"

I looked at her; she seemed anxious, and—if I read the signs right—in a gut-spilling mood. I couldn't help sympathizing, but truth was, I didn't *want* any of that right now. It was like the old line, "I feel for you—but I can't quite reach you."

So I said, "Not really. Thanks, though. Another time."

And feeling a little guilty but not too much, drove home.

Dauna wasn't home yet. Well, it was still early. I skimmed the paper, tried TV and found it wanting, put on some music and looked for a book to distract me. Couldn't find one I liked.

Ronnie Detweiler was still on my mind. In particular, her future. Once past the drastic, irreversible transition, where did she plan to take her life? Career woman, housewife, maybe both? Or a swinging single?

After about ten minutes I decided the overall concept was so alien that no evaluation of mine would be valid. By that time I *could* use another drink; I got out a beer and gave teevy a fresh shot. Prime candidates were two cop shows, a sitcom dedicated to the proposition that Loud equals Funny, and a documentary about industrial rape of the environment.

With the sound off, the sitcom wasn't too bad.

During a commercial, Dauna came in; teevy time ended. Wilford had sprung for a three-drink dinner, so all she wanted now was a diet pop for cold and wet. I fetched it, and sat down to hear the story. The way she looked, it had a happy ending.

"Not only a raise and perks, Mitch—a whole new contract!" She was unwinding her hair, shaking it loose from the coiled updo she'd worn for the occasion. "We put scratch marks and initials all over his version. *Strangely* is how our waiter looked at us." Swallowing the last of her sugar-free sweet water, she rattled the ice cubes. "So now I'm solid with *Westside Weekly* as long as the rag lasts. Or as I want to stay; whichever comes first."

I liked that news. I was sure she could pick up well with any of several local publishing setups, but it was nice that

F. M. *Busby*

she wouldn't have to try it while involuntarily unemployed.

I pumped her some more about the dinner; she was willing, and remembered several good lines from their dialogue. And, "Chuckie won't print any Detweiler story himself unless it's wholly favorable—but if my piece doesn't suit the *Weekly* I have clearance to peddle it any elsewhere I can." She laughed. "And he won't even fire me for it. Unless, of course, George Detweiler absolutely insists."

The prospect, I saw, didn't daunt her greatly.

There came a pause. I started to fill it by airing my nagging preoccupation with Ronnie Detweiler, but Dauna made a sour face. "I don't like any of that, Mitch; it bothers me. Can we change the subject?"

It took a moment to figure her reaction. Dauna has absolutely no use for gay men. Nothing to do with morals or religious bias but simply that those people are scoffing off their predestined duty to admire, covet and attend the female of the species. Lesbians are, in the abstract sense, helping to tip the ratio in her preferred direction. But Ronnie Detweiler wasn't.

So, shifting gears once more, I told her about Eddie Machell getting shot, and my fancy detective work that left my initial suspicion flat on its face. And then my more recent ideas concerning the strange inaccuracy of our sniper.

She said, "You think your Green Hornet, now, is mostly bluffing? More of a Green Paper Tiger? Maybe it's Japanese lantern time."

"How do I know? Ansel Borg died all the way. After that, either this inconsistent joker is playing games or he's a truly lousy shot. *I* don't know."

The hell of it was, I really didn't.

The next morning gave me an answer I didn't like. Coogan called early, wanting to see me in his office. His collar sounded too tight.

So I drove downtown. Every year the rush hour stretches out to include more of the day; my ride took longer than usual. I didn't mind; on one of our grey days with just a touch of drizzle, after a dry spell so that the pavement was oil-slippery, driving a little slower couldn't hurt. I skipped hunting for cheap waterfront parking and found a slot in a Gouge parking lot. The sign reads Gage but the prices don't.

Entering the Trosper Building's lobby I found a hassle. The guards, who are mostly for ornamental purposes, were trying to evict about a dozen robed, chanting Heavenly Sons of Rama. They were getting red-faced and loud about it, so I arranged my face in its best "I'm not really here, fellows" expression and edged around the main commotion, toward the elevators.

Only one stood available; the lights showed the others up at various floors and not moving. The man inside the open one wore cult robes but not the sloppy Heavenly Mohawk. He had his thumb firmly on Door Open. When I looked at him, he stared back as though I *really* weren't there.

I changed my expression. "You mind if I go upstairs?" I reached across and punched twenty-three. He kept his thumb where it was, and didn't answer.

I always like to give Nice its best chance, so I asked again. Same result. I sighed. "I'd be much obliged if you'd take your thumb off that button. I'm late for an appointment."

He looked straight through me. I gave him at least five seconds before my heel stomped his bare toes. I went on defense, and sure enough he took a few swipes at me to prove I didn't scare him. Then, silent after his first startled yelp, he punched buttons two through twenty-two, and gave me the finger.

All right; I gave it back, but used my pinkie. He looked puzzled; I said, "That's when you don't care enough to send the very best."

I'd swear he came close to grinning; he did shrug. "The hell with it; this was a stupid gig in the first place. I can't wait to get back into real clothes."

We'd passed the second floor; stopping, door opening

and eventually closing. Now it opened onto floor three. Paying me no attention at all, the man stepped out.

The door closed. One slow floor at a time I rode up to twenty-three.

Wondering, what the *hell* was going on?

Walking into 2310-14 I saw the young black guy sitting where Borg used to be. He had his own nameplate now; it said his name was Archer Green. I walked over and said, "Hi. Is Coogan busy, or can I go right in?"

Green smiled and waved a hand. All friendly, which was quite a change from his predecessor. "He's free; go ahead. I'd walk you in, but I'm behind with the mail." He picked up a brown envelope, a little bigger than legal-sized, and thick.

I was turning away when the idea came. But before I could turn back, the blast hit.

CHAPTER NINE

I was flat on my face. I must have tried to get my arms out in front of me. Not too well, though; one hand hurt, and my nose, too. The backs of my head and shoulders felt like being hit with a maul, and stung like a mild burn.

I couldn't track; I heard yelling but couldn't make words out of it. Nobody came to help me up; finally I managed it on my own.

My legs were eight feet long and made out of wet macaroni. I waded over to the wreckage of Green's desk and halfway fell on it, bracing with both hands. Emil the Stork grabbed my shoulder, holding me up; I hadn't seen him come in, but there he was. I looked across the desk and wondered why I wasn't throwing up.

Blood is blood, though, and a lot isn't that much different from a little. It wasn't as if the fragments of Green's head, noticeably missing from his neck, could be recognized as such. He was shy a hand, too; the other arm was under him, so I couldn't tell about that one. And the way he was lying, I didn't have to look at the unjoined end of his neck.

I turned around to Emil, to Coogan. "What the hell—?"

Pale as if his own blood were drained, his skin tinged slightly yellow, he shook his head. "Who—Banning, who would do a thing like this?"

He was wobbling on his feet, not too far from passing out. My own legs felt more solid now; I took Coogan's arm and walked him back to his office where he could sit down. From his liquor cabinet I poured us both some bourbon, not messing with sissy stuff like ice or water.

After a couple of sips Coogan looked a little better; color showed at each cheekbone and his mouth steadied. He still looked ten years older, but that was a fifty percent improvement. He took a little more Old Hammer or whatever the label read, and again shook his head. "Mitch—I don't *understand*."

I pulled up a chair and sat across from him. "Me either. Say—has anyone called the law yet? I mean, this one won't pass as any kind of accident."

He made a shaky gesture. "I did. As soon as I looked and saw—before I went out there." He emptied the glass; not waiting for him to ask, I fixed a refill. This time I did use ice, putting some in my own glass also. Coogan nodded thanks.

He wasn't done talking. "Banning—you know I've done a few things our society doesn't approve. But I've never physically harmed any human being, and I never would. This—this *monster*—with his guns and his death traps—I—"

"You sure there's only one?"

He didn't understand that either, so I explained. The Green Hornet who sent me the simulated letter bomb, who played games with Coogan's car and safe and elevators, not to mention color-coding his urine—that one probably blew up our mailbox, too, and pulled some kind of prank on Pedicord. And, most likely, was our shooter who couldn't quite hit anybody with a rifle.

"Those things," I said, "were designed to frighten. And aimed at individuals. But the transformer at Range A, and now this real bomb—these were *killing* moves, and nonselective. Whoever did them had no way of knowing who'd get the business. So"—I shrugged—"looks to me as if there could be two separate minds here."

"That can't be right." By now he was treating his drink with the respect good booze deserves. "But then, even one didn't make sense. Banning, what does he want?"

"What the hell; if it *is* all one person, he already told you. Half. Are you ready to hand it to him?"

Once again, Coogan gave me a suspicious look. "Is that why you're here? To negotiate for him?"

That one came close to lighting my wick, but I said, "I'm here because you called; you wanted to see me. Remember?"

His shoulders slumped. "Oh, yes. I'd forgotten. Banning, everything's going crazy. *I don't know what to do.*" He looked bad again; I waited, until he said, "It's Pedicord. He's gone!"

Missing, he meant, not dead. When the man didn't show for breakfast, Coogan went to his room and found it empty. The bed was mussed, had probably been slept in. "Some of his clothes are gone, and possibly one suitcase, but most of his things are still there."

"Was there a note, anything like that?" Headshake; he'd looked, but found nothing of the kind.

Okay; one more question. "You hadn't cut off his goodies, had you? Or threatened to?"

"I don't understand." The hell he didn't; eventually he admitted that he kept Pedicord's wheels on the ground with a hypo and the occasional batch of pills. "He was addicted when we met; I tried to help him break it. Without my help he'd be in the gutter by now, let alone doing serious work." His earnest look lacked the usual suaveness of phony sincerity; I believed him. "I have some connections, you see. From, uh, the time of my incarceration. I've got him switched to a heroin substitute, a so-called designer drug. It guarantees dependable strength and quality, and I try to keep him at a maintenance level."

"But when he's a real good boy he gets a high as reward?"

"An unstable personality; it seemed advisable, yes." But he insisted there'd been no problem that way, no hassles about the junk. The scary part, in fact, was that wherever Pedicord had gone, he hadn't taken his arm medicine along with him.

"Oh balls! Why didn't you say so in the first place?" Silly question; at the start of this, he'd still been trying to cover up. Still, the point needed saying. "That puts knobs on it, I guess you know. Pedicord didn't leave of his own accord. Somebody took him."

Before we could lift that idea off the pad, the cops arrived; we had to break off the session. Coogan pulled at my sleeve. "Don't say anything about Pedicord yet. All right?"

Sigh. I nodded, and we moved to the outer office where we could see all the blood some more. I was thinking that the police response had been a little slow, but then I saw a tall sergeant slamming a handcuffed Heavenly Son down into a corner chair. "Obstructing police business; we'll see how you like the slow elevators down at the Hall." I took care not to grin; apparently the push-all-the-buttons routine hadn't gone down well with our police contingent.

Nothing else was funny, nothing at all. The photographing and chalkmarking reminded me eerily of TV, until I remembered that TV doesn't show you headless bodies from the wet end. Finally what remained of Archer Green got wrapped up and carried away. Then the thin, quiet detective got around to talking with people.

It was Coogan's bailiwick so he went first: telling how he'd heard the blast, looked out and seen the results, called nine-one-one, and waited. The telling took longer than real time, but I think the detective knew Coogan had to unwind and get it off his chest; he stayed patient through all the repetitions.

As I listened, something nagged at me. I couldn't peg it down, not for little blue beans. So I made a mental shrug and concentrated on what I could hear.

Then it came my turn. I shook hands, a little surprised at the ritual, and sat facing the man. "Lieutenant Hanson," he said. Okay; same name he'd given Coogan, and why should he lie? Thin, with blond hair on its way but not gone yet, deep forehead lines, Viking nose, pale blue eyes that hardly ever blinked.

The guy impressed me, I admit it. To evade that gaze for a moment, I looked at the table between us and saw pieces of twisted, blackened metal and shreds of charred paper. Also featured was a blob of fused wiring.

I nodded down toward the stuff. "That was the bomb?"

"What we could find of it. Now, Mr. Banning, I'd like your statement." All right; in as much detail as I could remember, I began. Entering the building: I didn't know whether the Heavenly Sons were important, but the police had run into them too, so I told that part—leaving out the exact way I got the guy's thumb off the Open button. When I came to the blast itself, Hanson said, "One moment. You started to turn back? Why?"

Whoops. Did I want to open the whole can of worms, here? I tried to think fast; as sometimes happens, it didn't work. I said, "A while back I got a crank letter, a thick envelope with a sheet of plastic to pad it out. The letter pointed out that it could have been a bomb, but wasn't. This one—I guess it reminded me. But not soon enough."

Looking away from his squinting stare, on the table I noticed a shred of paper. On it were the letters: *erdesti*. The thing in the back of my mind came up for air. *Verdesting!*

I had to decide fast. Covering up one killing was bad enough; I pointed. "That matches the envelope I got. If I haven't thrown it out, I'll show you." My next breath came hard and shuddering. "I think that's what I saw, without actually recognizing it, that made me start to turn back to Green."

I kept it to that: a crank letter, a hoax bomb. Nothing as to what it was about. I took a quick glance back at Coogan and saw him relax. To Hanson, I said, "I'll look around at home; if I find that envelope I'll bring it down for you."

"Don't bother," he said. *Huh?* "I'll come help you look." Stupid, Banning! Sure—with the threat-letter still in it, to put the law onto investigating the Stork's caper. Well, I *said*, sometimes thinking fast doesn't work. . . .

Change the subject. I nodded toward the junk on the table. "Does this stuff help you much? Figuring out the source, maybe?"

His expression went wooden. "It's not police policy to discuss that kind of information." He waved my sorries off, saying, "Then what happened?" Well, the blast itself, and the horror we saw afterward; that was all of it. He thanked me; his stenotyper, a sergeant, punched a few more keys on his electronic notebook to close the entry, and I was all wrapped up.

Hanson beckoned to Coogan; with the facts on record, I suppose he wanted the Stork's guesses on motive. Getting up to make the chair available, I looked at my watch. Nearly eleven.

Idea. I said, "Excuse me, lieutenant. I skipped breakfast this morning. If nobody needs me just now, all right if I pop out for a quick bite?" Without much confidence in my ability to do impressions, I tried to look famine-stricken.

Hanson gave his okay, though. Before Coogan could say something and maybe screw matters up, I walked out. Fast.

The Heavenly Sons were gone; I rode an elevator down with only the normal quota of floor-stops. I quickstepped to the Gouge lot and drove home as rapidly as traffic allowed. On the high lope, as they say, I went up the tunnel. My quick frantic search located the Verdesting letter; now what? Half crumpling the empty envelope, I stuffed it well down into the cluttered wastebasket nearest my work desk, then put the plastic filler sheet into the appropriate recycle bin. Now the letter itself, which I did *not* want Hanson to see. I retrieved the plastic—there'd be no excuse for having one enclosure but not the other—and took it out the back door. A neighbor's garbage can, across the alley and two houses away, seemed like a good place for it.

And now, again, the letter. Hanson aside, I felt a need to hang onto it. But where?

When in doubt, always plagiarize from the very best sources. In this case, the late great Mr. Poe. I folded the Hornet's gentle missive in half and put it, as a bookmark, into a reference handbook on my work desk.

Next I made a sandwich, ate it fast, and drove back downtown. At Gouge Parking my stall was still vacant. A real break: there'd be no record of my car's absence. I went into Max's Lunch Bucket and asked the cashier if I'd left my raincoat there, making a minor fuss when she didn't remember my being there for lunch. She would now; I'd bet on it. And by sheer luck, on the way out I found a luncheon check someone had dropped, and pocketed it.

I hoped I wouldn't have to use the gimmick—because, TV to the contrary, amateurs have no business trying to fool the pros. And just by looking at him, I knew Hanson was a pro all the way.

I rode up to 2310-14 with my fingers crossed.

I needn't have worried. Hanson was on his last interview, which happened to be with Steve Broyles, and Ronnie in that guise was playing it very straight indeed. For a second there, I thought she intended to wink at me, but she didn't.

Then the thin detective stood. "I'm done here, for the time being." And to me, "Can we go out to your place now, and find that letter?" I looked over to Coogan; he nodded, so I did, too, and followed Hanson down to the street.

My address was entered into my statement but Hanson hadn't taken a printout, so I told him and he wrote it down. We separated; I got the Volvo and drove home.

I expected to wait for Hanson down front, but either he knew a shortcut or broke the speed limit worse than I did; when I got there he was standing beside an unmarked city car.

Walking up the tunnel stairs he stopped for a second, and grinned. "It's like something out of a movie. Your idea?" Before I could answer, he shook his head. "No. This was built a long time ago. I wonder why."

"Maybe somebody didn't like going out in the rain."

Upstairs, I went to the kitchen. "Would you like a beer or anything?"

Technically I suppose he was on duty, but he said, "One can't hurt. Thanks." I opened him a can; then as he watched, I dumped the jam-packed kitchen wastebasket and refilled it item by item, unsurprisingly finding nothing of interest. The same held true for the recycle bin devoted to paper.

Next, the living room. I leafed through miscellaneous stacks of papers, checked the near-empty wastebasket alongside the sofa, and frowned. Then I snapped my fingers and went into my working office.

Hanson followed. "What's the problem?"

"Trying to remember where the thing might have gone to. I was thinking through where I was when I opened the letter and where I could have put it." Sitting, I went through the major stack on my desk, and the piles of paper on the little table beside it. Not all the way down: at one point I said, "No. It was later than that," and went on to the next heap. So maybe, I thought, I could have got away with just sliding the letter *under* a stack. Or maybe not . . .

Hanson said nothing; he merely watched. Whether he was buying the act I had no idea.

I pivoted my chair and let my foot bump the wastebasket beside my desk, then looked down as though only the bump had brought it to mind. Leaning over, I began rummaging, and in a minute came up with the envelope. "Here." I handed it to him.

From a shirt pocket Hanson took the fragment from the real bomb, and compared. He nodded. "Same paper, same printing." He felt the envelope and looked inside. "Where's the contents?"

I looked some more—then, as in the kitchen, dumped everything onto the floor and fumbled through the mess.

After a while I shook my head. "Must have thrown the letter out." I paused. "If it got into the garbage, that's been collected since then."

I was waiting for Hanson to ask why I'd dumped the other stuff but not the envelope, when he turned it over and found the answer for himself. I'd used it to scribble some figures for the Seaboard job estimate; dead envelopes come in handy that way. So all he said was, "What was in the letter? Near as you can recall."

With all the driving back and forth, I'd had time to think of the answer to that one. I gave him the text almost verbatim: how it wasn't a bomb but could have been. At the end, though—the part about me getting out of the thieving schemes and so forth—for Pedicord and Coogan I substituted George Detweiler. George had enemies, certainly. So to Hanson, this should figure.

And I could see it did. He said, "I was wondering, you know, why anyone would have it in for an experimental project like Coogan's. Not that anyone wanted to tell me what it is." He paused, but I didn't bite; he said, "But Detweiler—getting where he is, he's torn up a lot of people."

The pale gaze zeroed in on me. "Now then, Banning; you tell me what Detweiler's connection is. And while you're about it, what *yours* is."

I'd wondered earlier why Hanson had asked me only about the blast itself, nothing about my business with Coogan. I told it fairly straight: how I'd heard that Detweiler was backing a big electronics project, and being a communications consultant, had applied for work on the telemetry-and-control end. I showed him my contract; the numbers brought a whistle. "Your specialty pays pretty well, doesn't it?"

"Only if I deliver—and on schedule."

"Yeah." He finished his beer, crumpled the can and dropped it clanging into the wastebasket. The dumped-out debris still lay on the floor; I'd clean it up later. He spoke.

"Like I mentioned, nobody said just what this big project is all about."

I shook my head. "Not me, either; that's part of the contract. If it had anything to do with the bombing . . ."

His eyes narrowed. "How do you know it doesn't?"

I spread my hands. "Proof or disproof of a new scientific principle? People don't kill over things like that. They kill over money or power or revenge or paranoia; you know that. So I can't see how the experiment's *object* figures in this."

All he did was wait; finally I said, "The information's not mine to give, lieutenant; please don't ask me to. Detweiler and Coogan are the principals. All right?"

After a while he said, "Fair enough. I—"

Out past the living room, the tunnel stair door slammed. From the sound, it was Dauna enthusiastic or at least vigorous, not Dauna angry at anything. Hanson swiveled to look; I said, "Lady coming home from work," and got up and walked out. He followed.

Looking happy enough, Dauna gave me the big kiss, and I made introductions. "Detective Lieutenant Hanson, Dauna Haig." I squeezed her hand.

She squeezed back, then took the hand loose to shake his. "Pleasure, lieutenant." And to me, "Mitch, I didn't know you knew any detectives. Is something happening?"

"Something already did. Tell you later."

Hanson's tipped-up eyebrow, I guessed, was reaction to our height difference, Dauna's and mine. Now it tipped back level. He said, "Banning. Haig. Not married; right?" One shoulder twitched. "None of my business; I'm just nosy."

Instead of blowing her stack, which for a moment there I expected, Dauna grinned at him. "If you weren't nosy, you wouldn't be much of a detective, would you?"

Hanson smiled back. "You got me." To me, now, he stuck out his hand; I'd never met such a handshaking cop in all my life. "All right; I'll be going. Thanks for the beer. And nice meeting you, Ms. Haig."

He said he could find his way, so I let him.

* * *

I sat down with Dauna to fill her in; she wouldn't get on with anything better until I did, so why fight it? At the blast part, her face went tight. "It blew his *head* off?"

"Most of it. I didn't look closely."

"Why?" Gripping a chair arm, her knuckles showed white.

"The Hornet, if it's all the same person—he's crazy. Has to be. So unless you're an expert on psychopaths, which I'm not, there *is* no why."

She pushed forward-hanging hair back over a shoulder. "What happens now?"

"Depends." I told her how far I'd leveled with Hanson and what I was keeping back. And then, suddenly remembering, about Pedicord's disappearance. "Maybe you were right the first time," I said, while she absorbed that development. Maybe I *should* get out."

"If you still can."

I felt the scowl come, and tried to smooth it. "What does that mean?"

"That maybe your Hornet wouldn't believe it. And if you're not around, close to Coogan, in touch with what's going on, you could get blindsided." She stood. "I need you, Mitch. Right now, I mean. Because, the idea of losing you . . ."

Straight to the bedroom, no stops. In bed, sometimes Dauna is cool and languid, sometimes a lot warmer, and now and then she heats up like an induction furnace. This time, though, she was all urgency and desperation. For a time I didn't think she could make it at all; when she did, her yell nearly took the roof off. Me, I was mostly just along for the ride.

I put a couple of TV dinners on to zap-and-stand while we shared a fast shower. We ate quickly, too, and had our coffee in the living room. Archer Green rated nearly thirty seconds on the news, and the item put Dauna back into reporter mode, asking questions. I recalled things Hanson

had said, back in Coogan's office, that hadn't really registered at the time.

"It was the desk," I said. "Reflecting the blast back up at
Green. That's what blew his head. Standing up, or sitting in
a chair with no desk, he'd have lost a hand or two, and died
of ruptured lungs if I heard that part right. But not as messy
as this was."

Dauna's eyes went wide. "You mean, if you'd been facing—?"

I hadn't thought about that, but now I nodded. "I guess
so. Looking away, not having time to turn back: that could
be what kept me alive."

I shrugged the idea away. "*If* I was that close to it," I
added. "I'm not sure I really was. After all, it didn't even
knock me out. Well, not quite."

I could see her begin to relax. Then the phone sounded;
I moved to get to it first.

Answering my hello, the familiar husky voice said,
"Have you got to where you like it yet, Banning? Every day
the Fourth of July?"

CHAPTER TEN

"**Y**ou chickenshit son of a bitch!" Until I heard me, I
had no idea I yelled that. I was shaking; so was my
voice. "You don't have the guts to *look* at your kills, let
alone do it face-to-face. You set your cowardly little traps
and don't give a rat's ass *who* you catch. Archer Green was
a nice guy doing a job; he didn't know the project from
Adam's off ox. Are you proud of yourself, you walking
piece of skunkturd? *Are* you?"

I heard his breath suck in. When he spoke, it came in a

quiet monotone. "You had a bad shock today, Banning, so I'll overlook that little outburst, this once. But—"

"Shut up. I'm not done yet." My voice had steadied. "You ever do any hunting? You know what a sound-shooter is? A guy who fires at a noise without bothering to find out what made it? Do you know how real hunters feel about shitkickers like that?"

"I'll take it as read. What are you trying to prove?"

"Just this. To call *you* a sound-shooter would be a compliment you don't deserve." I overrode his try at answering. "You're stupid, too. What if you'd got Pedicord? Where would you be then, trying to screw money out of a dead project?"

Incredibly, he laughed. I snarled, "What's so funny, hero?"

It took him a sputtering moment to kill the laugh. "*If* I'd got Pedicord? Just who do you think *has* got him?" I didn't answer; he went on, "Tell Coogan, stay close to his home phone. I'll call him tonight. And either he meets my terms or he can kiss the project good-bye. It's not negotiable; I get half."

And he hung up.

As I put the phone down I saw Dauna looking at me. I explained what the Hornet had said. She said, "Then hadn't you better let the Stork know what his little problem is?"

I checked the time; with luck, Coogan should still be at his office. The number didn't answer, though, so I called his apartment. Nothing there, either; I hung up.

"Let's eat." In the freezer I came up with a ziplocked brick of leftover turkey chili, dated not too far back. I gave the microwave my best guess for timing but it needed a second shot to melt all the way through and come up steaming. Dauna had a slice of wheatberry toast lying in each bowl, for foundation.

We had no Mexican beer, but made do with a can apiece of a local ale known affectionately as Green Death: the high-octane version, available only from our monopoly State Liquor Stores.

Afterward, in the living room again as we split a third can to go with our decaf, I tried Coogan's home phone again. This time the Stork answered.

It was no surprise that he didn't much like the news. When it came to the Hornet, Coogan used terms that definitely indicated a degree of military background. When he ran down I said, "I second the motion. But what do you intend to do?"

For a time he was silent; when he spoke next, he sounded unnaturally calm. "I'll agree, of course. Whatever he asks for. I know I said I wouldn't pay extortion. But this, now, is different."

"Oh? How so?"

"Because it will be merely a loan. For the rather short duration of the man's life."

Believe me, I was jolted. "Emil? Didn't you also say you weren't a killer?" And could never be, was how he'd put it.

"I'm not. But some years ago, as you may recall, I had occasion to meet more than a few who are. Some of them became my friends. And at least two, of those presently at liberty, owe me favors."

I thought about it, long enough that he called my name twice and asked if I were still on the line. Finally I said, "The first thing is, I didn't hear that—and if you say it again I still won't. The second: what if you can't find out who the Hornet is?"

"He'll slip," said the Stork. "Amateurs always do." He made a rasping laugh. "So do pros, sometimes; otherwise you'd never have heard of me."

I was wishing, just then, that I hadn't. Ever. "Then that brings up Item Three. I want to terminate our contract." He began to protest; I cut him off. "My part of the equipment's all in place and tested; from here on it's merely routine checks and adjustments. Machell and his crew have worked alongside me enough to handle those details just fine. So how about it?"

He didn't pause at all. "Out of the question. You'll

fulfill your contract, Banning—or haven't you read the penalty clauses? Renege on that contract and you'll forfeit most of your earnings. Of course, if you like working for free . . ."

Having had every intention of staying with the project all the way, I hadn't really looked at the penalty stuff. But knowing the Stork, I was pretty sure he had. I said, "That's your final word? You insist on keeping an unwilling employee, in a rather critical part of the project? Not to mention—"

He didn't give me the chance; I heard breath snort from his nostrils, and then, "Don't try to bluff me. You can't sabotage me with faulty work; your own reputation's on the line. And you can't expose *me* without explaining why you didn't do it months ago. Now if that's all you have to say, I want to clear this line for our murdering friend's call." Click went the phone; then came dial tone.

It was my day for being hung up on.

While I explained to Dauna what the latest was, I skimmed through my contract. Coogan had it right: if I walked out (extenuating circumstances were specified, but none of those applied), I'd forfeit most of the pay I'd already drawn. And losing such an amount, just now, would put me in the wringer more than somewhat. I explained that part, too.

Dauna poured us the last of the decaf; then she sat. "What is it you're trying to do, Mitch? If the tree falls, it'll make noise—whether you're there to hear it or not. Unless you can get Smokey the Bear to stop the axe work in time."

Right. Whether Coogan's hit man got the Hornet didn't depend on where *I* was working. "But I'm in too deep, helping cover the Borg killing, to blow the whistle to Hanson, now."

Dauna stared past me. "If it comes to that, Mitch, I heard your views loud and clear, second call back. If you're so crazy about trees, why do you want to protect a forest fire?"

I had no answer. Sure, I despised the Hornet. By rights, having him wiped off the books should brighten my whole day. Shouldn't it? And yet . . .

I gestured. "I don't know; I really don't. In theory, given outright murder, I favor capital punishment. Oh, not for some poor nit who gets stretched all out of shape and explodes, once in his life. Those are what rehabilitation's all about. But the nonhumans: pattern killers who repeat as long as they're on the loose, psychopaths who kill for money—they're better off dead and we're better off without them."

I shook my head. "But still—maybe it's because, in a way, I *know* the Hornet. If only by phone. And maybe, even in spite of Ansel Borg and Archer Green, I'm not wholly convinced he's one of the nonhumans."

Dauna smiled. "And Emil's no forest ranger."

"That, too." I shrugged, glad to put the mess aside.

And then George Detweiler called.

He was in his office. Coogan wouldn't tell him anything; what the hell was going on? Get my butt over there *right now*, and straighten things out. "I'll wait."

Sure; just like that. "One," I said; apparently it was my day for numbers, also. "My contract's with Coogan." *Not with you*, but I didn't rub it in. "Two. I'm on a date with a lady and a pitcher of Martinis." Well, I'd been thinking of mixing one.

He started cussing. I said, "Three. There's nothing I can tell you over there that I can't from right here." He shut up. "Questions?"

"Banning. *Please* come here. For this, the phone's not good enough. Bring the lady; you can have Martinis on me." A moment; then he said, "An hour here, maybe less. You can spare that."

I thumbed Mute and asked Dauna. She shrugged. "It's a nice evening for a drive." So I told Detweiler we'd be along.

He said thank you, just like a real person. Someday, maybe, his housebreaking would take, too.

We buttoned up the house. I drove us across the lake by way of I-90, to Detweiler's business stronghold. Light traffic, and this time I took the right exit; we got there sooner than I'd expected.

In the parking lot, except for a covey of the little Commutes, the black Continental sat lonesome. So the building's emptiness was no surprise. George had the main doors unlocked and the lobby lights about half-strength; climbing to the mezzanine I noticed that against the outdoor lighting all that glass looked quite ordinary; the tint hardly showed.

Approaching Detweiler's door I pointed to the "Executive President" sign; Dauna did a double take, and chortled. I didn't knock, just opened the door and followed her inside. At one time she'd have protested such outmoded "chivalry," but now she accepts that I grew up old-fashioned and lets it go.

George came from behind his big desk like a halfback going for the handoff. Making with the courtesies, he shook Dauna's hand ("Nice to see you again, Ms. Haig.") and then mine. He got us seated at a table near the big windows, and did things at his wet bar, resulting in three of those goldfish-bowl Martinis.

I've already mentioned the decor. As Dauna scanned it, her expression gave no hint to what she thought. Actually, this time around I was starting to like the place.

Our host brought coffee, too, not forgetting the sidearms. And then I realized what I liked about this setup: here was George Detweiler the big honcho, with no flunkies at all, doing his own chores for a change. I began to enjoy myself.

To help the feeling along, just for starters I beat him to the punch. As he sat down, I said, "What's the picture as you see it? That's where we have to begin."

He looked sidelong, to Dauna. "Ms. Haig's fully aboard, is she?" I nodded. He leaned forward. "This man Green, I'd never heard of him before, why was he killed? And what's happened to Dr. Pedicord? Something has. I needed him today, to get information for a press release in the near future; schedules are tight. Coogan wouldn't let me see him. Said he wasn't available, wouldn't tell me where he is."

He gulped coffee. It must have been hotter than he expected; hurriedly he took more Martini than is advisable in one chunk. "I can read Coogan. He's cagey, sure; but you don't get where I am without some ability along those lines. And that man's hiding something. He's scared." Leaning back in his chair, Detweiler said, "What's it all about, Banning?"

Hell. He already knew, nearly as much as I did. But I told him anyway. "It's still our little buddy the Green Hornet; the one who can't hit anything with a rifle but is hell on wheels at indiscriminate slaughter. He smells loose money where I doubt there is any, and he wants half. The terrorist stuff, apparently it's his way of leaning on the—on Coogan."

George's eyes went to slits. "On *the,* you started to say. On the what?"

Watch it! "On the project, of course. But Coogan's where the Hornet's applying pressure."

"Which," said Dauna, "is dumb. If it's money that dominates his little mind. After all, Mr. Detweiler, you're the Fort Knox in this crowd."

George liked that; for a moment he actually grinned. "You're sharp, Haig. But I can tell you why this hijacker's leaning on Coogan rather than me." He waited; obligingly, Dauna let her brows signal question. Again Detweiler bent forward; when he spoke, you'd have thought he was reading from stone tablets. "Because *nobody* leans on George Detweiler, and I think the word's gotten around pretty well." Satisfied with himself, he sat back; much more of this, and in an hour or so he'd complete a five-minute exercise program.

Now he frowned. "But what about Pedicord? I need him."

No way to break it gently. "The Hornet's got him."

George started up out of his chair. His eyes bulged; he talked loudly without saying much. I waved him back.

F. M. Busby

"The Hornet *says* he has Pedicord; Coogan says the doc's missing. Put it together, I think the Hornet's telling true."

Detweiler shook his head as if his ears were on fire; not, I guessed, in negation, but to clear his mind. I said, "If your next question is what do we do about it, you have the wrong number. I don't have the slightest idea. And I don't think Coogan has, either."

Since I didn't care for what ideas the Stork did have, I saw no point in passing them to George; he'd probably approve, maybe even abet. If they put it together on their own, that was a different problem. But damned if I'd help.

George wasn't all dumb; he couldn't be, even considering the way he acted sometimes. He scowled, overdoing the Thinker bit, then said, "If it's money, I could feed some through Coogan." He grinned. "Don't worry; I'd get it back." I wasn't worrying. But then he said, "I have contacts."

Straight-faced, I didn't say his eyeballs looked pretty naked from where I sat. I waited, and he went on, "Not directly. But I can find people who'll take care of the Hornet for us." He looked over to Dauna, then back to me. "You have a better idea?"

It was Mafia Night at the old homestead. I shrugged. "Not even a worse one. Though hiring a killer is about as bad as I can imagine." Somehow, while I wasn't paying attention, I'd polished off most of my oversized bowl of gin. I finished it, bottomed-out my one cup of coffee, and stood.

"Do whatever you want to, Detweiler; you will, anyway. But if you play it the way you're sounding, count me out."

He came around the desk like Student Body Left. Just short of bowling me over, he stopped. "Let's get one thing straight, Banning. Are you on the team, here, or not?"

Of all ex-athletes, football veterans generally seem to lead in the flabby-gut division. I looked not at Detweiler's face but at the best spot to plant a fist. Granted, he outweighed me better than three to two. But nobody takes a surprise in the solar plexus and does much for a while.

Then I heard him chuckle; I glanced up at his face and did

a double take. Looking amiable, he said, "Level with me, is all I'm saying. So which is it?"

Quick think. "All right. I helped you cover Borg's death. But you weren't the predator. If you ever are, don't expect any help from me. You won't get it."

He nodded, then ignored me entirely as he turned to Dauna. "Little lady, I'm delighted that you came along tonight. And I trust you'll use your soothing influence on Mr. Banning."

Little lady? Not breathing, I waited. But Dauna smiled. "Mitch decides things for himself. So do I. Thanks for the hospitality."

She walked out. Not looking back to see Detweiler's reaction, I followed.

I'd finished my entire half-pint of gin, twist and all, while Dauna had left most of hers. So, for obvious reasons, she drove while I sat back and tried to think. I wasn't bashed, just glowing a bit; my head still worked. But as we left I-405, followed I-90 to and across Mercer Island, and approached Seattle's skyline, I didn't find much to work with. Coming off the floating bridge and into the tunnel, I asked, "You think Detweiler would really put out a contract? On the Hornet?"

"If he knew which tree to lop, Mitch, he might very well hire a logger." Very precise and clipped, her voice came. "But the way it is, all he can do is yell. Try to scare the squirrels out of the top branches."

As we came out of the tunnel, a top-heavy camper, going about 20 mph slower than everybody else, changed lanes right in front of us. Dauna hit the brakes; she's too good a driver to lock wheels and skid, but I slammed forward into my safety harness pretty hard.

What Dauna said would have done a drill sergeant proud. I glanced over; her jaw was set. She gunned the Volvo: out left, then up alongside. By this time the camper decided he'd made a mistake; his lane read Right Lane Exit Only and he wanted back out. Dauna ignored his signal and held pace beside his front wheels until we reached the exit.

The guy had no choice; like it or not, he was heading for Tukwila or someplace.

Having shown the camper what she thought of him *and* George Detweiler, Dauna moved to the lane we'd be needing soon.

For a time I said nothing at all. Then, "Nice job." Navigating the I-5 interchange, she didn't answer. I said, "Some people don't know how to drive." No response. I said, "If I'm going to pin a medal on you, you'd better pull over for it. Or you'll flinch when the pin goes in, and we'll hit something."

Then she laughed, and everything was all right.

Even that late at night it was still one of those days. When we came out the tunnel and into the house, the phone was chiming its head off. Looking to Dauna, deliberately I turned away from the instrument. In the kitchen I poured myself a glass of nonfat. Then I went back and picked up the phone.

Husky voice, not so confident now. But still recognizably the Hornet. Well, who else?

"Banning! Pedicord's gone crazy; he says he's going to die. What can I do? You know anything?"

Adrenaline sobered me in seconds as alternatives chased through my mind. I said, "Try a doctor." No answer. "Or you could go back to his place and fetch his goodies for him."

"What goodies? What do you mean?" And quickly, "I can't risk a doctor, Pedicord yelling kidnap all over the place. So tell me about the other thing. *Fast.*"

CHAPTER ELEVEN

In the background I heard muffled yells and thumps; did the Hornet have Pedicord locked in a closet? I wondered what the neighbors were thinking. If the Hornet *had* near neighbors . . .

I said, "Didn't the doc tell you he has a habit? I'd think that's the first thing he'd blab, right about now."

"Damn you, Banning! Get on with it." But I wanted to know what Pedicord *had* said, so I persisted. Until the Hornet said, "Just to let him go. That he has to get back to his apartment."

So I told him. "From what I've heard, which is second-hand, the timing's just about right for your pigeon to be hitting heroin withdrawal." Okay, heroin substitute; what difference? "So have fun with it. Or go out and make a score for him. Of course you'll need the equipment, too."

People surely did cuss a lot, lately. When he stopped, he said, "I don't have that kind of connections. Wouldn't know where to start; sure as hell I'd get busted. So—Banning, *you* go get the stuff. Unless he's run out of it. Do you know?"

"If he had, he wouldn't be wanting to go home, would he? But leave me out of this; I don't even know where he'd be likely to stash it. Anyway, your business is with Coogan. Ask *him*."

"He's not home. We've already talked, and he's out making a delivery run. Money; the down payment. So it's up to you."

I didn't ask how the delivery was set up; he wouldn't have told me. And if the Hornet ran true to form, I'd probably be finding out about his methods soon enough, the hard way.

So it took some thinking. I had no burning urge to make

life easy for the Hornet. But if Pedicord were really suffer-
ing, I'd just as soon he didn't. I said, "I'm no break-in artist;
I'll need the keys."

From the silence, he hadn't thought of that. Seeing no
quick, safe way—from his viewpoint—to handle the matter, I let him sweat. And used the time to tell Dauna as
much as I could, in a hurry, of what was going on.

When he spoke again, I took my finger off the Mute
button.

"Here's how we do it," he said. I listened.

It sounded like an overkill of flimflam, just to let the Hornet
off the hook of running his own errand. I suppose he wanted
someone else to do it because Coogan might have the apartment staked out. At any rate, following instructions I left my
phone off the hook, so the mastermind could be sure I wasn't
calling anyone. Such as tipping off Detweiler. I couldn't cross
him up, either; once I left, driving south in the Volvo, the
timing would be too tight for any shenanigans.

Dauna looked an inquiry. Pointing at the phone, I motioned her to follow me to the tunnel stairs. Closing that
door behind us, she said, "You're going to do this? Why?"

"Pedicord's a flake, but I'd hate to see the poor son go
snap-crackle-pop."

"Well, if you have to, you have to. Be careful." We had
a good-bye kiss; then I went below and drove as instructed.

Once I hit the boulevard I watched for a Shell station on
the right at a six-way intersection; sure enough, someone
was waiting at the curb. "Someone you'll know," he'd said.
"But this person doesn't know *me*, so don't bother trying
to pump." How he could have set it up so fast, with his
phone tied up monitoring mine, was something else I
couldn't guess.

I pulled over and stopped. Ronnie Detweiler handed me
a small envelope.

The feel told me it was keys inside, all right. I looked at my
watch; I could spare a little time to talk, but not much.
"Ronnie? Do you know what you're into, here?"

Her headshake swirled the auburn wig. "No. I hoped *you* did." Her story was simple: the doorbell rang, and she found the unsealed envelope pushed under her door. In it were the keys, a note, and half a fifty-dollar bill. The note said to deliver the keys to me, time and place specified; she'd find the other half of the fifty in her mailbox, after. And I realized we were less than two blocks from her place.

Not bad, Hornet; not bad at all. Now, though, I had to scat. "Thanks, Ronnie. When there's time, we'll talk."

Fifteen minutes later, right on sked, I parked as directed: behind the building in which Coogan and Pedicord lived, and at the lot's darkest corner. Then I went inside and upstairs.

The key worked as advertised; I put on some lights and looked around. The place was sixties-vintage and the decor spelled "furnished." Elderly furniture with worn spots; new, it might have been pretty good stuff. Light green walls with an off-white ceiling. The builder hated comprehensive lighting; itsy-bitsy wall lamps took care of the living room, but not well.

The phone rang; I went to it. "Errand boy speaking."

The Hornet wasn't amused. "Have you found the stuff?"

"Just got here. How'd you happen to pick the lady for delivery?"

"Never mind that. Start looking. Leave this call alive." He wasn't missing a beat; I still had hopes of finding an angle, but not many. I set the phone on a sofa cushion and flipped a mental coin. It came up bedroom, so that's where I started.

That's where I finished, too. My hunch was that nut-genius Pedicord wouldn't use old junkie tricks like the baggie in the toilet tank, and it paid off. Not to enumerate all the places I looked without success, two pair of shoes sported shoe-trees that were truly unique. Good enough for him was good enough for me; I put everything back together and stuffed the four shoes into a bag from the kitchen.

I went to the phone. "Mission accomplished, *mein Führer*. Acquisition of specified material, that is."

"Stop clowning and pay attention. Do you have everything that's needed?"

"To my unpracticed eye, the package seems complete."

"All right, now listen." More instructions came. Accordingly, again I left the phone live while I went downstairs and outside, where I placed the bag under my car's front seat. Then I went back up and checked in with Big Brother.

"It's there. Now what?" He told me. So I hung up and went to the front window that looked out over the street, pulling the drape back so that anyone outside could see me clearly. For a moment I wondered if I'd been set up for target practice. But if he needed me for later . . . I relaxed.

As the wait dragged on, past ten minutes and then fifteen, relaxing didn't come so easy. But then the phone rang again.

"Midnight Window Displays. Banning speaking." It wasn't midnight yet, but so what?

The Hornet sounded more cheerful. "Have your fun. You can go home now. Leave the keys in the mailbox on your way out."

"Sure." Then I said, "The lady got fifty bucks for a two-block jaunt. What do I get?" Any info I could jolly out of him was pure gravy.

"You already got it. I shot to miss you; remember?" It was a hard line to top; I was still trying to think of something when the click came, and dial tone.

I stood, thinking. Go home, he'd said. But not when. So it was within the letter of our contract, I felt, to finish prowling the place first.

I didn't find much of interest. Some letters signed Gretchen, or sometimes *Deine Liebchen*, were all more or less to the point that yes, she did trust him, and she understood, and someday they would be happy together, and the baby was fine. She used purple ink and dotted her *i*'s with large imperfect circles; the paper was perfumed.

In the same small carton lay a wristwatch, a massive gold thing, studded with various-colored jewels. There was even what looked like a ruby imbedded at the center of the thick crystal. Whether the gaudy object related to the letters, I couldn't know. A recent present, maybe; a tag was still attached to the wristband. I closed the little box and put it away again.

The desk hadn't come with the rent; it was grey metal and fairly new. Two of the drawers stood empty, but in the top right, under a loose stack of hand-scribbled sheets written in Higher Mathematics which lost me, I found the draft of a paper. By "paper" I mean an article written for consideration of one of the topflight scientific journals. The ones I can't translate.

Its title read: "Infinitesimal Transit Times as a Function of Synchronization in Near-instantaneous Transfer of Nontrivial Mass over Significant Distance: a Hypothesis."

Then the subtitle, or maybe you could call it a blurb: "Artificial singularities can be shown to have mathematical properties which resemble those of random congruence. In this paper Dr. Olin Pedicord describes his hypothesis and explores the possibility of demonstrating unique applications of that characteristic under controlled conditions. Footnotes and appendices outline the boundaries indicated by his previous research, and the conclusion points out possible ramifications."

Why, I couldn't have said it better myself!

I tried reading into the essay proper, but didn't know enough of the specialized jargon to make sense of it. I put the drawer's contents back more or less the way I'd found them, turned the lights off, and left. Key in the mailbox, yes. I went down to my car.

It started without blowing me up or anything, and I drove home.

Dauna was in bed and asleep. The way her clothes lay all over the bedroom told me something of what her late evening mood had been. We weren't in sync that day, was all. I decided I'd better call Coogan.

Answering on the second ring, he didn't sound sleepy. I

said, "Banning here. The Hornet says you've started paying
him off. How much, so far?"

Ouch. He was perfectly correct that the amount was
none of my business. But I wanted to know anyway. "Are
we sharing info, Emil, or aren't we? I have some too, you
know."

So he told me. I whistled. "You've ripped twice that
much off Detweiler, already?" Because, *half*, the Hornet
had said.

I'd ruffled the Stork's feathers; his voice went harsh.
"Don't be any more naïve than you can help, Banning.
After you saw George Detweiler tonight—and when we
have time, I want to know more about that—he phoned
me. I'd just heard from the blackmailing toad's anus who
calls himself the Green Hornet, threatening to kill Dr. Pedicord if I didn't make a payment this very evening. I was
debating: to take a chance on using Detweiler's money
without his knowledge, or—"

"Or cut your losses? Drop the project, Pedicord and all;
take the money and run?"

"Crudely put, Banning—and a bit off the mark. Because
I could not abandon Olin Pedicord; once one has taken on
a stray puppy . . ." He sighed. "At any rate, Detweiler told
me what he'd learned from you and authorized me to use
project money. As bait. So I did."

"Catch anything?" If they had, I'd be surprised, but no
such luck. Coogan related how the drop had been set up:
nothing quite the same as my own assignment for the Hornet, but with similar safeguards.

Coogan was told to drive a fixed route, staying in the
right-hand lane. If a car sat to his left at a red light and its
tape deck played "Penny Lane" or "Strawberry Fields," he
was to chuck the bank draft packet across, through the
open windows. Then kill his engine and give the other car
one light-change's worth of head start. "He said there'd be
another car behind, with the driver armed. So I shouldn't
think to try anything cute."

I guessed that last part to be a bluff, and said so. But I
couldn't blame the Stork for caution; the Hornet could

have had a stooge do the actual pickup, while he handled the backup role himself. Emil had no idea either way; he tried to sneak a look at the other driver, but saw only a hat and shades. The car itself was a nondescript compact. And of course the license plate was smeared with mud or something.

"Detweiler was furious," Coogan said. "*He* had a car following, a block or so behind, waiting for a blinker signal from me. But of course I didn't dare give one."

"Way it goes, sometimes. You want to hear about my own run around the block, over the past couple of hours?" He did, so I told him. And added, "I had a hunch the bugger might be more slippery than we were primed for; remember? Sorry to be such a good guesser."

Yeah and sure, but the Stork was more interested in Pedicord. "Do you think he'll be all right?"

Forgetting Coogan couldn't see me, I shrugged. "Well, he's got his candy, and the Hornet has his payoff; for a while, anyway, Pedicord should be okay." Another thought. "I don't suppose you wangled any idea of when the doc gets turned loose, or the bottom line on what it takes to spring him?"

"Another installment like tonight's. Then, a week before project test deadline, the Hornet promises to release him."

"And you trust the Hornet's word." Actually, Coogan didn't sound very confident; maybe I shouldn't have pushed the point.

He said, "Of course I don't. But what choice do we have?"

I said something noncommittal and we wrapped it up, Coogan saying that tomorrow we'd meet at Range A.

I looked in on Dauna; she was still gone for the night. I sat around and skimmed the evening paper, then joined her. I hadn't thought I was sleepy, but lying down was the last I remembered.

I got up early, for me, but Dauna was long gone to work. I did a quick job on my personal needs and postal backlog, then headed the Volvo out into grey, misting weather.

Slowpoking traffic held me up; I got onto the freeway later than I liked. But the left lane moved well; when I reached my exit I'd made up most of the time. I cruised on in along the back roads with no hassles, and arrived at Range A right on schedule.

Walking from the car to Coogan's office I paused to watch Detweiler's Continental zoom in like a jet landing on a carrier. He jounced to a stop and came jogging toward me. I waited; he arrived puffing a little. I said, "So you made a payoff. Think you got your money's worth?"

His breathing improved fast. "If Coogan weren't scared of his own shadow we'd have *had* the bastard. I sent a car over, two men I can trust, to follow him. We didn't know the Hornet's plan ahead of time; Coogan was supposed to signal when it was time to move in, was all, and he didn't. Next time, though . . ."

I looked at his flushed, swarthy face, and didn't like what I saw; another minute and he'd be drooling. I said, "From the grade of runaround the Hornet gave *me* last night, next time he'll still be one jump ahead. But have fun."

I started to move away; Detweiler grabbed my arm. Maybe he felt me tense up; at any rate, he let go. "Sorry. But I need to know what you're talking about, there."

I told him. Not in detail, of course. I stood thinking, long enough—I hoped—to keep straight who was supposed to know what; then I gave him the basics. That the Hornet had talked me into picking up something for him and rigged it so I couldn't spot him or finger him. George wanted specifics; I didn't give any. "It's not in your area, Detweiler; you don't have what the Army calls 'need to know.' If you did, I'd tell you." After being loud about it for a while he settled for what he had, and we walked on to Coogan's prefab.

The Stork was edgy; we'd kept him waiting. When we went in, he rose behind his desk. "It's about time. I have a demonstration for you, Mr. Detweiler, and it takes a lot of power. If you'd got here much later, we'd have had to cancel for today. Or else delay start-up of your Riverside plant longer than we'd already scheduled." He shrugged. "Let's go."

He set a quick pace; I moved up alongside. "I thought your power consumption depended on mass and distance. Are you actually going to transmit something?"

He looked over at me. "Not unless you count air. But we're energizing the superconductors; we don't need Pedicord for that. And the initial drain is considerable. The detailed explanation is out of my field; Machell can tell you about it, if you like."

Machell, huh? I'd wondered; now I asked: "How did Eddie Machell get to be such a kingpin all at once?"

For a moment Coogan broke step, scowling. "With Borg gone I needed someone to head up the crews. Machell learned rapidly; I could see he was going to be my best choice for the job. That's all. Even though he and Dr. Pedicord aren't precisely Damon and Pythias."

"They don't get along?" I remembered seeing only one incident of friction, but I could have missed a few, at that.

"Working to learn his job so quickly, I'm afraid Machell gave the doctor the idea that the man was trying to pick his brains. Olin does have a secretive streak, almost paranoid at times."

We reached Origin, the sending station. I hadn't been inside since the major assembly work got rolling; the neat, professional look of the completed installation impressed me. I walked over to the transmission chamber housing and looked in.

The curved sliding lid was transparent; standing on the third step of the little climb-in ladder I saw how the dull-finished metal chamber hung in its cradle of spiraled support members. I knew how it would pivot, coming up to present its lidded end for the guinea pig to climb into. Tixo, that would be. But not today. This time we'd see a lot of power used to warm up all the gear and stage a dry run. Good enough . . .

I felt a hand on my shoulder. George Detweiler was trying to look past me. I grinned and stepped down so he could have the ladder. He looked, nodded as if the gadgetry made sense to him, and stepped down himself just as Tixo came in.

Detweiler gestured to the little Indian. "Ready for a test run, are you?"

Coogan translated; at least that's what it looked like, though he talked twice as long as George had. Tixo showed his brown-toothed smile. He came over to me and we did our knife ritual, touching each other's foreheads and ending with the knife back in its sheath. I had no idea what George Detweiler thought of our game, and didn't ask him. Then Tixo went to the ladder and climbed it.

At a small control panel Coogan pushed a green button. The housing's lid slid open. Another button—his hand was in the way, so I didn't see its color or exact location—and motors whined; the transmission chamber pivoted up and opened. Tixo climbed inside, sliding his way carefully into the angled chamber. "He knows this is just practice," Coogan said. "For the real test, of course, we'll be using the duplicate controls in the safety area."

Now I watched the chamber pivot down again, to its original horizontal position. The housing closed. I wondered how Tixo felt. In his shoes I'd have been a mite claustrophobic, lonesome at the very least. As though reading my mind, Coogan said, "For a real transmission he'd be in there for a warm-up period of not quite one minute. Then about the same at the far end, to allow the fields to decay to safe levels. But this time—" His hands moved; the housing opened and the chamber rose again, twisting in the odd path its spiral supports imposed.

The chamber, too, opened. Tixo's hands gripped its rim; he pulled himself out in one agile move; neglecting the ladder, he dropped to the floor. He was grinning as though he'd just invented sex; I gathered that the little guy enjoyed his starring role. Watching him, only in peripheral vision did I notice the chamber-housing button itself up again.

Detweiler began a question, but Coogan overrode him. "Now we'll go into the safety booth, and energize." Again he led. Detweiler and I followed; Tixo turned to go outdoors instead.

The booth was bigger than its name sounded: about eight feet square in open floor space, not counting the equipment racks—control consoles and instrumentation—that lined two walls. The place had its own door to outside. There were six chairs; Coogan motioned George and me to take our pick.

I'd been here before, of course; quite a lot of my own gear sat among the other gadgetry. But I looked around anyway.

The mirrors were new. This place was shielded from the radiation and other effects we could expect when the accelerators and so forth got hotted up. So we couldn't view the experiment directly. We would see the transmission equipment area by reflected light: light that entered the booth itself from the side facing *away* from the heavy artillery. Well, I'm all for safety, every time.

Sitting before a console that made the one in the transmission room look like my autodialer, Elihu Coogan flexed his hands. He reminded me of a cathedral organist; all the Stork needed were the candelabra. First looking up at the reflected view, he touched fingers to the keypunch array.

Then the action began.

CHAPTER TWELVE

There came a whining and a rumbling. For moments the whole building vibrated, but then something-or-other came up to speed and ran more smoothly. Once or twice the lights dimmed, but steadied when the sounds died.

Glancing back over his shoulder to us, Coogan said, "During the energizing process, the superconductor helices take a lot of current. Once operational, though, they're largely self-sustaining; we'll use only a small fraction of the starting load."

I watched the mirrors. Overlapping slightly, each

showed a segment of the transmission room. Pale coronae flickered around anything metallic and sharp-cornered—but nothing arced across, anywhere, so I quit worrying.

The chamber housing, the guts of the whole thing, was what I wanted to keep tabs on. And now I saw things happening. Our mirrors showed only about half the chamber, rising above the surrounding framework. Our view hazed: inside the housing, blue ionization flared. It surprised me there'd be so much loose field potential floating around. But I knew very little about the specific types and magnitudes of energies needed to build Pedicord's "singularities." So I shut up and watched.

Inside the chamber housing, the seeing got worse. Foggy. Blue flicker already obscured the chamber; now, apparently inside the housing, a whitish sheen appeared. Detweiler said, "What's that?"

"Water vapor," said Coogan. "Whatever's inside, condensing on the cover." Not sounding at all amused, he laughed. "You turned down Dr. Pedicord's request for dehydrating equipment, I'm sure you'll recall."

"You said there wasn't any danger involved!" Petulant, George sounded, like a little kid's "See what you made me do!"

"That is correct." Coogan's voice stayed calm. "But the moisture does produce this whiteout condition." He paused, then chuckled in a more relaxed way. "It's not important. We couldn't see past the ionization anyway, and the chamber's only sitting there, throughout. You're not really missing anything."

His hands moved; the whining began to wind down, like a high-speed turbine coasting toward a stop. Not all the way, though; at a soft pitch, barely heard, the sound leveled off. "We'll leave it on standby," Coogan said. "More economical than shutting down and starting up again. All right?"

Under Coogan's stare, Detweiler nodded. "Is that all?"

"For this time." Rising, Coogan checked his console once more and turned away. "Shall we go now?"

Detweiler got up too. I went to the console. I said, "Did

you do the full routine? Transmission and all, just as though there'd been something in the chamber?"

"Of course. That was the whole idea." Coogan wasn't paying me any attention; I looked down at his controls. Some of the keys, the ones he'd used, were wiped clean. Others, a whole block of them, had thin coatings of dust. And the labels weren't all that hard to read.

The Stork was lying. I wished I knew why.

Coogan and Detweiler headed for the direct door to outside. I was a little behind them, so I heard raised voices before I saw who was arguing. It was Eddie Machell, pudgy face flushed and blond hair mussed by fingers he was running through it, chewing on Coogan. "—supposed to be here when you energized! Those were Dr. Pedicord's instructions and you know it. Why, you might have ruined the equipment. I—"

Coogan waved a hand. "Nothing's damaged; go check, if you like. Machell, I did nothing—nothing at all—except routines with which reading and listening have made me thoroughly familiar. You were not here on time. And why, may I ask?" He didn't wait for any answer. "So, to maintain the agreed schedule at Mr. Detweiler's Riverside plant, we proceeded without you."

With no physical change at all, the air went out of Eddie Machell. Not the resentment—in the muscles around his eyes, that much still showed—but the will to stand up to Emil the Stork. Eddie's gaze shifted off somewhere toward left field; he said, "I was worried, that's all; this project, it's so *important*. All right then, Mr. Coogan. If you don't mind, though, I will run a check. I mean, even if I'd conducted the tests myself, I'd do that."

"Certainly; of course." As Coogan shifted into magnanimous gear, Machell's mouth twitched, but the man only nodded and went inside. Coogan turned to Detweiler. "Shouldn't you notify your Riverside facility that it's all right to begin operation now?"

Detweiler grinned. "No need, Coogan. I've left standing instructions: at the end of any test schedule, start the plant in ten minutes unless I call and say to hold off." George was pleased with himself, anyone could tell.

I doubt that Coogan was impressed but he faked it dutifully. Detweiler strutted a little and asked a few pointless executive-type questions before he climbed into his Continental and tried its best to imitate a jet fighter.

I don't know. If *I* wanted my driving to give that kind of impression, I'd drive something that could do it.

I was still watching George's dust, wondering about a few of many things that weren't clear to me, when Coogan spoke. I jumped; somehow I'd expected him to be halfway to his office by now. What he said was, "Banning—I shouldn't mind arrogance; I have a lot myself, and know it. But Detweiler . . ." His mouth moved; he almost made a face. "That man outclasses me too much."

Reading past the literal meanings, I said, "You didn't catch his act at its peak. Feel lucky."

Coogan laughed. He touched my shoulder, then quickly withdrew his hand. "It's a trifle early, Mitch. But may I offer you a drink?"

"Conference?" He nodded. "Sure thing. Lead on." And not much later, in his office shack, I sat with my feet up on an empty carton, sipping at bourbon graced by ice. Ice water side. Figuring nothing the Stork did was purely social, I waited.

Right again. His first query, as he leaned forward, was, "What did Detweiler tell you? Before you came in this morning?"

I sorted through my mental file of who was supposed to know what. "You were right, last night. He's purely bugged that you didn't signal his troops in the other car, to swat the Hornet."

"How could I?" But the Stork looked more relieved than otherwise. "Is that all you talked about?"

I wondered, did everyone in this mess figure me for an all-purpose news source? The role could have its advantages: swapping info with folks who weren't spilling directly to each other, I could wind up with more scoop than any of them.

It wasn't easy to keep everything straight. I sipped water first, bourbon second; that's not how a chaser is supposed to work, but bourbon has all the flavor. Then I answered. "He let me know he'd authorized the payoff, so scratch that one from your secrets list." And what else had George said? "He was all pumped up on the idea that next time he'll pop the Hornet for keeps. I think he won't, and told him why."

"His talent for protective procedure?" The Hornet, Coogan meant. Some people use pronouns for everybody, and expect you to keep track. I nodded anyway, and Coogan said, "Don't you think that between us—and I include Detweiler; give the man his due—we can outmaneuver this extortionist?"

"If we ever find out who he is, he's done; it's Parachute Night and cross fingers the nylon opens. But as of now, well, we've seen how easily he can keep us from communicating when time's a factor. So I wouldn't—"

The Stork cut in. "CB sets; Citizens Band. Communications the Hornet can't control. Detweiler can procure the equipment, and perhaps facilitate the licensing procedures." He grinned. "And if we can't get licenses immediately, George Detweiler can probably take care of any trouble the omission might cause."

I took a small slug of bourbon. "It's a permit, not a license. And the last I heard, the FCC had pretty well given up on enforcement." I had a nagging hunch that Coogan was missing a better answer, but I couldn't pin it down.

Still, I could see why Emil Storchesson had played the con successfully for umpty years before he finally slipped. He could think on his feet, was why. Or even, as now, sitting down.

I said, "I think you may have come up with a possibly decisive factor." I don't usually talk like that, but he was somewhat contagious. "If the Hornet thinks we're cut off from each other, and we're not . . ."

"Precisely." Coogan took some bourbon himself. He didn't use a water side, but did nurse his drink. Which was good; I'd hate to have to depend on working with a drunk. Now he pointed a professorial forefinger. "We don't try to finalize the situation on our first attempt. We are careful not to let our advantage be known. We simply try out the system, see how well it works for us, and how it might be improved. But the next time . . ."

"That's when the Green Hornet gets swatted?"

I didn't like the way he grinned.

"For keeps. That's correct."

Not for me it wasn't; not yet. The way I felt, I didn't want any more death lousing up my piece of this universe. But I realized I didn't exactly have the choice.

"Why is it you have to *kill* the guy?" The answer in his face was the same as why do you climb the mountain: because he was there. And remembering Borg and Archer Green, I couldn't find good cause to argue.

Hell with it. I tipped up my glass and took my leave.

Too early for lunch; I went back to Origin. Over the transmission room's door the red light glowed, and from inside came the sounds of something winding up. Also I smelled ozone.

So I knew the door wouldn't open, and that if it would, going in was a bad idea. So I went out around and into the safety room, where I found Eddie Machell doing arcane things with the controls.

When I shut the door, he heard and looked around. "Oh. Banning. Stick around; I'm just activating the distance rig, since Coogan didn't include it in his test." I'd thought power drain would be a problem on that one, too, but I didn't ask. In the mirrors I saw ionization building around the smaller setup, but nowhere near as much as the big unit had made. Then, as Coogan had done, Eddie wound his equipment down to standby.

He checked indicators, made an adjustment, and nodded. "Okay; it's shipshape." He stood. "What's on your mind?"

"Nothing special; a little time to kill. Thought I'd check

out balance and timing on my own circuitry. Now that it's been used for real, more or less.''

"Go ahead." He shrugged. "It's on the nose, though, near as makes no difference." He came over and stood facing me. "Do you know why Coogan pulled that trick? Running initial start-up without me?"

"Only what he said, that he couldn't afford the delay. For what it's worth, he chewed Detweiler, too, for being late. Said that a few more minutes and he'd've had to cancel the demonstration. Far as I know, that's all there was to it."

Eddie Machell frowned. Not at me; he had to be looking at something in his own head. "That lanky stork never does anything for simple, obvious reasons. So—"

With no thought, I'd said, *"Huh?"* Then I realized: Machell couldn't know Emil's past; he'd reinvented the nickname on his own.

But Eddie looked at me narrow-eyed. "You said what?"

I put a hand to my mouth. "Sorry; just a burp." I turned and walked past him, to check out my gear. "Might's well get at this stuff; there's just about enough time to run the checks, and still catch lunch ahead of the rush."

Whatever his point might have been, for a few seconds I expected him to push it. But he said, "Sure. See you around," and went out.

I began my test routines. For the most part Machell was right; almost everything was on target. Time delays on two telemetry channels had drifted nearly to the edge of optimum range, though, so I recentered them. Putting the test gear away, I felt I hadn't wasted my time.

Heading for my car, I passed Coogan's office hut and saw him bent over his desk. He didn't look up. There was nothing we needed to say, anyway.

The morning's weather had cleared; now the sun tried to beat its way through haze and the air felt muggy. The Volvo was hot inside; I rolled my window down. Not for the first time, I wished I'd sprung the extra tab for factory air.

Going toward the freeway, traffic was light but slow.

Once on the concrete snake itself, I had enough breeze to cool me.

Freeways. Love 'em or hate 'em: environmental disasters, but awfully convenient. Exiting back to street speeds, I felt the heat sock down again.

I'd set my taste buds for the Prairie Corral's luncheon steak, rare, complete with their Martini special that comes in a miniature carafe, nesting in ice, and fills your glass thrice.

The Corral's parking lot was full, though; inside, I'd be in for quite a wait. So I drove home; instead of the Martini I settled for iced tea.

Nothing in the mail inspired me, though two items did require answers. From the fridge I sandwiched liverwurst between caraway rye with hot mustard. Tea and sandwich weren't exactly steak and Martini, so before I ate I put a stemmed glass of slightly adulterated gin in the freeze compartment for later. Thus motivated, I felt up to answering the mail.

I was halfway through my first reply when the phone rang.

Somehow I knew who it had to be, and it was. The husky voice said, "How were your tests, Banning? Does the thing work?"

I wasn't in the mood; I said, "Go to hell," and hung up.

Of course I knew the sonofabitch would call back; this time I said, "Just a minute," and went to fetch my Martini and some ice water. Might as well enjoy *some* part of this.

"Go ahead."

"Same question, Banning. Does it work?"

"What's the matter? Are your sources on vacation?" But I was wasting my own time as much as his. "All right: this was merely a dry run, warming up the equipment. No attempt to transmit any physical object. As far as it went, I gather the test was satisfactory."

"What does that mean?"

"The gear took power without blowing up. All readings fell within the predicted range." Well, I assumed they did;

otherwise Coogan would have said something. Or Machell would have. "And the ancillary equipment—" Mine, I meant. "—it didn't behave too badly, either."

"Ancillary. Sure. What's that?"

"Try auxiliary. Control and telemetry. Is that better, or do you want a dictionary for Christmas?"

I took a sip from my Martini glass, still frosted from the freezer. The Hornet said, "Banning, you don't sound healthy; maybe you need more exercise. Like running a few more errands. I could think of some." While I searched for a better answer than the obvious two words, he said, "In case you're interested, Pedicord's all right now."

That stopped me. "I—I'm glad. Thanks for telling me." Then I had a thought. "While we're at it, why did you grab him in the first place?" I didn't expect any real info, but you never know.

Briefly the Hornet laughed. "Why? Because Coogan wouldn't pay off, before. Now he has, and will. That's the grabbing part. The holding, now: well, you'd be surprised how good Pedicord is about explaining things, when he wants his fix. Such as the way his gadget works, and how to build one." For quite a few seconds I heard only line noise. "You like it, Banning? You see what I could do with that?"

"Not exactly. Tell me, why don't you?"

"You need a diagram? *Whatever* happens here with Detweiler, there could be other markets. Like overseas, for sure. With Coogan's money—and I have to hand it to him, sneaking that much loot past Detweiler—I can do a damned good presentation." And again he asked, "You like it?"

First blackmail, then murder and kidnapping, and now a hijack: a jerk of all trades, this one was. I shook my head. "Not especially. But then I don't like anything about you, and never have. So why don't you give my ear a rest?"

He chuckled; oh, was the Hornet ever in high humor! At this stage, I realized now, insults made him feel good: powerful, on top of things, sniped at by the powerless. "Sure, Banning, anything you say. One thing, though; I've decided that when Coogan makes his next payment, *you'll* handle the delivery. If you want to see Pedicord in one piece again. Any objections?"

No objection of mine would make any difference, but I let him wait anyway, while I chose my words. "What if I told you to fuck off? Are you childish enough to kill Pedicord, just for *that*?"

"But you won't! You're a bleeding heart, Banning, and we both know it. You couldn't take the chance."

The hell of it was, he was right; I couldn't put a life on the line for a minor point of pride. The Hornet, apparently, could. If one of us were sane, the other wasn't. Q.E.D. I said, "You don't know me as well as you think—but I'll do it. If I ever see you in person, though—"

"Oh, you will, Banning. You will, and that's a promise." He hung up. I couldn't give myself many points in the exchange, so I sat back and thought about other aspects.

When the Hornet went into gloating mode his husky tone slipped a little—and then the voice sounded familiar somehow. But whose was it? Someone recent, I was sure of that much.

All right; who did I know, lately? The only person I could think of, who had acted on the Hornet's behalf in any way, was Ronnie Detweiler. Okay; so Ronnie seemed like a nice girl. Or at this point, a nice intermediate-stage person. But certainly she had motivation to rip George off.

Did the voice *sound* like her? I couldn't be sure; she and Steve Broyles used quite different tones. I wondered if Ronald Detweiler had any acting experience. Verdict: case unproven.

So in this setup, who else did I know? The only possibles I'd worked with at all closely were Larry Des Palmos and Eddie Machell. Well, both of those men had their own problems, but somehow they didn't strike me as likely candidates.

And who said the Hornet had to be an insider? I'd thought so, but maybe the "sources" line was for real, and what we had was an outside hijacker. Then why did the voice, when it slipped, almost ring a bell? False recognition, a chance similarity to some friend or acquaintance?

I wished I knew. I wished my Martini hadn't got warm during all that fruitless speculation. I wished my metabolism would allow me to finish it without blurring matters around the edges.

The hell with the whole mess. I put the glass back in the freeze. I set dinner up to cook and went to soak in a luke-warm shower, cooling off the slow way.

The first I knew Dauna was home was when a glassful of cold water hit me in the back, right in the middle of my second chorus of "The Dutch Company." So I blew the high notes, badly.

I dished up the chow and made coffee; we ate and talked. Dauna said, "The wizard has his magic candy; he'll live. The Stork's getting ready to deliver his next bundle. The Hornet's playing tin soldiers. Mitch—where does all this leave *you?*"

I wasn't sure, and said so. "Except, in the middle. He has me pinned there; they all have." I spread a hand. "I don't like it much. But what can I do?"

Pouring coffee, at first she didn't answer. Then she said, "Not much, it seems. Until the junkie genius is back safe in his own beddie-bye. But after that, Mitch: what could anyone do about it if you simply pulled a Houdini?"

"A what?"

"A vanishing act. An escape artist routine."

I thought, before saying, "I have no idea what would happen."

She reached, touching my hand. "You can't afford to worry about it. Stop trying to put body English on the whole world."

I wasn't finished. "Detweiler has no handle on me. None at all. Oh, he could swing weight, but why should he bother?" I found myself squinting. "Coogan, though; the early-termination penalties he wrote into our contract. I see two possibilities."

"One," said Dauna, "is that if necessary you pay the

man, and we learn to prefer beans to steak for a while. What's the other?''

I had to laugh. ''Actually that wasn't one of my picks. No; my thought was that if Coogan's on the level he'll come out too rich to bother with me. And if he's on the con, he won't be hanging around long enough to sue anybody.''

Palms spread, she shrugged. ''Then what frets you?''

''The Hornet, I guess. What else?''

Dauna nodded. ''Body English. Like I said. Mitch, you can't allow yourself to feel responsible for what a cornflake does.''

At head level she was right, but my gut didn't agree; I understand there's a lot of it going around. Looking for a way out of the discussion before we drowned in it, I said, ''Anything good on the teevy?''

She gestured no-comprende. Checking the paper I spotted an old British comedy series on PBS reruns. ''It's coming up in a few minutes. Shall we?''

I've never understood why having half the cast in drag was supposed to be so side-splitting; nonetheless, watching those classic old Monty Python shticks did get us thoroughly out of serious mode.

CHAPTER THIRTEEN

Detweiler liked Coogan's CB-net idea; he bought up a few sets before I had the chance to tell him there might be a better way. CB, you understand, was old hat by then. And had been for some years. Nowadays the standard mobile natter toy was the cellular phone. I'd never owned either, myself, but did have some idea of their respective capabilities.

No matter; George was in the saddle, so giddyap. Once

again he had someone scrounge for bargains, and came up with a mixed-brand collection of used gear. Mostly in the fancier models, and at least half of the units needed no major repairs.

And again he'd acted on a brainstorm of his very own, not bothering to check with anyone to see if it might work. Privacy gear; scramblers. Nobody builds stuff like that to work with CB; there's no market for it. But George dug up half a dozen old privacy units designed for point-to-point radiophone.

Not to get too technical about it: the levels were wrong, the impedances didn't match, and power supplies to run the units off car batteries simply didn't exist.

Bottom line: there was no way to get there from here. Detweiler gave me a look that said it was all my fault.

As the old saying goes, up to then I didn't know the half of it. The other half was quite an education. I'd seen CB jargon stereotyped in TV commercials, but still the reality jarred me. A lot of people, no doubt perfectly normal in real life, did talk hillbilly when using their rigs. When we got our sets working and tried them out, running around a little to see how well we could keep in touch on the move, George Detweiler fit in perfectly: "good buddy" every other sentence, and all the numerical jumbo which I have mercifully forgotten. His anonymous storm troopers (meaning, employees I hadn't met personally) seemed uncomfortable with the lingo and used it sparingly. At least they weren't stuck with any fancy "handles"; Detweiler tagged them as Delta One, Delta Two, and so on.

George himself was Delta Supreme. Of course . . .

The Stork played CB games not at all; he read the info book but used none of the code numbers. Just words, every time. He did have a handle; I think he chose it to tell me I didn't scare him any. First time I heard him say "Chimney Bird to Delta Supreme" I thought he had his brains in backwards, but then I realized Chimney Bird would fly right over George's head. And that maybe the Stork did have a sense of humor.

My own handle carried no deep symbolism; I used Flagman which had a limited link to Banning by way of "banner," and let it go at that. As for talking Appalachian, sometimes I entered into the spirit and sometimes not. Depending on how I felt. Meaning, I didn't exactly believe CB was a way of life.

George was, however, a good organizer. He or some employee came up with good innocent-sounding code words to cover various situations. George himself wanted to use DDT as code for the Hornet, but settled for Flyboy.

After we played network for a while, experimenting with signal range and learning about blind spots, I began to think the idea might even work.

But on that aspect, for some time all we could do was wait.

During that time the Hornet called me only once. "You can relax, Banning. I won't need you just yet."

Feeling antsy I said, "I don't need you at all. Never did."

The man laughed. "That's your problem." He paused. "Two weeks, maybe a little sooner. Then Coogan follows up on his down payment."

"And?"

"As I said before. You'll make the delivery."

I was drinking coffee; I poured a warm-up. "Another fancy hide-and-seek game? What is it this time?"

He giggled. Slightly drunk, maybe? "I'll tell you when the time comes, not before. I wouldn't want you to waste your energy, trying to figure how to beat it."

"Or maybe you're afraid I *could*." Well, I hadn't really expected any advance breaks. "You have something more?"

He said, "No," and I hung up.

Early evening storm clouds darkened the sky; I put some lights on and closed the drapes facing downhill. I liked that night view: lighted windows, and rows of street lights decorating the opposite hill. But lately, any time I looked out at all of it, I heard that damn bullet again. It bothered me, going chicken this way, but I never seemed to find time to psych myself out of it. As they say, though: Real Soon Now . . .

Dauna was out on an interview; she'd told me to expect her when I saw her. I watched a few yawns' worth of TV and bedded down early. Whatever time Dauna got home, she didn't wake me.

In the morning, though, she got me up. To take an incoherent call from Elihu Coogan. Why he was in his office so early, he didn't say. Just: "Get down here! I've got to talk with someone and you're it."

Trying to keep the snarl out of my voice I told him I'd be there in an hour. Being rousted out of the sack at that time of day wasn't anything I appreciated.

Pouring each of us a cup of coffee, Dauna emptied the pot she'd been working on and we sat for a bit. I couldn't answer questions because Coogan had made no sense. She told me about the article she'd worked up last night and it sounded good.

Coffee finished, we kissed good-bye, which was unusual because most mornings she's gone before I wake up. After she left I showered and all, had breakfast for a change, and dressed.

Driving downtown, I could feel a muggy day coming on.

Trosper Building, Suite 2310-14. Behind the new reception desk sat Tixo. Again he'd reverted from friendly mode to grudging acceptance. I wished I knew what went on in his wizened skull, but aside from language lessons one way or the other, I wasn't likely to find out. I returned his nod and went into Coogan's office.

At nine in the morning he was drinking bourbon; he offered me some but I shook my head.

"All right; what's it about?" I sat across from him, elbows on his desk and chin in my hands.

"Look at this." It was an envelope, addressed to one Edsel M. Allert, c/o Progress, Inc., Transportation Specialists. Just the way the firm's name read on the suite's outside door. Except that on the envelope, the *g* in Progress wasn't set crooked.

I felt my eyebrows rising. Coogan said, "Read the letter!"

So I did.

> *Dear Mac*
>   *You didnt give me any adress except where you work, I hope you get this alright. Mac I dont think you should do what you said. I know you feel Docter Pedicord cheated daddy but two wrongs dont make a right, you know that. I dont see how you can get away with it anyway, once they know who you are your going to get fired for sure. Dont get in any trouble Mac, daddy wouldnt want that ever. But good luck anyway.*
>   *Your loving sister*
>   *Alice*

I put the handwritten sheet, green ink on pink paper, back in the envelope and handed it to Coogan. "The Hornet, you suppose?"

He slugged down some bourbon. "Damn it, Coogan! *All* we need is you slopping yourself into a blue funk. Now get your ass in gear and tell me what this is all about."

He shook his head, but did push the bottle away. He wasn't all that drunk yet—just working on it. He said, "You saw the name on the envelope. Allert. I told you about him, I think. Man who worked for Pedicord, got paranoid and thought Olin was stealing his ideas. And then, long after Pedicord had to fire him, died of cancer. Remember?"

I did now, sort of; it was the kind of thing you hear but don't save on disk, so to speak. I said, "Passing the fact that opening other people's mail is a Federal offense, I get the picture. This letter is from Allert's daughter to Allert's son. And it seems the son is on your payroll."

I frowned. "Edsel? And then Mac? I don't get it."

The Stork cocked his head forward. "Middle initial M;

I suppose Mac would be a nickname. Does it matter? What does is what you just said: the son *is* on my payroll." His shoulders twitched; the shudder ran up his neck and tensed his face.

With a deep breath he regained control. "Well. Now we know who the Hornet is, and why. What we don't know is who the murdering bastard's *pretending* to be. The name he's using here."

He punched an intercom button; faster than you'd believe, Tixo brought in coffee. Unpredictable again, the little guy gave me a shiny brown grin. I pointed to his knife, aimed fingers at his forehead, smiled and waved a hand to indicate we could skip our routine this time. Tixo did it all right back to me; I saw it was giving him a real kick.

Maybe some days he was bothered by nagging irregularity.

I figured the party was over, but as I stood to leave, George Detweiler came in. "All right, Coogan; this had better be good, getting me over here when I'm busy as hell." I waved a hand and started for the door, but he said, "No, you stick around. When Coogan's done, I have a couple of things on my mind."

I sat again, while George got the same info I already had. At the end, Coogan said, "Detweiler—what can we *do?*"

George didn't speak; I said, "You haven't messed up the envelope? You steamed it open, didn't you?" Coogan nodded. "Then why not reseal it, and put it back with the rest of the employees' mail?"

"And see who picks it up; yes! Keep an eye on the boxes. Here at the office first, then out at Range A. I—"

"No." That was Detweiler. "I mean, Banning has the main idea right, but forget the Peeping Tom part." Sure enough, George had a more sophisticated plan. Nothing new: for years, variations have been used to find out who's tapping the till. The only question was whether to dust the envelope with stuff that stains hands green, or the kind that fluoresces under UV.

The latter sounded fancier so that's what they chose.

George made a phone call, then said, "Give me the letter. I'll have Delta One take care of it."

I didn't ask how; the mechanics seemed obvious. The only catch was, the Hornet could be wary enough to leave the bait untouched. I didn't mention that idea. Coogan said, "You had some things to talk about?"

Detweiler nodded. "Scheduling. When do we test for actual transmission? When do we get Pedicord back so we *can* test?" Coogan looked helpless; George slapped the desk. "If necessary we'll go without him; between you and Machell it should be safe. Not on a human, maybe, but trial runs with inanimate samples. Right now, though—"

Scowling, every inch the Executive President, he said, "This blackmailing Hornet sonofabitch, this Allert. There's more than one way we can go after him." George leaned forward. "Coogan? Tell me everything you know about the Allert family."

Swallowing first, the Stork began. Aside from what we'd already heard, he didn't have much. The Illinois hometown of Bernard Allert, who'd worked for Pedicord, was also daughter Alice's address on the envelope. Only vaguely, through Pedicord, had Coogan heard of Bernard's off-spring. There'd been a son back from Army service in Europe, who had gone into technical work. Then a daughter, who would be Alice our letter-writer. And another son—but near as Coogan could recall, that one should be too young to get work on a project of this sort. So . . .

Coogan spread his hands. "That's all I know. Perhaps if Dr. Pedicord were here . . ."

"And if the dog hadn't stopped to crap," said George, "he'd have caught the rabbit." Sometimes I found myself disliking Detweiler a bit less than usual. "Anyway," he said now, "you've given me my next move."

Coogan looked puzzled but I thought I saw it; Detweiler proved me right. "Edsel M. Allert was in the Army. I have connections that can get me his records, *fast*. Including description, pics if any, and his fingerprints." He grinned. "Like it?" The Stork nodded; I was thinking it over.

George harrumphed at me; I made a delay gesture and

said, "It's good, yes. But don't count chickens yet." Eyebrows gained altitude; I said, "The Hornet's no dummy. A whack, yes—but a smart whack. We've found that out the hard way."

Detweiler snorted. "Smart won't change his prints."

I didn't bother to mention a guy I'd known, who'd fixed it so someone else's prints were on his service records. I said, "You haven't fingerprinted your employees, have you, Coogan? Not me, anyway."

"We'll do it tomorrow," Detweiler said. "All right, Banning?"

I shook my head, but Coogan's brow cleared. "I see Mitch's point." I waited and he said my own thought: "There will be objections; bound to be. On an organized level. And I'll be very much surprised if we can find out who instigates them."

There it was: the Hornet had an inside pipeline and he'd know how to use it. Unions get their backs up at any hint of infringement on their members' rights. And that's all the Hornet would need.

After only moments, Detweiler said, "We'll try it anyway. Sooner or later the bastard has to slip. What we do is give him all the chances we can manage."

Regardless of how I felt about George Detweiler, I was beginning to see how he'd carved his way to where he was.

At Range A the next morning, it turned out Coogan and I were right. An hour after the fingerprinting notice hit the bulletin board, a shop steward arrived from town with the draft of an Unfair Labor Practice complaint. Somebody had moved fast; my guess was someone riding figurative wings and packing a nasty green stinger.

Saying he needed to make a quick run to the nearest village, a little more than halfway to I-5, Detweiler stalked to his Continental and did his usual imitation of a jet takeoff. I still thought it stunk, compared to what he could have done with a Ferrari. With all the things George had going for him, class wasn't one of them.

In the Stork's office, he and I were using up the last of an

overly mature pot of coffee when a delegation knocked and
came in. It was made up of the top-level peons, near or even
into management grade, including Larry Des Palmos and
Eddie Machell.

Des Palmos did the talking. "Look, Mr. Coogan, I'm
sorry about this. Our group here, we want you to know
that we don't personally object to the ID verification procedure. But if we didn't back the union's stand—well, the
whole crew would walk."

He looked down at his feet. "We just wanted you to
know how we feel."

Coogan put on a good face and made with the polites; the
little gears in his head had to be revving up, though. "No
hard feelings at all," he said. "I understand perfectly." He
gestured toward his little side bar. "In fact, gentlemen, why
don't we all have a drink on it?"

He set out a tray of glasses, a bowl of ice, and bottles.
After a little "You first"-ing, Des Palmos fixed himself
bourbon and water. A black man named Arnold used ice
with his, and Eddie Machell poured a shot neat into his
own tall glass. In between, the three whose names hadn't
yet registered with me made their own choices. Lastly,
Coogan and I served ourselves.

Arnold and Des Palmos sat down; the rest stood. Some-
one mentioned the Seahawks' chances in the coming sea-
son; Machell picked up on it, but then the subject died. Des
Palmos upended his drink and looked around at the others.
They followed suit, though Eddie looked at his glass, rub-
bing his thumb along its side, before he emptied it; there,
I gathered, was a man who appreciated good bourbon.
Standing, Des Palmos said, "Thanks for the hospitality,
Mr. Coogan. We'll get back to the job now."

While he said that, George Detweiler stalked in. "All
right, Coogan: *now* what?" The Stork tried to shush him;
finally George blinked and said, "Conference? Okay; I'll
wait." He sat in the chair Larry Des Palmos had vacated,
and glared; looking uneasy, the six men left.

Scowling at the little table beside him, Detweiler picked
up the empty glasses and dropped them into the bar's small

sink, making a minor splash. "If you're done fraternizing with the hired help—"

"You idiot!" Eyes wide and mouth working, Coogan pointed to the sink. "You've ruined it." George's own mouth hung open. "Why do you think I fed good liquor to those gloating hypocrites?"

I caught on before George did. "To get fingerprints; right? Cagey stunt, right out of Sherlock Holmes."

"But—" said Detweiler.

"But now"—Coogan almost shouted—"you've mixed the glasses up, put *your* ham-handed prints all over them, and put them in the damn *water!*"

Slugging down his own drink, he reached for the bottle again, then thought better of it and sat behind his desk. "All right, Detweiler; what else do you want?"

Face red, holding onto his temper with both hands, George took his deliberate time fixing himself a drink, then returned to his chair. Conforming to the trend, I found one for myself. My drink was still largely intact; I sipped on it and waited.

Now Coogan sat quiet; finally Detweiler said, "I'm sorry I spoiled your stunt." Slightly appeased, the Stork nodded. "I wasn't so bugged that the Hornet beat your try, the way you both predicted; what burned me was seeing those fat-heads celebrating their victory on your tab." He was sailing on the right tack; the Stork's ruffled feathers smoothed visibly.

George leaned forward. "I came in here to ask you what's next. But actually I have a pretty good idea how to proceed for the time being. I'll need full access to your personnel files."

Coogan looked attentive; Detweiler continued. "I've got young Allert's prints. Their code-listings, rather, not pictures. The codes are good enough, until we have a close pair to match up. And . . ."

He hadn't had to go to the Army after all; Edsel M. Allert had done some work down at the Cape, for a Boeing sub-contractor. Around the time of the first Heinlein Station launches. "I've put the Delta team on it, backtracking the people *I've* hired, who've had access to Range A since the Hornet first gave sign. The newer ones we needn't bother with—and the same goes with your own files." He downed his drink. "Are you with me?"

Coogan nodded. "Of course. Name your representative, and the downtown office will cooperate fully."

They talked some more; they even asked my opinion, but I had nothing to add. They were closing in pretty well, it seemed to me, on the Hornet's past trail. In present tense the CB caper, if the gear worked as well as everyone hoped, looked like a good shot at the guy. Offhand, I wouldn't bet much on his future.

But considering the way things had gone lately, I wouldn't bet a whole lot against it, either.

CHAPTER FOURTEEN

We broke for lunch. Detweiler was going back to town. Or rather, to his Bellevue office; he'd be cutting from I-5 to the Eastside freeway, well north of the county line. Going out the door he turned and said, "Let's do another CB team exercise tonight; set up a few problem situations and solve them. Begin at nine o'clock; all right?"

Dauna and I had nothing planned; I nodded. Coogan said, "Quite satisfactory. What starting points are you assigning?"

George shook his head. "None, this time. In real action we might not have much advance warning. So start wherever you please; part of the drill will be getting the team oriented."

"Not bad." That was my contribution. "I'll be there." Detweiler did a double take, grinned, and closed the door behind him. After checking the afternoon's chore list with Coogan, I left also.

I hadn't brought a lunch, so I drove out to the small town that lay toward the freeway. I'd eaten there before, both at Marge's Café and in the Club Montmartre. In Marge's you could see what you were eating, so that's where I went. The food wasn't great, but at least they kept you waiting for it. As Dauna said once, "We're lucky they don't give us all we pay for." I knew where that line came from; originally it applied to government and taxes.

I parked not far past Marge's and walked back. Going inside, I saw the place was fairly well filled; no booths or tables were empty. A few vacant stools at the counter, but as I turned that way, someone yelled my name.

Not quite a yell, actually, but loud enough to cut through the noise. I looked around and saw Larry Des Palmos and Eddie Machell at a table, along with someone I didn't know by name, from the morning's delegation. One vacant chair; Larry waved for me to come over. Well, why not?

They held menus but hadn't yet ordered; Larry gave me a look at his. But first, introductions. "Mitch Banning, Orville Hackett. Orv keeps track of supplies; he's not out here much."

Larry grinned while he said all that; I decided he wanted to make sure I knew it was Buddies Week. So I grinned too, and shook hands. Orville was a skinny guy, pale-faced with black hair. Standing, he'd top me a little, but tall he wasn't. We mumbled hellos. I looked at the menu just as if I didn't already know it pretty well; it was the standard model, which takes only about two readings.

Our waitress was a young kid, probably still in high school. Without the makeup, and with her hair combed, she'd probably have been pretty. I ordered salad and oyster stew, neither of which tend to come out greasy. I didn't notice what anyone else ordered. Then, drinking rank coffee, we waited.

So far, nobody had said much; considering the situation, I didn't mind at all. But as soon as the food arrived, Des

Palmos asked: "Mitch? That fingerprint stuff; what's it all about?"

Oyster stew doesn't take much chewing, but in the interest of keeping my answers slow, I got some mileage out of the salad. "Well, Larry, it's no secret there's a lot riding on this project." Chomp, chomp-chomp. "Maybe Detweiler or Coogan, or both, simply decided they needed to beef up security."

First line of defense, but no one seemed much impressed by it. "And there *have* been some hairy incidents. Whatever you know about those, though, is how it's going to stay; I'm not authorized to help out with guessing games."

Larry's grin lost something. "You mean *we're* under suspicion?"

I couldn't believe a crew chief could ask such a dumb question. I said, "We, meaning anyone who's had access to Range A. Hell yes, of course we are. How else?"

Hackett's voice came out thin. "Those incidents you mention. Then the police must have some prints from them?"

I did half a headshake. "Maybe so, maybe not. Nobody's told me." It was a good misleading line of talk; I was glad he'd thought of it. Whether or not any of these three could be the Hornet, word of this talk would spread. Couldn't hurt.

Machell hadn't said much; now he spoke. "Plain old security, though, starts out by checking for criminal records. I imagine they've already done that?"

Now I shrugged. "Wouldn't know. Seems likely." I spooned up the last of the stew; final score was three tired oysters in all that milk. Not meaning to, I found myself scowling in Eddie Machell's direction; when I noticed I was doing it, I stopped. "You have to understand, Eddie: any time I'm in on Coogan's and Detweiler's conferences we're talking tech, not exec."

In a sense, I suppose, I wasn't entirely lying.

We'd all finished eating; for a wonder, the young woman brought coffee without being asked. I couldn't take any more of the stuff and requested iced tea instead; eventually it arrived.

Meanwhile, Hackett and Des Palmos were trading guesses about the fingerprint bit, coming nowhere near any version of the truth. Finally Eddie Machell slapped the table, not hard. "We're spinning our wheels. It's probably just security, like Mitch says; if you don't have a criminal record you don't need to worry." He stood. "I'm not."

We fed the cash register and went out, splitting to our respective cars; the others had all come in Machell's. I started off first; he convoyed behind me, back to Range A.

On a hunch I went to Detweiler's field office and checked the mail tray. The Allert letter was still in the pile. It would have been safe to handle it; only the letter inside had been dusted. "That way," George had said, "we won't get false leads from people sorting out their own mail."

It was nice of him to explain his reason; otherwise we might never have guessed. In my esteem he moved back a space.

The highlight of a dull afternoon was a quick thunder-shower that caught me walking from Origin to Coogan's office. A little later I drove home over wet pavement, squinting through an oily splash my wipers kept spreading around, but also smelling the clean freshness of rainwashed air. With the CB exercise coming up that evening, I left the Volvo curbside and walked up the outside stairs.

As usual, most of the mail hit File Thirteen unopened. I put Dauna's pet casserole on for slow heating. Then I sat down with the paper, and for once completed the cross-word without interruption.

And also the Jumble puzzle. I like those because they use a nonlogical, nonlinear aspect of the mind's patterning function. Dauna can do them as fast as she can read and mark; I have to work at it, to get away from my habitual left-brain way of thinking. You might think being stoned would help, but I tried that, during my year for dumb stunts, and it didn't.

The first scramble was XOICT; in the blank boxes just

below, the fourth letter was circled. No problem: TOXIC. Next came HETTE, fourth letter circled. TEETH, so toward the final answer I had an X and a T. Then STIIMF, second letter. For minutes that one stumped me, because I'd slipped and let myself "hear" the scrambled version, mentally.

So I went to the final word: GYRENE, third letter indicated. "Damn!" The hardest ones are those that already make a kind of sense, but still have to be shuffled into the "real" word.

I scanned the Clue panel, a cartoon with caption. It showed a figure with an anchor tied to its neck, standing on a cliff over the water. Caption: "Sometimes the only way out."

Mumble, mumble, then *Aha!* EXIT, so I needed an *I* and an *E*. MISFIT popped to recognition fast, but ENERGY took longer.

I yawned and stretched, releasing tension. In the Sunday paper they use six words, six letters each. I get most of them.

I skimmed the paper, reading a piece here and there, eyes passing over the ads without noting their content; that reflex developed spontaneously some years ago, and I'm grateful.

In another swipe at the Creighton-Ogsberth bill, Hod Neill had Berlinda telling Thom Tumb that the government was only trying to do him a favor: carrying money around in his pockets made him look lumpy. Thom agreed. "Yer right, Berlinda. Nothin' the gov'ment hates worse'n lumpy pockets. On other people." The universe, I decided, couldn't be all bad.

I put the paper back into reasonable order—Dauna likes it neat whether she reads it or not—and went to soak residual tensions out with a long hot shower. Yes, we do try to help conserve water and energy (I flashed on GYRENE); it was a long hot *trickling* shower, not a big gushy one.

Toweling off, I heard the front door close; Dauna called my name. I yelled "Hi!" full-bore; with our acoustics, from where she was she'd have heard nothing less. Still dripping, I took the towel along and went to greet her. After we'd kissed, I finished drying and put on a light robe.

Obviously, I saw, it was Talk Time.

Dismissing her own day, Dauna asked how things were going on the Hornet front. As she bared her feet, wiggled her toes, and stretched like a cat, I brought her up to date.

She did not seem pleased. Undoing her hair, shaking it down loose, she said, "You still don't know a thing, really, do you? Not you and not Coogan and not Detweiler. Allert's only a name."

"Well . . ." I went over the angles George and the Stork were trying to work. "Tonight we're doing another CB exercise, running around like TV cops only not so loud. It might help."

Shrugging, Dauna grinned. "Cop shows bore me. How about we impersonate an X-rated movie, instead?" Which was a great idea, except that we were both too hungry to wait dinner.

After it, while our meals settled, we talked some more; nine o'clock loomed sooner then we expected. And along about then, Dauna said she'd changed her mind about cop shows; she decided she'd like to ride along.

I saw no reason why not, so we went down to the car.

Right on time, Detweiler called. Leaving out the jargon, Delta Supreme was calling Deltas One through Three, plus Chimney Bird and Flagman, in that order. After each call he waited until he got a response, giving location. Deltas One and Two, riding together this time, reported from East Lynne, code for Detweiler's office complex; sometimes George surprised me. Delta Three, lacking a code word for his position, admitted right out loud that he was passing the north end of the university campus. Unfortunately for him, Seattle has three universities; finally the poor guy had to cough up an actual street and a block number.

"Chimney Bird to Delta Supreme." Coogan tried to sound bored, but I could hear the excitement of a little kid playing spies. "At the sanitarium, leaving northbound."

Sanitarium was a cutie: for TB, which meant the Trosper Building.

In turn, I allowed as how Flagman was standing by, just outside the Holland Tunnel—our underground stairway—waiting instructions.

Delta Supreme gave a few, mostly having everyone move around. Chimney Bird and I were to rendezvous near a six-way corner: 12th and Union and Madison, just east of First Hill; in twenty minutes His Supremacy would expect us to call from there. The Stork was closer than I was, so I left in a hurry. Our meeting point was a tavern parking lot; maybe we'd have time for a quick beer.

Detweiler hadn't given his own location, and nobody asked.

Actually it wasn't all that quick and easy. All too often some outsider would horn in on the conversation, usually with funny-ha-ha comments. Now and then I could hear George working up a head of steam, but he had sense enough to avoid antagonizing anyone, which could only make things worse. I could see, though, that this gimmick was by no means the cure-all Coogan expected. Especially when one Delta or another hit a blind spot and George couldn't get answers.

By dint of offensive driving I made rendezvous ahead of sked. Coogan was surprised to see Dauna with me. She smiled at him. "I might do an article on CB itself, the way the scene's changed since the glory days." The Stork nodded, and joined us in going inside for a quick beer.

The place was clean, and the crowd was cheerful enough, but the only vacant seating was next to one of the loudest jukeboxes I ever heard in my life. We were short on time anyway, so we drank up faster than I like. When we got back out to our cars, Delta Supreme was not being happy. Where the hell had we *been?*

Well, screw it; my watch indicated we were right on time. "You said twenty minutes, Delta your Supremacy, sir, and twenty it is. If you want us to keep an ear hung in there between schedules, say so. Flagman out."

He hit his Talk button; I could hear the hiss. But he didn't say anything. Maybe he was thinking he had no direct payroll handle on me. When he spoke I heard the effort of trying to sound like a man reasoning calmly instead of one who was pissed off quite a lot. For a novice he did it rather well.

"Delta Supreme here. I expected that all of us would stay on the goddamn—would give full attention—throughout the entire exercise. From now on, is that understood? Delta Supreme out."

Well, sure; in a *real* maneuver. No point in explaining; I gave him some agreement soft-soap and signed out.

Over the next hour or so, Detweiler directed us through various exercises. Sometimes it worked and sometimes not; once, Delta Two got lost in a blind spot for almost half an hour. And Delta Three, behind time on making station, took one chance too many and got a ticket: speeding, and running the amber. George could afford it, but my hunch was that Delta Three would be someone else next time; this guy had too many strikes on him.

Finally our Führer was either satisfied or else gave up, and we all went home.

Shucking shoes and a few clothes, Dauna and I sat around drinking decaf and doing a postmortem. "Mitch, do you think this razzle-dazzle can actually make the flyswatter work?"

"Maybe." I thought about it. "If the Hornet depends again on keeping us isolated from each other, we can short-circuit that to some extent. Get extra troops to X marks the spot, and so forth. But I don't think these CB rigs do a solid enough job for what we need." Brooding a moment, I decided. "I'm going to try to sell George on springing for cellular phones."

Then of course I had to explain why. Luckily she soon got bored, and let me off the technical kick.

She was brushing her hair, out to one side so the long strands almost floated off the end of each stroke. She said,

"What happens if you make your big try at the Hornet, and miss?"

I sipped some decaf; it was cooling, so I gave it thirty seconds' microwave. While it heated, I said, "Nobody mentioned that problem. And I guess I haven't allowed myself to think about it."

"Somebody has to, don't they, Mitch?"

"I suppose." I looked at her. "You realize I'm not the one running this show."

Her return gaze didn't let me off the hook. The phone's chime, just as she began a reply, came as a relief.

Not for long. When the other party answered my hello, I pushed the Mute button and turned back to Dauna. "Speak of the devil." Her brows lifted; I nodded and released the button. Into the phone I said, "Well, well; surprise. We were just talking about you."

"And being kind, like it says in the movie. All right, here's the word. Tomorrow night, my next payment from Coogan. He'll give you the money according to my instructions. Then after you get home from work, stick close to that phone. Any questions?"

Suppressing the urge to needle him, I said, "How's Pedicord doing? And when—"

"*I'll* say when; don't you forget that. He's all right; for a junkie he's really fine. Plenty of elbow lube, and I'm holding him down to maintenance—I think. He won't run out too soon. Now then: are you set for tomorrow night? Any snags? Conflicts? Other commitments?"

As though he could see me, I shook my head, then realized and stopped. "No. Nothing. I'm clear for that time."

"Good. Then that's all." He paused. "Oh yes; one more thing. You don't have to wear out your fingers, doing all that walking. I've already instructed Coogan. Then I waited two minutes and called back. His line was busy; so was Detweiler's. Yours wasn't. Does that tell you anything?"

Not a whole lot; not anything I hadn't known already. And in case the Hornet wasn't fully cognizant, I explained. "This is Coogan's problem, his and Detweiler's. Not mine.

I'm in it only to the extent that you've dragged me in. After first trying to scare me out. Sometime let's sit down and open up a keg of nails and you tell me how it all works. But meanwhile—"

"Meanwhile you're wasting my time, Banning. Good night." He hung up. I hadn't kept score on which of us hung up on the other the most—but my hunch was, the Hornet had a big lead.

Dauna had an expectant look, but I was busy punching numbers. Between Detweiler and Coogan I picked the Stork. When he answered I said, "We've both heard from the Hornet, and I think you've reported to George, so let's go from there. I have a point to make."

"Indeed." Sounding miffed but hiding it behind a pose of boredom. "Very well, I'll listen. Though how you propose to alter the situation, I have no idea."

"You will in a minute." I gave him Dauna's misgivings: what might happen if the flyswatter took a full swing and didn't connect. I didn't take time to credit her: most people forget that details which are important to the speaker may have no importance at all to the listener. I kept my pitch down to cases, and wound up with: "His most likely reaction to a missed try would be killing Pedicord immediately."

After a time Coogan answered. "Not necessarily. This man wants half, he says, of sundry indefinable proceeds he expects to materialize in some way I can't imagine. Why should he kill the goose, so to speak, who lays the golden eggs?"

His words were a bit tangled; even the Stork, it seemed, could get rattled sometimes. But I caught his meaning. And thought about it. The answer wasn't all that difficult.

"The Hornet's ambivalent, Emil." His breath caught, a little; I'd used the old name deliberately, hoping to jar him into seeing this mess in the round, not just the playacting side of it. "He hates Pedicord and wants money; whether he's hotter for loot or revenge probably varies with his blood sugar level." Coogan tried to cut in but it was my dance. "And he'd know you're ready to go ahead, partially at least, *without* Pedicord."

Coogan waffled but I withheld the syrup. "Listen! You've mentioned that part with others present: Des Palmos and Machell, for two. And if you think they don't leak things around to impress the peons, you haven't worked many projects. So the Hornet knows, all right. Whoever he is, with Range A access."

A longer pause, before Coogan said, "And do you propose a solution? Do you have a plan?"

Another easy answer. "A negative one. For tomorrow night's delivery, the flyswatter routine is off. At least, I won't cooperate." Additional thought. "If I catch you and Delta Supreme trying to work it anyway, I'll abort the mission."

Coogan didn't answer. I said, "You can tell Detweiler that. If he doesn't like it he can get somebody else to tote the bale. Except, likely the Hornet wouldn't go along with that."

The Stork's next words, he was obviously choosing carefully. "How am I expected to sell this to Detweiler?"

"Tell him we can't risk a swing and a miss until Pedicord's back safely. Period, end quote."

"Well . . . Olin's not absolutely essential. Still, though . . ." Then I guess he realized how his words sounded. "To the project, I meant. At this stage. Most certainly I feel responsible for Dr. Pedicord; I've told you why. I would never—"

"Sure not. Any more than you'd use a needle to keep a man in line. We're all Boy Scouts here, aren't we?"

He said nothing; suddenly I was sorry I'd made the crack. After all, he'd convinced me of his concern, earlier. "Cancel that, Emil. The way things are, we're *all* strung out."

"Yes. All right, Banning; I'll try to get George Detweiler to see your logic. Can I call you back later?"

I looked at my watch. "Before midnight, yes; after that, save it for morning. We'll have all day to settle things."

"I suppose so." He sounded tentative. "Very well; I'll see what Detweiler's reaction is and get back to you."

He didn't, though. Dauna and I were doing a little quiet necking when the phone sounded again. It was Delta Supreme, mad as hell. When we were done he was even madder; we came nowhere near agreement. Finally he said, "It's late. We'll clear this up tomorrow."

"In my book, Detweiler, it's cleared up right now. I won't change my mind. Let me make delivery without interference, or get yourself another boy and see how the Hornet reacts to that. End of transmission. Flagman out."

With the phone hung up, I looked over at Dauna. She said, "Who did you say wasn't running this show?"

CHAPTER FIFTEEN

I was in no hurry, next day, to lock jaws with George Detweiler. It wasn't that he scared me, these days, but I had a hunch the argument would expand to fill all available time. So as I saw it, the smart thing was to begin the hassle as late as I could manage. After lunch, I decided, would be about right.

Not at all by accident I slept in a little late, took my time showering, and did a leisurely job with toast and coffee and orange juice. About the time I was due at Range A, which was well before Detweiler ever showed up or was likely to, I called the project site and found myself talking to Eddie Machell.

I made it quick. "My work outside the project's been backlogging, and there's not much lined up to do at the Range, so I won't be in before lunch. Pass it to Coogan and Detweiler; okay? And thanks, Eddie."

Before I left for Range A, I really did quite a lot of work.

* * *

Morning had been foggy and overcast, but heading for the freeway I saw the sun beginning to make a dent. As happens sometimes, the haze burned off fast; by the time I hit the county line the sky showed blue and clearing. This wouldn't be a hot day, though. Just pleasantly warm.

The gas gauge sat lower than I liked, so after I was off I-5 I stopped at the gas station across the corner from Marge's Café, and filled up. Gas costs more up there than in town, but that's what I got for not paying attention. On the other hand, the kid pumped it for me; I'd almost forgotten about that service.

On arrival at Range A I decided not to check in with Detweiler, whose Continental was in the lot, or even with Coogan. I walked over to Origin, where I found Eddie Machell coaching a young woman in transmission chamber procedures. I recognized her: Nancy Ohara was Japanese, but kidding around, the gang usually pronounced it Oh'Hara. I waved hello to both of them.

Eddie nodded; Nancy pushed at the bangs that fell across her eyebrows, and grinned. Seeing they were busy I didn't intrude with chitchat, but went to check on my own gear.

The installation had been under power long enough that most circuits had stabilized pretty well. Still, routine check-ups never hurt and sometimes help.

This time I found myself with a real glitch. Not a matter of readjustments, but an equipment failure: a whole channel bank was dead. Sixteen channel units wouldn't go out all at once; it had to be something else. By the same reasoning: since other banks were working, so was the master oscillator. Ergo, the frequency divider unit for the one bank had turned up its toes; I plugged a spare in and all was well. I red-tagged the failed module to go back to Detweiler's shops for repair.

The dividers themselves were nothing but strings of ring counters, so no retuning was needed. Having sweat the older type some years ago, I did appreciate the simplified design.

When I work, I guess I concentrate a lot; as I looked around, I saw that Machell and Ohara had left without my noticing. For coffee, maybe, and when I went around to the oversized closet we used for coffee breaks at Origin, I wasn't too surprised to find them there.

I pulled a chair over and poured myself a cup. "Well, how's the OJT going?"

Nancy giggled; Machell glared as if I'd called him a bad name. "What the hell do you mean by that?"

Caught totally off guard, I stammered a little before I said, "The transmission chamber. You were showing Nancy through the drill; right? What else would I mean?"

His face got red; Nancy put a hand on his sleeve and said, "Earlier today Mr. Detweiler made a remark, a rather crude one, to Ed and me. To the effect that the safety booth certainly made an ideal love nest, and in that context he also mentioned on-the-job training. So Ed thought—"

Machell scowled. "Oh, hell, Banning. Guess I shouldn't be so sensitive. But I thought you'd heard Detweiler's line and were needling me."

I shook my head. "Haven't even seen the man today. I was purely talking shop, folks." I looked at Nancy; there was something more here. But damned if I'd ask.

She told me anyway. "The sensitive part is that Ed and I are *not* lovers. But we might get that way. Not in the safety booth, though." Blushing, she looked even cuter.

I didn't have to answer; the bell saved me. Or, to be more accurate, the intercom.

"Is Banning up there? I saw his car in the lot. This is George Detweiler, and I want to see that sonofabitch right now!"

With Machell watching, not to mention Nancy Ohara, I had to decide how to handle being cussed out by the Big Cheese. Unobtrusively, or so I hoped, I took a deep breath; then I flipped the Talk switch. "As one sonofabitch to another, Detweiler, what's on your mind?"

Sidelong, I watched Machell; he seemed suitably impressed, so I forgot about him and said, "I don't have to cuss any more if you don't. You're in your office?" He grunted something that probably meant yes. I checked my watch. "I'll be there in fifteen minutes."

Detweiler didn't answer. I poured more coffee. Machell said, "Why fifteen minutes? He wants you right now. You're going to keep him waiting while you drink coffee?"

"That's right. It will do his soul good."

Nancy smiled like an angel. "And perhaps he won't be so quick, again, to call you names."

I shrugged. "Something like that. With the Detweilers of this world, you can't afford to give an inch they haven't already taken by main force."

Eyes narrowed, Eddie Machell nodded. But the way he looked at me, the intensity of him just then, I wondered whether I'd said the right thing.

Until I finished my coffee and left, no one spoke much. What they might have said afterward, I have no idea.

Detweiler, when I joined him, looked at his watch. "You're nearly half a minute late."

"Sorry about that." I did a fast calculation. "Three percent error isn't all that bad. Now what's so urgent?"

I watched him work up toward pounding his fist on the desk, and then decide not to. I pulled up a chair and sat. He said, "You know damned well. And you don't want to have to talk about it, so you've been avoiding me. You can't deny it!"

"Why should I? It's perfectly true. I've said what I have to say, and I hate to waste time repeating myself."

But of course I had to. For content and results, the argument might as well have been between two recordings. After about a half hour of it, I said, "Look, Detweiler; let me put this so that even you can understand it." Among the insults we'd been trading, that one was minor. "Neither of us can tell the other what to do and make it stick. I know you like to think the principle works only in your favor, but this time you're wrong. I can't stop you from trying for the Hornet tonight. But if you do, with Pedicord still at risk, I'm out of it."

He started up again, saying the same old things, until *I* hammered the desk. "That's it, Detweiler. That's it, that's it, that's *IT!*" My breath came ragged. "You can talk until the cows come home, George—but you won't change a thing, so there's no point." I stood. "And to save you the wear and tear, Delta Supreme sir, I'm leaving. Now."

I had almost reached the door when he said, "Banning? Once Pedicord's safe, will you cooperate?"

Awkwardly, in midstride, I stopped. And turned to look at him. "Sure. Up to a point, that is. I won't be accessory to any killing. Will that do?"

His lips parted but his teeth didn't. "If the Hornet didn't insist on you doing the payoff . . . or *does* he? I have only your word for that. I wonder—did you *really* get shot at?"

"He shot to miss; he said so. Same as with you, I expect, and probably Machell, too." Then it got through to me, what he'd said. "Detweiler: do you think *I'm* in with that maniac?"

He frowned. "I wouldn't have thought so. But you seem awfully concerned that he stay healthy, and you're road-blocking our efforts to pin him down. What am I *supposed* to think?"

When he spelled it out that way, I could see his point. But still . . .

I spread my hands. "Right now it's Pedicord's health that worries me. Though I can't ever agree with hiring someone killed, either: private justice isn't really my shtick."

George leaned forward. "Banning, if I promise you there'll be no attempt to take the Hornet tonight, and no intention of killing in any event, will you help us try to *spot* him?" He waved a hand. "I was mad as hell when I talked hit man; you know that. It wouldn't be a smart move, really. There's better ways to block somebody out of play." He waited, while I tried to guess whether I could trust him, then said, "All right?"

"No more private justice?"

"Everything legal." He grinned. "Well, more or less." So I gathered he had a few cops in his pocket.

The idea didn't surprise me much, and when it came to using dirty work on someone, it couldn't happen to a nicer fellow. I nodded. "All right; you're on."

Then I got outside fast because I had to laugh, and

George Detweiler wouldn't have understood. The laugh had nothing to do with him or with the Hornet. All it was, suddenly I had this mental picture, of a right-wing comic book hero.

He was in the Army, and his name was Private Justice.

I might as well, I decided, look in on Coogan. I found him at the phone, while Larry Des Palmos sat holding a clipboard and obviously waiting. Coogan said, "Yes, Mr. Detweiler. I understand. If that's the best we can do, we'll have to accept it." He put the phone down, gave me a hello, and said, "Let me clear a few things up with Larry, and I'll be right with you."

So I sat while they discussed last-minute modifications. Then Des Palmos went out. Coogan turned to me. "So you've decided to cooperate. To some extent, at least."

"Say what Detweiler told you; I want to be sure we're reading from the same menu." He recited, and George had put it pretty straight. I nodded. "That's right. As long as we don't endanger Pedicord, and killing's off the agenda, our peerless leader can pull the rug out from under the Hornet any way he wants to. Dirty or not, I don't care."

Coogan smiled. "That's better. Detweiler was beginning to wonder about you—and frankly, so was I." He stood and went to his little bar. "This calls for a drink. Ice with yours; right? and a water side."

I nodded, thinking that with the Stork, more and more things called for a drink lately. Not that I was any teetotaler myself, and the stuff didn't seem to be running away with him. When he handed me my two glasses I said "Cheers" and sampled each in turn. Sitting down, Coogan responded in kind.

Scratching at his beard he said, "This evening, if you have any opportunity at all, can you try to expedite Dr. Pedicord's release? We're nearly ready for a real transmission test. With or without Olin, in fact. Detweiler won't let us hold off more than one more week; delays are costing him."

Hell yes, I'd try. Nearly every time the Hornet had called

me, I'd made a pitch to get the doc loose. Coogan knew this, too, but I told him again anyway. And then, "Do I tip him to your deadline? Assuming the grapevine hasn't clued him already."

"You may as well mention it. But not the details." He filled me in a little. First try would be small objects in the larger, short-haul system. Next, more small stuff but over the longer route, to downtown. After that: well, Coogan didn't want to risk Tixo without Pedicord on hand, but George was pushing him to agree, if need be, to that contingency.

"You could use guinea pigs first."

"What?"

I'd finished my bourbon; the Stork looked an inquiry, but one was enough. "Who says the first live try has to be Tixo? It makes sense to do animals first: mice, guinea pigs, you name it."

Oddly, my suggestion seemed to startle him. His nails worried the side of his chin; knowing how an angry pimple can set up shop under cover of foliage without one's noticing, I bet myself he had one. I said, "You mean nobody thought of this before?"

"Why, I— You see, Dr. Pedicord designed the testing schedules. I gave no thought to changing any of it; that part's not my line. But—" His eyes narrowed. "Yes; I think I see how to arrange matters, and satisfy Detweiler for a time, even if the Hornet won't release Olin just yet."

Suddenly it struck me how strange it was, that we were all accepting the man's kidnapping and imprisonment as just a snag in the project. But then, everything about this setup had been strange. My brief, involuntary laugh sounded hollow. "Much longer, and the Hornet can claim legal custody. Under the doctrine of adverse possession."

The Stork wasn't up to jokes just then; the line brought a blank stare. It was time to leave so I did.

But not before one more hang-up. Coogan said, "Don't forget to take the money." Right; this time it was cash. I'd forgotten I was supposed to pick it up during the day; now he handed over a brown paper package sealed with mailing tape. By shape and heft it could have been a medium-sized book. I didn't ask the amount and Coogan didn't tell me.

"All right," I said. "Today I go straight home and wait by the phone. I doubt the Hornet will give me any chance to call you or George; last time he sure's hell didn't. So somebody who *can* connect had better be at his CB set." Coogan agreed, and this time I did manage to get away.

Outside in the sun I guessed the temperature at around seventy-five. I'd left the car facing east with the windows down, so the inside was reasonably comfortable and I wasn't stuck with a sunbaked steering wheel. I drove down to I-5 and had a quick scoot home.

In the oven a nice hunk of pork shoulder was slow-roasting; it looked and smelled fine. Inspecting the mail I found mostly junk and a few bills, but also an envelope with the Verdesting, Ltd., letterhead logo. A skinny item, obviously not a bomb. No stamp or postmark; the Hornet had delivered this, or had it done privately. Well, well . . .

Inside was a single sheet with a few typed lines on it, all caps:

> BANNING. *VITALLY IMPORTANT YOU FOLLOW ALL*
> *INSTRUCTIONS EXACTLY—REPEAT, EXACTLY—*
> *TONIGHT. IF YOU WANT TO SEE PEDICORD ALIVE*
> *AGAIN. KEEP THIS IN MIND AT ALL TIMES.*

And again the crude drawing, green-inked, of what was probably intended to be a hornet. The guy would never replace Norman Rockwell. Or even Picasso.

Why the letter? He could say all this on the phone; in fact he probably would. Emphasis? I shrugged; the Hornet had a weird mind, was all.

I unfolded the paper and worked the crossword and Jumble. GAWJIS stumped me until JIGSAW popped to mind and gave me a circled W. The cartoon showed a dog with a sore foot and was captioned: "Can make paws hurt."

The answer was WASP. I wondered if Somebody was trying to tell me something. If so, He wasn't getting through.

I turned pages. As usual, city government was a circus—but why did it have to be *all* clowns? And today the funnies didn't fun me much. The governor was lambasting the press, which is a losing game because the press does the editing. President Little Joe declared a bold new policy on something or other; I didn't read far enough to find out what, because either it would be window dressing or Congress wouldn't pass it.

Mainly I was killing time until Dauna came home.

After she'd showered and put on a robe not especially planned for modesty, I brought her up to date. She liked the parts with George Detweiler, which embarrassed me because I was trying *not* to show off.

She read the Hornet's note. "Damn. Mitch, I wanted to tag along with you tonight. But this—I guess I can't. Even hiding on the car floor, behind the front seat . . ."

"No. We don't try to pull *anything* on this guy, if there's the slightest chance he could catch us at it. Not just now."

"Too right," she said. "But once he's played his ace in the hole, you can throw in all the chips and call his bluff."

I wouldn't touch that metaphor with gloves on.

The pork roast came out tasting as good as it smelled. The salad was all right too, I guess; I'm no greens freak but eat the stuff because everybody says it's healthy. We had coffee in the living room.

When the phone rang, anyone else at the far end would have been a letdown. "Banning. Listen carefully. You won't have to take notes, because there's not much of it. For now."

"Listening. Go ahead." Dauna looked questions, but she'd have to wait. Repeating the Hornet's words, back to him, couldn't help but make him suspicious.

He said, "Put your woman on the line."

Not bothering to explain our views on possessiveness, I

said, "You want to speak to Dauna? What for?" Her brows
went up.

"If that's her name; yes. I'll tell her; she can tell you."

I shrugged and handed her the phone. She said, "Hello,"
then listened, looking ever more peeved as time passed. I
could hear a tinny rattle of voice, but no words.

Then she cut in on him. "That's ridiculous. None of this
has any connection with me. I have *work* to do, and you're
telling me to waste my whole evening. . . ."

Whatever he said next, she shut up. And then nodded.
"All right. You're a damned maniac, though; if ever I get
the chance I'm going to tuck your ears in your mouth." He
must have asked something; she said, "So you can hear
what you sound like."

Pause. "Yes. All right. Here he is." Shaking her head,
Dauna gave me the phone back.

The Hornet was laughing. "Is she always like that?"
Then, "All right; that's the small stuff. Let's get down to
cases." And he gave me my instructions. The first installment, that is.

When the call was done I looked to Dauna. I didn't
expect to have to ask, and I was right. "You know what that
tin Hitler told me? To leave here when you do, and drive
way down to Southcenter Parkway, and waste my time
watching a sappy movie." She made a face. "I've already
seen it, and it stank!"

Per the Hornet's orders, the phone was still off the hook.
"He doesn't want anyone here making calls—or receiving
any," I said. I picked it up; he was still on the line, too.

The hell with him; I touched the Mute button. Now he
could tell the line was still tied up, but couldn't hear anything Dauna and I might say. I listened; he didn't like my
move at all, and yelled for a few seconds until he realized
I might not be hearing him. Then he mumbled, "You
smartass!" and shut up.

Dauna was waiting to hear how my part of the caper was
supposed to go, so as far as I knew at that point, I told her.
Concluding, "He shouldn't know about the CB rigs, but
he's fixed it so we can't use them tonight—or not for long."

Dauna shrugged. "One of these days he'll outsmart himself." We talked a little more, then got ready to leave. At the designated minute we went down the tunnel, got in our cars and drove off. At the first corner our routes separated.

For a moment I almost envied Dauna her lousy movie.

CHAPTER SIXTEEN

Only about five minutes to the first checkpoint, so I tried the CB and after a while got Detweiler. "Listen fast; I don't have long." I explained. "Once I make the pickup, there can't be any calls coming in here; I'll cut my receive volume off, to be sure."

"Delta Supreme to Flagman. Is that all you have? Just go to the gas station and take on a passenger?"

I stopped for a red light just as it went green; suddenly I was short a couple of hands for all the gear. When I was moving again and had things sorted out, I said, "The passenger must have more instructions for me. I'll try to get all I can, as soon as possible, so that—"

Detweiler cussed a little. "What good will that do, if you can't forward the info?"

"I said *listen*, George; try it once. I can lock the Talk button here. You can hear me but I can't hear you; get it?"

Quite a pause before he said, "Oh." He chuckled, and I wasn't sure I liked the sound. "Good thinking." Perversely, my reaction was: *George likes it—so what's* wrong *with it?*

All I said was "Yeah." The station was only a block ahead; I pulled over and stopped. "If you have anything more, Detweiler, say it fast; I'm due for pickup and almost there."

"Umm. No, I think that's all. Just be alert, will you?"

"Sure thing. Flagman out." I cut Receive down to an inaudible level, and as advertised, gimmicked the Talk button. With a litterbag hanging over that part of the dash, the rig hardly showed and didn't look special. I didn't know how well the mike would pick up conversation, but figured I could sneak in a little loud paraphrasing of anything crucial without rousing too much suspicion. I started the car rolling.

It was the same Shell station at which Ronnie Detweiler had delivered Pedicord's keys. And once again it was Ronnie waiting.

Only not quite; she was in the Steve Broyles getup.

And on the other end of the CB line, George Detweiler would be listening.

There wasn't time to figure who was supposed to be on whose side. I pulled up short of where Steve stood outlined against twilight glow, got out of the car and walked to meet my passenger.

"What are you doing? I'm supposed to go with you." It was the Steve voice, which helped me with the identity situation.

"We'll go in a minute. But I need to tell you something, outside here. I don't know your tie-in with the Hornet but I think my car's bugged. Whether it is or not, you have to give me the delivery instructions—and I'd advise you to be very careful at keeping cover as Steve Broyles. You understand?"

"Yes. Of course. Should I tell you what you're to do, the first part, out here where it's safe?"

Damn! Had I set this up right? "We don't want anyone to know we're suspicious; let's just get in and follow orders, shall we? Say everything you're supposed to say, and make sure you keep in character. Right, Steve?"

"Right." In the car, Broyles said, "Drive south, for now." I started off again. Checking my watch I saw we hadn't wasted enough time to matter.

Traffic wasn't heavy but it moved slowly. Noodling along, I waited for my next clue; finally Steve said, "Pretty soon along here, head west for downtown. Do you know the shuttle bus loop?"

"Vaguely; I've never ridden it. Why?"

A no-windows van cut in front of me. I hate those things; from behind one you can't see a damn thing, such as where you're going. Interrupting my complaint, Steve said, "All right, I'll navigate. Take the next right." I did. "Now you're supposed to pick up the free shuttle route where it crosses Fifth at the north end of the loop, and follow the next bus for one full circuit."

Steve hadn't spoken up too well. Putting a little exasperation into my tone to justify its loudness, I said, "Find the shuttle crossing Fifth at the north end, and *follow* a bus around the whole damned loop? Hell, that's half an hour, maybe more."

Getting into the spirit, I went on. "Oh, I get it. To make sure we're not followed. A second party behind us, tailing the stupid bus all that way and never passing it, would get pretty conspicuous." My big dramatic sigh wasn't all faked; the idea thrilled me not at all. "Okay; what comes after that?"

Headshake. "That's not the way it works. One step at a time is all I'm supposed to give you." Well, it had been worth the try.

We got down to Fifth-and-whatever. The bus came and I followed it, bored as hell, around the full loop. Most of the bus zones were long enough to let me duck in, but twice I was left hanging out in the street, with people honking at me for being so cluck-headed as to block the intersection. Both times I pantomimed engine failure and got away with it.

When we entered the north cross-leg again and neared Fifth, I said, "Can we get off now?" Steve nodded. "Which street do we take? And which direction?" I hoped the mike was getting everything out where it might help; otherwise I was wasting good acting talent. Or maybe I wasn't as good as I thought.

Leaning closer to me, Steve whispered. "From now on, if possible I'll *point* directions—and don't you comment on them, either. If the car *is* bugged, we have to take more precautions than we've been doing."

All right; I could whisper too. "I expect the Hornet did it, and he'll want to know we're on track, so we'd better do *some* talking."

Steve pointed left; I had to juggle lanes fast to make the turn. "Then let me do the talking, Mitch. Since I know how the instructions go."

The hell of it was, if you ignored my standpoint, and Detweiler's, Steve's idea made perfect sense. I tried to think of an angle, but couldn't.

The car behind us was a black Continental, not exactly the least conspicuous model on the market. Okay: George's move, and to my mind a pretty stupid one. But at the moment there wasn't much I could do about it.

I'd been watching for a different tail, one that with any luck would be the Hornet, but I hadn't seen one. Just George, and what he thought he was accomplishing I couldn't guess.

At Steve's cue I headed up toward the I-5 freeway, with instructions to go north. Behind me Detweiler was practically tailgating. Coming up slowly to a red light, I had an idea. I said, "If that parade float behind us isn't the Hornet, I hope it gets lost pretty soon. Otherwise the Hornet might think it's following us, that something's fishy."

I was taking a chance. If Steve recognized George's car, he might say something that would tip his ID. But he merely glanced back, apparently noticed nothing, and looked ahead again.

When the light turned, George dropped back a little and changed lanes. He let two cars pile up behind me and then switched left to follow again. Well, it was some improvement.

The Mercer on-ramp is left-hand access; going up the long approach I said, "How far do we go on the freeway?"

"I'll tell you when it's time to get off." Strike two. But as soon as I'd jockeyed us from the ramp directly into the fast lane without getting us killed, a trick that always surprises me, Steve said, "Cross fast. Second exit, the one for the Evergreen bridge."

It wasn't a bad idea; without the CB we'd have lost George for sure, because in the Volvo I can thread the needle where a Continental can't. I could have waited until the last instant before picking my hole through the next-to-exit lane, and Detweiler would have been on his way to Canada all by himself.

Listening, though, he simply began cutting over immediately. With half a mile to work with, he was right there when I made my own cuts. Back a little, but with only one car between us.

Still following orders, I stayed on eastbound 520 only about a mile, then peeled off into street traffic short of the bridge approach, and looped around to backtrack the way we'd come. Entering I-5 south there's exactly the same kind of mean crossover we'd just had northbound; for a moment I thought the Hornet was in a rut, but now the word was to go north again, instead. George was three cars back now, so I had no chance to pull misdirection even if he weren't listening. I wished I'd gone along with Steve's idea of merely pointing the turns, without words. But I could hardly suggest it now.

Back on I-5 we proceeded toward cooler climes. And kept silence, until at a spot well out of town, between two exits and at least a mile from either, Steve said, "Pull over and stop. On the shoulder."

If you were the Hornet and wanted to be sure nobody extra was hanging around, it was a good place. I followed orders. In the mirror I saw Detweiler slow briefly, then decide he'd have to give it up for now. The Continental picked up speed; just as we stopped, it went past like a tornado.

Turning to Steve I asked what we did now. "We get out. Leave the package under the seat. And put the hood up, standard distress sign." I knew that, but didn't say so. "Then we climb the bank and sit behind those bushes, out of sight."

I did the first part. When the hood was up, I said, "What if good ol' Smokey sees our SOS and comes to our rescue?"

Steve had started up the graded hillside; he stopped. "That's why we go out of sight. The Patrol won't stay long with an empty car; they're too busy."

Why argue? I followed, up the hill; then we sat waiting. Nothing happened except traffic passing below, two hypnotic streams of lights separated by the median strip. With twilight long gone, both front and rear lights wove patterns. I wished I had a camera, one that would take time exposures. You see that kind of pic sometimes on the Sunday Pictorial.

After a while I said, "Is this all? Do we just wait until the Hornet makes pickup, or is there something more in case he doesn't show?"

In dim light I barely saw the headshake. "Not now. I tell you one step at a time. Remember?"

"We're outside now. Unless you think he's bugged these bushes."

"I don't know; I don't think so." Steve clutched my arm. "Mitch? I wish I didn't have to be Steve right now." I waited for it. "Because Ronnie could use some cuddling."

"This," I said, "is no time to break character."

We kept waiting.

When a small generic-looking car pulled in behind the Volvo and stopped, my hunch said rental. The headlights stayed on, so I couldn't see whoever got out until someone walked up past them. A weird figure: tall, in some kind of dark robe and oversized headgear. It turned in the light and looked up toward us; I saw it wore a mask, too. Then it clumped ahead to the Volvo. For a while nothing happened; then my car's inside light gave its dim glow and I saw the door had opened. The pause then was longer than need be, to find and take the package; the Hornet was having a look-see. Then the door closed and the figure straightened. It waved an arm at us: greetings or good-bye, maybe even thanks. Then it clumped back past the glare of headlights, got into the car and drove off. Except for the obvious horsepower difference, takeoff was much like one of George Detweiler's.

Steve and I stood, brushed grass and so forth off our clothes, and walked back down the hill.

My watch said we'd shot a major hunk of evening, and for very little accomplished. In an irritable mood I said, "Don't get in the car yet; stay back until I check it out."

"Why? Do you think he's left a bomb, or something?"

Actually that idea hadn't occurred to me. But it made a good cover, so I nodded. The thing was, I was tired of tailoring everything I said, to suit the ears of George Detweiler. No doubt he was eager for a report; well, that dumb tailgater could wait and hear it at *my* convenience. At the driver's side I opened the door and made a show of checking for contraband intrusions. While I pawed the glove compartment with one hand, the other unlocked the CB handset's Talk button. Then I beckoned Steve aboard.

Until we were moving he didn't speak. Then he said, "We're done now. We can go home."

At the next exit I looped across and onto the southbound lanes. I kept visualizing the Hornet, moving in and out of headlight glare. I said, "Why the flaky outfit? Disguise, sure. But what if the patrol pulled him over for something?"

Back in character, Steve Broyles chuckled. "There's some kind of costume contest tonight, down at the Center. I recognized that getup: it's the villain from a series of old space opera movies. Don't you remember those?"

"Vaguely." I hadn't thought of Darth Vader in years. I said, "So if he did get stopped, he had his story ready."

Something else bothered me: so much so that when some moron cut in front of me, leaving no space *and* hitting his brakes, I was lost in concentration and damn near creamed him. When I'd managed to miss rear-ending the fughead, and recovered from my adrenalin jolt, the answer came to me. "The costume's close to seven feet. But inside was a short guy."

Steve said, "Huh?" I explained. The awkward gait was platform shoes, high and heavy. And the arms looked long hanging down, but didn't reach out that far: padding on *top* of the shoulders. "And I bet he was looking out through the mouth of that mask, if not lower." And of course the headdress . . .

As I talked I paused and glanced over, when I could, to see Steve's reactions. But if what I said was news to him or wasn't, I couldn't tell. I quit trying, shut up and drove. Back in town I let Steve off at his apartment—not Ronnie Detweiler's—and went home.

Dauna wasn't back yet; well, she wouldn't be. I looked at the phone and left it just as it was. It could wait.

What this occasion needed was a little festivity.

After I polished off my eggs, scrambled with ingredients that would bring the Galloping Gourmet to a dead stop, I realized I hadn't done my homework. Bad sign; I shook my head and put the phone back to service. On the third ring, Steve answered. He was, I noticed, still in character. "Steve? Mitch Banning some more. A question or two?" The answering grunt sounded amiable, so I put my feet up and began. "How did you get hooked into tonight? Tell it from the top?"

After a pause the story began. After work there'd been a letter waiting. Like mine: all caps, no stamp or postmark. Maybe the Hornet was what we needed to replace the Postal Service—but I got my mind back on track.

The offer was: take the assignment and keep the enclosed portrait of Ben Franklin, or expect trouble. Then followed instructions, to be memorized and passed to me a step at a time, as indeed Steve had done. "And I wouldn't be hurting anyone, and a hundred bucks beats a kick in the head, so—" The nervous laugh was somewhat Ronnie. "You see?"

"Sure. Hey, I'm not blaming you for anything; I just need all the info I can get. Thanks; that should do it for now."

After I hung up I still felt restless. I realized I'd been waiting to hear from George Detweiler, loud and angry and probably cussing up a storm. But he hadn't called; I won-dered what was up.

Then, suddenly, I got another idea. I went down the tunnel, backed the Volvo out and parked it at the curb. Then I cranked up the CB. "Flagman to Delta Supreme. Do you read me?"

Until George was done boiling off, like what the bleeping hell I bleeping well thought I was doing, I stayed shut up. When he slowed down enough to hear anything, I said, "Which comes first? What happened at your end, or at mine?"

Even with repeating himself, his end didn't take long. When Steve had me pull over and stop, leaving Detweiler hanging out to dry, he'd barreled to the next exit and cut back to the nearest side road, figuring to re-enter one stop back and sneak up to park where he could see us, but far enough away that the Hornet wouldn't notice.

Dumb idea; no chance. But I didn't say so.

Anyway: going southbound he'd met a pickup truck taking its half of the road right up the middle. Dodging around it he'd wrecked a front tire and maybe that whole corner of his Continental, on a rock. "If I ever catch the hayseed hick . . ."

I waited while he got that outrage off his chest; then he went on to tell the rest of it. Delta One was supposed to go pick him up, but the CB signal must have been too noisy. Delta One misheard the directions and got lost; George had to wait over an hour before the guy called in again, from someplace way the hell over by Richmond Beach. With any luck, presumably this time he'd zero in on target and get Detweiler out of there.

Before I hit my Talk switch, I made sure I was all done laughing. It was time for business; I said, "We'll pass it that your tailing me could have blown the whole delivery. So—"

No; we weren't going to pass that. At least, George wasn't. "Wiring your Talk switch or whatever you did, Banning—it didn't pan out. Nobody except Coogan could hear you, more than just a few words now and then. So somebody had to get close enough to listen until we had some solid info, and I was nearest at the time. I knew it was touchy, but what else could I do?"

Leave it alone, I thought to myself, but no point in push-ing. Instead I said, "Well, you did take the hint and drop back. And the way the Hornet doled out his instructions, no chance you could have got an edge, anyway. Well, the delivery did go through. . . ." I paused. "You ready to hear that part now?"

He was, so I told him, including my guess about the size of the guy in the spook suit.

His response came in slow words. "Are you sure about that?"

Caution bloomed; maybe a tall guy *could* fake it the way I saw. Eyes shut, I watched the Hornet again. "Ninety percent, yes; that much, I'm sure. But not a hundred."

For a while, silence; then the set burped again. "You had a passenger. Who? And why?"

Think fast. "Not a passenger, a guide. Somebody the Hornet drafted, I think; nobody I'd know again." Okay, so I lie sometimes. "All right?"

"I suppose so." Detweiler didn't sound happy, but when did he ever? Signal, dropping off, blurred his next words, then came more clearly. "Delta One's here; now I can get out of these boondocks. I'll talk with you tomorrow, Flag-man."

Over and out. Roger, sir. I garaged the Volvo and went back topside.

I thought I wanted only a beer, but when I opened the fridge I realized I was hungry *again*; this outdoor nightlife, I supposed. All right: liverwurst on caraway rye, with mus-tard and a little horseradish. I didn't bother with a plate; paper towels don't need washing. I took my stuff to the living room and sat down. About halfway through the sandwich, the phone chimed.

I considered not answering, but on the other hand I

might miss something important. Sighing, I lifted the hand-set. "Flanagan's! He ain't here, lady; he just left."

Dauna gives that line very little credit for funny, but it does slow people down a bit. I waited; then I said, "It's your quarter. Use it or don't."

"Banning?" The Hornet; I didn't answer. "I promised you'd see me, didn't I? Satisfied?"

How to play it? All right: "You're a big one, that's for sure. I don't recall the movie that well, so I can't rate your costume on points." I took a bite of sandwich, chewed and swallowed, while the Hornet said nothing. I went on. "Anything else on your mind? I trust the package filled the bill. I didn't see the inside, of course."

"Package? Oh, yes. I counted; it's all there. Coogan knows better than to short me. Banning?"

I saw no reason to say "Yes?" or anything else. I waited, until the Hornet said, "You were followed tonight. Who was it?"

I grinned; maybe he could hear it in my voice: "No comment." He began to protest, then stopped; I guess he realized he was pushing something that wouldn't go. When he went silent I made the point clear. "The day you start leveling with me, fella, that's when I give you the same treatment. Not before."

More silence; then he said, "For a man living such a vulnerable life, Banning, you're awfully brave. Think about it."

Remembering Coogan's request I suppressed the flip an-swer that came to mind. "I'm willing to *trade* info. Sure, I recognized the car; I expect you did, too. I didn't see the face." Yes; when possible, tell the truth—but not necessar-ily all of it. "Now then: Coogan needs to know when he gets Pedicord back. Detweiler's rushing him to test the action no later than a week from now. Doc or no doc. With live subjects. Which could be dangerous."

The man laughed. "I suppose it could. Too bad, though; that's how it has to be. I'm not done picking the man's brains yet, and until I am . . ."

"Can you give me a date? Something I can tell Det-weiler?"

After a time I thought he wasn't going to answer, but he did. "Ten days, maybe twelve. And when you come to get him, Banning, you'll bring another package. Just like to-night's; same amount."

The Hornet hung up, giving him a bit more of a lead in The Great Phone Contest.

CHAPTER SEVENTEEN

Cold sandwiches don't lose anything by sitting for a while; I finished my liverwurst on rye. Along with the beer, which had warmed more than I really like. I decided I was tired of beer. The clock said too late for coffee, but I wanted some anyway. I was setting it up when Dauna came in.

"Hi! How was the stinking movie?"

I expected anger or maybe the sulks. But she came over, grinning, and gave me a big hug and kiss. "I would not know; I left it unwatched." It was her punchline, so I waited for it. "When I came out of the Ladies Lair, across the hall an office door showed light. The manager was there, and the technician, and two tickets people. Plus a bottle and a blackjack game. I won forty-three bucks."

I had to laugh. She ditched her coat over a chair and visited the bathroom. When she came back, the coffee was ready and poured. She looked at it, nodded, and sat. "And how was *your* evening?"

Thinking back through it, step by step I told her, pausing whenever she had a comment or question. Such as "George Detweiler will never replace Sam Spade" or "So now the Hornet's doing his Fu Manchu impersonation." And finally, "Detweiler's really set on barging ahead, without Pedicord?"

I nodded. She said, "Then you'd better tell Coogan where his choices lie."

"I intend to; I'm only just off the phone with the Hornet." Also, I'd halfway expected the Stork would make the call, soon as he got home. But all right; I tried Coogan's apartment and heard ten rings. I hung up, trying to recall his office number without looking it up. So naturally the phone sounded. "Three guesses." I picked it up.

"Banning?" Coogan, yes. "How did it go? Did you learn anything? There's no sense out of Detweiler; he's angry about anything and everything. He did a certain amount of swearing, then told me to talk to you."

"Sure." I sighed and went through the whole story once again. Most of it, rather: I saw no reason to name my passenger-guide. Unlike George, the Stork didn't ask.

When I came to the Pedicord part, I heard a groan. "That's bad, Mitch. Extremely unfortunate."

"You don't think Detweiler will hold still for ten days? That's only three more than he had in mind."

"The week was his maximum; he'd make it tomorrow if he could. And now, with a third payment demand—originally, you know, there were to be only the two—I'm certain he'll insist on bulling ahead before he pays the Hornet another cent."

Uh-huh: why throw more money without some indication that Pedicord's gadget would *work?* I said as much, then asked, "You'll have to get this money from Detweiler? The Hornet's cleaned out petty cash?"

"Tonight's payment, Mitch, was largely *new* money from Detweiler. Why do you think he's so angry?"

"Not getting his own way; that's all it usually takes. For two things, he missed the Hornet and he piled his car. And it cost him more in the pocket, too?" I whistled. Coogan didn't speak, so I added, "As I see it you'd better do a real con job tomorrow, on George. Or else be ready to test in a hurry."

"Those alternatives were already apparent to me. Well,

thank you for the report. Not good news, but at least I know where we stand." Saying good-nights, we ended the call.

Brows raised, Dauna waited to be filled in. I said, "Straight or crooked, you have to admire the Stork for guts."

I explained; when I was done, she nodded. "From now on we let each other know, at all times, where we're going to be." I asked why, and she said, "When they fire that goojie up, and squirt things through the fourth dimension or whatever it's supposed to do, I intend to be there!"

Next day, unless you count a lot of arguing, not much happened. Detweiler cracked the whip; in response, Coogan dragged his feet. He didn't have a prayer of getting his ten days, but he surely gave it the old college try. Finally Detweiler said, "Tomorrow I'll announce the test date. You'll prepare accordingly," and stalked out.

Looking at the rest of us, Coogan shrugged. He had quite a crowd assembled: Des Palmos, Machell, Nancy Ohara, Orville Hackett and Ridge Arnold were all present. Ridge—at first I'd thought the name was Rich—was short for Ridgeway. Now the black man stood. "If the Czar names the date tomorrow, my guess is he'll make it the day after. I want my end of things to be ready. So if we're through here, I think I'll start now."

"I suppose," Coogan said, "that we have to proceed on that assumption." He looked around again. "Arnold's right. I suggest we all follow his lead."

Everyone began moving out. I think Coogan wanted me to stay and talk, but I didn't feel like it; everything that could be said, had been. Avoiding his gaze I walked out between Machell and Nancy.

Outside, the three of us headed toward Origin. Nancy asked a couple of technical questions I didn't understand; Eddie answered as if his mind were mostly elsewhere, then said, "Let's wait until we get there. I can show you better than I can tell it." I thought he was a little short with her, and expected her to feel rebuffed, but she only smiled. Maybe their love affair had taken off, after all. I didn't ask.

In the transmission chamber room and then in the safety booth, I checked through my gear again. By now the job bored me, but I took care not to skimp the routines.

One sync channel was almost off the high end of its range: workable but far from optimum. Well, to date I'd left all the far-end adjustments centered and done the compensating at Origin; now, I saw, I'd have to modify that policy. The channel was to Catcher Two, the smaller one, downtown at the Trosper Building. I got on the phone but couldn't raise anyone in the office who could be talked through the routine by remote control. So as soon as Machell and Ohara were between sequences, I explained the problem.

Eddie nodded. "Let's have a look." I showed him what was needed. He said, "Sure, Mitch. Call me when you get downtown, and one of us will jiggle readings with you until we have both ends well away from the edge."

He looked at his watch. "Time for a break. Have some coffee before you go?"

"Why not?" Around the corner the pot was ready; when we each had our various preferred mixes, we sat quiet a moment.

Then Machell said, "What's making Detweiler so antsy? Do you know?"

What I didn't know was where Eddie stood in the whole mess: how much he knew, and how much it would be wise to tell him. I said, "Just impatient, I suppose. He's gone fairly deep into this project, and then there's been all the trouble. He wants to see some action. In a way, I can't really blame him."

Machell frowned. "I think there's more to it than that."

"Oh?"

And Nancy said, "What do you mean?"

He shook his head. "I don't know for sure. But there's a lot going on that nobody's telling us about."

"If you're right," I put in, "maybe we're better off not

knowing. I didn't especially enjoy getting shot at; did you?"

He shrugged. "Who would? Maybe you've got the right idea. The job feels weird, though. Makes me nervous." Nancy put her hand on his; he smiled at her.

I finished my coffee and rinsed the cup. "George Detweiler's weird, period. Let's just do our work and draw our pay; there's a lot less worry that way."

Nancy grinned. "Do up a catchy tune for that, and you'll hit the Top Forty."

"Yeah, sure." Leaving, I said, "I'll call you in about an hour, probably; could be a little less." Machell waved agreement.

When I-5 got me into the downtown area, I found my usual exit blocked by a jackknifed truck; getting back from the next one made it well over an hour before I called. Machell knew his business; in about two minutes we had the channel centered, so we went ahead and optimized the rest of the bank.

Routine checks showed my other gear to be mostly on the money; what wasn't, I fiddled into line. I looked at Catcher Two's chamber housing, apparently a scale model of its big brother at Range A, but it didn't tell me anything.

I stepped into the side office where Steve Broyles worked, but a middle-aged woman sat at the next desk, so we couldn't say anything important. "Hi" and a handwave; I turned to go.

"Just a minute." Steve got up. "It's early for lunch, but I missed breakfast. How about you?"

I wasn't hungry yet. If Steve wanted to talk, though . . . "Sure." We rode the elevator down, mostly in silence, and entered the building's ground floor coffee shop. Steve ordered soup-and-sandwich with coffee; I took iced tea. I said, "Something on your mind?"

"I'll be glad when this job's over. Keeping in character is a real strain."

"I wouldn't be surprised." A genetic male, first temperamentally and now hormonally inclined in the female direction, playing a male role. How Ronnie kept all the pieces straight, I couldn't imagine. "I'd think you'd want it to last. For the money."

Steve grinned. "I have the money—or will have, soon."

I didn't know Steve's salary, but wouldn't have figured it to pile up savings so fast. My expression may have shown those doubts; he said, "Not to worry, it's all set up with my fairy godfather."

"Umm. Anyone I know?"

"If you explain your magic, it won't work any longer."

That was all he'd say. I switched to what I felt we *should* be discussing: asking about his contacts with the Hornet, trying to unearth some new clue. Even a small one.

I drew a blank. Our kidnapper-cum-killer-cum-black-mailer simply left no kind of useful trail. Steve told me nothing I hadn't known already, which certainly wasn't much. A little later he returned to work and I went home for the day.

I spent the afternoon catching up odds and ends. The mail brought a job offer: an outfit in Alaska, dissatisfied with commercial circuit performance as applied to its specific wants, wanted to set up its own radio net and to hire me to design it. The proposal wasn't entirely in my line; I'd need to call in Al Hubbard or somebody for the antenna work and to deal with the FCC. By the time we split the take . . .

I shook my head and wrote a quick note, thanking the company for its consideration but pleading backlog.

If it hadn't been for Coogan's project coming to a head, I'd have taken the job anyway. It read like more fun than not, and I wouldn't have minded seeing Alaska again for a few weeks. It's a great place to visit, if your timing's right.

Ridge Arnold's guess missed by only one day; next morning Detweiler lined us up, so to speak, and told us, "Day after tomorrow we run the thing. We run it with whoever we've got, and we run it for real. Understand, Coogan?"

The Stork blinked. "If you insist, I suppose so. But inanimate objects, only. Dr. Pedicord—"

"I know, I know." George waved him off. "For the live tests, I'll give you until the first of the month." Which was one day after the Hornet's *earliest* earliest proposed date for delivering Olin Pedicord. "After that we go, regardless."

Coogan kept trying. Pedicord, he said, might not be in the best of conditions for conducting critical experiments. Not after two weeks of imprisonment. What he didn't say, but must have been thinking, was that if the doc ran short of venous delight, it might take a little maintenance time to pull him down off the ceiling.

Spoken or unspoken, none of it made any difference. Delta Supreme had given the word; the stone tablets would be along later.

As I was leaving, Tixo came in; suddenly I realized I hadn't seen him for at least two weeks. Maybe longer. The little guy motioned to me, so I stepped aside and let everyone else go past.

Today his happy side was up; we did the knife and fingers-to-forehead bits, and Tixo's grin wouldn't quit. Coogan spoke to him—a little sharply, I thought. The Indian nodded, and went into the next room.

"Where's he been lately?" Coogan stared at me. "Our little chum there; he hasn't been around for quite a while."

"Oh." The Stork nodded. "He's been down with some kind of flu. A severe case, whatever it was."

I nodded. "Hospital?"

"No. He should have been hospitalized, but by the time I saw how sick he really was, the poor man was delirious. I couldn't get near him. The knife, you know."

I suppose I stared. "You just let him sweat it out?"

Looking uncomfortable, Coogan said, "I brought him food; sometimes he ate, sometimes not. And plenty of water, of course. He always got to the toilet somehow, but never when I was around. I mean, I deduce as much because he did not foul his bed. He knows about aspirin, so I left him a supply and I'm fairly certain he used a reasonable amount. Though if so, it didn't seem to help greatly."

He frowned. "What did help, unless his recovery was

due to sheer vitality, was some gummy green substance he may have brought from his home area. I've seen it before; Tixo is secretive, but when he uses stimulants he tends to minor lapses. And this morning I found shreds of the stuff by his bedside."

"Did you save it?" Coogan nodded. "Have you thought of having it analyzed?" He looked blank. Exasperated, I said, "Coogan, if there's a chance that Tixo's native gunk helps with the flu, it could be a big thing, medically."

He frowned. "I know nothing about medicine."

I laughed. "Translate medical into financial. How much do you suppose we're talking, in American money?"

He got it; his face cleared. "Oh yes; of course. Thank you for the suggestion, Banning. I'll look into it."

"Good." I had an afterthought. "Don't forget to cut Tixo in."

"I will keep you advised."

I left then. Not that I had anything in particular to do, but the Stork's words smacked of an exit line and this was his office, not mine. Walking away, it struck me that between them, Detweiler and the Hornet had really shaken up Emil Storchesson. When somebody else had to tell him where the money was, he was not—definitely not—his real self.

Methodically I checked my equipment at Origin, then at Catcher One. Bored out of my skull and finding no surprises, I did that.

Before the transmission tests themselves I went plodding through the same routines three more times, including visits to Catcher Two at the sanitarium—alias TB, aka the Trosper Building. Once the afternoon of that same day, twice on the next, and of course once on T-day itself.

On that morning I got up considerably earlier than usual, so I could give every piece of my gear one last checkup as close to T-time as possible.

And then, finally, the whole thing was on the line. All that could be done had been done; all the elements of this complex situation had acted to bring the project to its moment of decision. Whatever maneuvers Coogan and Pedicord and Detweiler and the Hornet were up to, this would be where they all proved out. Or maybe didn't.

The cards were dealt; all the chips were in the pot.

If Coogan had a good hole card, it was time he showed it.

CHAPTER EIGHTEEN

I went out to Range A's parking lot to meet Dauna; she arrived in plenty of time. Her engine sounded like riot night in the gasworks, but it always did. I'd given up urging her to see a mechanic; as long as it got her around, the choice was hers.

We walked to Origin. By now of course the transmission chamber room was closed, its warning lamp glowing red; we went to the safety booth. Inside, I saw we were the last to arrive.

At the main console, Coogan sat. Behind him, a little to the left, stood Eddie Machell. He'd be at Catcher One for the live test, I recalled; today, though, Nancy Ohara had that spot, with a couple of helpers just in case. And at Catcher Two, Ridge Arnold had charge.

Sitting in a huge thronelike chair I'd never seen before, George Detweiler was something to be noted. I found his pose of regal majesty so hard to believe, I didn't even try. His cigar held a good two inches of undropped ash; beside him, holding a clean ashtray, stood Larry Des Palmos. Sitting at a rear corner, Orville Hackett wore an expression that said he wasn't really there and preferred it that way. Alongside, Tixo looked as though he was guarding Orville, but that had to be serendipitous.

I guessed we were all here. I had no idea why people

stood when we had chairs to spare, but it was none of my business. I pulled one over, a few feet to the side of George and with a slanting view past the Stork to the control panel, and sat. Dauna brought another, and perched beside me.

Detweiler scowled. "If we're done arranging the furniture . . ."

I gave him my best cheery smile, right off the top shelf. "Good morning, Mr. Detweiler. We're not late, I hope."

George grunted; Coogan turned to look at us. "Banning—Ms. Haig—our power-drain time-slot isn't due for a few more minutes. I was about to outline the parameters of today's experiments." I loved it when he talked like that, and as he continued, he didn't disappoint me. "Mr. Detweiler has inspected the test object, which is now in Number One transmission chamber. I wished to utilize a unique subject, and Mr. Detweiler agrees that I have chosen well: a bundle of five-dollar bills, consecutively numbered. These have been weighed and photographed, for purposes of comparison after they have undergone transportation by this radically new method."

He cleared his throat. "I believe I've covered the necessary background. Mr. Machell: one minute, *mark*. As agreed, you will bring power up to operational level, and I will activate the transfer process."

No matter how often I saw it, I still found the proceedings impressive: shudder of resonances building, flicker of ionization, water vapor fogging the casing outside the transmission chamber. But this time something new was added. When Machell nodded, Coogan punched buttons and turned knobs—and the building *groaned*. Lights dimmed once, and again; then some kind of backlash flared them up, brighter than their usual level. Something whined, the pitch of sound rising past normal hearing range, then burring my nerves as it passed the little sensitivity peaks we all have, up at the high end. No ionization glowed inside our safety booth but I know static charge when I feel it.

Abruptly, Coogan moved two controls; the whining peaked, and our entire surround *jerked* sharply. Then, slowly, seeming to take half of forever, it all wound down.

My ears still tried to echo the vanished screaming howl, but it was gone. At nearly the moment I accepted the return to normal, Coogan turned to the intercom. "Ohara? Results?"

The squawkbox needed adjustment; Nancy's voice came distorted. "Just a moment, Mr. Coogan." Then a pause, and this time it wasn't the intercom that put the squeak to her tones.

"It—it works, Mr. Coogan. It *works!*"

She must have run all the way. Out of breath, clutching the banded bundle, Nancy Ohara arrived in half the time I would have expected. She went to hand the bills to Coogan, but Detweiler reached out a hand and she gave them to him instead.

George peeled the band off and leafed through the stack; then he nodded. "The numbers match, and I don't see any kind of damage."

Coogan came over and took the packet, now loose. He sniffed it. "No gross chemical changes, certainly. And the colors appear to be correct."

Eddie Machell cleared his throat. "Were you going to recheck anything, Mr. Coogan, before the second run? Timing's getting close."

Second run? Maybe Coogan read my mind; it was to me he turned as he said, "While we have the power allotment we're going to run this same test sample through to Catcher Two, downtown." He checked his watch. "In less than five minutes. So we'll wait and do the comparative weighing and photography after that operation."

He held out the bundle. "Would anyone care to inspect these now, before I retape the lot?"

I didn't, but Dauna raised a hand; Coogan passed her the stack. She looked at it; near as I could tell, she rubbed a bill between her fingers, riffled through for a quick look, then shrugged and gave it back.

Coogan, in a hurry, replaced the tape and left the safety booth. In less than a minute, by way of the mirror system we saw him use the local controls to open the smaller chamber's housing, then the chamber itself, and set the packet inside. Quickly he closed things again, then returned to join us.

"Time, Machell?"

"I'm cranking it up." Again the chamber room glowed with blue flicker: not so impressive in the miniature version but still nothing to play tag with. All the earlier indications came again, of powerful forces in action around us. Not as strong as before but enough to make me shiver a little. Sound climbed the frequency scale; the floor jarred my feet. Then, as Coogan's hands moved at the panel, came a pause. And I waited, while all of it whined down to eventual quiet.

Coogan gestured; Machell moved to the nearest phone and punched numbers. Brief wait, then he said, "Ridge? Did—?" He listened, and turned to Coogan. "The package made it. Do you want Arnold to bring it out?"

Emil the Stork smiled. "That's hardly necessary. We're done here, for today. Button it down, Machell; then we'll go into town and inspect the test object at Catcher Two."

Not until Dauna and I were crossing the parking lot did I realize what a tremendous thing I'd just seen. Pedicord's invention could turn the world inside out; I was barely beginning to envision the possibilities. I said as much; Dauna shrugged.

I looked at her; she said, "Aladdin's lamp lit up on schedule, Mitch. But we haven't met the genie yet. He could still be from Central Casting."

I didn't get it, and said so. Dauna shook her head. "I want to see that money again. Then maybe I'll know something."

In our separate cars we drove to I-5, where our individual driving routines soon had us losing track of each other. Dauna used to like the fast lane until she caught two tickets driving there; now she avoids it.

Downtown, parking was tight; I took the last vacant space in a Gouge lot. Sometimes you have to settle for what you can get.

Ridge Arnold admitted me to 2310-14; I was first to arrive. He said, "I'm not sure I can let you have the test object until Detweiler and Coogan get here. You can look at it, though."

"Understandable; thanks." So I didn't try to touch the packet, let alone take the tape off and leaf through. On the top bill the serial number showed; all I remembered were the last four digits, but that much fit. I wasn't sure why I wanted to check, unless to be certain the Stork wasn't playing some kind of sleight-of-hand trick. If he were, it was a hell of a good one.

Now others came in: our entire homey little group from Range A; Dauna wasn't even the last to arrive. Detweiler had first look at the money bundle; untaping, he looked through carefully. Then Coogan, then Machell, and then me. However it was supposed to go from there, I took a bare, brief look and passed it to Dauna. She turned it over and her expression went absolutely poker-faced; in silence she handed the stack to Nancy Ohara.

After that, I didn't notice; I was watching Dauna but not learning anything.

Coogan's attention was all on George; the Stork reminded me of a puppy expecting a biscuit for remembering to go on the paper. He kept saying, "What do you think *now?*"

Detweiler, who seemed to carry his own share of confusion, finally answered. "Coogan, you're planing on the first step." That was thunderboat talk; Seattle's a hotbed of hydro fans, and the big boats don't get up speed until they "plane" up out of the water, with just the prop and two small hull areas touching. Sponsons, they're called. "As it stands," George continued, "I'll make you a substantial offer for fifty-one percent of this device. But if you can transmit *life*, man—that's the top step, and it's worth a whole extra decimal place."

Cagey. Percentages, decimal places: no mention of any solid figure. But Coogan beamed; apparently he heard the right grade of jingle.

"We'll give you what you need, Mr. Detweiler. With Dr. Pedicord's help, or without it."

I saw Dauna look to me, then toward the door. She was right; for now, we had all we were going to get. I made our excuses to Coogan, who hardly noticed, and we left.

Outside, waiting for the elevator, Dauna said, "Central Casting, all right. I don't know how, but that last bundle was phony."

Suddenly I was gripping her arms, hard. She winced; I made a conscious effort and relaxed my hold. "What says so?" My voice sounded funny and faraway.

"This does." She wiggled her right thumb. I waited while she took a deep breath and let it out. "When I had my hands on the money, before the second test, I marked a bill: used the point of my thumbnail, hard enough to leave a little crease. You know; the way cardsharks make 'readers' out of a straight deck. I passed the bottom bill—somebody might have noticed that—and creased the one directly above it, turning the bottom one back for an instant."

She shook her head. "When I checked the stack just now, that dent wasn't there."

A sinking feeling hit me; somehow, I'd lost something precious. "I—I guess I really wanted to believe in that thing." Then, "Wait a minute, though. . . ."

I had to try it, of course, with the small wad of bills from my wallet. My own thumbnail was too short to do business; I handed her the money. The way she held it, I couldn't see what she did. But when she turned the bottom one back, the dent in the next showed clearly.

"Maybe it just doesn't stay very long." I was still trying.

"Here, Mitch." I took the bills. "Wiggle it. Smooth it out, bend it. Not taking the stack apart, though." I did those things, then looked again; not quite so distinct now, the crease still showed plainly. Giving a tired shrug, I put the money away. Who knows? It might come in useful someday.

"How do you suppose he did it?" I asked her. "The serial numbers have to be right; that's the first thing Detweiler

checked." The elevator arrived; descending, I guessed at
possibilities. At Range A, some kind of pneumatic tube
could have done it—except that we'd been able to use the
Navy's old cables, so no trench had been dug between
Origin and Catcher One. Therefore, no such tube should
exist. And if it did, I thought, it could hardly be big enough
to hold Tixo, so what would be the point? And a tube to
downtown was impossible on the face of it, if only because
of the time of transit.

We reached the lobby and went outside. I said, "We
need to talk, but it can wait until we get home." We separated to get our cars. I reached home first, but not by much.

Sitting in the front room I went over my guessing some
more: all of it aloud this time. And got nowhere. Dauna
had a dreamy look—until suddenly, eyes wide, she sat up.
I said, "What—?"

"The genie, Mitch. What if it's Santa's elves, instead?"

For once the translation came clear immediately. Sure; the
Stork had said he knew a few killers, from prison. "You
mean Emil's graduating class might have included one or two
high-grade counterfeiters?" Smiling, she nodded. "You're
right; it could be. The bills looked good to me, though. And
apparently to George. In his current mood, I doubt he's
thought of having a Treasury agent check them out."

Her smile changed to an urchin's grin. "Are you going to
put a flea in his ear?"

"No. This is between him and Coogan, and Detweiler's
a big boy now. Big *man*, to hear him tell it. No; if the Stork
can take him, he's going to get taken." Still, I felt myself
scowl. "You don't think I should horn in, do you?"

"Of course not. For one thing, we're still blue-skying.
We don't *know*."

"True." Then I had another idea. Now that a little time
had passed . . . I brought out my wallet and looked again
at the bill Dauna had marked. *No mark.*

For a moment I couldn't breathe; Dauna looked at me
strangely. Then I turned the bundle around. The mark was
at the other end.

"Dauna?" Her brows went up. "At Range A, did you mark both ends of that bill? Or just one?"

"Just the one end."

"And downtown, did you check both?"

"No, but—Mitch, I'm sure I checked the *same* end."

"Left, or right, looking at it right side up?"

"Left—no—oh, dammit! I was certain, but—" Her mouth twisted. "Mitch? Do you think I could have checked the wrong end?"

"It's not what I think; what do *you* think? Could you have?"

Fingers stiff, pulling hard, she ran her hands back through her hair. "I thought—actually I *wasn't* thinking—I assumed I'd turned the packet the same way as before, just automatically. Visual recognition without noticing consciously. But now: I try to visualize, right end or left, and I don't get any mental click either way." She said a few words which would have been bleeped out of the Late Movie, then shrugged. "So. What's our position, navigator?"

"Same as before, I guess. Dead lost."

My best move, we decided, was to head back downtown and try for another look at the test sample. If Dauna had the right guess, there were three identical packets, but two of those were probably still at Range A, and wouldn't be lying around loose in any case.

So I went to the Trosper Building. Suite 2310-14 seemed to be running about half-speed. The young woman who'd replaced the late Archer Green, who in previous turn had taken the place of the equally late Ansel Borg, gave me clearance to Coogan's sanctuary. I found the Stork alone, and about half-bombed. Still talking well enough, though.

"Well, Banning! *Now* what do you think of the product of Dr. Pedicord's genius?" He offered me a drink; I settled for ice water.

"I'm impressed. Confused, but impressed." Words of truth aren't always heard the way they're meant; I was counting on that. "Have you weighed and measured the test sample? Taken its pulse and blood pressure?"

Coogan laughed; at this high point he could take a little kidding and even enjoy it. Yes, he'd supervised the weighing and photographing, including exposures under ultraviolet and infrared. After that, Detweiler had taken the packet for further testing at his own labs, down at his Riverside plant.

I polished off my glass of fluid, thanked the Stork, and left to follow the trail.

The odds beat me. I found the labs all right; Detweiler's new replacement Continental was there and so was he. He looked surprised to see me, but in his current expansive mood he played Welcome Wagon to the hilt. "Come in, Banning. I'd offer you a drink—in fact, as soon as we wrap up this last test, I will. Come along."

He rattled on, something about acid or alkaline balance in the dyes used in Uncle Sam's private scrip; when we entered the small cubby, almost filled by a tilt-top drafting table, I saw why. There, spread out on a big blotter, were the five-dollar bills, with Honest Abe looking dyspeptic in all fifty copies. Each and every chemically-stinking one of them was soaking wet; no thumbnail dent could have survived.

So much for that idea. I listened to George build air castles and tried to get some idea of how much money he'd been talking about earlier to Coogan.

He never did get around to that drink. After a time I excused myself and went home.

Dauna loves Martinis but only on a sociable level; she'd set a pitcher up to chill, for when I got back. Now while I gave my report we had a round; truth to tell, it did ease frustration somewhat. "So apparently," I said, "Detweiler's satisfied that the boodle is kosher. Frankly, I'm surprised the question crossed his mind at all. Anyway, he's happy as a campaign contributor getting a new tax loophole for his birthday."

Dauna's frown lines showed, then vanished again. "Well, King Midas wasn't terribly smart either."

I disagreed: For all George's arrogance and occasional childishness, I'd seen him operate. "He's out of his field here, is all. His weak spot is that he'd never let himself realize that."

"You'd make a great shrink, Mitch."

"I already did; haven't you noticed?" She doesn't often feed me a straight line. "My mother washed me and I shrank."

"Oh, *you!*" She set her drink down and came at me like the Seahawks' front four when they're all healthy the same week; barely in time I got braced for the wrestling matches.

My main problem is that she gets me laughing and then takes advantage. By the time we'd pooped ourselves out enough to get rid of a little steam, we ended up in the middle of the rug.

And—well, why not? The buttons, we could sew back later. Except that as sometimes happens, we lost a few.

We'd knocked one end table over; by luck, the glass was empty *and* didn't break. I used my shirtsleeve to wipe off a little dust, and poured a refill. The rug made good sitting, with our legs stuck out into a patch of late sunlight. Dauna said, "I hope you've learned your lesson, you big bully."

"Oh, I have, I have. Women will take you in."

I shouldn't have said that, not while she had her glass to her mouth. She sputtered, coughed, and almost spilled her drink. Finally, wiping away tears, she said, "Please keep in mind that I do *not* like Martinis up my nose."

"Right. In the glass, yes. Mouth, ditto. Nose, no." I topped off her refill, then visited the bathroom. While I was in there I heard the phone sound twice, then stop; presumably Dauna answered it. When I came out, though, it was hung up.

I didn't have to ask. "The Hornet just buzzed. You're to buzz him back at seven-thirty. Sharp."

I looked at her; she held up the phoneside notepad. "Oh, yes. This time he left a number."

CHAPTER NINETEEN

I grabbed the slip of paper and looked. The general area for the exchange was a little south of us, but that didn't help much; your friendly operator won't ordinarily give you the address that goes with a number. Oh, I've gotten around that policy a few times: given a name *and* the number, ask if this is the Joe Doakes who lives at an address you improvise at random; quite often they'll reel off the correct one without stopping to think. But with the number only, no chance. Aloud, I mentioned the problem.

I could almost see the canary feathers at Dauna's lips. "I tried a call. It's a pay phone, at a bar. The bartender answered; he said no one had used that phone for at least the past half hour."

"So the Hornet called from somewhere else, keeping his own number under wraps." I considered the possibilities. "Dauna? Maybe, just maybe, he's slipped for once."

We talked about it. Stake out the bar? If Detweiler knew, he'd want to sic the CB team onto it. And I couldn't trust George; he'd go independent on me and blow the whole game.

Besides, all we were after for now was an ID make. So it was up to Dauna and me; the only question was how to play it.

"You can't go," she said. "The Hornet knows you, and you have to be here making the call."

"He knows you, too. You've been to Range A with me, and five gets you a bundle, he has you tagged."

"As me, yes. But not the little lady who's going to strut her stuff at Henry's Dive-in. After dinner, you'll see."

So we ate early. After coffee she began dressing up and making up: getting into character.

Maybe twice before I'd seen her wear the curly black wig. She arranged it, now, to cover her forehead and shade her eyes. Still, the eye makeup, including costume-style blue false lashes, made quite a send-up. The rest wasn't quite so extreme, but the pattern of color and highlights changed her apparent contours, especially in the cheekbone areas. And something subtle with the lipstick, which generally she used sparingly if at all.

Add a padded bra and long, bulky sweater; they put several extra pounds on her looks. With the lights down she stood hipshot and gave me the heavy-lidded pout that's enriched more than one movie star. "What do you think?"

I closed my eyes and opened them quickly, getting a flash impression. "You're right. If I saw you in a bar, not knowing, I don't think I'd recognize you myself."

"Or want to, probably." She waved off my disclaimer. "That's all right; the *idea* is to look faintly ridiculous, someone not to be taken seriously. I gather that it works."

Grinning: "Let's say, I'm glad all that stuff comes off."

She was not, I made it clear, to do anything but look: at the Hornet when he took my call, and if possible without drawing his attention, at his car when he left. Including plates, of course. "Then call me. If it seems like a good idea I'll call Detweiler, but the odds say no on that. But don't go up to the Hornet; don't try to follow him. None of that. Agreed?"

She nodded. "Getting stung isn't one of my major ambitions."

So a little past six-thirty, she left. With nearly an hour to kill I tackled the paper. The crossword was boringly easy, even with several definitions omitted by printer's error, but the Jumble fooled me. The overall answer was clear from context, but for some reason SOIVIN stopped me cold; I had to settle for an incomplete answer. Minutes later I flashed on VISION, but by then it didn't count. Waiting, I drank more coffee than my nerves needed and watched the clock pretend not to move at all.

At seven-thirty straight down, I punched out the num-

192

ber. The line was busy. *Two slips in one day, Hornet.* Any
moron, hindsight told me, would know a bar's phone
could get tied up at any time by some drunk.

Nothing for it, I decided, but to keep hitting Redial.
When I finally got a ring and an answer, I'd lost count of
the attempts.

"Mitch Banning?" It wasn't the Hornet on there. It
was— I knew the voice, but couldn't place it.

"Name yourself."

"Don't you recognize me, Mitch? Ronnie?"

"Oh for Chris'sakes! What are *you* doing there?"

"Earning another hundred dollars, what did you think?"
I didn't answer; after a moment Ronnie said, "The message
is, you can pick up your missing doctor the evening of the
twenty-ninth." A fast count made it one short of the Hornet's minimum ten days; the guy must be getting generous.
"And," Ronnie continued, "you're to tell Coogan that a
little housebreaking may be in order, whatever that
means."

Sure; the juice supply was running low, maybe even out.
Well, that was the Stork's problem, his and Pedicord's. But
I'd pass the word, all right.

"Anything else?" I couldn't imagine a reason to go to so
much trouble, and waste a Ben Franklin to boot, to pass
this info at this time. I mean, it didn't seem that urgent. On
the other hand it had been a time since I'd seen Pedicord.

"Not that I can think of, Mitch. And there's some
woman standing behind me, waiting. Maybe I'd better—"

"What's she look like?" I thought I knew, and I was
right. I sighed. "Put her on the phone. But don't go away,
Ronnie. I want to talk with you some more."

The next voice, not talking directly into the phone, was
Dauna's. "Stay put, Red, if you want out of here with both
arms on." Then, "Mitch? This bimba in the wig; is she part
of anything or just a lucky accident?" And suddenly I realized that Dauna had never seen Ronnie Detweiler in her
own person.

I explained. "The Hornet sends Ronnie two zeros and some info to pass. I told you about that, before."

"So we've been had again. It *was* too good to be true, the Hornet coming anywhere near a butterfly net. Now then; what about the Detweiler? Let her go, or bring her along?"

Now admittedly Dauna was playing a standard spy-story role, but less than an hour in the bar and here she was doing Sam Spade. I decided I'd prefer the legendary Emma Peel, and wondered what on earth Dauna had been drinking.

But I said only, "I'd like to talk with her again for a minute, then she can go. And speak nicely; she's been cooperative." Well, so had Dauna; I paused briefly, then said, "You're doing fine, honey. Come on home and get congratulated."

"You bet." Then she talked away from the mouthpiece again, but I could hear fine. "Mitch tells me you're one of the good guys in the white hats. Sorry to come on so strong, Ronnie. Now he'd like to talk a little more. I have to go, so good night."

Each said something I couldn't catch, then Ronnie spoke to me. "Mitch? You had something more?"

"Except for thanks, not a lot. But, did you get your instructions in the mailbox again?"

"Yes. No stamp or postmark. And—really, I think that's all there is to tell you."

I wasn't so sure, but settled for it. Dauna, a little later, came home sober. Well, I hadn't really thought she was bombed in the bar, just oversaturated with old movies.

We chewed the situation over and came up with no new clues.

Tomorrow, I decided, was time enough to tell Coogan.

The Stork next morning had some fair-sized shakes; I gathered he'd built himself a workmanlike hangover. I didn't learn this right away; at the downtown office his receptionist checked with him and put me on hold.

I sat down and decided to get acquainted; since she'd taken over the job I hadn't been in here much, and then

usually just passing through to Coogan's office or the
equipment room.

Tillie Trosper grinned and told me she was no relation to
the building. She was a shortish brunette—"stacked" is the
operative word—with pale skin and grey eyes. Her black
hair, even cut quite short, was wavy enough to look like a
lot. Her accent, but not her word choices, sounded Canadian.

When I asked her, she shook her head. "My family and
I lived in Alberta when I was small, but we're all Ameri-
cans." So are Canadians, of course, along with Mexicans
and Guatemalans and the like, but I let the point go. She
was explaining why Moraine Lake in Banff National Park is
more spectacular than the more celebrated Lake Louise a
few miles distant from it, when the Stork buzzed and called
for me.

Standing up, I smiled. "All right, Ms. Trosper; if I get up
that way, I'll check out your advice." Then I went inside.

At least Coogan wasn't treating his ailment with hair of
the dog; what jiggled in his cup was hot tea laced with milk.
He offered me booze; I said tea would be fine. Once we got
sat down, I told him the news. "And it sounds as if Pedicord's either low on juice or soon will be. You'd better
stock up."

He gulped tea and looked pained, indicating that his was
as much too hot as mine was. "Unless the Hornet has kept
Olin on shorter rations than I'd care to try, he's run out
some time ago." He made a face. "Oh, *I'm* stocked. My
delivery schedule carries a safety factor, to avoid untoward
delays. I've also obtained new accessories, in case those the
Hornet took are lost or mislaid."

The Hornet hadn't taken the hardware; I had. But who
was counting? I sampled a couple of wheat crackers from a
tray on Coogan's desk. Unsweetened, unsalted: not bad. I
wanted to change the subject but could think of no good
way to ask him if the test runs had been gimmicked. So I
said, "If we could make contact with the Hornet, you
mean, we could get the doc his happy dust; right?"

He shook his head, then winced. "Banning, I have no

such intention. Olin's drug shortage may be the only thing that will force the Hornet to release him to us." He gestured. "You see my position, don't you?"

I didn't, not really, and I guess it showed. He protested, "Banning, I didn't do this to Pedicord; he was addicted when I found him."

"So you've said. At any rate, the twenty-ninth gives you three days to shape him up for the live run, with Tixo."

The Stork looked unhappy. "Assuming a late evening release arrangement, which fits the Hornet's pattern to date, and a morning test run, three days' leeway is on the optimistic side. I might have forty-eight, perhaps even fifty-six hours, to produce Dr. Pedicord in a presentable and capable state of being." He moved his head and neck the way you do to crack tensions loose. "Sometimes all the breaks go the wrong way."

Not much I could add to that; I asked how Tixo was feeling. "Getting healthy again? No relapses?"

The last thing I expected was a smile, but Coogan did. "While he was recuperating, feeling better but still weakened, Tixo developed an addiction of his own. Television."

I had to grin. "Was it soap operas that hooked him? Or the game shows?"

Coogan shook his head. "Neither. He loves commercials."

Unable to top that line, I said, "I don't have any more news just now. You heard from Detweiler today?"

He filled his teacup again, then found only a few drops left in the milk carton. He shrugged. "Yes, he called. As you might expect, he pushed for an earlier live test. Now, with your information, I think I can talk him out of that."

A thought came. "Then don't tell him the release date; just say that Pedicord can be ready to squirt Tixo around by the first of the month."

A friendly scowl is a contradiction in terms, but that's what the Stork gave me. "There's a saying, Banning, about teaching your grandmother to suck eggs. Heed it."

Meaning: none of my business. Right. I said, "Oh yes

indeed, boss-man sir," and asked what I was supposed to be doing between now and the first.

The answer was, not much. Between now and the twenty-ninth, check my circuits through twice, and call in each morning to see if anything more was needed. "When Pedicord's back," Coogan said, "revert to the normal daily maintenance schedule. But until then there's hardly a point to it."

Good enough; time to leave. In the outer office I exchanged a little more chat with Tillie Trosper. Now I know from experience that I am not universally attractive to woman: the species. But I got the distinct impression that if I were available, so was she. The other impression I got was, she'd be a lot of fun. While no system of sexual ethics is perfect I've always found virtual monogamy the most comfortable. Tillie's attitude, though, emphasized its major obvious disadvantage.

The hell with it; I went out to wait for the elevator. When it arrived, George Detweiler emerged. I said "Good morning" and stepped in and punched the Lobby button; the door closed before George could start a conversation, or call me back to Coogan's office if that's what he had in mind.

Just then I purely didn't need a session with Delta Supreme. I went home.

Calling in every morning and checking my circuits a mere twice made for a dull week. I found myself wishing I hadn't firmly, yet kindly, made my unavailability so definite to Tillie Trosper.

Oh, well . . .

From Coogan I knew that Detweiler wanted to talk with me. Or rather, at me. Not sharing that wish I made a point of dodging the interview. I didn't stay home much, especially evenings; I saw more movies that week than in the previous six months. The two times I did go to Range A and to the Trosper Building I checked with my spy network, Nancy Ohara and Tillie Trosper, making sure George was elsewhere. Both women seemed to enjoy our little conspiracy; they had no idea what it was about, but since both disliked George Detweiler, it didn't matter.

On the twenty-eighth, though, George caught me. I got home hot and sweaty, eager for a shower, and forgot to make sure the phone's ringer was turned off. So when I came out, dripping, the damn chime was sounding. I lack the temperament to ignore it for long; I said one short word, then lifted the handset.

Without even announcing himself as Delta Supreme, Detweiler cut loose. "Where the hell have you been?" No answer to that one, so I waffled. He said, "Never mind. We have to discuss tomorrow night's project. Operation Pedicord." I could even hear the capital letters. And I gathered that one way or another, Coogan had spilled the timing after all.

"What's to discuss?" Then I thought of something. "If you want to work the comm net again, though I can't think why, you should scrap those CB rigs and spring for cellular." He knew what cellular phones were, of course—but I was bemused to learn that even in his outsized Continentals he'd never had one. Every time I discovered a new blind spot in George Detweiler, who was always described in the financial pages as a Man of Vision, it surprised me all over again.

Now he said, "You think they'd do a better job? How?"

"Hell, yes. They—" But why waste *my* time? "If you want how, George, talk to the phone company. They're not paying me to sell their toys."

I did tell him, though; some, anyway. Cellulars cost, but on a mobile basis they do nearly anything your home phone can do: in particular, for our purposes, conference calls. Unlike our CB setup, privacy gear is available; private links, they're called. Plus Mute buttons, Redial, number memory of various capacities, and speakerphones. And with the radio signal stations spaced the way they are, the signal coverage beats CBs all hollow.

Not wanting to overload George, I skipped the business of punching up your call number and seeing it on a screen before you hit the Send button; save a few thrills for later. I said, "So if you want to upgrade your Delta setup out of the Keystone Kops level, I'll try to cooperate, to put some salt on the Hornet's tail. Somehow or other, though, he'll cross us up."

Detweiler sputtered; I said, "Face it. Every time, he has new tactics and we don't. Now if you have a good new idea, Detweiler, I'm listening, I really am."

After a moment he said, "You're a smartass, Banning, but sometimes you do think. I'll get somebody on this cellular thing; we'll have them by tomorrow. And now, you listen." I did that. He said, "The Hornet's primary trick is, call you and then make you leave your phone off the hook so you can't call out."

I shrugged; so what else was new? George said, "Tomorrow that won't happen. You'll have a second phone."

Now I listened because I wanted to. Here was an idea I hadn't considered. I said, "How?"

"Tomorrow I'm having the full crew on duty at Range A. All day. That includes you. If we're right, it also includes the Hornet." So far, so good; I waited. "So he can't be around to see your new phone being installed. And there won't be an extra lead-in, to tip him off."

I thought I knew why, but asked him anyway because he was busting with it. He said, "Your phone's on something they call subscriber carrier, and in your group there's a vacant channel. The installer simply goes in your back door, which you leave unlocked tomorrow, and adds the channel terminal and the phone."

He paused for effect, then said, "How do you like it?"

"A lot." Why, I didn't even begrudge George Detweiler having a good idea for a change. "This could give us an edge. Maybe not enough, but it has to help." A sobering thought came. "What happens with the regular channel terminal, the pole-mounted one? Those only work on the basis of one channel, one phone."

He chuckled. "My friend at the phone company, he's taking care of that. Your line already carries two channels;

it's just that until tomorrow you can't hear the second one."

I knew George was only repeating facts he didn't truly understand, but all right; what I gathered was that it would be a haywire job but should work well enough. I said as much—or rather, the complimentary parts—adding, "When the time comes, who do I call?"

"Me. On my cellular, which I'll have in the car by tomorrow afternoon."

"Will you have the number in time to give it to me before then?"

"Oh shit. I think so, but maybe not." I could visualize his lower lip sticking out, the pout I'd seen so often lately. "Then call Coogan, at his apartment. I'll have more time to work with him than with you anyway, the way the Hornet always chivvies you around."

"You should try the experience." But that was fruitless repartee. "Good enough," I said. "That's how we'll do it."

He told me a couple more things I'd need to do next day, and we signed off.

The first item was to take my Volvo in to have the cellular phone installed. This wasn't any while-you-wait job, so Detweiler had arranged for one of his people to leave off a car for me, at Emerald City Cellular. George himself, I gathered, had had someone sent out to his home, to install his phone during the night, overtime pay no object.

Enroute to Range A I drove in cautious mode; I didn't need to be pulled over while driving a car owned by someone I didn't even know.

Arriving at the site I hoped no one would notice my change of vehicle, but as I headed for Origin, Eddie Machell walked up and said, "What happened to your Volvo?"

"In for its 30-K checkup. They gave me a loaner." My dealer has no loaner policy, but that was none of Eddie's business.

*   *   *

Considering how little there really was to do, Range A had a great air of busy-busy. Taking a little longer than usual so as to keep out from under other people's feet, I checked my own equipment at both ends of the big rig and found it doing fine: solid-state circuits either fail in a hurry or last for years. Mostly, that is. And all of it had been working under power long enough, by now, to do most of any drifting it was ever going to.

I reported to Coogan; today he seemed excited, eager. I said, "Everything's fine in my area. And I checked Catcher One directly, to be sure. Should I run downtown and do the same for Two?" Something I could have done before coming out here, but with luck he wouldn't think of that.

He was too busy lighting a cigar to answer right away. "We have no tests planned over that routing in the immediate future," he said finally. "When we do, I'll give plenty of advance notice."

"Sure thing. But I'm all done here. Can I go home, or do I hang around all day and twiddle my thumbs?"

Like a kid with a new toy, the Stork grinned. "Stick around until after lunch, my boy. I've planned a little surprise; truly, you wouldn't want to miss it."

"If you say so." Looking, I could see that something had him hyped-up quite a lot. Something emotional, not chemical. In fact he wasn't even drinking.

He wasn't telling me anything more, either.

So I went over to Origin and watched Machell put the bigger transmission chamber through its paces twice; with nothing but air inside, the power drain was relatively nominal. Then I walked to Catcher One and saw Nancy Ohara monitoring the indicators there.

The Catchers, both here and downtown, took little in the way of control work; given some extra bucks, most of that could have been put on automatic. Now, though, Nancy did it all manually on her key panel: opening and closing the chamber housing and the chamber itself, swinging the latter from operating position to loading or unloading stance, and vice versa.

After a time I was fairly sure I could have done it myself. Not the sending end, though; that one had some controls I'd never figured out. And since it was none of my business, no one had bothered to tell me.

That train of thought sent me back to Origin. If I kept watching, I might learn a little more; it couldn't hurt anything. But this time George Detweiler was there, standing in the middle of things and asking loud questions. George didn't know enough about sophisticated electronics in general, let alone *this* rig, to ask anything that made sense; I could see Eddie Machell working up a burn. In a TV cartoon, smoke would be rising from his collar. But on the whole he kept a cool front.

The next time the apparatus wound down, though, he flipped the Ready switches off and stepped back. "It's in shape; no significant variations over the past three tries." He looked at his watch. "Let's break early for lunch, gang, and come back about ten minutes early, too. We'll start the show at one sharp, if Mr. Coogan agrees."

"What show?" said Detweiler. "Coogan won't tell me anything, and I think I have a right to know what's going on."

"Sorry, Mr. Detweiler." Eddie smiled, but he wasn't fooling anyone. Well, George, maybe. "Mr. Coogan gave me strict orders; he wants this demonstration to be a surprise. And I want to keep my job."

Detweiler turned to me. "Banning?"

"You know as much as I do. Maybe more."

He glared at me, then at Eddie, and walked out. Machell said, "I wasn't kidding about lunch. Let's go."

As we passed Coogan's office he called to me from the doorway. I went over. "What's up?"

"Your friend Dauna Haig. If possible, she should be here for this."

My watch said there was plenty of time, if I could reach her at the magazine. "Use your phone?" He nodded. I waved to Machell and the others to go on ahead, and went inside.

On the second try I got through; Dauna was out but Ned Farringen said he'd pass the word. I said, "Tell her it's the Detweiler story. I'm at the site north of town, and if possible she should be here before one o'clock."

Ned was agreeable. Well, maybe she'd get the word in time and maybe not; I'd done what I could.

As I hung up, Coogan said, "One o'clock? I hadn't set the time yet." I explained that Machell had made it tentative, subject to the Stork's approval, and Emil was happy again.

Going to the door I saw that the others had left. I must have looked hesitant, because he said, "If bread and cheese would suit you, perhaps a few cold cuts and an impromptu salad, my refrigerator is your refrigerator." He *was* feeling good.

So why not? I thanked him, he got the fixings out, and we had quite a pleasant snack: good coarse tasty bread, Swiss cheese, salami. The veg part was lettuce and celery and tomatoes and cucumbers, and we each had a bottle of Mexican beer alongside. Not much talk while we ate, but over coffee I said, "Since I'm going to be writing up whatever this is—along with Dauna—do you really have to surprise me? I mean, if it's important to you, to do it that way, all right. But—"

"A moment, Banning." He poured the last glass from his beer bottle and motioned me to do the same. Then he said, "A toast! To proving, this afternoon, that Dr. Pedicord's system can and will successfully transport living organisms."

CHAPTER TWENTY

Instead of sipping, I'm afraid I gulped; a rude thing to do to an inoffensive beverage. Coogan didn't mind; he laughed. Then he reassured me; today's subject was not Tixo, but a lab animal. A white rat, in fact. "You suggested guinea pigs; remember? But these little rats are even smaller, less massive. Machell's calculations indicate that at this time of day we can make the test without danger of causing a power overload. There's margin, he says, because a potline at the aluminum plant is down for repairs. Whatever *that* is."

"And you're satisfied that Eddie knows what he's doing?"

"I checked. I asked him to make some estimates that Olin had already calculated, which Machell had not seen. The results came out very closely, within reasonable limits of error as Dr. Pedicord had explained those to me."

I had to hand it to Emil. With no real scientific or technical background of his own—and to the best of my knowledge he had none—he was finding ways to check up on folks who knew much more than he did. Well, nobody works the con game for twenty years or so before getting caught, without a certain degree of native intelligence. In Florida, as I recalled, he'd run into a very unlucky string of coincidences.

And here, now? There was still the Hornet to think about.

Not trying to hide the fact that I was suitably impressed, I asked more questions. Again, as with the stack of bills, the subject would get a lot of before-and-after testing; I didn't try to keep track of all of it but did make a few notes.

At twelve-fifty I heard Dauna's car pull in. The unser-

viced V-dub still sounded like a demolition derby in a mine
field, but once again it delivered her safely.

I went to the door and waved. She came over and had
coffee while Coogan filled her in. "Please keep the details to
yourself, if you don't mind, until the test run is completed.
I wish this to come as a surprise to George Detweiler, and
I have my reasons."

What I'd been thinking, Dauna said out loud. "George
is a sucker for dramatic effects, and you can use all the
leverage you can get; right?" He didn't protest. "I won't tip
the kayak."

Other cars arrived, including the gang back from lunch.
At Marge's, probably; I was grateful to Coogan for sparing
me that experience this once.

They walked past, up toward Origin. As Detweiler's new
black Continental zoomed in for splashdown, we followed.
So George was the last to enter the safety booth.

His big chair still dominated the place. He sat, and said,
"Well? Whatever this is, are we ready to start?"

Coogan moved the drill well. Larry Des Palmos went
somewhere, and in about two minutes came back with a
little white rat in a light, plastic cage. When Coogan made
his big announcement, George nearly dropped his molars.

Now came a lot of bustle: the rat was weighed, its pulse
and temperature recorded, and Nancy Ohara snapped several Polaroids of the little beast crouched in Coogan's
hands before he returned it to the cage.

He took the pics, looked at them, then handed one to
George and another to Eddie Machell. "Keep this one for
checking," he told Detweiler. "And Eddie, that print goes
in the files. Adequately labeled, of course." The rest he
stuffed into his shirt pocket.

Now he turned to the waiting group. "Are we ready? If
so, will Mr. Des Palmos please take the subject and place
it inside the transmission chamber. Mr. Machell, please
operate the chamber controls. Then, when the sending
room is vacated, bring the chamber up on-line and go to
supervise at Catcher One. Once you've signaled readiness,
I will activate transmission myself."

"Just a minute!" Detweiler made the interruption. "Let me see that rat." Des Palmos handed him the cage; in a moment George had the animal in his hand. "Give me a marker pencil, somebody." Eddie Machell brought his out but Des Palmos was closer; it was his that Detweiler used to mark a black X on the creature's side.

"There." He put the rat back in its cage.

"Wait." Now it was Coogan's turn to interrupt.

George scowled. "What's the matter? Something bother you?"

The Stork waved his hands. "Only that now, of course, we will need new pictures, to show the subject as transmitted."

So Detweiler held the rat up for Ohara's close-up shots. Again Coogan gave a print to Detweiler, one to Machell, and kept the rest. Now Larry did take the caged animal away, and soon, by way of the mirrors we saw him set it gently into the open transmission chamber. As he rejoined us, Machell at the controls pivoted the chamber down to its operating position, closed the transparent cover over it, and began revving up. Again came the ionization—and, as I'd come to think of them, the other Special Effects.

When the place was sparkling and making noises to his satisfaction, Eddie stepped back and nodded to Elihu Coogan. "Everything's go. Give me a couple of minutes, once I get over there, to make sure of Catcher One. We don't want any mistakes; you've impressed me with the importance of this test. I'll signal Ready as soon as possible."

He left. I expected Ohara to go with him, but she went to stand beside Coogan so I guessed he wanted her for backup or something. We waited, everyone very still except for George Detweiler, tapping fingers on his chair arms.

On Coogan's control panel a red light blinked. Whether that was the signal or whether I only happened to notice then, I don't know. But now he was moving switches, and once more the building groaned and shuddered. Ionization and condensation had long since hidden the chamber, but still I stared at its masked location; when I glanced aside I saw everyone else staring, too. In side vision, Coogan's hand moved again. Something went *whoosh* as the lights flickered briefly; the building jarred. And then, as in previous tests, it all began to wind down.

I don't know about anyone else, but that's when I noticed I was long overdue for some oxygen. It took me a while to catch up.

Ionization faded and died; the steamed-up cover lifted; the chamber swung up and opened. *Empty*. A lot of ragged breaths came out, including mine. If the timing at Catcher One was the same, then Machell and his crew, carrying the caged rat, made good time getting to us.

Coogan took charge; the pictures and earlier tests were repeated. "Everything within limits," the Stork reported. "Pulse and breathing a little rapid, which is understandable." Understatement if ever I heard one. "Temperature normal—and that's something we'd worried about, Dr. Pedicord and I. And the pictures—well—" He handed Detweiler the cage. "Inspect the animal itself. Does it seem to have been harmed in any way?"

George took the cage as if it might be booby-trapped. He looked in, then opened it and took the small animal out. With a finger he stroked the white fur and the black X. Then he put it back inside. "As far as I can tell, it's all right."

In a dark room, just then, I think Coogan might have glowed and shot sparks. "All right," he said. "Machell, Des Palmos, Ohara—all of you. Button the equipment down to normal standby and report to my office in twenty minutes." He couldn't stop grinning. "I have a case of chilled champagne that deserves your attention."

Well, nobody ever called Emil the Stork a piker. It was a good party. I watched myself on the bubbly since I had a little job, concerning Dr. Pedicord, on for the evening. But the need for moderation didn't spoil my fun noticeably.

Not even when Coogan slipped me the money bundle for the Hornet . . .

* * *

Driving home—Dauna and I ran out before the champagne did—I took it cautiously. That stuff seems to hit me harder than its content merits, possibly because it tastes milder than it is.

Thinking back, I had to chuckle. Not only had George Detweiler doffed his pomposity and become positively hail-fellow, merry-merry-be, but Tixo had added an unexpected note. Two glasses of bubble water inspired the little Indian to song and recitation.

Not much of a song. Same line over and over; it sounded something like: "The sputsfa you!" Then he'd gone into a kind of cheerleading routine; he'd yell one phrase to one side of the room, then turn and do a different one the other way. Again, the same set of syllables each cycle. One almost made sense: something like "Last felon" except eliding the "t" quite a bit. But "Tay skrate" had me baffled.

Until now, in retrospect, everything clicked. He hadn't been using his native tongue; he'd been reciting lines from beer commercials. As yet, English pronunciation wasn't exactly Tixo's strong suit.

I had a stop on the way, at Emerald City Cellular to pick up my Volvo and leave off George's loaner for whoever would be picking it up. While I was there I asked the shop foreman a few questions.

Okay, the new handset and its base were mounted on the dash, where the equivalent CB stuff had been. The transceiver module, about the size and shape of a medium hardback book, reposed under the passenger seat; its power and handset cables routed beneath the floor mat.

The little antenna stuck up inside my rear window, looking like a toy. To emphasize that impression I decided to hang some kind of plastic ornament over its tip.

We didn't have the "private link" scramblers after all; they weren't in stock. But with more than eight hundred channels, accessed at random, anyone trying to listen in would have himself quite a haystack.

I listened, though, while the man talked me through the

operating procedures, which weren't all that difficult. Then I headed straight for home.

First order of business was to inspect the new additions to my telephone enjoyment. The second phone sat closely alongside the old one, which didn't seem too smart to me, but probably Detweiler hadn't given his tame installer much of a briefing.

Over against the wall by the phone jack, the subscriber terminal looked like part of someone's stereo or VCR, inexpertly disassembled: no case, just the cluttered chassis.

I tried the new set, dialing the *Times* Sportscores number; it worked, but the handset cord was tangled so I unwound it. I wasn't used to cord phones; I'd fallen in love with cordless when the innovation first appeared. I didn't have much luck with the early ones: neighbors' phones interfering and what have you. The second generation was better, until I realized they could be "tapped" without trace *or* a court order. I lost a couple of job bids that way: eavesdropping by an unscrupulous competitor.

The one I had now was a real whizzer, with built-in privacy gear between base and handset. This wasn't the fancy encryption you can get on a digitalized line, which is too expensive for my tastes. It worked on the old-time principle of dividing the voice frequency band into subbands, which you can transpose and/or invert to your little heart's delight.

Mine's a five-bander, and I forget how many combinations that allows, but only a few of those are good for really solid garbling. The company picks ten of them for you. On any call, the Priv button assigns those ten to your one-through-zero buttons. Assuming Dr. Fu Manchu is listening, or maybe the IRS, you can change setups any time you want to. I hadn't used the change feature lately, but it was there if I wanted to.

Giving Murphy's Law its due respect I tried that set, too, and was pleased to find that on this occasion Murphy had struck out. I hoped the bill for the extra stuff was going to George, not me, but the problem didn't worry me a lot.

Nothing more seemed to need doing here; I checked the

mail. My concentration on Coogan's project obviated picking up much other new work, and most of the older jobs were ending, phasing out. So I couldn't expect much input and found little worth noticing. I set two items aside for later and dumped the rest.

Ordinarily this period before dinner would have been a good time for Martinis. But after Coogan's party, more booze was the last thing I needed. Coffee, though, seemed a good idea. When Dauna came in I had it ready. Drinking the stuff, we talked.

"What do you think?"

"I dunno, Marty; what do *you* think?" It's a proven fact: too many Late Movie reruns can be hazardous to your repartee.

Setting her cup down, Dauna said, "I couldn't spot any wires, Mitch. But I still can't quite believe Peter Pan's flying all by himself."

"I have the same hunch, in triplicate. But *how?*"

She coiled part of her hair around one hand, then smoothed it loose again. "Maybe that's the wrong question, for now. What if we give 'why?' a try? And how many?"

I was slow today, no doubt of that; but then I saw it. "Besides Coogan, you mean? Who would have to be in on the shtick?" She nodded; on the fingers of my left hand I started to count. Thumb first. "The Stork himself. Eddie Machell for sure; if anything's fishy, he'd have to know. Nancy Ohara, his understudy: maybe but not necessarily. Larry Des Palmos a near certainty; he came in as a contractor's man during construction, and switched to Coogan's payroll later."

I paused, thinking: who else could there be, high enough on the totem pole to qualify as a suspect? Orville Hackett functioned basically as a supply sergeant in civilian clothes; no reason for him to be in the Stork's confidence. But in the only test of Catcher Two, Ridge Arnold had operated that facility. So, six fingers wrapped up my list of possibles. "Of course," I added, "there could be a few spear-bearers who don't know what's really going on, but draw a little extra money to keep shut up about things they don't understand."

Dauna tilted an eyebrow. "With Machell as a suspect, how about the person who touted him to you?"

Ronnie Detweiler? I shook my head. "Ronnie couldn't have known anything at that time. Machell used her, is all, to get an in with me on the hiring end."

Dauna's expression accused me of wetting on the rug. "Not what she knew then, Mitch. What she might know *now*."

I was stumped. "Oh hell, I need some more coffee. It won't do much good, not until the champagne wears off all the way, but I need some anyway."

It didn't help, so I went in the bedroom and took a nap, which did. Dauna got me up for dinner; with a couple of pork chops under my belt, plus the inevitable vegetables, my head came back on-line.

"All right. I'll see what I can get out of Ronnie, if at all. Not tonight; the Pedicord business preempts everything else. But the test doesn't come off until the first. That leaves me tomorrow and the next day."

Wholly sober again, I nursed coffee while we waited for the phone to sound. My original phone, that is. Usually the Hornet's "business" calls had come in early evening, but tonight was different. I tried killing time with the paper, but as the other shoe didn't drop and still didn't drop, my concentration went from fitful to hopeless. For the first time in months the Jumble baffled me; I got two words out of four and no clue at all to the final answer. Hell, I couldn't even finish the crossword.

Then the phone rang. Reaching to the sound I picked it up before I noticed it was the wrong one, the one installed just today. "Yeah? Who is it?"

"Delta Supreme to Flagman. What's holding things up?"

"I can't move until I have some word, can I? Now get the hell off here. I'll call back when there's something to say. Through Coogan—or do you still want it that way?"

"Uh, yes; that's best. But here's my cellular number."

I repeated it back to him, wrote it down, gave him mine in turn, and hung up. I started to explain to Dauna.

"Never mind," she said. "It had to be Detweiler."

Almost another hour, the Hornet kept us hanging. When he did call, he said, "Tonight bring your woman along. If you can."

"You want Dauna to ride with me? I'll ask her." She nodded. "Any special reason?"

"Pedicord may need some lifting and carrying. Not much, but all by yourself you're a little light for the job. All right?"

If we ever met in person, he might be surprised what I'm not too light for. But I said, "She says she'll come. What next?"

I never liked hearing the Hornet laugh. "You have a CB rig in your car, I noticed. So I got myself one, too. We'll have much better communications tonight, you and I. In fact I want to hear you talking to me, or listening to me, at all times."

The channel he specified wasn't the one I was used to.

But that was the least of it. CB? I no longer *had* CB; what I had was a high-tech cellular phone, complete with buttons I hadn't even tried yet and a liquid crystal screen for showing me that I'd punched the wrong number. Sorry, Mr. Green Hornet, sir, go out and get yourself a whole new system in the next fifteen minutes.

I was hyperventilating; I tried to stop doing it. My thoughts weren't going anywhere so I shut up and listened.

The Hornet's only further instructions were to leave the house immediately, head for the nearest arterial, and turn south. Plus, as usual, leaving the phone off the hook. Except that this time, "Leave that damn silencer button alone!"

And, of course, bring the money. . . .

I recovered enough to know what I had to do next. Stall. "Understood," I said, "and agreed. One thing, though." No answer, so I went on. "Don't get antsy, but before we hit the street I need a john stop. Dauna probably does, too. And a couple of other little matters." He started to fuss; I said, "I'm not driving all over creation with a full bladder and that's non-negotiable. Over and out."

Until I heard a grudging grunt that I decided to take for a yes, I kept listening. Then, with the Mute option forbidden, I wrapped the handset in a pillow and stuffed the lot down the wastebasket. And while I was at it, took the whole thing to the far corner of the room.

Still breathing like a marathon runner, I stood there. Dauna looked at me wide-eyed. "Mitch! What's wrong?"

"Everything. Wait here." There was a chance I might still have the CB set after all; driving home, I hadn't really noticed. Two at a time I went down the tunnel stairs to check the Volvo.

Its inside light was too dim to help much so I pulled the halogen lantern out of the trunk. Nope, the cellular gear was in place and the CB wasn't. Shit*fire!*

Wait a minute; the installer wouldn't have swiped a customer's discarded equipment. The trunk? I looked some more, and there under a greasy towel I found the CB handset. *And* its base module. Needing three hands I made do with the two I had, grabbing the loose gear along with my spare tool kit.

Up front again I laid things out on the seat. I didn't know where the screws had gone, so I stuck the little module atop the dash with duct tape. The antenna feed had been stuffed back down through the hole there; I fished it up and reconnected it.

Power. . . . The installer had preempted the CB feed, changing connectors; the two types didn't match. Wondering how my hands could be so steady I cut the plug from the CB cable, stripped the wires, and connected them to the ignition switch. With luck, maybe even to the right places.

When I was done I turned the key to Accessories position and switched the rig on. Under my hillside there wouldn't be much signal, but the receiver hissed properly with background noise. The send side, I'd have to take on faith. But aside from Murphy, no reason it *shouldn't* work.

I was halfway up the stairs before I realized how badly I'd blown a perfectly good out.

All I'd've had to tell the Hornet was, my goddamn CB had gone on the fritz and I couldn't get parts before Monday.

Too late now.

CHAPTER TWENTY-ONE

When I reached topside, Dauna looked to be in need of some facts; as briefly as I could, I gave them.

"The whole web's coming unstuck?" She had that much right; I nodded. "Well, I'm glad it's not just you. So now what happens?"

"We're late already, cutting out of here. Now we get later."

On the new phone I put a call to Coogan. "Don't talk yet. Just listen." I described the monkey wrench the Hornet had thrown into the works, and what I'd tried to do in lieu of repairs. Then I told him about the Hornet's very own CB scheme, including the channel he'd have me using.

"So now what do we do for communications? I can't have the cellular phone blatting while I talk to the Hornet. Or even ringing. And he's going to be listening like a narc at a dope auction. Do any of the Deltas—?"

No, the Stork assured me; from Delta Supreme on down, the posse had done away with CB capability. "However," he said, sounding calmer than he had any right to, "I have a duplicate CB rig here at the apartment, with a rather good antenna." Had I known that? If he'd told me, I'd forgotten. What the hell, take it as given. . . .

"So I will do the CB listening. And of course"—beating me to the reminder—"maintain silence thereon. I will also, on the cellular conference circuit where George Detweiler is displaying a deplorable lack of patience, relay to him whatever you deem advisable. Is this—"

"What *I* deem advisable? How'm I supposed to tell you that, past the Hornet's big ears? Oh shit, listen." Damn, I had to get this straight. "My cellular's useless on this; tell George they gave me a defective one, or that it went sour on me, or—" No, that was wrong; now *I* was getting rattled. "Don't tell him a thing; stewing about me may occupy his mind and keep him from thinking up something really stupid."

What else? Oh, yes: "And whatever you hear on the CB, use your own judgment on what you pass to Detweiler or don't."

Time was eroding my life span; I said, "I *have* to get out of here. Before the Hornet decides we're crossing him."

"Yes. Well then, Banning—"

I hung up on him. Dauna was ready at the door. I started in that direction, then stopped.

Call it power of suggestion; right then I *did* need a john stop.

In the Volvo, first I hung a little velvet mouse to the end of the cellular antenna. Then I checked out how to turn off that phone's ringer and speaker. If a call came, maybe I'd spot the little green light and could listen on the handset; with luck it wouldn't be loud enough to carry over to the CB mike.

What else? I killed the cellular handset's mike with the Mute button; it's a toggle, so I didn't need anything to hold it down. I hung the set over a small cable that looped across under the dash. That left the cellular hookswitch free to hold the CB talkset. All right so far . . .

Then we could roll. Once clear of the garage, belatedly I followed the Hornet's instructions: switched CB channels, and called. "Banning to Hornet. Come in please." Well, he hadn't specified any other nom-de-CB, and I might as well make things easy for Coogan.

After some cross talk from other people, the Hornet

answered. "Banning, if you're trying to pull something—! Where the hell have you been so long?"

Only one way to handle this. "The details of our bodily functions and personal hygiene are truly none of your business." That stopped him; I said, "Can we get on with it?"

"Yes. Locate yourself to me: current route and next major intersection." I spotted a street sign and complied. The Hornet said, "Call off the cross-streets as you approach them; I'll tell you your turnoffs. Mainly, Banning, I want to hear you often enough to be sure you haven't left this channel. Got it?"

"Roger, Kemo Sahib." I obeyed happily; after all, his very own routine was keeping the Stork better informed than any trick I could have managed.

Pretty soon he had us going west on North 85th. "Turn left on Aurora," he said. Which is old Highway 99. But at 85th they don't let you do that. Not wanting to bother the Hornet with small stuff I went straight through, circled to my right by way of the gas station/minimart, and headed south as directed.

We crossed over the ship canal, skirted the east side of Queen Anne hill, and were nearing stoplight country. Or possibly not: I said, "You want us to go through the tunnel and down the viaduct?"

"No! Peel off there! At the first light, turn left."

Maybe the Hornet was from out of town, which meant the personnel records might yet tell us something more. In any case he hadn't been near Aurora Avenue for some years; twice in a row he'd blown his directions. This time I said, "Can't do it. No left turn. I'll have to go ahead two more blocks"—two, because of the one-way streets— "then left, and come back."

Quicker than I expected, he responded, "Never mind; go right instead. We'll use an alternate site."

I couldn't get over in time; I had to go through and turn right twice, bringing me up against a long wait for the left turn I needed now. When the Hornet asked for an update I said, "Traffic." As a navigator he made Wrong-way Corrigan look good.

Going west again I called off the cross-blocks as before. No great feat; those lights are timed so badly that I missed all but one. Then came, "Right at the next." I did it, putting us on First North. "Go up four blocks," which took us north past the Coliseum. Then a right, followed by a quick left into and through a small supermarket's parking lot.

The alley beyond featured, on its left, parking stalls behind a row of small businesses which fronted on the avenue we'd just come up. One of these had a lean-to attached, shading the slot alongside it from the supermarket lights. Naturally, that's where the Hornet had me park.

Cutting the motor I put the key to the Accessories setting, which also powered the CB, and listened to the rest of the Hornet's spiel.

"—and leave your parking lights on," he said. "That tells the Merchant Patrol, if any, that you're there legitimately."

"I am? Gee, that's good to know."

"If I wanted boffs, Banning, I'd watch reruns. Now shut up and listen. First, put the package under the front seat." All right. Next, we were to get out of the car, walk back the way we'd come in, turn right and keep walking. "All the way around the block. And don't shortcut down the alley when you pass the north end of it. You'll be watched."

I could see problems from hell to breakfast; if the Hornet saw the cellular base module, which now had the CB handset hanging on it, would he recognize the difference? If he did—no matter I couldn't use the thing—it was Katie bar the door. On automatic I said, "And then what?"

"Take Pedicord to his own apartment. I suggest you don't disturb the packaging until you get there, and that you take him in the back way." A pause; emphasis? "All right, get moving."

"Sure." But what to do? Sometimes there aren't any good answers. I hung the litter bag over the suspect gear and hoped for the best.

I should check with Coogan: see what else was happening. With the Hornet not expecting me on the CB just now, I reached under the dash and fumbled for the cellular handset.

"I said *move it*, Banning. Get your butts on the road and do it now!" I looked at Dauna. A shrug would be superfluous; I took the keys and we started walking. No sooner were we out of sight of the car than I forgot whether I'd left the parking lights on. If I went back to see, the Hornet would surely think we were crossing him. This time I did shrug. Then we proceeded.

At the sidewalk we turned west toward the first corner. "Does he really have a crystal ball," Dauna asked, "or was that last prod a shot in the dark?"

"What's the difference? Either way, it worked." I saw what she meant; if we'd been away from the car we couldn't have heard him. But either way it worked; yes.

It doesn't take long to walk around a block. Halfway, passing the alley at its north end, we stopped for a moment. Directly south of us a car was leaving, turning right, the way we'd come in. It cut the corner and partly missed the driveway; its rightside wheels jolted down off the curb. My quick impression was of a nondescript compact in dull paint, maybe the same one Ronnie and I had seen make the pickup on I-5 that night. No chance at the license number; too far and too dim.

Somehow I was certain the Hornet had come and gone, that the rest of our instructions were a dead letter. I turned to Dauna. "Let's go see."

Walking toward the car, suddenly I felt an odd kind of emotional impact. From the overall situation: in a way I'd been seeing it as a game, us against the Hornet. Now it struck me: in my car there'd be a real live person, a man who'd been held captive for—how long *had* it been? I'd lost track. And whatever kind of shape he was in by now, junkie or not he was in my car.

Or, of course, maybe he wasn't.

At first I didn't see him. Then, hearing the thumps, I looked behind the front seats. My inside light glinted off the steel-wool hair but something hid the face. And the way he was hunched together, making a kind of lump, I didn't need good lighting to figure the doc was tied up.

No one should be treated that way: I felt a sick pang. But remembering the Hornet's admonitions I said, "Take it easy, Dr. Pedicord. We're bringing you home now. The wrappings come off when we get there." For a moment he quieted; I said, "Hang tough. It won't be long."

Up front, I looked before getting in. Tension left me by way of a convulsive shudder. From all indications, nothing had been touched; the Hornet had been in too much of a hurry, for once, to snoop the car.

No two ways about it; sometimes you *can* luck out.

I started the car, and thus the CB also; it lit up and sounded off. "—the hell are you, Banning? What's taking you so long? If you're trying something funny—"

At my first chance, I cut in. "Hold it down to a dull roar, will you? We just got here, and eyeballed the consignment. What kind of shape's he in, anyway?"

"That's Coogan's worry; let him handle it. And why didn't you leave your trunk open?"

"You didn't say anything about a trunk." Or did he? I thought back; nothing clicked. "Dauna?"

"Not that I remember."

"Don't give me that! It's on my notes, and I check-marked it when you acknowledged. I—" There came a long pause; then, voice subdued a little, he said, "Sorry, my mistake. It *looked* like a checkmark."

Well. The Hornet, admitting he could be wrong? That was a first, for certain sure. I said, "If we're done here, I'd like to get Pedicord home now. He can't be very comfortable."

"Done for tonight, yes. Except, one more item. You remind Coogan that whatever, however, and whenever Detweiler pays him for this plagiarized machine he's built, I *get half!*"

"Sure. Banning out." I had the car moving now, out of the lot and heading for the closest route to Pedicord's digs.

The note with Detweiler's cellular phone number was in my shirt pocket. After retrieving the handset and releasing the Mute button I consulted the slip of paper, turned the speaker on, and for the first time made use of my new gadget. After a few rings George finished manipulating his Call Holding or whatever the setup needed, and came on the line to include me in his conference call.

He was boiling.

"—right on his tail, no way that heap could lose this car, but he slowed on the amber so I had to run the red. And this dumb cop—" The cop wasn't dumb enough to give a ticket to Howard Hughes, Jr., but the delay had sprung the Hornet—or somebody, at any rate—free and clear.

I'd wondered how much of my exchanges with the Hornet our Chimney Bird had been able to pick up on and pass to Delta Supreme. Quite a lot, it seemed, since George had reached the area in time to chase some likely suspect.

When he ran down, I started to fill him in. It wasn't easy; first he objected, "Why the hell weren't you on this circuit earlier?"

Oh, yes . . . "My new phone had a bug in the installation. Until we got Pedicord, I didn't have a chance to look for it."

"That's why you and Coogan went back to the CB rigs? Not bad thinking, except for the delay involved."

"More or less, that was why." Which beat trying to explain the real situation. "But eventually I did find the trouble." I cleared my throat. "Now here's where we stand."

When I was done he said, "All right, Banning, I'll meet you there and advise Coogan to that effect." He went silent; I decided he'd toggled his Mute key, and did likewise.

For getting across the ship canal, the Ballard Bridge was closest. I should have known better than to expect any more luck: we were barely onto the bridge when a boat tooted and the span went up. For myself I didn't mind the four or five minutes; it was Pedicord I was thinking of.

Aside from occasional thumps the man stayed quiet during the drive; I supposed he had to move a little, sometimes.

When we reached his block I pulled around to the back of the apartment building and found Coogan waiting. Dauna and I got out; I opened the back door and helped the Stork ease Pedicord to the ground and sit him up.

Dauna had the fingernails to get at the tape around his ankles; I got the gag cover off his face and pulled a wad of cloth out of his mouth. It wasn't as damp as you might expect.

Pedicord took a deep, shaky breath. I think he was going to yell, but Coogan said sharply, "You're all right, Olin. Now save it until we're inside." The doc nodded. Even in dim light he didn't look good.

Dauna was digging at the bonds on his wrists. "Save that, too," Coogan said. "Help me get him up to the apartment, Banning. I'll take it from there."

"Sure." One of us to either side and Dauna following, we got Pedicord inside the building and up to his floor. Coogan unlocked the door. With a hand on Pedicord's shoulder he moved the man on in, then turned to face us.

"The next few hours will not be pleasant, and you wouldn't learn anything anyway. I appreciate your help, both of you. But it would be best if you went home now and got some sleep. Tomorrow, if and when Olin is capable of telling a coherent story, I'll call you." I had no counter-argument; we said good night and Coogan shut the door.

Dauna and I went back downstairs and over to the car. As I drove out into the alley and turned toward the street I wanted, Detweiler's Continental passed us, going the other way.

If he recognized us he gave no sign. Dauna said, "I wonder if the Stork will let him in."

There was only one possible answer. "Frankly, my dear, I don't give a damn."

The line got more of a laugh than it deserved.

A little short of sleep next morning, nonetheless I got up early. I phoned Steve Broyles at home. "Steve? Any reason you can't call in sick today, for a good cause?"

"I suppose not. What's the cause, though?"

"I want a nice long talk with Ronnie Detweiler. It's important, and I'm in a hurry about it. All right?"

"I'll meet you at her place. Have you had breakfast?"

I walked over and looked into the kitchen. Dauna was setting up coffee but hadn't done anything about food. Was it my turn? I couldn't remember. I told Steve, "No, I haven't."

"If you can hold off until you get there; say, an hour? We can have it together."

I gave up keeping track of the pronouns that applied to whichever role I was talking to. "Fine. See you."

I went into the kitchen and explained to Dauna. It was my turn to fix the meal, all right, so I cooked hers and she made a point of how much she liked it—whether in appreciation or to rub it in that I was still hungry, I couldn't be sure. Then she readied up for work, I kissed her good-bye for the day, and she left. Not long after, I drove to Ronnie's digs.

Steve or Ronnie opened the door, wearing a T-shirt and female-style slacks. The sideburns and mustache were off, but hair and eyebrows were Steve's. "You're early, or else I'm running behind time. Just a minute."

As I closed the door, my welcomer went into the next room. A couple of minutes later, she came back wearing the auburn wig.

Ronnie smiled. "I hope your talk can wait. I can't think until I've had breakfast."

"Join the cult." So we had juice and bacon and eggs and toast and coffee. Pouring our first refills I said, "Eddie Machell. He came on the job as *your* friend. Tell me about him."

"What's to tell?" Ronnie's shrug gave no hint of Steve Broyles—nor, presumably, of Ronald Detweiler. "I met Eddie in a singles bar, not long after he came here. He was fun; we flirted a little and he picked me up."

"Oh?"

Her brows lifted. "I told him right away, as soon as he began to make a pitch. How it is with me, all that."

"And?"

She grinned. "Surprised as hell. Really set back on his heels. But Eddie's a good sport. He didn't even mind, when we stood up, that I was taller. With heels, anyway. He said the invitation still held; we could be 'jes' kissin' cousins.' We went out and had an evening on the town; it was fun, and from then on we were friends. We still are."

I looked at her—trying to see past the words, see if she were putting on any kind of act. I guess she misread the look; her hands went to the small unhaltered breasts outlined under the T-shirt. She said, "All right, they're not so much now. To be Steve, I had to ease off the hormones. But you don't need to stare, dammit!"

"Oh, hey." Embarrassment struck. "I didn't mean to. Really, I was thinking of something else entirely." *But don't ask me what.*

"Like what?" she said, of course.

In a moment I had an answer. "Machell, still; what else?" Partly the truth, yes. "What's his background?"

Ronnie shook her head. "Back east someplace. Midwest, the east coast; I think he's moved around a lot. He didn't say much, just the side remark now and then. And I didn't ask."

She gave me the hard stare. "What *is* all this? Do you suspect Eddie of something?"

"I don't know; he's one of quite a few people we have to check out. And since you were acquainted with him first . . ."

"You thought I might know something." She'd cooled down; now she said, "Well, anything you want to ask, go ahead."

I tried a few more leads, looking for any new info that might be solid, but if Ronnie knew anything she hadn't already mentioned, she couldn't get it up on screen. I stayed until we finished the coffee, then thanked her and excused myself.

Outside, getting into the car, I decided the breakfast had been worth the trip. Which was a good thing; otherwise I would have been wasting my time.

And no one likes to admit doing that.

* * *

The next step, I supposed, was to fine-tooth the personnel records of all our suspects. But with any luck, Detweiler would have his people already doing that. So I could wait and ask George, next time I saw him. Who knows? I might even catch him in a good mood and making sense.

Meanwhile, how about Pedicord? Either he would know something or he wouldn't. I drove along, looking for a pay phone for quite a time until I remembered the cellular. Then I pulled over. I can walk and chew gum at the same time, but driving in traffic while dealing tricky nuances with Emil the Stork is playing in a different league. The majors.

At Pedicord's number, Coogan answered on the fifth ring. He said I could come over and talk, but I can't say he sounded very enthusiastic.

CHAPTER TWENTY-TWO

Olin Pedicord looked tired, not to mention more than a little shaky, but he talked well enough. The only trouble was that he didn't have a whole lot to say. "I don't know *who* he is." His hands waved futility. "First I saw him in a ski mask. Then he took my contact lenses, and only let me have them on occasion; without them, at more than a meter's distance I couldn't tell *your* two faces apart."

There was more to it, of course: the other means the Hornet had used to make sure the doc couldn't identify him. "It varied," Pedicord said. "When I could see, he was masked. When there was no need for me to see clearly, in order to read my drawings and tell him what he wanted to know, he was a blur in dim light. And much of the time I had to wear earplugs, distorting his voice as I heard it." The doc shook his head. "After a time I gave up trying to outguess him; he was always one step ahead of me. And of course"—he shuddered—"at no time did he allow my nervous system to stabilize fully."

Well, the Stork had guessed that Pedicord had been kept on short rations, dopewise. I looked at Coogan, shrugged, and went on trying to find out what else had happened.

Mostly the Hornet had forced his captive to do up a full, annotated set of specs and drawings for his device. Just as he'd told me on the phone some time ago that he intended. Had I told Coogan that part? In case I hadn't, I did now.

Coogan shook his head. "Peddle it abroad? Yes, I think you did mention that. He can't, you know." Seeing my best skeptical expression, he expounded. "On his own, Olin couldn't have sold it to George Detweiler; he doesn't know how to sell. And neither, by my estimate, does the Hornet. *I* know how to sell."

He looked at me; I said, "I'm not arguing. But what do we do now?" I mentioned the matter of checking our suspects via the personnel files, and Coogan nodded.

"You may be wrong, Banning, in restricting your suspicions to more-or-less key people. Nonetheless I can give you this much information from memory, without consulting any files. Machell and Hackett are new to this area; Arnold and Des Palmos have been around longer. Ohara is local talent."

I shrugged. "None of it proves anything, does it? So the Hornet didn't know, or forgot, that left turns are barred at a couple of intersections. It could happen to anyone, hometown or not, who doesn't ordinarily use a given route."

Shakily, Pedicord stood. "I'd like to go lie down now."

Coogan gestured assent; the doc started for the other room.

I said, "Dr. Pedicord? The live test, with Tixo, is day after tomorrow. Will you be ready for it?"

I hadn't thought his flabby face could produce such a convincing snarl. "Right now!—if it were necessary. Since it isn't, I will get some needed rest."

He went into the next room and closed the door. Coogan shook his head. "Banning, you push at the wrong times."

"Yeah." Another thought came. "Our Number One suspect Edsel Allert comes from a Caucasian family; right? So unless he's adopted, he can't be Ridge Arnold." Coogan didn't comment. "Arnold or Ohara could be accomplices, maybe. But of our prime cast of characters, all we have are Hackett, Machell, and Des Palmos."

Looking over the top of his steepled fingers, the Stork said, "I still mistrust your tendency to center on foreground people."

I didn't understand, and said so. He frowned. "The Hornet has outguessed us at every turn. We're dealing with an extremely intelligent, resourceful opponent. He—"

"He's somewhat of a nut, too. Inconsistent, for one thing."

"Or possibly wishing to give us that impression. But I have not yet made my point." Brows raised, he paused until I gestured for him to continue. "Mitch? If you were the Hornet, what kind of cover role would you prefer to take on the project?"

I hadn't thought about it. "I hadn't thought about it."

"Well, I have. In Allert's situation I would choose to be as inconspicuous as possible. While still getting myself into a position to access a maximum of information. I would *not* try for a key job, such as Larry's or Eddie Machell's. Instead I would seek a quiet, seemingly inconsequential slot which allowed me to tap vital data while keeping an extremely low profile."

As Coogan paused, I thought it over. And finally said, "You realize where *that* idea leaves us, don't you? No place, is where. Back to Square One. Why, there must be sixty people on the project who more or less fit your pattern."

"I know," the Stork said. "I don't claim to like the possibility; nonetheless I am forced to consider it."

To that idea there wasn't much to say. So I dropped the matter and asked a few questions unrelated to it. The answers were that George Detweiler hadn't been allowed to see Pedicord the previous evening, that he'd gone storming away in a tantrum, and that Coogan had no idea how to get

in touch with him just now. Nor any such intention. I
didn't blame him.

Finding no particular reason to stay longer, I excused
myself politely and left.

At barely midmorning, the high haze greying the sky hadn't
begun to burn off. Plenty of time before lunch to run the
routine checks on my portions of Aladdin's lamp. I headed
out for I-5 and went to Range A. Detweiler's car wasn't in
the lot.

In Origin and then at Catcher One I went through my
bag of tricks. As usual lately, all systems were on the
money—but I didn't let the smooth going make me care-
less. The other putterers, such as Des Palmos, Arnold,
Machell, and Ohara, also seemed to be taking their chores
seriously. Over at the power board Larry was frowning at
an indicator. It looked all right to me, but he shook his
head, closed his test kit, and called for a coffee break. Done
with my own work, I joined the group.

Over coffee there was a lot of chatter, but not much said.
My guess was, the suspense was getting to people but they
were trying not to show it. Only Nancy Ohara let her
excitement be seen; suddenly she released an explosive
sigh. "Oh, if only it *works!*"

Looking at her, Des Palmos said, "We know, Nancy."
And Machell patted her hand.

She smiled at him. "You, too?" Everybody nodded, including me. For that moment I felt very close to the whole
gang. Even though I was reasonably sure that one of them
was a saboteur, kidnapper, and murderer.

But with luck, the rest might be honest. . . .

After the break I hung with the group for a bit. Back at his
power board Des Palmos studied a little longer, then
grinned and hit a switch. "Gotcha!" Seeing everyone look
around at him, he said, "Study the trees too long, you lose
the forest. I must have checked that setting a dozen times
without seeing that it was positioned for Catcher Two.
We're all right now, though."

With everyone relaxing, it seemed a good time for me to ease away. Outside, noting that Detweiler's black behemoth had arrived, I walked over to his office. The door stood open; seeing he was alone, I walked in. "Morning, George; how's it going?"

His expression changed. "That damn Coogan! What the hell's going on?"

Calming him down took some time. No, Pedicord had *not* been in shape to talk last night. No, Coogan hadn't let me inside either, and I was the one who'd done pickup and delivery. No, Pedicord still had no useful information. With Detweiler, of course, a certain amount of repetition was needed.

Finally he simmered down. "Well, for what it's worth, *I* have new information. On Mr. Edsel M. Allert."

He handed me some Xeroxed sheets and a small photo. The pic was none too clear: a young guy with a skinny face, light hair a little wavy, cut fairly short but still partially obscuring his ears, and a walrus mustache.

The sheets were descriptions. According to the Army, Edsel Allert was five feet seven; Boeing had him at five eight. Well, he could have got some of his growth late; it can happen.

Either way he didn't read like anyone I'd seen recently. And in the pic, the heavy-rimmed glasses were no help at all. I handed the stuff back. "Does it tell *you* anything?"

"Not much." George didn't seem much bothered by the lack. "I got some other things, Banning: on the phone, from Allert's home town." He leaned forward. "In high school the kid was quite a thespian." I felt my eyebrows lift; I hadn't expected Detweiler to know the word. "He acted in nearly all the school plays. And get this, now: he was especially good at voice impressions. Any celebrity you like; name it, he does it."

Yeah. The husky voice the Hornet used at first. I hadn't noticed while he gradually dropped it, but now I realized he'd done just that. Or maybe he'd had a cold for a while—or maybe some more, that's what he wanted me to think. No point in confusing George with those speculations; I said, "Then why did he bother to make Pedicord wear earplugs, more than not?"

That remark opened Pandora's box. Now Detweiler wanted to hear *everything*, such as it was, that I'd learned from Coogan and Pedicord. Trying, without much luck, to be brief about it, I gave him what I could recall.

And speaking of luck, mine was truly out; just as I was finishing the narration, Coogan walked in. And I had to stay and hear the whole works all over again, from the Stork's viewpoint.

One good thing. By then, Detweiler had cooled down enough that he hardly yelled at all. And when he was done asking the same questions over and over, possibly in hopes that Coogan would slip and give him some answers he liked better, George sat back and actually grinned.

"All right; now we know where we are." I didn't, but on the off chance that he did, I listened. "I've been trying the scientific approach; for the past week I've had a fingerprint man lifting impressions all over Range A."

He snorted. "Well, that was a big methodical waste of time. He got prints that fit the coding for Edsel Allert, allright—but no way to *pin* them to anybody."

"I don't understand. . . ." Coogan's voice was hesitant.

George looked pained; for once, I could see, he thought he had Coogan on the stupid end. "I have to send this guy sneaking, when nobody's around. So he never sees who's touched the places he's dusting." Fist, bang desk; right. "The hell with science; from now, we go to push."

Sure thing; I shrugged. "If you say so. But what if the Hornet does, too?"

Pulling out his desk drawer, Detweiler showed us a glimpse of a rounded, checkered gun butt. Big mother, from the look of it. But come to that, they put some good-sized frames on .22s these days. "From now on," he said, "I'll be armed. And I know how to shoot."

Well, so did I, and still do. The trouble was that shooting people has never been one of my preferred response patterns.

I grinned. "First, George, you'll need a target. So far, the Hornet hasn't given us one."

Then I left.

From the rest of that day, not much comes to mind. Or the next one, either. I did my chores, of course, and heard grumbling throughout Range A because on Big Test Day all troops not essential to the operation were excluded. "If they'd had the common courtesy to tell us in advance," one young woman complained, "I could have planned some good use for the extra day off. But this way—"

For what it was worth, she had my sympathy.

At home, when I got there, suddenly Dauna and I seemed to need each other a lot: reaction to strain, maybe. Not for sex, either; somehow we weren't tuned that way. Just to be touching, more, or at least in touching *distance*. Talk tended to trail off into silence.

For some reason I kept expecting more hassle to jump out and bite me on the leg; most of the evening I spent being on edge. But no one intruded on us: not Detweiler, not Coogan, not Pedicord. Even the Hornet didn't call, and you'll never know what a comfort that was. After a time I quit fretting.

That night, just before the big test, surprisingly I went to sleep easily and stayed that way all night long. The only dream I remember was from childhood. One of my favorites: I rediscovered how to swim in the air and it was the best fun ever.

Come morning I went to the kitchen and turned the page on the calendar. First of the month; time for happenings.

Like for starters, breakfast. Trying to do our eggs "over easy" I broke four out of six. I didn't *feel* jittery but my coordination knew better.

Eventually we had ourselves ready to roll. I did a last minute scan on my project file, making sure I left no piece of paper I might need on the site; then we went down to the garage.

For today, one vehicle was plenty; I drove the Volvo.

Once onto I-5, in the fast lane where I could drive my own system, my handling of the car improved more than somewhat.

I knew the guard at the Range A gate and the guard knew me, but on this day she demanded to see ID. "Mr Detweiler's orders."

"Sure," and Dauna and I showed our cards.

For a weekday morning the parking lot was practically empty: aside from the project vehicles that lived here all the time, only four cars were there ahead of us. Detweiler's I saw, and Eddie Machell's; the others I wasn't sure about.

We walked over to Origin, and seeing the sending room empty, went into the safety booth. Machell and Ohara hovered over the control console; George Detweiler bounced out of his throne to greet us. "Where the hell's Coogan? I haven't been able to raise him all morning."

I wussed at him. "He'll be here; it's early yet." Unless, the thought came, the Hornet had stung from a new direction. No point in airing that idea; George was keyed-up enough already.

All around, we said our hellos. The others present were Ridge Arnold and the logistics man, Orville Hackett. I wondered what he was doing there. Then I looked at him and wondered something else.

Skinny, with black hair, and more or less the right height: could this man be the Hornet?

I had my own equipment routines to do so I began. But every now and then I'd sneak a glance at Hackett. I wished I had the blurred picture Detweiler had shown me, for comparison.

Orville's hair was by no means kinky, only a little on the wavy side. And he wasn't wearing glasses. Neither difference, nor both together, added to any real objection. And Edsel Allert's walrus lip-fringe had obscured his mouth pretty well.

By the time I finished at Origin and left to check out Catcher One, I decided that without a fingerprint make there wasn't any way I could say yes or no on Orville

Hackett. And again it struck me that this was no time to stir up George Detweiler.

All I could do was try to keep an eye on Orville.

Catcher One was a fast read, few adjustments required. Walking back to Origin I saw Coogan's Toyota pull in and park. Then he and Pedicord and Tixo went into the building. I found them in the sending room, being yelled at by George Detweiler. "Today of all days, Coogan!"

By gestures more than by words, the Stork got Delta Supreme to shut up and listen. As he said, "That police lieutenant, Hanson. Sheer bad luck that he chose this morning to want to go over the data again, about Archer Green's death." I'd seen Hanson around Suite 2310-14 a time or two since the bombing, but all we'd said were standard, casual hellos. So, what was up now? I listened.

"I explained that today was urgent business," Coogan said, "and he did keep it short. I got away as soon as I possibly could, Detweiler."

Harrumph-snort-frown. "Did he have anything new, Coogan?" Headshake. "Then what do you say we get our ass in gear?" He looked at his oversized digital watch; if I wanted one like that, I'd pick the kind that doesn't take both hands to consult it. "Our power drain window," George said, "comes up in half an hour. Let's don't skimp ourselves on the leeway."

Nodding, Coogan began giving some instructions on his own, including a few in the language that, here and now, only he and Tixo understood. Today the little Indian was in his happy mode; he'd given me a grin and the fingers gesture, even though we were on opposite sides of the room and couldn't do our knife ritual. Considering what he was going to attempt this morning, I was glad to see him cheerful.

Now it began to move. My stomach tightened. Everything we'd worked toward, these past months: now it was up for grabs. As we all, except Coogan and Tixo, trooped around to enter the safety booth, I thought about it.

Detweiler saw a billion dollars riding on the next hour.

Coogan saw money, too, but how much and by what means? As to Pedicord, I was convinced by now that the man genuinely envisioned a great scientific breakthrough. But what part of his dream came from dope?

Aside from Nancy Ohara, whose enthusiasm couldn't be hidden, I didn't know how the rest felt. And except for one man, it hardly mattered. The Green Hornet. I didn't know who he was, but I would have bet a bundle on his presence here.

Looking around from one to another I had no clues at all. Under my arms the sweat glands prickled.

Through the mirror system I saw Tixo climb into the transmission chamber. Coogan shook the man's hand with both of his own, then took one look around the room and walked quickly out of it.

As we saw the chamber close, and then the housing over it, the Stork joined us. He motioned, and three of the group left for Catcher One: Machell, Ohara, and Ridge Arnold.

We waited until Nancy called with the ready signal. Then Coogan said, "All right. Dr. Pedicord, full test procedure. For the record, our subject is a consenting human being."

He took a deep breath. "Activate!"

And Pedicord began to operate his controls.

"Just a minute!" In his throne-chair, Detweiler halfway stood. "What about all the weighings and measurements? The photographs?"

This was Coogan's show; he wasn't taking interruptions. He looked at George as if George had spilled his milk. "We have those records long since. On a test as important as this, do you think we'd wait until the last minute?"

Detweiler sat.

The rising sounds, the building shuddering more strongly than ever before, nearly drowned Coogan's last few words. Impatiently the Stork turned back, to watch over Pedicord's shoulder. Again blue pulsations filled the sending room; before condensing vapor could fog the chamber's housing, the flicker of crackling discharges hid it from view.

Our lights dimmed, flared up again, then momentarily dipped almost to darkness. Something, or maybe everything, cracked like a sharp, drastic seismic burst. I found I was hanging on to someone's chair and someone's shoulder, but couldn't look away to see whose. Then as the lights came up and the screaming noise wound down, we squinted through the blue glow for first glimpse of the chamber.

Before the howling whisper died away entirely, the fogged cover opened; under Pedicord's guidance the sending chamber swung up and its cover lifted.

"Empty!" I don't know who yelled that, or if we all did.

Then came Ohara's voice. "It worked. Tixo's *here!*"

I saw Dauna's unbelief and Detweiler's bulge-eyed glee. Pedicord seemed dazed as the Stork, smiling, shook his hand.

Except for a kind of confused wonder I wasn't at all sure how I felt, myself. Was I really awake or was this the second feature, following the one in which I swam in the air?

I didn't get a chance to figure it out. Again from Catcher One, Ohara called.

But this time in a harsh scream.

"He's dead! Tixo's *dead!*"

CHAPTER TWENTY-THREE

The universe went into slow motion. Detweiler froze in place, expression and all. Pedicord went slack-faced; his mouth worked but no sound emerged.

It was Coogan who acted. Grabbing the doc's shoulder he yelled, "You idiot! The buffer field; you must have had the damned *phase* inverted."

Pale of face, the Stork shook Pedicord hard. All the doc could do, it seemed, was waffle; if he knew what was going on, you couldn't prove it by me.

"Don't argue!" Coogan shouted. "Start setting it up again—and this time get it right." He hit the intercom switch. "Coogan to Catcher One. Arnold! Get Tixo up here right away, direct to the sending room and into the chamber. We'll have to put him through again—and quickly, before brain deterioration begins. If we want to save his life." To me it sounded like pure gibberish, but what did I know?

I heard Ridge Arnold acknowledge; Pedicord kept saying, "But you can't—"

Coogan turned on him; I'd never heard such a biting tone in my life. "Shut up, Olin, and do what I tell you! It's life or death; can you understand that much?" Something was drastically wrong with this picture, but I wasn't sure what. At any rate Pedicord nodded, mouthing words that seemed to satisfy Coogan, and turned back to the controls. For a couple of seconds there, I almost convinced myself I knew what was going on.

And then Coogan bent over, clutched his gut, and groaned. I started toward him; so did Larry Des Palmos; he waved us back. Shaking his head: "Of all the insane things to happen! Excuse me; diarrhea, cramps—I thought it was over, but this strain . . . I'll be back as soon as I possibly can." He clumped toward the door, then looked back. "Banning. Please help Arnold get Tixo into the chamber. And *fast*." Hesitating, he added, "Olin! As soon as they've cleared the sending room, begin transmission immediatedly. With or without me. Do you understand?" Pedicord nodded, and finally Coogan minced his anguished way out the door.

I stood, trying without success to read faces. Dauna gripped my arm. "It's a long time until Easter. But if you're going to assist with the Resurrection, hadn't you better move?"

When I reached the building entrance, Ridge Arnold was already coming in. With Tixo like a rag doll over his shoulder, Ridge was panting. I ran ahead, to let him into the sending room.

The chamber's cover was up, and its lid open. Now as Ridge climbed the ladder he could use some extra hands; that's what I was there for. As he eased the little Indian's legs and lower body into the cylinder I tucked the arms in to Tixo's sides and supported the lolling head so that he slid in smoothly, without any of him catching at the rim. Then we stepped down and back, and turned to leave.

"It's not that he's so heavy," Ridge said as we hurried out, "but I was running, trying to make good time."

"Sure. And you did, too." The door closed behind us; now Pedicord could get on with it. We moved toward the safety booth. I found I was rubbing my right thumb against its forefinger; both felt sticky. I looked. What I saw was a minor smear of blood, with no cut to account for it.

I paused. Yes; this was the hand that had cradled Tixo's head. I turned—but we were almost to the booth and I heard the sound of the apparatus beginning its windup.

Ahead of me Ridge held the door open. "Are you coming or what? Hurry up!" I did, and he closed the door.

Detweiler was saying "Too much time; the brain—"

Looking back over his shoulder, Coogan cut in. Whatever his problem he'd made a fast recovery. He said, "There's a slight stasis effect. I have to count on its being enough."

He punched the intercom switch. "Machell!" All of us heard Eddie acknowledge. "Stay on those controls, do you hear me? Don't leave them, not even for an instant. I'm not having any more screwups, Mister, and I'm holding you personally accountable."

Eddie Machell's assent sounded more like a growl, and the way Coogan had talked to him I wasn't too surprised.

Then Nancy Ohara spoke, voice both shrill and chill. "Are you saying *I* made the mistake?"

Coogan shook his head. "No. No. It was here, all of it. But *this* time—" Now the howling rose, and the flickering; Emil the Stork turned to watch Pedicord. I should have been used to the effects by now but still they awed me. By the time the "earthquake" hit, though, I was braced for it.

When the winding-down began, it seemed to take almost forever; until the noise fell to silence, we waited. Then came Ohara's voice, trembling.

"He's alive!"

Trying to speak, Pedicord only sputtered; Coogan shut him up and turned to me. "Come on. Banning, you and I are going over there. *Fast.*"

I didn't stop to think, or to notice what anyone else did; going out the door I was right behind him. Outside, trotting to keep up with the Stork's long strides, I gasped out, "Mind telling me what's our hurry?" I got some breath back. "And how come you leaned on Eddie so hard just now?"

Stopping short, Coogan grabbed my arm. "I needed to find out something, and I succeeded. When we get there, Banning—watch yourself!" And again now, we were moving.

"Watch, *why?* And what was it you found out?"

A quick, guarded look he gave me then. Before he said, "That Machell is the Hornet."

Going into Catcher One I couldn't claim much for clear thinking. Tixo, coming out of the receive-chamber room, was being hugged by Nancy Ohara. Machell stood to one side; maybe it was only imagination that made him look, to me, more frustrated than pleased.

Tixo let Coogan shake his hand; then he gave me the fingers-salute and I returned it. No knife in the act this time, though, nor did Tixo smile. Not that he looked sullen; serious as hell, was all.

Maybe he had a right to look that way; maybe dying took

the fun out of things. I shook that idea off; he couldn't have been *really* dead.

Leaving Ohara to cut Catcher One down to standby, Coogan started herding the rest of us back to Origin. Remembering his most recent advice I made sure to keep Eddie Machell in plain sight. He kept lagging, letting others pass him by; then, about halfway between the buildings, Eddie stopped cold.

Only the Stork and I were with him; the rest had moved ahead. Machell said, "Coogan. You know, of course; you can't help but know. But if you ever hope to collect another dime from Detweiler, you'll keep your mouth shut." And the Green Hornet grinned.

From his voice on the phone I'd guessed I wouldn't like to see the sonofabitch smile in character, and I surely didn't. As he added, "And I still get half; don't you forget it!"

Lips tightening, the Stork nodded; again we moved ahead. I felt dazed, remembering: dead or not dead, when Arnold and I boosted Tixo into the chamber he'd had no breath or pulse, not that I could detect. Yet now, up ahead, I saw him moving along spry as anything.

At Origin everyone was still in the safety booth. Flushed and beaming, George Detweiler gripped Tixo by the shoulders, patted him on the back, then shook Coogan's hand. "You did it, man! I've called my main office; they're sending the contracts and checks by special courier."

The Stork didn't look anywhere near as pleased as a person might expect. Nonetheless everyone began congratulating everyone else; before I noticed, I caught myself shaking hands with Eddie Machell. I started to pull away but he gave me a warning look; I decided against doing anything conspicuous.

Dauna started kissing everyone and vice versa; when Nancy Ohara came in she got the same treatment and seemed to withstand it admirably.

I saw Coogan pull Detweiler aside; all I heard was: "—to seal it right now, no waiting on the red tape. Five percent,

like earnest money in real estate." And George, beaming
like the Buddha himself, pulled out his checkbook and
began writing.

Pedicord, I noticed, was carefully easing the main chamber's power down from ready to standby. Suddenly it
struck me that today I'd seen *two* miracles: not only a man
brought back to life, *but resurrected by having been instantane-
ously transported through space.*

I shook my head. My mind wouldn't handle all the fac-
tors; I was literally overloaded. In more than one way:
suddenly I had to visit the washroom. But just then I saw
Tixo leaving the booth and figured he was probably on the
same errand. All right; I could wait.

To distract myself I went over and listened to Coogan
and Pedicord making their pitch to George. First order of
business, it seemed, was to beef up the power systems. And
move Catcher One to a greater distance, or else duplicate
it. Then to replace the Tixo-sized chambers with larger ones
of more general utility. The Stork emphasized what we
already knew, that only the chambers themselves needed
replacing; their housings had been purposely sized to allow
for this expansion.

Uh-huh; Detweiler scribbled cost figures. . . .

Tixo was taking his own sweet time; I decided to go bang
on the door if necessary. When I got there, though, the
place was empty. I did my business and started back to the
booth, arriving just in time to meet Elihu Coogan, once
again bent over and holding his gut. "Oh, damn it! Excuse
me, Mitch—" I was in his way. "*Another* attack!"

Compassionately I stepped aside. The door ahead
opened again, and Eddie Machell came out of the booth.
His look dismissed me from consideration as he started to
go past, following Coogan.

It was his arrogance that did it. Without forming conscious intent I braced my feet and grabbed his arm, stopping him. Then my thinking cleared; I said, "Outdoors,
Machell. I want some answers."

He tried to jerk loose but my grip held. "Why should I talk to you, Banning?"

I hoped my grin was as mean as his had been. "So I don't start yelling my head off. Right here, right now."

He squinted at me. "You'd blow the whole deal, you know that."

"So what? Nobody's cut *me* in." I hoped my face wouldn't give away the bluff.

I guess it didn't; Machell nodded and we went outside. Around the corner, out of sight of both doors, we stopped. "All right; tell it. Start with how; the whys can wait."

I got the whys anyway; he was so full of himself that once he began he couldn't stop. "—stole my father's discovery and sent him off to die! Pedicord could barely understand it, let alone perfect the application. But Coogan got hold of him and planned how to cash in anyway. He—"

Could all this be true? It didn't matter; *he* believed it.

"You're Edsel Allert?" The skinny guy from the Army picture? Well sure; sometimes people do grow up skinny and then fill out. The bottom line read: yes, he was Edsel Allert and what did I care?

In a way this free flow of information worried me; a suspicious person might have thought maybe Machell wasn't planning for me to be talking with anyone else, later.

The name, though: Edsel McElhaney Allert; Eddie Machell. Amateur trick, modifying a real name to form an alias; very amateur. Still, it had fooled everyone long enough. . . .

Something else, though. "Are you all the Hornet there is?"

"What kind of stupid question is that?"

"It looked more like two. One who killed, another who took pains not to."

"Just me, Banning. Strictly a one-man show."

But why the mixed plans, I asked. The contradictory moves?

The Hornet sneered. "Confusion. Misdirection. It worked, didn't it? To start with, all I really wanted was to discredit Pedicord. And Coogan. And then, if I could, take my father's discovery to someone who'd treat it seriously, and *prove* his genius. Not like this farcical magic act of Coogan's."

"How about the money?"

He gestured scorn. "That's just gravy on the dumplings."

"But you're trying for more of it. Aren't you?"

"I'll take what I can. Who's going to stop me?"

The gun he pulled from his pocket, then, said it wasn't going to be Mitch Banning.

Sometimes I have this inappropriate reaction: when I should be getting scared I go calm instead. I shook my head. "Poor thinking, Eddie. A shot brings everybody outside. Not to mention alerting the gate guards."

Again he grinned. How could I have failed to notice, all this time, what a mean-looking bastard Machell really was? "Not if I shove it up real close."

He used it to gesture. "Back inside. I think you need to go pottie." I started to say I didn't; the revolver barrel jabbed my ribs. "Turn around and start moving!"

Actually the john was an even worse place for shooting, so I didn't argue. Going inside I hoped we'd meet a crowd, but no luck. Instead, just as we passed the Ladies, its door opened and Dauna came out. And before I could say something harmless, hoping she might go away safely, her expression changed and I knew she'd seen the gun.

Machell caught it too; stepping to one side he used the revolver to gesture Dauna forward. "Just follow Banning. I'll ride tail gunner." And to me, "The other john, like I said."

I said, "What if it's occupied? Then what will you do?"

"Reload, if I have to. Keep moving."

I did move, then paused at the john door as Dauna tried to put up an argument. "I don't have to go; I've just been. And besides, that's the *Mens*, so—"

"Shut up, Aunt Phyllis; it's unisex time." If her pitch was meant to distract him, it wasn't helping. As a wrestler I'd specialized in a fast, low tackle, first faking to one side. Here, that might have worked or might not, but the way he kept Dauna between us gave me no shot at it.

There was no place to go but in, so I went. At least the place was empty. I wondered where Coogan had gone now.

First, Machell locked the door. Then, keeping us both in line of fire at all times, he went to the washbasin, reached under it and moved something. And beside him a wall panel opened to show us a narrow, unfinished passage.

Again it was me in first, then Dauna, and finally the Hornet, who closed the opening behind us. The passageway went to our left; in dim lighting, barely enough to avoid bumping into anything, I led off.

It wasn't until I reached a branching corridor that I realized we'd entered an entire network of hidden ways. Any time we came to a choice, Machell said which way to turn. More than once, given just the two of us alone in there, I could have made a break for it: dash to get around a corner and take my chances. Because we passed other panels like the one we'd come in through, and that one hadn't looked terribly sturdy. But with Dauna there, hostage for my good behavior, I contented myself with trying to guess where we were in the building itself.

We went down steep, narrow stairs to a low-ceilinged room about fifteen feet by twenty. There was no other way out, just those stairs. I turned to look at Eddie Machell.

He motioned us to a corner, near a control console alongside a lump of machinery with a big, two-armed crank handle sticking out of it. Machell pushed a button; when nothing happened, he shook his head. "Forgot the safety interlocks." He shrugged. "Cranking it by hand is quieter, anyway."

With the gun he motioned again; at me this time. "Turn the crank: one or two turns clockwise." I couldn't have looked more puzzled than I felt. And now that the immediate threat had receded, I was getting realistically scared. I looked at Dauna: for all her face showed, she could have been concealing boredom. Machell said, "You wanted to see how it really works, didn't you? And maybe I owe you that much."

So I stepped over and applied muscle.

The muscle would have been okay, but on height and weight I ran a bit short. Still, I could have rotated those handles—but I had a better idea. Grunting and heaving, I stayed well shy of maximum effort. But instead of Eddie it was Dauna, at Machell's order, who came to help me.

As we moved into position, taking our stances to give each of us a good grade of leverage on the thing, she whispered, "He's going to kill us."

We heaved at the handles; again, purposefully I used less force than I could have. As we eased off, I whispered back, "He's going to try, you mean."

"Mitch! What can we do?"

"Watch for a break. Find a way to make one. He's not infallible." *Sure* I was whistling in the dark. But Dauna on edge with hope was a better ally than Dauna hopeless.

"That's enough stalling! You don't *have* to live any longer, if—" I know sincerity when I hear it so I put more whammy into our next push. Still, it moved the crank only a fraction; no point in making my previous sham too obvious. But then we gained a little more, and finally we'd done about a turn and a half.

"That'll do," said the Hornet. "You can see all you need to." Waving us back from the machinery, he pointed straight up.

I looked at the ceiling. Part of it had slid aside a couple of inches. And through the crack I was looking up into the transmission chamber housing, at the bottom of the chamber itself.

The significance escaped me, and I guess my ignorance showed. Again pointing upward, Machell made a twisting motion. Then I understood: when these ceiling panels slid farther apart, the chamber's spiral supports would pivot to bring the chamber down *here*. With its lidded end in position to accept or release a test object. Certainly the movable section was heavy enough to provide adequate shielding between here and upstairs.

At Catchers One and Two, no doubt, similar facilities would be found.

I hadn't been breathing; with a shudder I began again. But—how did the subject *get* from here to a Catcher? We'd met the genie from Central Casting, all right, but still I had no idea how he did his trick. And Dauna was shaking her head. . . .

I looked again: at the opening above, the stairs, and a lot of solid concrete. Nothing else. I started to ask the How question, but Machell said, "Cute, isn't it?"

When I did ask, he shook his head. "Crank it shut again." We obeyed. I didn't bother to make it look difficult; that ploy no longer meant anything.

He raised the gun. "That's all you get, folks; I'm running out of time. Which means you are, too. You'll have to take your questions to the big Answer Man in the sky."

No doubt about it; Edsel McElhaney Allert was enjoying himself. I wasn't, though.

"Wait!" Scared was too small a word now; try petrified. Sweat came from unlikely locations; I couldn't breathe right. "Wait!"

He laughed. "What for? You think you can make a deal, promise to keep your mouth shut? I wouldn't believe you. I can't afford to."

The hell of it was, he was perfectly correct. *I* wouldn't have believed me. "Look. Maybe . . ." Suddenly I knew I loved Dauna even more than I'd realized; what I was trying to come up with was some kind of deal to get *her* out of there alive.

But there was no such thing, nothing that Allert would buy. Not fast, I began to edge toward him. "The gun, Allert; upstairs, they'll hear it." Headshake. Well, he knew the shielding better than I did.

The revolver waved me back, but I stayed put. For the first time I took a good look at it, as good as the dim light would allow. Short-barreled .38 on a light frame; if Allert knew handguns at all, he wouldn't try heavy loads in that piece.

With training, you can jump an armed man and live through it. Unfortunately, in Unarmed Combat I'd never mastered that maneuver very well—but at this point, what else did I have going for us? Given the caliber and probable load, if by great luck I did get past the gun and take it away, I might take a peripheral hit on the way in and still survive. Maybe, even, mostly in one piece.

The idea didn't thrill me much. But I did some deep breathing, or tried to, and braced myself to jump. As Allert cocked the hammer for single-action fire, and aimed.

I'll never know if I could have made it. As I paused, teetering at the edge of decision, peripheral vision caught a hint of motion.

Dauna? But my startled gaze went past her, to the stairway opening beyond. And I saw that Tixo had two knives now.

I tried to put my mind on hold, freeze my expression—as Tixo made his silent approach, hands at his sides, with a thumb and two fingers holding the blade of each gem-handled knife.

But Machell's face tightened; he swung around. Seeing Tixo he went pale: the gun's short barrel gave its sharp, ill-tempered bark. In the confined space, concussion stabbed my ears. At least a yard from Tixo, concrete dust flew.

He'd been hell on wheels with a rifle, but handguns weren't Eddie's speed at all. He was shifting, taking a two-handed grip for better aim, when my brains unfroze and I jumped him.

I jumped sloppy and hit sloppy, but I did get his arm down; his second shot spanged off the concrete deck. Allert bucked, trying to throw me loose; my feet slipped but I didn't lose the hold. The gun crashed again. I winced; the blast shock, this time, nearly made me let go. But my feet scrabbled to get me upright for a better grip: arms around the man's chest and neck, then one hand lunging for the gun itself.

For a moment I had it: my grip clenched around the cylinder. That's one thing about a revolver; once it's fired, it won't shoot again until that cylinder turns to the next notch.

My grip was at an angle; I couldn't hold it. As he broke the gun hand loose I settled for a desperation grab that caught his upper arm against his side and hampered his aim.

For a moment we stood deadlocked. Looking across the top of Machell's shoulder, I saw Tixo start his sidearm throw.

First I couldn't dodge; then I did, a little, and the blade lost itself in Allert's neck.

Blood made a fountain, spurting from the wound and missing me by inches. Allert went limp, taking me to my knees before I could disentangle.

Whether he was "dead when he hit the ground" as they say, I have no idea. As he lay there, though, the question was moot.

Dauna helped me stand up; if either of us said anything, I can't remember what. As Tixo came forward, face stretched into agonizing grimace, I wasn't awfully sure we wouldn't be next.

But he came to me, two-finger touched my forehead, handed me the unused knife, and waited while I returned first the salute and then the weapon.

He nodded; maybe he tried to smile. Reaching down, he pulled his other blade out of Edsel McElhaney Allert and wiped it clean on the dead man's shirt. For a moment I saw both knives together. Despite what we'd just seen, the weapons didn't look well-balanced for throwing—but near as I could tell, they were identical. Jewels and all. As Tixo sheathed them he looked up at me; for the first time ever, I saw those dull-pebble eyes reflect light. From tears.

With no thought, my arm went around his shoulders. "Thanks, buddy. I owe you." He couldn't know the words, but maybe the tone helped.

How much he understood, I have no idea. His face showed grief as he pulled at my sleeve and pointed to the room's far corner. Squinting, I made out a bundle of some kind: a roll of canvas, it looked like. I followed him to it, Dauna close behind me.

For a moment Tixo stood; then he squatted to pull at the canvas. Folded back, it uncovered a man's head.

Even in the dim light I recognized the dead face.

Tixo.

CHAPTER TWENTY-FOUR

Shrill-voiced, Dauna said, "I will *not* have hysterics." And she didn't. The way our hands clenched together we'd have bruises later, but at the time I didn't notice.

"Twins," I said. "That explains a lot." It surely did: everything from teleportation and resurrection to the unpredictable ambivalence toward my personal self. And the time at the Trosper Building, when he'd come close to being in two places at once. Dizzied, I said, "I had plenty of clues; I should have guessed. But who'd expect such a thing?"

Suddenly I realized and appreciated how fast Coogan had adapted when Nancy Ohara reported Tixo dead: finding a way to put a temporary save on the mess, bulldozing Pedicord into going along with his impromptu scheme, then faking the upset gut so he could go set it up. Crook or not, the old Stork had moxie.

Besides him and Pedicord, how many were in on the plot? Ansel Borg, of course. The Tixos, following orders without knowing what they meant. And later Machell. Ironic: doing the exact opposite of Coogan's speculation, the Hornet had nailed himself a key spot, privy to *all* the inside scoop.

Now I realized what a smooth job Machell had done on *me*, pretending ignorance in his Hornet guise. Hell, if he and Coogan could have teamed up, and the transporter actually worked, I wouldn't put it past them to clean out Fort Knox.

And was anyone else in the cabal? Maybe, maybe not.

Right now, it hardly mattered. Tixo had his own ideas.

He did a workmanlike job tying the knots, and on the whole I couldn't blame him much. After he pulled the canvas up to cover his dead twin he began to shake; while he hacked out dry sobs I hugged him as though he were a hurt child. Then, backing away a step, he began our knife ritual. But when I did my finale, returning the weapon, he looked apologetic but pointed it at my navel. I couldn't bring myself to argue, let alone try to fight. And Dauna hadn't said anything in some time.

So now my belt confined my ankles. The end of it came up to be held firmly by my knotted shoelaces, their other ends looped around my crossed thumbs. Hogtied was the word for it, in the old West.

Wiggling and fidgeting I tried to get a finger hold on the laces. Absolutely no luck. Dauna had the same situation; her own tie-up was somewhat different but equally effective. And we were each tied also to stationary supports, unable to reach each other.

After a time we lay back and tried to relax. I wondered where the outside entrance was, to the trick basement under Catcher One. . . .

I felt nowhere near as desperate as I probably should have; somehow I was certain Tixo hadn't left us to die there. Not that I understood the inside of the little man's head; for all I knew, my upcoming death was what he'd looked apologetic for. But I didn't believe it. For one thing, his last words before leaving had been, "A few gotha dime Vega tha bear." So he as well as his twin had been exposed to TV commercials. A few more sessions and his English might become positively fluent.

So for hours we lay there. Quick rushes of talking came between long periods when neither of us found a word to say.

For hours. Then when rescue came, it turned out we'd been there roughly sixty-five minutes.

So much for keeping calm.

Capcek, the tall deputy who had come out to deal with the gimmicked transformer, turned us loose. Someone found a nearer exit than the way Machell had brought us down. Dauna broke for the Ladies and I made equally fast time getting to its counterpart; being tied up has a strange and urgent effect.

In the safety booth George paced, Pedicord sulked, Nancy and Hackett and Arnold sat mute. Larry Des Palmos brought coffee to Dauna and me, snuggled up together in Detweiler's big chair.

I appreciated every nuance.

Capcek asked questions. Since I had a few myself, I tried for balance between input and output of info. I didn't manage it, of course, but did learn enough to help my guessing.

Such as: Coogan didn't come back from the toity so Detweiler got antsy. He went looking, came back empty, and found Machell and Tixo also missing. Being George, he ranted some. Largely at Olin Pedicord who, I gathered, mumbled a few things Detweiler found suspicious, then clammed up entirely.

Frustrated out of his mind, Howard Hughes, Jr., blew up and called the law.

By the time Capcek arrived George had driven Pedicord, who looked to be running seriously late for his fix, to the ragged edge. The doctor fell apart, I was given to understand, and showed the deputy a way into the clandestine passageways. Which was lucky for me, because while the doc *thought* he knew what happened to the Tixo twin, he didn't know for sure. So he led Capcek directly to the room under the transmission chamber. And thus to me, and to Dauna.

As best I could, I tried to edit my own testimony. Having heard no mention of any Green Hornet or kidnapping or previous murders, I took the chance of making none myself. If Pedicord's head were working at all, maybe we could still keep this simple.

Why? Sheer self-preservation, for one thing. The fancier it gets, the longer you have to hang around for it. Given a choice, "material witness" was not a role I cared to play.

So what I told was what "everybody knew." The apparently successful test of the transport machine, followed by Machell's killing and the discovery that Tixo was twins. No way of hiding any of that: too many people knew bits and pieces. If I tried to cover for the surviving Tixo, Capcek would pin me.

I didn't testify to seeing Tixo kill Machell. But only we three and Dauna and Coogan had been absent from the safety booth, and none but Tixo carried knives. Anyway, it appeared that circumstantial evidence from others had already fingered the little Indian for Machell's death.

Well, either Coogan would get the two of them away free and clear or he wouldn't; no point in worrying about it.

I could see Detweiler fuming up a storm, and when Capcek finished with me, George cut loose. "Pedicord, you damned *fraud!*" The doc cringed. "And can't anybody find Coogan?"

Ridge Arnold spoke. "He was gone when Deputy Capcek arrived. At least his car was."

"What kind of car?" At Capcek's question, between us we described the red Toyota. No one remembered the license number.

The deputy nodded. "Could have been the car I met, going west, just before I hit the turnoff to here."

"Who was in it?" Detweiler said. "Did you see?"

Capcek frowned. "Let me think." It didn't help him much; he'd had only a quick look and paid no great attention, since for all he knew, the car wasn't necessarily from Range A at all. Two people, though; he remembered that

much. A driver wearing a hat and shades, and a passenger
who sat taller.

"Coogan?" George said.

Capcek shook his head. "No. Balding, I think. Glasses.
And I didn't see a beard."

Detweiler bought it. But Detweiler had never seen Emil
the Stork without his Elihu Coogan trimmings.

Dauna looked to me. I knew, or at least hoped, that we
were thinking along the same lines. My own figuring didn't
take long. The readout was that so far as I knew, the Stork
in his own person wasn't wanted in this state. If he'd
managed to get to town and cash Detweiler's check ahead
of the stop-payment call, could be he'd earned it. The way
I saw things just then, George had his money's worth in
entertainment value alone.

And Tixo? He'd killed his twin's murderer, and for all I
knew, maybe that was the Code of the Amazon. Anyway,
all through this mess the poor little devil had been out of
his league; I didn't want to see him in court, confused,
unable to communicate or understand.

I *didn't* want that. And with the Stork looking after him,
maybe he had a chance.

I knew my attitude flunked all legal standards and most
ethical ones, but that was how I *felt*, damn it! Looking over
to Dauna, watching the play of expression on her face, I
nodded. And was relieved when she nodded back.

For a moment I almost relaxed. But then Detweiler
started yelling again.

It was Pedicord who triggered him. At one edge of my
attention I'd noticed the man talking to him: "—all Coogan's fault, Mr. Detweiler; he never had any real faith in my
work. He's the one who arranged all the trickery—didn't
give me a fair *chance*; put the money into adding useless
fakery, for show. On the larger installation he totally omitted the real—"

And George blew up. He stood, shaking his finger like a
school headmaster. "You damned charlatan! What I'm

damn well going to do—! They'll lock you up and lose the key. You and your halfass scientific doubletalk! When I'm through with you, you can try it on your parole board!"

I had to hand it to Olin Pedicord then; he was being blown out of the water, but he didn't back down. "All right, Detweiler! If *you* weren't such an unmitigated cheap-skate—! But even so, I'll show you. My singularity device *does* function."

And turning away, he ran out the door.

Detweiler shrugged; he asked Capcek some inane question or other, halting the deputy's move to go after Pedicord. I wasn't certain where the action was until the mirrors showed Pedicord entering Origin. At the door he stopped, removed one shoe, and placed it at the lower door-hinge. When he moved on into the room, the door didn't quite close.

A hand gripped my shoulder. I looked around to Larry Des Palmos; he said, "He's jammed the safety interlock." We watched as the doctor went to the smaller chamber, the one that fed Catcher Two.

Somebody—Capcek, I think—said, "What the hell?" Nobody said anything more as we saw Pedicord pull his wristwatch off. It was the one I'd seen in the cardboard box at his apartment: truly a flashy ornament, studded with enough jewels to make a good bicycle reflector. Maybe he was wearing it today to celebrate the big occasion. Now he held it up, waved it, then put it into the chamber.

"What's going on?" Capcek. "We'd better—"

Whatever he had in mind was already too late. Pedicord went to the duplicate, local controls, and began pushing buttons.

Behind me, Des Palmos said, "Oh, Christ! He's bypassing the *other* safety circuits. There's not supposed to be any way—"

That's when the building groaned, and blue glow sprouted.

* * *

All I could do was watch as his damned gadget wound up
the same as always, firing potential fields around at random
and shaking the whole place. It hurt my ears.

I saw Pedicord leave the controls and run for the door.
I saw blue firelike streamers stretch to engulf him, merging
with the blue bolt that snaked out from the doorknob as he
reached for it. With that door ajar, maybe the air currents
drew the ionization; I wouldn't know. But in midstride
Pedicord jerked and fell, skidding and then only twitching.

The machine didn't stop; effects built until we had our
minor "earthquake." At that point the lights went out.

I'd been half standing; now I found myself slumped back
in the chair. Through wraith-light of ionization I squinted,
trying to see what was happening. Fat chance.

And then, inside the sending room, something blew up.

All I could see was smoke. For a moment, until I realized
I was seeing it only through the mirror system, the stuff
seemed to strangle me.

"Ridge!" Larry Des Palmos shouted it. "Disconnect the
Origin and Catcher Two feeds, so I can restore power
here." Arnold said something affirmative; shortly we had
lights again and I could see the two men at the separate
power boards.

I ran to Des Palmos. "Larry—you cut *all* power? Knowing what that would do to the superconductor fields, the
stability of the particle accelerators?"

His face stiffened. "I'm trying to save a man's life."

Standing close to him, I kept my voice low. "Your own
ass, you mean." His eyes widened; I shook my head. "No,
I'm not out to nail you." I heard someone behind me, and
spoke louder. "But it didn't make sense. Pedicord had
already died."

Capcek's hand swung me around. "Who says he's dead?
What makes you so sure? Let's get to him right now!"

I couldn't think; I said, "Come on, then." On the run, I
led the way. Behind me I heard talking, but didn't look to
see who else followed.

Inside Origin most of the smoke had cleared; the first

whiff made me cough, though. Capcek bent over Pedicord and straightened him to lie flat. He checked the mouth to be sure the tongue was clear, then reared back and slammed his fist into Pedicord's chest. Someone gasped; the "cardiac thump" does look a bit drastic if you haven't seen it before.

Capcek tried twice more, then shook his head and crouched to apply mouth-to-mouth. But after two or three breaths he raised his head. "Can anyone else here do this? I have to go call the aid car."

"I can; I've had the course." It was Nancy Ohara; Capcek stood and she took his place. She knew her stuff, all right; she settled in and took up a steady rhythm, just like what I'd seen in cop shows and medic operas on teevy.

Capcek went out; that left six of us standing around. Dauna came over and squeezed my hand. Arnold and Hackett stood to one side, and Detweiler went up to Des Palmos. "Is there any chance," he said, "any chance at all, that the thing *did* work?"

Larry shrugged. "We can take a look. The small chamber itself should be intact." George nodded; the two went to inspect the wreckage. The housing's cover had blown clear; the rest of it looked as if someone had given it the "smoke test" at high power. Well, in a way, someone had. . . .

With Dauna still holding my hand we moved over to see, too. The chamber's lid was jammed, but by main force Des Palmos pulled it open. Detweiler gasped. "The watch! It's gone."

He started to say more; his face showed exultation. But Des Palmos said, "Hadn't we better check the catch box?"

Dauna's quick grip told me she understood as well as I did. George took a little longer, before he shouted "You were in it! Des Palmos, you were in it all the time!"

He swung around. "All of you were! I'll—"

Larry shook his head. "No. Just me. And Machell, of course, but he's dead. The rest here are clean. All of them."

In the silence, suddenly I found answers to questions I hadn't thought about. Such as, how had Coogan—and Tixo—known Machell was the Hornet, the one who'd killed the other Tixo? Now I knew: it was because Machell had been the only conspirator at Catcher One, the only person who *could* have done the killing.

And I'd wondered how the hidden structures had been kept secret. Well, sure! The construction workers had no idea what the project was about. When they left, the hidey-holes were sealed off so we regular, aboveboard tech types never saw them.

But Larry Des Palmos had worked both sides of that fence. Ruefully, I shook my head.

Detweiler waited; finally Des Palmos shrugged. "Working for the building contractor, from the start I couldn't help but smell something fishy. Then one day I overheard Coogan talking with Ansel Borg, the man who got fried when the transformer went bad. And I saw how to cut myself a slice of pie."

He frowned. "I was into heavy money trouble, Mr. Detweiler; I still am. Maybe you can't understand that. But it's the reason why I—"

"It's why you joined a criminal conspiracy; I understand that much, all right. Des Palmos, you're going to—"

Larry cut him off. "You can nail my hide, I suppose. If you don't catch Elihu Coogan, I'm the only one left. But with four men dead of this mess—five, probably"—he looked over to where Nancy Ohara still worked over Pedicord—"maybe that's not too important to me, now." He had guts; I'll hand him that much.

"I went along with it, yes. And when the contract work ended, I pressured Coogan for a nice high-paying job on the project. I *did* that job, though. And I did it right."

Fuming, Detweiler gestured toward the chamber housing. "About you, I'll decide later. Right now let's see what happened to Pedicord's watch." What had happened to Pedicord himself, I noticed, couldn't have concerned George less.

We waited. Des Palmos couldn't raise the chamber's supports to get at what he'd called the "catch box." He went outside for a couple of minutes; when he came back, he said, "I have power on the mechanical controls. May-be . . ."

At the console he manipulated switches. The chamber creaked back and forth, moving a little farther each time. Then something snapped and smoke came out, not much, nor for long. Des Palmos brought a pry-bar over. "Now, I think . . ."

He set the bar and pushed; things moved a little. His face reddened; veins stood out on his neck. Stepping up, I added what push I could manage and the resistance gave. I slipped and fell, not very hard; Des Palmos barely kept balance. He pulled the bar out and set it down, kneeling to reach in and scrabble under the chamber.

In a moment he rose, one hand holding something. "The watch isn't there. But this was."

What he held out was a packet of five-dollar bills.

Beating Detweiler by inches, Dauna grabbed it. She turned back the bottom bill and showed me the one above it. And there, of course, was the dent her pointed thumbnail had made.

We didn't try to explain to George; he wasn't interested. "The watch!" he yelled. "Pedicord *did* transmit it. Some-body call downtown. I—"

"Sure." I was on it already. Progress, Inc. didn't answer right away; the person who eventually came on the line was Tillie Trosper. Considering the way Detweiler was fussing around me, I asked my questions in fairly quick order. When I had the answers I hung up.

I looked at George. "Things blew at that end, too. Some young fellow—Steve Broyles, I think she said—he's trying to hold the fire down with CO_2 extinguishers until the Fire Department can get there. But the girl on the phone: from what she says, she doubts there'll be much left to analyze. Not that she put it that way, exactly." What she actually said was: they won't find squat.

Standing alongside George as though they were buddies, Des Palmos said, "But even so, doesn't the reaction at the far end, resulting from the explosion here—doesn't that prove there *was* some kind of successful transmission?"

George's face went happy again. But I knew better. Oh, Larry *could* be right. But I had a simpler explanation, and was pretty sure it fit. When Des Palmos cut our power, and all the controlling fields went to hell so that things blew, my very own telemetry channels fed the readings on down to Catcher Two. And at that end the equipment tried to conform to, or compensate for, the conditions at Origin.

So everything went crazy there, too. I mean, what else could be expected? You might think a fuse or something would blow, to protect the works. But if anyone finds out how to put a fuse inside a particle accelerator I wish he'd tell me. Especially in the supercooled circuits.

Looking at Detweiler, though, I decided it wasn't the proper time to tell him any of those things.

Capcek came back and relieved Ohara; Pedicord wasn't responding but the deputy kept at it. Then the aid car arrived. Sooner than I'd expected; it must have been fairly near already. It carried a real doctor: an officious type with patent-leather hair, but he did seem to know his business. He hooked Pedicord up to various gadgets unidentifiable to me, shot stuff into his chest and rolled up a sleeve to bare a limp arm.

Then he cussed. "This man's been shooting something! Does anyone know what?" He frowned. "Speak up. It could prove critical."

Tentatively I said, "Heroin, I think." Then, remembering what Coogan had said, "Or some designer drug that substitutes for heroin."

The doctor only nodded, gave further instructions to his helpers, and left to inspect our other casualties. Detweiler took it harder; he came and grabbed my arm, then looked embarrassed and let go. He was learning. . . .

"Banning!" Hoarse-voiced, now. "Dr. Pedicord was a dope addict? And all along, you knew?"

I shook my head. "*Not* all along. Not until the Hornet

had him." Only part truth, but knowing and suspecting aren't one and the same.

Headshaking must have been contagious; Detweiler did it too. "That's another thing. All this, and still we don't know who the Hornet is."

With an effort, I got my mouth closed. The trouble was, sometimes I lost track of who knew what. "Oh, for God's sake, George! Machell was the Hornet. Why did you think Tixo killed him?"

My luck was running true to form; Capcek had come over, close enough to hear me. "You saw it, did you? I thought so."

All right. No point in holding out, so I admitted that much. "And you'll swear to it in court?" Capcek said.

"If need be, I will." Before that point could be taken any further, Dr. Slick-hair returned. He'd found what had killed Tixo: puncture wound at the nape, between two vertebrae, doing the spinal cord no real good whatsoever.

I looked at my right thumb and forefinger. The little smear of blood must have rubbed off on something; no trace remained.

Almost, it appeared, it was time for school to let out. Capcek did have a few more questions. Nancy Ohara admitted that during the first "transmission" operation of Tixo to Catcher One, Eddie Machell had left its control booth for maybe two or three minutes. The timing would have given him the crucial few moments to kill Tixo before the "transfer" was complete. The young woman sounded shaky, and looked it; I decided she and Machell had gotten their romance under way after all. Well, I liked Nancy Ohara and hated to see her hurt. But she was well shed of Edsel M. Allert.

Finally Capcek closed his notebook. With no great amount of approval, he looked around the group. "All right. I have it now, I think. Most of it, anyway. Three people dead here today; I don't like it one bit. A lot of funny stuff, too. But the fraud aspects didn't happen in my county. And that's one thing that does please me; I don't have to bother with them.''

His look became almost a glare. "The deaths, though. Machell killed the one Indian, and the other one got him for it. Pedicord—the aid car hasn't given up on him, but that's just the way they are—he did it to himself. Accident compounded by carelessness, and/or stupidity.''

He moved one shoulder, not quite a shrug. "So I have a set of closed cases. I don't like them, as I've already said, but they'll clear through channels and I can get on with my backlog. So once I've put out an APB on Coogan and the Indian, I'll settle for what I've got.''

The deputy shook no hands nor offered to; he left without good-byes. I was relieved to see him go but I couldn't argue with his attitude.

The man had it right, all the way.

CHAPTER TWENTY-FIVE

I was pooped. Detweiler wanted to jawbone some more, but I talked him into putting it off until the next day. At his office across the lake.

Nobody else had much to say. Ohara looked purely beat: droopy, and hurting. I went to her and took her arm, gently. "Nancy—we're in the book; come see us. We talk, we serve good drinks; if you're lucky and hit Dauna's day to cook, we even feed good meals.'' After a moment she made a try at smiling, and nodded.

One more thing happened. The aid car people took Olin Pedicord out on a stretcher. The sheet was up over his face. Everybody looked, but no one said anything.

Then Dauna and I left. Getting down out of the project area, then onto the public road to and through the village, and onto the freeway where I automatically got into the left lane, I drove but didn't talk. And Dauna, after a couple of tries, didn't push it. What I did was, I brooded.

How much of all this was my *fault?*

Five men dead. Starting with Borg, then Archer Green, and today a Tixo and Pedicord and the Hornet himself. Eddie Machell, Edsel McElhaney Allert, the Green Hornet: he'd killed three of the five on his own account, one way or a lousy other, before the backlash got him. And Pedicord: a lot of *his* desperation was the Hornet's doing, too. Sure . . .

But what if I'd spoken up at the start? If I hadn't fallen over my own feet helping Detweiler cover Borg's death, how many more would have followed? Any at all? Or would Coogan and Company simply have run for the tall brush, leaving the Hornet with no one to sting?

Why had I done what I did? I thought about it but came to no real conclusion. Except, perhaps, that I'd still been trying to make somebody give me back my pants, from when I was a frosh at prep.

I felt no pride. None at all. And certainly not about getting back, in a way, at George Detweiler.

We came home. The mail was all trivia and I put the paper aside for later. The hell with moderation; I mixed a big pitcher of Martinis. While it chilled, we went to bed.

For the first time in my entire life I found myself banging away like your basic savage; even when I noticed, I couldn't stop. Dauna gasped once, but made no other protest. When it was done—when *I* was done—she said, "I didn't kill your baby, Mitch." Then I cried, and we held each other, and she said, "Let's go have some drinks. When you can, you'll tell me."

We got up, acting as if everything was okay. I brought out the Martinis and poured for us. Ice water sides and all, though mine didn't get much play. Dauna phoned out for pizzas; I guess she felt no more like cooking than I did. Then she went to take a shower.

I unfolded the paper and tried the Jumble. At first it

worked. DEIXO gave me OXIDE; circled were the X and I and E. Then KROST. STORK, of course; the coincidence bothered me, but I had an S and an O toward my solution. When I came to THORNE I felt a chill: HORNET, with E and T indicated.

I looked at the "clue" cartoon. A cop waving traffic along; the balloon read "Keep moving." The caption was: "On the freeway, it can keep you going." So I looked at the last scrambled word, DOLCEY, and after a moment flashed on CLOYED and had C and L and D for my final letters. So: X I E S O E T C L D. The answer space indicated a six-letter word and then one with only four.

I suppose the answer was something obvious and easy. I don't know, because T-I-X-O sprang out to my attention and I couldn't get rid of it, and the other letters wouldn't make a word anyway.

Crossword and all, I threw the paper into the recycle bin and never looked at it again.

Dauna rejoined me, sitting unclothed as she blow-dried her hair. The goojie makes noise; we had to yell a little to get through. I refilled our Marts. She said, "Now that I have my story, Chuck Wilford won't print it."

My nod meant "Probably not" or maybe "Who's surprised?"

"The *Times* likes it, though. Including full byline, and word rates nationwide if AP picks it up."

The nod still worked. She said, "So maybe I need a new job. We'll see." Then, "What about *your* story, Mitch?"

Headshakes work, too. "I'm not writing one."

With the dryer she pushed her hair up so I could see the raised eyebrows. I said, "You're not saying anything in yours, are you, about Coogan's other identity?" The quirk of her mouth didn't tell me anything. "Anything *I* wrote would have to center on that."

I leaned toward her. "You and I, Dauna: we're the only ones who know that Elihu Coogan was Emil the Stork. What say we leave it that way?"

She smiled. "Let's drink to it." We did. Then the pizzas

arrived, doing wonders for my blood sugar level and a little something for my state of mind. I didn't even creeb about the anchovies.

Then, after an hour or so of loud but basically harmless comedy on the teevy, we tried bed again.

This time things went better. Dauna said, "Hurricane all gone?"

I said I hoped so.

Next morning I stalled around, delaying my drive across the lake to see Delta Supreme. Even though Detweiler as chief source of company assets was handling the liquidation of Progress, Inc., and would in that capacity be disbursing me a chunk of nice money, I wasn't looking forward with enthusiasm. But a little before ten I quit puttering, tucked a copy of my contract and my stack of project worksheets into the briefcase, and drove off through drizzle.

Grey skies and poor visibility did little for my morale.

At Detweiler's fief, parking was tight; I had a hundred-yard wet scamper to the building. Inside I walked up to the mezzanine and came to the door that still read Executive President. This time I knocked.

Detweiler himself let me in; he was alone in the office. He offered a drink; I settled for coffee. Facing across his big desk, we sat. While he inspected the papers I'd brought, I waited.

Finally he scribbled some figures on the margin of one of my sheets and shoved it over to me. "There it is, Banning. Overall agreed figure, minus payments advanced to date. With various adjustments, also as agreed. Any questions? Or will you settle for the amount specified, right now? It's Coogan's payroll I'm closing out, but all the company's current balance came from me, so a court order gives me *de facto* authorization to liquidate. And *somebody* has to wrap the mess up." As usual, he had to spell out what everyone already knew.

"Nice of you," I said.

He made a thin-lipped smile. "I'm not taking as much of

a bath as you might think. We've recovered most of the Hornet's ransom payments: one installment in a money belt on the body, and the other two from trick hiding places in his car."

George frowned. "An odd thing. From each packet, ten percent of the money was missing."

"Maybe he tithes."

"Oh, I doubt that." Then, brows lowered, he caught on. But he passed it, to say, "What hurts is Coogan, getting away with that check I gave him. I phoned in a stop-payment, but he'd already cashed out and vanished." His right hand clenched. "One more day, dammit, and they couldn't have handed him all that cash. The Creighton-Ogsberth bill, you know?" His voice grated. "Just one lousy day!"

So Cretin-Hogsbreath, the cash-restriction measure, was passed and signed? And in effect immediately, it seemed, under the usual lock-the-barn-door emergency clause. I'd been skipping the news lately. Keeping my voice mild, I said, "You were the one, George, who insisted on rushing the tests."

On his swarthy face, color heightened. "Well, it won't do him any good. There's no way he could wash all that money, this soon. And when he does try, the Feds will nail him."

The Stork? Fat chance. Maybe George and I hadn't kept track of Cretin-Hogsbreath, but you could bet your sweet violets that Coogan had. Even if he wasn't safely out of the country by now, he'd have contacts who'd be able to convert his contraband currency into something negotiable, and likely at not too bad a discount. Detweiler might not think so, but I had faith.

Hell. For that matter, I could probably figure how to do something of the sort myself. Not so neatly, of course . . .

Enough of that topic. I took a quick look at the figure Detweiler had written. The decimal point sat where it should, and the first two digits fit, so why argue?

"I'll settle."

"Shall I punch it in, Direct Deposit?"

"I'd prefer a check." So he brought out his fancy leather-bound check dispenser, the kind with the long duplicate stubs. He filled in the blanks all along one set of forms, and eventually tore off the end piece and handed it to me. For all the pomp and circumstance it looked like any other check in the lower end of six figures. I nodded, said thanks, and started to get up and leave.

"Just a minute," he said; I sat again. Well, I might have known there'd be more to it. He leaned forward. "Banning? How much did you know? Or suspect? I'd hate to think you knew all along."

I tried to sift it through my mind: what *he* would be asking about. What he knew and what he didn't. I'd lost track. I said, "For sure, not until I saw one live Tixo and one dead one."

"But you did suspect something? On what basis?"

I hedged. "When something seems too good to be true, it usually is."

He wasn't done yet. "Another thing I can't understand. Machell: what *was* he after? If it was money, then why did he try to wreck the deception by killing Tixo?"

I'd wondered about that myself. First the Hornet would milk the project, then try to derail it completely. The only way I could figure it was that greed and vengeance kept tripping over each other. Well, Coogan had said the older Allert was paranoid; maybe he meant it literally, and maybe he was right. I said, "When he was getting ready to kill me, and spilling his guts to a certain extent, he said he did it all for misdirection. I think maybe he lost track and got in his own way."

Time to change the subject. "What are you going to do now?"

"About the transport machine?" He shrugged. "Not much; it's too dangerous, with all that high voltage floating around, to set anyone to troubleshooting. I'm closing out Range A as a failed research project and cutting my losses, taking advantange of the R-and-D tax write-off. What else would make sense?"

"You still hold the specs, don't you?"

"That's right. Every single numbered copy. So what?"

"Well, I understand the U of Wash has a pretty good Physics Department. It might welcome a research grant to evaluate what you have."

"Oh?" His patented sneer. "And then what?"

"If the results look promising? Hire some help you can trust, this time, and see what happens. If you want to."

"No." When the firefighters cooled Catcher Two down enough, Detweiler told me, Steve Broyles and Tillie Trosper had volunteered to sort through the debris. Now he said, scowling, "They found something, damaged, that they thought might be Pedicord's watch. Offered to send it out for me to look at. But—"

I leaned forward. "Hell, George! That would *prove* the thing worked."

He shook his head. "I won't be fooled again, Banning. The five-dollar bills: I heard your woman explain how she'd marked the ones Des Palmos found at Origin. And the two Tixos. The damned *rats*, for Chris'sakes! Remember when I marked the one, Machell had to trot quick over to Catcher One? *Sure*, he had an emergency; he had to mark the goddamned duplicate rat, was what."

Detweiler glared. "I can be screwed over; anybody can, in unfamiliar territory. But once I know the score . . ."

His grin was so smug, I had no qualms at leaving it that way. But George was overlooking something. The Stork had never dared put the transporter solidly on the line. He hadn't let any real test be made: only the fixed ones, with duplicate subjects at the Catcher ends.

But *Pedicord* believed in it. And when, desperate to the point of crazy, he made his own suicidal demonstration, he did it *off the cuff*. With neither opportunity nor reason to have a duplicate planted at Catcher Two.

I gave the matter a quick study. If I really wanted to, I could probably argue George Detweiler into an effort that might well wind up making him several billion dollars.

On the other hand, he'd probably yell a lot. And I hadn't slept very well; I was tired. Anyway, there was no hurry about it. I sat back and listened to George.

"Oh, I've turned Pedicord's papers over to my own re-search people, to look at when they have the time. On a quick scan, they haven't made much sense out of them. If they ever do, that would be a different story. I still own the development rights—the license on them, kept alive by this mickeymouse research effort—for some time to come."

"Good enough," I said. George's researchers are fine applications specialists; the Detweiler Commute attests to that much. But theory experts they're not. I stood. "Then we're done here; right?"

"Not quite, Banning." He stood, too. "You're enjoying this, aren't you?"

I gave him my best innocent stare, but he wasn't buying it. Frowning, he said, "Seeing somebody take me, I mean." And I knew he saw something in me that I didn't like much.

I said, "Enjoy it? Not enough to stomach killing, I don't. But still . . ." For a moment, what I enjoyed was watching George Detweiler hang on what Mitch Banning had to say.

I said, "How does it feel, for a change, to have *your* bare butt hanging out?" And I hadn't expected to let loose with anything of the sort.

He blinked once, then nodded. "People don't forget, do they?" I couldn't argue. "Well, neither do I."

The pause quivered with yells that didn't come. Then he said, "You want to buy a few CB rigs cheap?"

"No, thanks."

"Well, then." He seemed to be looking for something to say; then he found it. "Good-bye, Banning. You're not my idea of the ideal employee, but you did good work for your money."

He offered a handshake. Why not? I took it. He didn't try to crunch my knuckles or anything, so I guess that part was okay.

I turned to leave, but at the door I stopped. "George. Whatever—I don't hate you any more."

His forehead wrinkled. "Hate? I never hated you." He looked puzzled. "I don't understand. Banning, you were never important enough to hate."

I said "Sure." Or maybe something else. I went down the

stairs past the tinted glass, out through the drizzle to my car. Starting it, revving up, and leaving rubber on the asphalt as I got out of there.

I was almost to the freeway entrance before I heard myself asking, "What the hell *else* did you expect?"

Something I needed to know. After I-90 got me across Mercer Island and then the lake, I took the exit over to I-5 and then dropped off that freeway into downtown. A block from the Trosper Building I spotted a space vacant, pulled in, and loaded the meter. I crossed the street against the blinking red DON'T WALK and entered the building at a dogtrot. After about a year and a half, an elevator let me out on twenty-three.

In 2310-14 a lot of the mess had been cleaned up. Tillie Trosper sat at the reception desk; she gave me a cheery enough greeting and said, "They're paying me for another two weeks, until Mr. Detweiler closes out the whole smorgasbord."

"That's nice." There was no subtle way to open the subject; I said, "The watch, or whatever, that you and Steve found in Catcher Two. May I have a look at it? If it's still here?"

"Sure. We wanted Mr. Detweiler to see it, but he said it was just another fake and we could—well, you know how he talks, sometimes."

Did I ever. But now, to cases. Tillie opened a drawer and handed me something.

It was the watch, all right, or had been: the gaudy oversized gold hunk with a lot of gems on it. To one side the settings were empty and partly melted; I looked at the stones still in place and tried to guess whether they were the real thing or expensive-looking glass.

No question in my mind: this was the watch I'd seen in Pedicord's apartment. And from the brief glimpse I'd had, I was *almost* certain it was the object he'd placed in the chamber. There could hardly be another like it—unless, even in extremity, he'd been relying on a previously planted, deliberately distinctive ringer.

But would he risk his life on a mere trick? At the time, I'd taken his actions as a desperate plea for belief. The trouble was, I'd never known Olin Pedicord in any depth.

I turned the wrecked timepiece over in my hands. At one edge the backplate had sprung loose by about a millimeter. I pried at it—but the other side, for a short distance, showed back and case melted together.

I'm not sure why it was that suddenly I wanted to see the inside. But I did. So from the back room, what was left of the Catcher Two installation, I brought a maintenance tool kit.

The third screwdriver I tried was the right size to pry the back of the watch loose. The works, I saw, no longer could; no surprise there. What did jar my sense of wonder was the inside of that back cover. There were letters engraved on it.

Toward the heat-damaged side some characters were blurred to illegibility. I squinted at what remained . . .

> *To Olin*
> *th Love*
> *etchen*

. . . and remembered the letter written in purple ink.

Gretchen's dreams wouldn't be coming true, now. For seconds I was hung up on the very moot question of whether Pedicord ever intended to do right by his *Liebling*. *Nil nisi*, I decided.

Another, related matter fretted me. Pedicord's apartment must be cleaned out by now, its contents ransacked by police and possibly Detweiler's people also, before being discarded. So the letter was gone, and the address with it. Gretchen, poor Gretchen, would wait and wait, never knowing that her baby was half-orphaned.

On the other hand, did the kid need a junkie daddy?

I thanked Tillie and took my leave. Not mentioning that I was also taking the watch.

I left a receipt, though. In the drawer. George could look at it any time he wanted to, and call me, and I'd give the watch back.

Any time.

CHAPTER TWENTY-SIX

No matter how I sliced it, though, there was still some-thing missing in this charade; if I thought hard enough, maybe I could find it. And finally I came up with an answer.

Machell pumped Pedicord; there's another set of specs. Changing directions, I drove to Eddie Machell's place.

Only yesterday, he'd died; at his door one newspaper lay lonesome. The lock was a credit card special; I went inside, and found I wasn't first in line. The place was a right mess.

I prowled it anyway. But I didn't expect to find what I wanted, and I was right. When I came upon the little stack of letters addressed to Edsel M. Allert, plus a few other things pinning down Machell's true ID, I knew the answer.

Against all reason, cops hadn't searched here yet. But Emil the Stork had. And unlike me, he'd got what he came for.

I let myself out. Driving home I found I was hoping that someday, somewhere, Coogan would line up a crew that could make the device work. Which in some measure would depend on whether he *believed* it could.

I got home and Dauna wasn't there. I tried to put my mind to work; it had to be good for something, and now was as good a time as any. Eventually, over coffee, it gave me a readout.

One more thing needed checking; it wasn't even a good long shot, but still I had to see for myself. I trudged down to the car and took off again. To park, eventually, behind the building where Olin Pedicord had lived and possibly in the very same space at which Dauna and I had delivered him wrapped for parcel post. On the door upstairs, once again the credit card worked; inside the gutted apartment, so did the lights.

Beyond the usual bereft air of rented rooms between tenants, Pedicord's erstwhile digs had a pathetic, almost raped look. Because the place wasn't cleared out, really. Police and maybe Emil before them had rummaged and taken what suited their needs; all else had been left as debris, scattered and meaningless.

I wasn't sure what I was looking for, so I had no idea where to start. All right, take the easy parts first. The bathroom was simple enough: cabinets, clothes hamper, and the junkie's safe deposit box, the toilet tank. Nothing. As expected.

Bedroom. The mattress was ripped apart, its innards a mess all over the floor. The dresser's drawers much the same, and its upright empty shell retained only dust bunnies. Bedside stand overturned, drawer space vacant. I pawed through piles of clothing from the stripped closet and found nothing useful, not even in the pockets.

The kitchen held a wider grade of miscellany, places to search and items to look through and discard, but the result was still No Sale.

Which left the living room-cum-office. Formerly upholstered furniture sprawled dissected; a fast slashing search had seen to that. Around the thoroughly emptied desk lay miscellaneous papers but nothing of import: bills, receipts, a laundry list, coupons—One Free Entree—from a restaurant chain. Those I pocketed; Pedicord had no more use for them, and you never know.

One filing cabinet lay on its side; the component drawers were stacked loosely beside it, and more scattered papers required fruitless inspection.

The other cabinet, still upright, was a different matter; its empty drawers came out on slides, against stops, and weren't detachable. Absently I shoved them closed, one after another.

The bottom one wouldn't go in all the way, but what the hell. Anything this old . . .

Oops, wait a minute. I pulled it out again and tried to

reach my hand in and down behind, to see what might be in there, but my arm wouldn't stretch that far. Okay, tip it over. But a bottom panel frustrated me.

Oh come *on*; anything you can put together, you can take apart. There had to be some way. Carefully I began to look over the details of this assembly. It took a time, but finally Bingo.

The top came off. The heads of six screws, long since covered by so many coats of paint that their outlines could barely be distinguished, revealed themselves to the laborious chipping action of my penknife's tip. Back in the kitchen I knelt to sort through cookware and a few miscellaneous tools to find a rusty screwdriver. A half hour, two skinned knuckles and a wealth of creative cursing later, one framework of dried and aged wood grating against another, the top came free.

So. I laid the decapitated object on its side, pulled all drawers out to their fullest extent, and went in, head and arms. The wadded papers at the far end, crunched around one corner of the lowest drawer so as to be wedged against both the bottom and left side, looked faded. Carefully I pulled and wiggled, hoping not to tear them, and finally they came away.

Mostly, at least; some fragments ripped off and stayed stuck in there, out of sight and out of reach, but as I brought the sheets clear and partially smoothed them, a quick glance showed that I'd lost nothing but blank margins. Those didn't concern me; when my creaking knees brought me upright, I sat on the ravaged arm of a once-overstuffed chair and inspected my booty.

Most of it was written in Higher Math. Not all, though— and what text and sketches I did see made it clear that I'd salvaged a well-aged copy of the plans for Pedicord's matter transmitter.

Not a complete one: checking the scribbled page numbers I saw I had recovered roughly the latter third of the fifty-four-page work. Not exactly a working proposition.

Looking more closely, I found two things very puzzling. First, the handwriting—or rather, printing. I'd seen the doctor's scribbles; what I had here was neater, more precise. But maybe this was written before he got on drugs. . . .

Then there were the comments at the bottom of each page. Every time, the same irreverent "BLA." Why would anyone keep saying that about his own work? But even without a drug habit, I supposed a man could have his down days.

Once more I looked around the room. What I had was little or no help, but I decided to keep it for souvenir value. Folded more carefully, the pages went into my jacket pocket. Then, closing the door behind me, I went downstairs and out to my car.

Home again, I found Dauna drying off from a shower. Over dinner, one of my better efforts at gourmet thawing, I told her of my half-hope that Emil might someday, somewhere, actually build a working model.

She laughed. "If he can trust himself not to pick his own pocket, I'm all for it."

For the rest of the evening we managed to say nothing more about any part of Project Detweiler.

Before I went to bed that night I took a better look at the old, incomplete matter-mover plans. Trouble was, the first page in my possession began partway into some kind of complex function derivation; since I had no idea of its starting point, I couldn't tell if it really went where the conclusion indicated it did.

Finally I gave up and shoved the wrinkled pages into a drawer. After that I forgot about them.

Or tried to.

Over the next few days I worked toward putting my life back to normal mode. After such long and intense involvement in the project it wasn't easy, but I gave it my best shot. Customers called me, and I called some possibles myself. I picked up a few small jobs, nothing that tied up very much of my time.

One of the first things I did, though, was get off a sizable check to Liliane at Hilo on the Big Island. With only the project salary coming in for the past few months—no money from other jobs and no writing income at all—the support payments had been running chronically late. Not late enough to elicit one of Liliane's more volatile letters, but definitely on the laggard side. As usual when it came catch-up time I made my apologies by way of paying a couple of months in advance. With that nagging guilt off my mind, I hoped I could settle down better.

But hard as I tried to get comfortable again in the old rut, I couldn't. Too many things still bothered me.

I wasn't surprised when Steve Broyles, after collecting a final paycheck, simply vanished. But Ronnie Detweiler was gone, too; neither her phone nor doorbell brought any response. After the first few days I quit trying; maybe she'd left town.

Then one afternoon, a few weeks after the balloon went up, Ronnie called me. I was using a lot of scratch paper on problems concerning a rather dull piece of work, and welcomed the chance to set it aside.

Ronnie asked me to come over. "You can help me take care of some excess champagne, Mitch. It's chilling now."

When people want to surprise you it's not polite to ask questions. "Half an hour," I said, and hit the timing almost exactly. This time when I rang the bell, the door opened.

Deliberately posed, Ronnie stood in the doorway. No wig today: the Steve Broyles haircut, now grown out a little, was styled into short auburn curls. As I took time to see the rest of her, she smoothed an unruly one back.

Again her eyebrows formed slim winged arches, and under the sheer, pale green robe I saw the breasts had regained their earlier contours and maybe more. She said, "You like?"

"Well, your chestal area's made a comeback." She looked disappointed. "Hell, you look great!"

Ronnie let me in then, and pulled a bottle from the ice bucket. The way she took hold of it, I saw she intended the big "Pop!" with wine gushing all over, so I said, "Let me?"

and eased the stopper free. Waste not, want not. Then we sat.

She raised a toast. "To *me!* Maybe you haven't noticed, but with this robe it should be obvious. I've had the operations."

"So that's where you've been." She nodded. I tipped my glass again. "Congratulations, I guess."

"You *guess?*" I'd said the wrong thing. "I achieve what I've wanted as long as I can remember, and you *guess?*"

I felt my face redden. "I'm sorry. It's just that I—I can't possibly identify. You know? But—you do have my sincere congratulations. Because it's *your* wish that's come true."

Then it was all right. I even felt free to ask how she'd managed it so soon. The money, for basics . . .

She looked cautious. "I'm not sure . . ." Then she grinned. "But *you* wouldn't tell, would you?" Not waiting for any answer, she said, "Eddie Machell. All I did was ask you about a job for him, but he said he owed me. When he gave me something out of his first pay, I thought it was nice of him and forgot all about it. But then he kept doing that, every payday."

And? There had to be more, and I thought I knew what it was going to be. "And—?"

After a moment she nodded. "Yes. That wouldn't have been enough, not this fast. But—" She paused while I refilled her glass, then said, "Three times, right out of the blue, he gave me *big* sums of money. I couldn't think why; when I'd ask, he'd say I was his lucky charm, or his agent. Except that once he looked at me sort of funny, and said it was for insurance."

So much for Eddie Machell, devout tither. In a way, though . . .

Another thing. "Something I want to know." I asked.

She shook her head; the curls bounced. "Not really. Oh, I had suspicions, but I didn't *want* to believe he could be the Hornet."

I remembered the mean grin, the short-barreled .38. Ansel Borg and Archer Green and the little dead Tixo. "He was, all right. Take my word."

"Oh, I know that now. And I finally figured out why he paid me the big money. He thought I knew *then*; he was buying me off."

And so much for Santa Claus. Too bad, Virginia . . .

Ronnie had more on her mind. Like my male reaction to her, now that she was ". . . a real woman. Well, as real as I'm going to get, and I *am* happy with the result."

Searching for an answer both honest and ego-stroking, I came up with, "You're an attractive person. Attractive as all hell. But now or later, keep in mind that I'm taken."

Her grin took an impish cast; I wondered if I'd made a stupid, egotistical assumption. But what she said was, "You're off the hook anyway." Impish changed to wry. "After all my struggle to become a woman, it seems I'll be a gay one."

Huh? "But all along, you could have—"

"No. I couldn't. You don't understand; it's *different*."

She was right; not even a little bit did I understand.

Ronnie wasn't finished; she said, "What did it was being Steve; the status and respect he had, just as a matter of course, that I'd gotten used to doing without. Oh, not with everybody—not you, for instance. But overall, after a while the unfairness got to me." She gestured. "You could say it politicized me. Put me off men altogether. For now, anyway."

Feeling confused but determinedly amiable, somehow I got through the rest of that conversation. When we hit a pause I checked my watch. "Oops. Good booze and good company, but I'm due home."

One last toast: mostly, I suppose, to affirm that we still liked us. Then, most graciously, Ronnie saw me out.

Actually I didn't need to be home just then—or, for that matter, anywhere else in particular. The day had turned sunny; being indoors didn't suit my mood. On a whim I worked my way over to I-5 and headed north. Toward Range A.

I know perfectly well you can't go home again. And why. It's because it's not there any more. But still I had a hankering to go look, to see what there might have been to see all along, that I'd missed at the time. Color me morbid, but that's not how it felt.

No gate guards now, and only a few cars in the lot. Near Origin I saw a number of pencil-protector types; some of George Detweiler's research people, those would be. They went straggling toward Catcher One, leaving behind a man I recognized: Larry Des Palmos.

I walked over, we said hi. He added, "Don't say it. I was surprised, too, when Detweiler asked me to stay on and help shepherd his tame research boys."

"Just one jolly surprise after another, our George."

Then I asked, "Are they finding out anything?"

"What I tell them, mostly." I waited. "Not, for instance, that a lot of the gear was just to put on the Frankenstein show."

"The what?"

"Are you simple or something? All that high voltage display, the ionization coronas, the noise, the earthquake substitute. The real working high voltage circuits are tucked away safe where they belong; none of the special-effects stuff had doodly shit to do with sending anything anyplace, and none of it was in Pedicord's original plans."

"Pedicord. He *said*—"

"Right. Coogan let him buy and install real hardware for the Catcher Two link, but then he had me add Show Time. On Catcher One . . ." He shrugged; no need to spell it out.

Oh-kay. The electrical pyrotechnics, I could see. And of course the condensation, fogging the chamber housings, was purposeful. To make *sure* no hugger-mugger could be seen.

But the "earthquake"? About that part, I asked.

"Easy. There *are* some heavy-duty machines involved. Coogan just had one of them, at each location, mounted badly: one corner off-level and a bit loose, maybe. Enough to build vibration 'til all hell wouldn't have it."

"So a lot, maybe most, of Detweiler's money went into wool to be pulled over his own eyes?"

"You could say that."

"Have you told him? Are you going to?"

Des Palmos gave me a pitying grin. "Me? I'm not paid to be an expert, just a hardhat strawboss." The grin turned wry. "If Coogan had been on the level—and I wish to hell he *had* been—I could have done him a lot of help. And still could. Assuming Pedicord had a real McGuffin, and now I think maybe he did."

What Larry thought, I knew for a fact, but he wasn't my idea of first choice to confide in. Instead, "Help? How's that?"

"I have more info than you might think." Then he gave me a sidelong look. "Never mind. Maybe it wouldn't be enough, anyway."

Whatever he'd started to reveal, that door had closed. I said, "But to George, I gather you're not offering."

He shrugged. "Detweiler's getting exactly what he pays me for. Sure, he's given me a break here, sort of, but it's not all gravy. And I'm not forgetting he killed Pedicord, bullied him out of his mind so he tried that test with the interlocks cut out and a big chance it would kill him." Then, more quietly, "Don't ask me why, but I kind of liked that crazy old skagger."

He pointed a thumb toward the Catcher One building. "So the stuff in there, let the Ph.D.s sort it out."

And wasn't that more or less the same decision I'd made? I had no license to point fingers. I said, "Well, have fun. Nice to see you," and went away.

While thinking: with all his cunning, Emil the Stork had truly outfoxed himself this time.

Driving down I-5 I passed the off-lanes to I-405, the Eastside freeway to Bellevue. Which brought George Detweiler to mind again, this time so solidly I couldn't get him out.

All else aside, the man deserved to know what he had: that the singularity device wasn't the Frankenstein's-lab thing we'd all thought it was. And mainly, that it *worked*.

I pulled off to the shoulder and stopped. By the time the cellular phone had been due for removal, along with the second one indoors, I'd played with it enough to decide it was worth keeping, so I'd had it transferred from the Detweiler Industries account to my own. Now I punched up Detweiler's office number.

His secretary took my name and put me through with less delay than I expected, but when Detweiler answered he said, "We have nothing to say to each other."

"Wait, George! There's things you need to know."

"Not from you, Banning." I tried to put a word in, but he overrode me. "Get this straight, and get it for keeps. If you offered me everything you have in the world, which probably isn't all that much, and threw in your girlfriend and your firstborn son if you ever have one, I'd spit it all right back in your face. You have used me, Banning; you've tricked me and insulted me. Now get the hell off this line. And if you ever come near me again . . ." He didn't finish it; abruptly, he hung up.

I'd tried. But sometimes you break something, there's just no fixing it. Maybe in this case it was broken from the start.

I waited for a hiatus in the flow of cars and gunned back onto the freeway. After a while I began to feel good again. Driving on a sunny day in light traffic will do that for you.

What the hell? I *had* tried.

At home I found Dauna lounging in her nakeds. "Mitch!" Arms open, she rose to greet me; I went over for a big hello with kisses. "I won the war. Bulletins follow."

"I shall return." And in a minute or so, carrying a beer, I did. Snuggling seemed like a good idea. "Bulletins, you said?"

She laughed. "General Haig outflanked the Wilford forces and carried the day. Chuck *hated* my Aladdin's lamp story. But when AP picked it up for big, he lowered his flag. Unconditional surrender. Now he wants an expanded version for the magazine." The next laugh was more a snicker. "Actually I had help from Howard Hughes, jr. He came out so heavy-handed, demanding that the story be killed locally when it already was, that he put Chuckie's back up. That's when I got the Seal of Approval."

She wriggled loose. "As part of the settlement I get treated to dinner with Chuck and Ned. I'll need a shower."

So I'd be eating out of the freezer. Oh, well . . .

I turned on TV. PBS was doing a series on genetic engineering. What caught my attention was a line of research aimed toward allowing choice of just about any given characteristic—eye color, for instance—from either parent.

As a short man attached to a woman who probably didn't want short kids, I found the possibility quite interesting.

While I mulled the idea, Dauna came out, dressed to go. She handed me an envelope. "I forgot to put this on your desk. It's all the mail you got today. It's like you're retired. Are you?" Not waiting for an answer, she kissed me and left.

I looked at the envelope: no return address, and the usual illegible postmark we get these days. Opening it, I unfolded the single sheet I found inside.

> A note of appreciation, my boy. Judging from the news releases, you haven't seen fit to apprise the authorities concerning past events or identity matters that are really none of their business. My thanks to you, and be advised that my diminutive associate wishes you well and regrets the circumstances of your recent parting. We are relocating the enterprise at a considerable distance; you may wish to keep abreast of news from abroad.

No signature, only a drawing. If I hadn't known from the text, I doubt I could have figured it out.

The Stork couldn't draw any better than the Hornet had.

When Dauna came in, happy as a clam at high tide and just slightly on a glow, I knew what she'd have in mind for next. First, though, I said, "Announcement! Announcement! Battle plan!"

She squinted at me. "Dauna—for the next week or two

let's go someplace. So far that it costs ten bucks to send us a postcard." She nodded.

I didn't check the postal rates where we went, but I bet we came close.

CHAPTER TWENTY-SEVEN

Home again, we were barely unpacked when the Alaska job fell into my lap and took us north for a couple of months. Yes, this time Dauna came along. She wangled an assignment, with national syndication, on outstanding achievements in native schools; while bush pilots flew me to places not on the maps, she visited Innuit towns from the Arctic coast to Kotzebue Sound and Bristol Bay.

A snowmobile got me from a place I can't pronounce to one I can't even spell, where I installed some specially altered equipment for a rather exacting client. A plane held together only by the pilot's devout faith delivered me to Fairbanks, where Dauna met me with the plane tickets for home.

Two months up north, and we must have spent at least four days together. Not exactly what I'd anticipated. So a long boring airborne time later, when we arrived home via the shuttle from Sea-Tac East, I looked forward to further R-and-R.

Which, for a welcome change, we could afford quite a lot of.

After warming up two months of accumulated chill, home was in good shape. I made coffee and settled down to the answering machine. For so long a trip I'd patched in an extra tape deck.

I did find quite a lot to plow through, sampling each call and flipping ahead past sales types and fundraisers.

Two job offers were past the bid deadline; any time you leave town, that's the chance you take.

Ronnie Detweiler sounded plaintive. ". . . hasn't turned out much like I expected, and dammit you're about the only person I can *talk* to, so call once, won't you?" There was a pause, then, "Oh yeh, Mitch; this guy called, a kid more, got the bum's rush from my dear brother and sounded like maybe you could do him some good. So I hope you don't mind, I gave him your number."

If Ronnie wasn't a mite bombed she gave a great imitation. "Call now, act without thinking." Okay, I would. But later.

I caught several seconds of borderline porn bait from a 900 exchange. I really don't know why our peerless leaders license something on the one hand and prosecute it with the other.

Possibly this is why they're rich and I'm not.

When Dauna came to sit beside me I lost track of one call and had to reel it back. A rather young-sounding male voice, saying, "Mr. Banning, I need to talk with you. This is very important; I will pay you your normal consultant fee for your time. Please return my call; thank you," and he spelled out his number. Adding, "Extension two-twenty-three."

I called it; a motel switchboard operator answered. I said, "Security check, sorry to bother you but we need confirmation on identity. Room two-two-three. How listed, please?"

Even over the phone, that grade of indecision is evident. Finally she said, "Two-two-three? Mr. Allert, Mr. D. L. Allert, of Chicago."

I must have looked like the rube wondering which shell the pea was under; as I hung up, Dauna said, "Did you see a ghost or was that the IRS?"

I explained. "I suppose it has to be a relative. But whatever he wants, I don't have it for him."

And so much for that. By now we were pretty well

unwound from travel. The rest of the phone tape could wait for morning.

I slept later than intended and got up to find that Dauna had already gone out and replenished our more perishable foodstuffs. For once I ignored cholesterol; this day was made for eggs and toast and Canadian bacon. Pouring my third cup of coffee, I picked up the phone. At the motel a different voice answered; I asked for two-two-three.

He must have been sitting beside the phone, just waiting; he picked it up before the first ring was done. "Hello?"

"Mitch Banning here." Neither saying his name nor asking it: *your move.*

"Uh, thanks for returning my call. When may I see you?"

"You have my address. Can you find the place?"

"I bought a map."

If it had all the tricky one-way street segments right, it beat any I'd seen. I checked my watch and decided to give him a break in case he got lost, which was not unlikely. "Ten-thirty all right?" He said yes. "Okay; see you."

Dauna's brows drew down. "You're sure this is a good idea?"

"What's to worry? If the guy meant any funny business, why give warning?" I checked my watch. "Going in to work today?"

"Afternoon will do. I want to see this Allert person."

"I don't, especially. But he came all the way from Chicago, or so he says. So I may as well get it over with."

At ten-twenty-eight he came climbing up the outside steps.

Dauna went toward the bedroom. "I'll stay in there a few minutes; if I hear anything I don't like, hello nine-one-one."

"Sure." At our rarely used front door I let the guy in. He was young, all right; barely out of college, if he'd gone there.

"Mitch Banning." I put my hand out; as we shook I eyed

him. Any resemblance wasn't to Eddie Machell as we'd known him, but more to the skinny-faced picture.

He was an inch or so taller, if that mattered. I waited.

"Del Allert. I, uh, didn't want to give my name over the phone because—well, I thought you might not want to see me." No kidding? "You see, I'm Eddie Mac's brother. I can't help that."

When he grinned he looked even younger; well, Eddie hadn't seemed anywhere near the thirty his records indicated. I said, "Quite all right, Del. Now what brings you here?" And I didn't mean whatever wheels he happened to be driving.

"The newspapers." I'd walked him on into the living room; now I indicated a chair. He sat, then leaned forward. "Eddie Mac's death, and Olin Pedicord's."

"The papers told it straight: one slightly suicidal accident and one eye-for-an-eye killing. The provocation, plus two other murders Eddie did all by himself, brings the box score up to five. Did you read about those, too?"

He waved me off. "I'm not here to justify Eddie Mac. It's about my dad's work, that Pedicord stole when dad fired him."

Another paranoid? Carefully, "That's what Machell said."

"Who?"

"The name Eddie used here. And that's why—"

"I know. Look—let me tell it. I was there."

By "there" he meant the time of collaboration between his father and Pedicord, and its end. Bernard Allert, Del said, hired Pedicord to help develop the singularity device, partly because Allert was weakening due to a prolonged fight with cancer but also because Pedicord had genuine insights into the processes and effects Allert wished to produce. Salary was fairly low but augmented by a contractual share in any eventual profits.

"Wait a minute." This didn't fit. "The way I heard it, your father worked for Pedicord."

"I have Dad's financial records. At home, that is. Including Social Security deductions, and those can be checked."

All right, so somebody had lied. Probably Pedicord to Emil, but no matter. It was time to get Dauna in on this, so I called a pause to bring her out and introduce them. Young Del was visibly impressed; whatever Dauna felt, she wasn't showing. Polite enough, but keeping her reactions to herself.

It was too early for booze and maybe our guest was a bit young for it; I suggested coffee, made a fresh pot, and did the honors. With everyone set up, I said, "So Pedicord was the employee; we'll take it as read. Then what happened?"

For some time things went well, then Allert began to find irregularities in the other's work. Pedicord blamed the lapses on stress and promised to do better; needing the man's help, Allert hoped for the best. He was nearing a critical stage of development, ready to begin translating the specs into equipment that could handle *objects* rather than mere particles. "He'd already transmitted alpha particles," Del said, "which proved a major point because they carry a detectable mass but no charge."

He shrugged. "Transferring charge doesn't mean much; there are too many other ways to do it." But with this more clear-cut grade of transmission to demonstrate, Bernard Allert was close to signing up a sponsorship package: three high-powered investor groups. They had to be; to transmit tangible matter, the kind you can pick up and heft, he needed supercooled particle accelerators. Those don't come cheap.

"He had a feeler out for partial governmental funding, but Eddie said he'd better stay clear of that; they'd want control. And by that time we had nearly enough backing without it."

But then, "Dad caught Pedicord shooting up; they had a row. Dad fired him, and paid off more than we could really afford, for whatever share he may have earned." Del didn't know, nor did any of his family, how Olin Pedicord managed to get away with the research data: notes, mathematical proofs, proposed equipment specs; nearly everything, paper *and* disc, was gone. "He couldn't get the hard disc out, but he wiped it. And took along the guts, the most important hard-to-get parts, of the breadboard model."

Pedicord's paper had claimed actual transmission of alpha particles. Assembling his demonstrator around stolen apparatus?

Del grimaced. "Dad tried to rework the basic equations from memory, something to build on, later. But with the medication and all, his recalls were shaky. And there wasn't time; he didn't last three months. So the whole package fell apart."

And then? "Eddie Mac came home from the Cape, from the hospital there, a week before dad died. Still had the cast on and a lot of bandages. He always wore his helmet, riding that cycle, or he'd've died; even with it, he was never the same. Just like all those pills he had to take, cortisone or something for his shoulder, pudged his face out and part of it stuck."

Which explained some discrepancies.

"So Eddie got hurt," Dauna said, "and your father's research data was stolen, and he died. What did you do then?"

Bernard Allert had sworn out a warrant on Pedicord: theft of the data, which made it fraud to accept the kill fee on future gain. But the man had vanished. "Mom hired a detective agency, but we couldn't afford them for very long. Settled for their newswatch service: they look for names or happenings and send you clippings; then they'll follow up if you authorize it."

"But it didn't get you much."

"No. There was one magazine article, all about—"

"We saw it," Dauna told him. "The man who built black holes in his basement."

"Yes. A blind lead, though. Pedicord gave the interview, collected his fee, and went away. The writer had no idea where."

To take even that much of a chance, the good doctor must have been well juiced. But the magazine piece, most likely, was what brought him to the attention of Emil the Stork.

We were off the subject. "Eddie. What did *he* do?"

Young Del looked distressed. "I'd never seen him like that; he'd always been easygoing. But now it was like something was driving him. I mean, dad had been hurt and angry, and for good reason. And mom was dog set on getting our own back, which was natural enough. But Eddie Mac got to brooding. You never knew how he'd take things. Sometimes too calm, sometimes so mean that even Alice shied away from him. Our older sister, she is."

Alice the letter-writer, not of the greatest literacy. "She wrote to Eddie," I volunteered. "I saw the letter."

Embarrassment showed. "Alice is—she's a very sweet person. But while Mom was carrying, she caught some kind of fever, and Alice—well, she's what they call 'differently gifted.' Which sounds like candy-coating—except, I think perhaps she really is."

That was nice. But, "About Eddie, you were saying?"

"I don't know where he got his leads, but one day he just said he was heading west, and left. Wrote Alice one letter, we found out later, saying he'd caught up with Pedicord and was going to fix his wagon for keeps, but not to tell the rest of us anything until he said so. And she always minded Eddie."

Dauna's nod indicated sympathy. "So you couldn't know . . ."

"Not until the clippings, which the agency didn't get around to sending for quite a while. And then I came out here myself."

Right, but how . . . "How did you get to Mitch?" Dauna looked puzzled. "I don't recall his name in the write-ups."

"No. It was just all the deaths, and Eddie Mac with both his real name and another one, being one of the victims but maybe a killer too, and a man named Coogan wanted for embezzlement. Along with some shadowy Oriental character, possibly a spy." I guessed the out-of-town papers had embroidered things a little.

"And all this happened," Del went on, "at some secret project, shut down now, run by something called Detweiler

Industries." He spread his hands. "It had to be the singularity device; what else would Pedicord have?"

"So you looked up George Detweiler." He nodded. Of course; this kid was the guy Ronnie had mentioned. For a while there, I'd forgotten her message.

I sighed; that woman was *always* sending me Allerts. At least this one went by his right name. "And asked him what?"

"For information. A chance to show him that what he'd bought wasn't Pedicord's to sell. To arrange some sort of fair settlement, a share in the device and future repayment of at least part of his losses, if he'd release it for development. I think mom and I could get dad's backers rounded up again, or new ones; she did a lot of the contact work the other time."

"And good old George, the picture of fairness and generosity . . . ?" I waited for his reaction.

"Picture of scatological abuse is more like it!"

"Just testing. He threw you out?"

"Not physically, but close to it. And threats, of course."

Of course. Del continued. "Going down the stairs I met this woman. Redheaded, very striking. I guess she'd heard some of the loud parts. She just took my arm and walked me down, over to the company cafeteria for coffee. Pretty soon I was telling her the whole story. She grinned a lot, but sympathetically; you know? And then she wrote down your name and address and phone, and told me to look you up. Said if anyone could or would help me, it was you."

And obviously hadn't said who *she* was. So neither would I. All I did say was, "The trouble is, I can't think how."

Well, there were a couple of things. At my desk I rummaged through papers left over from the project and found a copy of the personnel listing, with addresses and phone numbers. Spreading it out, I looked for names to check. "Some folks you might talk to; they may not be much help, but it's something to do."

Who, though? Des Palmos, if he happened to feel chatty.

Nancy Ohara. Ridge Arnold, perhaps. Even Orville Hackett. I almost checkmarked Steve Broyles before I remembered he didn't exist any longer.

I handed the sheet to Del Allert. "Just the ones I've marked; I don't see anyone else on here who could do you much good." Afterthought: "With Nancy Ohara, be tactful. She and your brother were starting to go together some; she took his death pretty hard. Not to mention the other stuff."

Sober-faced, he nodded. "I'll be careful." He pulled out a checkbook. "And what do I owe you, Mr. Banning? What are your usual consulting rates?"

I waved the idea away. "No charge; I'm not working. Ask me about digital transmission problems, you pay for the answers. But not for this. I'm just sorry I can't help you."

"Then I guess I'll be going, and thanks. Nice meeting you, Mr. Banning, Ms. Haig."

He started to leave; I said, "You'll be at that motel for a while?" I'd heard the name on the phone, but it hadn't stuck.

"The Regrade Hacienda, yes." A quick smile. "One lone stucco arch in front, and it's a hacienda."

He'd been gone maybe two minutes when I remembered something else and ran to the door. "Hey! Come back."

Too late, though; his car was just turning out of sight. As I went back in, Dauna asked, "And what would that be all about?"

"Some papers I found, at Pedicord's. Part of an old write-up on the singularity device. I guess I forgot to mention it."

"So you did. What kind of write-up?"

I thought about it. "A lot of math, some text, a few rough layout sketches. The math starts in the middle of a major derivation; without the initial conditions it doesn't compute."

"You are not," she said, "playing in my ballpark. But if these papers are a dead-end proposition, why call the young knight errant back from his quest?"

"They might help him someway. I don't *know* they're useless; I only gave 'em a quick scan."

She gave a decisive nod. "Then that's settled."

"What is?"

"That you won't be satisfied until you know for certain."

"Don't be silly!" But she'd already left the room, to change clothes and head for work.

Now where had I put that stuff?

A little later I sat down with the faded papers, some nice fresh blank sheets, and my little "scientific" pocket calculator that can outdo the very best computers of two decades earlier. Without it, I wouldn't have had a prayer with Pedicord's math.

Differential calculus makes sense: apply a few known principles and turn the crank. Integral's frustrating; if the function's not in the tables, maybe you can get lucky substituting variables or maybe not. And on differential equations my budding skills caught frostbite. *Except*—looking at the forbidding mathematical expressions, I remembered the book that helped me crack Diff Eq 139 in my senior year.

It was in a box at the back of the spare room's closet. I hauled it out, wiped the dust off, and settled down once more. Armed with the Transform equations of Fourier and Laplace, I prepared to battle the paper demons of Olin Pedicord's making.

When Dauna said over my shoulder that it was six o'-clock and I could either eat now or starve until breakfast, the score was not in my favor. I'd been so involved that I hadn't heard her come in, let alone do things in the kitchen. Now my nose came alive and smelled dinner. "Uh—thanks; I'll be right there."

I was also dry; ignoring thirst takes real concentration.

What we ate was some kind of chicken goobly Dauna clobbered together from odds and ends in freezer baggies. It went great with beer and I said so. "Good," she said.

"And are you making any strides toward supplanting Saint Albert in the pantheon?"

"That's gods, not saints. In a pantheon, I mean. And no, Einstein's place is not in danger. On the other hand . . ." I grinned at her. "I'm not done yet."

So, taking coffee with me, back to it. And a few hours later, found that for the most part I could vouch that starting from a summary point on page thirty-six, the derivations and transformations did follow. Leading to results that actually fit the mathematical description of a singularity.

Not that I knew that definition—but I did know how to find out where to look it up. It can be expressed in several ways, but in every one of them, some quantities must become infinite.

Offhand you'd take that to mean "you can draw it but you can't build it." Yet Pedicord *had* built one, gonked-up though it was with Coogan's trick effects. The sketches and equations before me made it clear that Pedicord's intended results—as distinct from Emil's—depended on what happened to the shapes and values of converging fields; if one quantity not too clear to me were made to simulate infinity, mass placed at one nexus could no longer exist there and must appear at the second, conjugate locus.

But we all know that infinite quantities can't exist.

Infinite *ratios* can, however, even though your pocket calc won't divide by zero. Just as a point on a beam of light can move faster than light itself, if it's far enough out and you swing your source with sufficient speed. Nobody's found any use for the effect but there it is.

So—Pedicord's end result was the key to producing his singularities. The only trouble was, I still had no idea of his starting point. Meaning, how in the name of all that's halfway reasonable could anyone *build* the thing?

CHAPTER TWENTY-EIGHT

The answer turned up sooner than I expected and from an unexpected source.

Not right away, though. Next morning I had a call from Chet Baird, the attorney who had saved me from being totally skinned alive when my marriage came apart.

His news was, Frankenstein was adopting my kids. Liliane's new husband, Frank Ansteen; coming out hurting from a divorce, you take your kicks where you can. But, "What the *hell*—?"

The late support payments, all last summer. Under a new law over there, I'd compromised my parental rights. Chet tried, but couldn't reach me to attend the hearing in person; basically we lost our ass. "And on the payment issue, appeals don't fly."

So my kids were now Pat and Nicky Ansteen. What Chet did manage to get was me off the support-payment hook. Which didn't thrill me as much as some might think.

I did feel a perverse throb of pleasure at having sent Liliane a fair bundle in the kids' name, when legally I didn't have to but she couldn't know I didn't know that.

If you follow me, and I'm not sure I do.

I made a totally unrelated call, wrote a check for Chet's fee, and put it in the mailbox on my way to the car. So I could navigate rain-slicked streets to visit Ronnie Detweiler.

She hadn't changed much: more bust, maybe, and more hair. But she had a nervous edge, an aura of discontent. As I shucked my dampened jacket she offered a drink; too early, but thanks. I sat facing her own favorite chair. "Now what's up with you?"

"Coffee, anyway," she insisted, and brought me a cup.

Must have started it as soon as we hung up; it tasted fresh and good.

She sat. "It was a jolt, Mitch—finding I resent men too much to be straight." I nodded; that was safe. "So all right, I'd try gay. Hey, I always *liked* women. But now . . ." She gestured. "If I make a move, they shy off."

Her face and voice showed real distress. Stalling, I sipped coffee. Then, "Up 'til then you get along okay?" Her turn to nod. "Then it must be the pitch itself; right?"

Ronnie shook her head. "How could it? Look, Mitch—okay, I was miserable being a guy. But I *was* one, so I tried to do it right." A wry smile. "Don't ever think my masculinity died a virgin. I know how to make a play. Very damn well, in fact."

"As a guy, yes. And these women, the ones you're interested in—maybe that's how they hear you. And a lot of them *hate* guys. As in romance, anyway."

She fought the idea. "That's crazy. I appreciate your trying to help, but it just doesn't make sense!"

I shrugged. "Okay. Then what does?"

Her lips compressed, rubbing in and out; she sniffed a couple of times. "Oh shit! Mitch, what am I going to do?"

Yes, Big Mouth; what indeed? "Uh—pretend, maybe. Dump your guyside experience and pick a role model. Be *her*."

Ronnie blinked. "You think that'll do it?"

Now how would I know? "Could it do any worse?"

"I guess not." Almost at the same time we stood and moved toward the closet where I retrieved my jacket, then to the door. I still had one arm caught in a sleeve when she wrapped me in a pro-league hug and perpetrated one of the most X-rated kisses I'd ever felt. Freed and getting my breath back, I watched her face change. "That was just for fun. But you know? If your idea doesn't work, maybe I could swing the other side after all."

When in doubt, smile. "Blessings be thine, either way."

With which, I was gone from there.

* * *

At our house I saw a car parked in front; up on the porch a man sat huddled against the door. I took the Volvo into the garage, checked for mail that hadn't arrived yet, and climbed the indoor stairs. Topside I hung my jacket to dry. At the front door it was no surprise to find Del Allert waiting.

"Come on in." His coat was wetter than mine and got the same treatment. "You had lunch? I haven't."

"Oh, you don't need to . . ." But why not? From the veggie bin and a can I mixed tuna salad and made sandwiches. Over those and coffee—I did offer a beer, but in cold drinks he stuck to soda pop and I didn't have any—I listened to what he had to say.

Unfortunately he was a good storyteller. A poorer one would have got to the punchline sooner.

Orville Hackett had left the area for points south with no COA entered; basically a supply sergeant in civvies, he wasn't much loss to Del's investigation. Ridge Arnold, now working in southern Idaho, would be useful in building and operating a new device, but not during the design phase.

Which was also true of Nancy Ohara, whom young Allert *had* found. Mostly, though, she'd talked about his brother. "What happened was an awful shock," Del said now. "She hadn't suspected—he was always gentle with her, moody and withdrawn sometimes but never mean or belligerent or anything." Earnestly he asked me, "She's a very nice person, don't you think?"

Yes, I did, but it wasn't getting us anywhere. "How about Des Palmos? You reach him?"

Del leaned forward. "That's what we need to talk about. He says there's no chance of getting specifications from Detweiler's people. And that the ones for the larger units are worthless, anyway. I don't know why; he didn't say."

"Never mind; he's right. But it's not important. To you, I mean. So—what is it you want to talk about?"

Humph. "The man has something he wants to sell, and it may be at least part of what I need. But I can't afford to buy it."

What *I* needed was information; I looked inquiry until he said, "It's a partial copy of my dad's original descriptive specs, that Pedicord stole. There should be over fifty pages, though, and all he has is the first thirty-four."

All he has . . . ? On a sudden hunch I said, "What was your father's middle name?"

"Lewis." He looked bewildered. "Why?"

Bernard Lewis Allert. The BLA on each page I'd found wasn't any kind of scoffing comment; the guy simply initialed his work. And no wonder the printing didn't look like Pedicord's.

I saw no point in loading young Allert with these facts, not just yet. I said, "Later. And what's Larry asking?"

He let out a long breath. "Fifty thousand dollars, and ten percent of any eventual proceeds."

His face showed strain. "Mr. Banning, what can I do?"

I thought. "Larry Des Palmos isn't all bad." Not the way he stood up to Detweiler, and felt bad about Pedicord. "But he's an angle shooter, trying to peddle stolen property; he may not know its history, but sure as hell *he* has no bill of sale."

I sat back. "What he needs is a fence. I'm volunteering."

No more questions; I was fresh out of answers. "Go on home, Del. Back to the motel, I mean. You've got cable there; find something worth watching." He didn't like it much, but he left.

I took a look at my balance sheet. Fifty K was way too much to ante, but I could float a respectable dicker.

I called Des Palmos at the former Range A. Yes, he'd be home during early evening. He'd moved, so he told me his new address and phone. Then, what did I want?

"Just to talk a little. If you're not too busy."

"Seven o'clock?" Fine by me; we hung up.

I should have spent the afternoon writing up proposals for the few job invitations on hand, that hadn't expired yet.

I didn't, though; I stewed over the pitch I was going to put to Larry. Because the job I really wanted was to help make the singularity device work.

If it made me a bundle in the process, that was fine, too.

* * *

Dauna came home tired. Luckily I'd dropped my frettings and had dinner ready: lamb casserole with fresh fruit on the side.

Over the meal I brought her up to date. She didn't ask many questions, but when I was done she shook her head. "You want *us* to buy into Cloud Nine Transit? Not even knowing if the trolley works? And hey!—doesn't George the Scourge still hold cards in this game? Are you making a play for those, too?"

"He won't talk to me, remember? Anyway, I bet Mama Allert's sponsors have a tame lawyer for that chore. And Detweiler's a businessman: given a chance at his money back *and* the option to hang in and make a lot more, he won't cut off his own nose."

"I would still rather play poker with a man called Doc. Using his deck."

"Hmm. Look—if you want, I'll do this strictly out of my side of the cupboard. I can, just now." We keep all our loot in joint setups, right of survivorship. But in practice, mostly we each spend our own funds and keep our own accounts.

"Oh? How about the support payments?"

Oops. I hadn't told her that news; now I did. "It bugs me, sure, getting blindsided when I'm out of town. But for this setup it unties my hands." I saw her looking dubious. "Oh, I won't get into the trust funds." Planned to help the kids later on if they needed it, those were building slowly; this sneaky adoption hadn't changed my intentions on that score.

Dauna shrugged. "So you're off to outslick Larry Des Palmos. Well, if you insist on going over Niagara Falls, you'd better hurry before the tide goes out." She was playing fast and loose with geography but I didn't criticize. "Would you like me to come along and make sure the barrel's seaworthy?"

"Nope, but thanks; just gimme a kiss and I'm gone."

* * *

Larry's new place had plenty of room for a single guy, plus a southward view of Lake Union and our overgrown sky-line. He stepped over to his built-in wet bar. "What's your pleasure?"

"You have any beer never promoted on TV?"

He laughed; like me, he felt that most nationally adver-tised brews are made for people who don't like beer. "No other kind."

So we sat, he in the armchair and me at one end of the big sofa. "Cheers." He added, "What's on your mind?"

"Hear you have some papers for sale."

"The kid told you, did he?" The superior grin. "How do you rate the Hornet's little brother?"

"Not so dumb as you might think."

"Got you running point for him, has he?"

"Not exactly. Call me the appraiser. Let's see what we're talking about."

He wouldn't show me a lot; afraid, maybe, that I'd re-member too much. But the first page told me what we had, here. And I'd seen Pedicord's paper, which most likely he'd cribbed from this, and understood close to half of it. What I wanted to see was the last page. Two reasons: to make sure it fit onto my own stack, and to prove something to cock-sure Larry. For leverage.

Such as, when he finally let me look: "Oh jeez! Del told me your copy was only partial, but *this* bad?" Quickly I flipped back a couple of pages. "See here? He's run some derivation to a break point and laid the equation out, what-ever it means. But from here . . ." I ran my finger down that page and the last two. "He's into a whole new set of trans-formations; you see that?"

"I guess so."

"It's not finished, Larry, and he's given no indication of where it's supposed to *go!*" He still didn't get it. "Without more clues, it'd need another Einstein to take this where Allert must have. To where it would make some kind of sense."

Which was all very true. Nothing said I had to tell Larry Des Palmos that I personally had the end results but couldn't make them work without this part he had right here.

So I didn't. Everything I told him was absolute truth. Just not all of it.

He settled for twenty thousand advance on a two percent share. No bad return for finding some papers and guessing what they were. You could say I'd done little more, my-self—but I was also putting up the twenty out of my own sock.

With a little creative hand-editing, one of my standard job contracts fit the bill okay. "I'll have Del sign it tomor-row, and send you a copy. Meanwhile here's half your advance, for earnest money." I wrote the check.

Des Palmos seemed pleased enough. He'd asked big, but I felt he hadn't really expected to collect much.

On the other hand, next day I signed with Del Allert for six percent across the board in consideration of a full set of specs and my twenty thousand investment. Hey, he'd have paid fifty if he'd had it, plus *ten* percent share, for the incomplete version. I'd kept Larry and me, combined, well below that same ten.

I mean, besides getting Del the complete works, I'd put him fifty thousand ahead. Sometimes I am so damned phil-anthropic I can't stand myself.

I'd even stocked the abhorrent soft drink most flashily advertised on teevy. Anything to make a visitor feel wel-come.

Not that I'd be working this job *pro bono*. I showed my Coogan contract to Allert who was sipping his Diet Boop-sie with undue respect, and pointed out a few options. "Agreed sum for communications and telemetry—design, installation, and testing—plus expenses. Payments, less ad-vances to date, at completion of each project phase. That's how we did it before. But this time I'll be doing more than just telemetry; wouldn't you say?"

"I was hoping so."

"Then I will. But—I was going to say, we could also set this up as a straight salary contract."

The figure I named made him pause but not exactly wince, so I added, "With per diem allowance for out of town work." *Ease off a little.* "Whatever's standard T/DY in the given locality."

His frown eased; I wrapped up. "So how do you want it? Am I on salary, or a subcontracting mercenary?"

He looked at me dead serious. "The latter would be best."

"Why's that?"

"I'd rather have an independent-minded colleague than an insubordinate employee."

When I got my grin under control I didn't tell him the cause of it. Which was, this kid knew by instinct what George Detweiler might never learn.

Writing up that contract took a bit longer; Dauna came home in time to trade hellos with Del on his way out. Shucked of outer garb and settled down with a cup of hot chocolate she pumped me for the latest, then said, "I am all for bold venture and the like. But are you flying this kite, or riding it?"

"When I find out, you'll be the first to know."

I remember the golden age when airlines vied in offering *convenience.* Then Ronnie Raygun introduced deregulation as a spur to competition. Now a few surviving outfits run us through overloaded hubs where we spend more time on runways than in the air, wondering if our luggage will make it this time. A good connection is when you get out the same day.

What with tandem shuttles at each end, it took United American ten hours to move Del Allert and me from Sea-Tac East Satellite through Denver's B hub to the newest remote satellite field serving the Chicago area.

So when I met Susan Kay Allert at her home in a Chicago suburb, I was pupaed out of my cocoon and ready to bite small nails if I couldn't find large ones.

I hadn't expected to stay with the Allerts; I'd thought to womb it at a convenient hotel and use a rental car. But from the time our flight landed, Del called the shots: pick up his car at a security lot, ride to his home, hi mom.

One look at Susan Kay, standing at her front door while the chilly wind played with leftover snow, let all the steam out of my misgivings. This pastel blondish woman had to be in the neighborhood of fifty, but even at close range you'd take her for ten years less. Vidstars do it, sure—but here we had strong light and minimal makeup. Now I knew how Eddie Machell came up looking younger than his years. And Del too, I suspected. She was shorter than either, about my own height. But the prime datum was, I liked her right off the bat.

I said hello, it's a pleasure or whatever, and shook hands. Looking over half-glasses, the reading kind, she said, "Mr. Banning, eh? You'd be the one, I imagine, who second-carded Bernard's papers out of some pipsqueak or other? I'll enjoy keeping an eye on you."

"Well, you're a pleasant sight yourself, Mrs. Allert." Two could play. She chuckled, told Del to show me up to Eddie Mac's old room, and announced that dinner would be in twenty minutes.

The hour was late for dining; I guess she knew airline food, and recognized hungry travelers when she saw us.

I washed up a little—twenty minutes wouldn't do for my kind of shower—and went back downstairs. The house was large, old, and well kept; its only obvious updates were modern lighting and, as I learned later, the kitchen. Even the TV was a boxy old glass-tube model; so far I hadn't seen it turned on.

Helping Mrs. Allert in the big old-fashioned dining room was a younger woman. "Alice?" Del said. "This is my friend Mitch Banning from Seattle. He knew Eddie Mac."

"Hello, Mitch Banning."

"Hello, Alice." The older sister, damaged before birth by her mother's illness, showed no obvious handicap. Her features seemed heavy until she smiled; then, though she had to be past thirty, suddenly she looked childlike. Dark blond hair hanging straight, past her beltline, added to the effect.

The smile ended; she said, "Eddie was always good, before," and turned away, going back to the kitchen for another load.

Dinner was pot roast with carrots and onions and potatoes and celery and turnips at the very least; stuffed, I wasn't ready for pie afterward. Rhubarb, called pieplant here, and extremely good. I hadn't allowed for it, was all.

Everyone talked pleasantly enough, but still the shadow of Edsel McElhaney Allert loomed over the gathering.

Upstairs, after sharing TV long enough to be polite and then catching my overdue shower, that shadow didn't keep me awake.

CHAPTER TWENTY-NINE

Del's calls home had alerted Susan Kay to start rounding up funds; i.e., sponsors. Still, prior to their arrival we had a couple of days to firm up a presentation.

From the library we cross-checked Pedicord's journal paper against a crisp new copy of the Allert specs; the doctor, I was surprised to find, had derived some valid simplifications. I'd brought data from the Stork's showboat setup; by deleting obvious scam components from the Catcher Two units I made a ballpark guess at the true power load. Still big, but not so prohibitive.

Singularity transfer ate power in two ways. First, to enable the gear, ready it to move mass. That part went up with the fourth power of the transfer capsule's interior effective radius, which is merely the radius of a sphere with the same volume.

Volume being a third power quantity, why the four?

Even Del, nearing his Ph.D. in the quarkly arts, had to waffle. "Well, considering spacetime as a four-dimensional phenomenon . . ."

Since the device's operation didn't require my understanding, I let him off the hook. We would build what we could afford, governing our capsule radius by the fourth root of the budget. "But cheaper than dad figured," said Del. "Or Pedicord. New superconductors. Easier temperatures, more stable materials, available at industrial prices. And of course the overgrown Range A accelerator was only camouflage for the trick, the man-sized capsule." Along with the fancy pivots, to get a chamber in and out, safely through the Frankenstein effects.

Okay; singularities primed, we'd have to goose the transfer itself, hit the *Kazanga!* button. Power for that step looked to vary with the square of the mass to be moved. Or almost; the curve fit only approximately. (One would-be sponsor argued later that squaring a pound differed from squaring sixteen ounces. And these people control the destinies of thousands.)

Allert's equations, though, indicated that swapping two masses took less energy than one-way transport. Bernard hadn't addressed the mechanics of providing return ballast, but the possibilities looked interesting.

Come to think of it, Coogan and Pedicord had said that exchange was easier; they just couldn't afford the extra gear.

Alice came into her daddy's old study to announce lunch. By now I thought I understood her a little better. She wasn't slow; what she did understand, she caught immediately, but abstractions went right over her head. Her thinking was totally Aristotelean: yes or no, black or white. Her IQ wouldn't add very high, yet in clear-cut situations she was competent. But the outside world held too many unknowns; she was safer here.

At breakfast the first day she'd thrown me a curve. After a big smile of greeting her face went serious. "Are you the one, did you kill Eddie Mac? I hope not." I assured her I wasn't, and left unstated the fact that Eddie had fully intended to kill both Dauna and me. Alice gave a nod, and brightened again immediately. "That's good." Satisfied, she dropped the subject.

Now I followed her to the kitchen—the dining room was reserved for dinners. Susan Kay had gone out; Alice and I sat down to soup and sandwiches, split pea and roast beef respectively, plus coffee. After a few bites took the hard edge off my appetite, I began to wonder what was keeping Del.

Then he came in, waving several sheets of paper. "It's two different components, Mitch. Linear for exchange of masses, and varying as the square for uncompensated transfer."

Are you sure? Well, look at this. Yes, it certainly seems. . . . Right; this way it fits the *curve*.

And it did. Draw a graph: a straight line slanting up, for exchange, and a rising curve for uncompensated transfer. Where they cross, the same energy will do it either way. And if you swap unequal masses, power drain is linear up to the smaller number and goes by the square for the difference between them.

Over the long haul, the trick would be holding that difference to a minimum. Preferably zero.

One thing for sure; the deeper we dug, the better the cost picture came to look. Still a little blurred, though.

The rest of the day we worked at clarifying it. The telemetry and control circuits, I thought I knew. And without George Detweiler's ego in the way I could shop around and get some real equipment bargains. But I'd missed a point.

"Timing," said Del Allert, looking up from his dad's original spec.

Like where, I asked. He showed me a rough sketch, the saddle-shaped function: two parabolas and a hyperbola at right angles in 3-D. "We need exact sync on the transmit pulses at each end. Any lag pushes you out along one of those curves and ups the energy drain. Even nanoseconds can cost a bundle."

Well, Catcher Two, the only leg actually built to work, had lacked any transmit gear at the far end and relied solely on brute force; still, we'd synced pretty closely. But the idea of perfect simultaneity hadn't entered into it.

And come to that: given any distance to speak of, the concept couldn't apply. Citing Einstein's relativity, I said so.

Del shook his head. "Not in the singularity pair itself. No matter how far the gap is, time doesn't enter that equation. It's your control signals that have to achieve sync."

Yes. "I figured on delay circuits anyway. But not this tight." When it came to graphics Bernard Allert's computer was terminally awkward, pardon the pun, so I used scratch paper. "See? And for fine-tuning, rechecking as needed, we swap small identical masses back and forth, and fiddle for least drain."

His frown cleared. "I like it."

I shrugged. "Why not? It may even work."

Automatic matching of return ballast is what stumped us. Oh, it could be done, but not economically. For starters, at least, singularity devices would be fed by hand.

Next morning I slept late and skipped coffee. With four prospective sponsors coming I didn't need a caffeine assist. Del and Susan Kay drove to the satellite airport to meet three of them. I had little hope of their early return, but the travelers got lucky; even after making a lunch stop, the entire crew wheeled in a little after one.

As I came to the front door and stepped outside into chilly gusts of breeze, there they were: Susan Kay in a bulky jacket and trim slacks, Del dressed for a hike in the woods, and three suits. Hagen Bellisle and Leigh Ortison, one dark and the other pale, a pair of fortyish MBAs who needed more exercise, could have been twins who didn't happen to look alike.

They didn't bother me. Who did was Royce Geardon, a scrawny little guy crowding sixty; at first sight I guessed he could use the other two for munchies and most likely me with them. I decided to watch him. For whatever good *that* might do.

As the chitchat went along, nothing that concerned me

after the introductions, everyone filed past and inside. I stayed to watch a superstretch limo negotiate the turn at the end of the block and make its stately way to park directly in front.

Not that those oversized showboats are all that unusual. But ordinarily they don't come in shocking pink.

Once halted, this locomotive calf did a trick I'd seen only in commercials: when the door opened to reveal a seated woman, the seat and its section of floor swung out and sank slowly to the ground. All the woman had to do was stand up and walk.

It was, I decided later, a very suitable first view of Annelise Vanden Huik.

Her dress matched the car—or possibly, it struck me, vice versa. She was old and tall, very erect and trim, standing poised for a moment before she walked, briskly if a bit stiffly, from streetside to the Allert front porch.

Her face, I saw, was holding its own: fewer age wrinkles than you'd expect. Maybe a little chin lift but nothing obvious.

I didn't believe the light brown hair, worn in a smooth style sweeping back to end neatly at the nape, but the color was soft, not jarring. Understated, like her makeup.

The chauffeur stayed put; she approached alone. A few feet away she said, "Young man, do I have the Allert residence?"

Odd phrasing. "This is it, ma'am." She had to be the other sponsor, whose name escaped me just then; I added, "I'm Mitch Banning; Del and I have worked on the specs together."

I was right; she nodded. "I am Annelise Vanden Huik. And unless there is some arcane reason to stand out here in this wind, may we go inside?"

"My pleasure." As I opened the door for her, it really was. The suits were known quantities, more or less, but this one was a wild card. I couldn't wait to see Geardon try to crowd her.

* * *

They knew each other; it was "Hello, Royce" and "How good to see you, Lise"; the tension wasn't obvious but I could feel it. The non-twins introduced themselves with surface courtesy, as if they thought this old lady was trying to bat out of her league. And maybe she was.

Or maybe not; in the back of my mind, bells rang. Vanden Huik: decades earlier, Annelise had been a tabloid staple: "madcap heiress" to an eminent industrialist and state politico whose Holland birth sparked her scandal sheet nickname, the Dutchess of Illinois.

Headlined were the disputably bigamous second marriage, the two children whose fathers' names she never revealed. And once, barred from driving in the Indy 500, she tried a midnight speed run and was breaking the lap record when she spun out. Her right tibia needed bone grafts; the femur now had an alloy rod in it.

When she inherited her father's corporate holdings, a veteran raider thought he saw easy pickings. I don't really understand finance, but somehow the man ended up not only broke but under indictment.

Anything this old Tartar was in on, I thought, should be interesting.

To a considerable extent, I thought wrong.

Much of that day's talk remains a merciful blur: fiscal structure and options and John Maynard Keynes knows what else. Maybe Del followed it, but my comprehension tended to go on hold; I found myself studying details of facial expressions, speculating on what lay behind them.

I used to have the same trouble in Economics 203.

Things perked up any time someone asked about the device itself: its limitations, possible best uses, how long the construction would take once we had a site and materials and a crew. And of course, what was it going to *cost?*

The latter depended on how much gadget they wanted to build. I passed around a sketch, my idea of a feasible test capsule. A cylinder with hemispherical ends, one foot in diameter and two in length. "This," I said, "is something we could build and test without breaking the bank," and nearly everyone nodded.

Another factor would be how much of a leg they had up on the infrastructure. Such as Detweiler with the old transmitter site. "Do any of you have a comparable prospect?" Nobody answered, but Vanden Huik's lips tightened briefly, like a poker player assessing a two-card draw. Then Hagen Bellisle got into the tax benefits of phased funding and limited partnership, riveting my gaze to a bit of salad green that perched coyly beside an incisor when his lip raised enough to show it. Until Alice brought coffee and he somehow rinsed the fragment loose and swallowed it; with that source of amusement gone I found life bleak indeed.

Especially since I wasn't up to coffee myself, just yet.

Then, blessedly, talk cut away from whether to go public with stock sales to what do we use for bait. "What can the device *do* for them?" Vanden Huik asked.

Del took it. Transport capacity, size and mass? X pounds for Y dollars, and his figures were possibly as good a guess as any. Each transmission necessarily separate, exchange of mass cheaper than one-way transfer; having been through all this earlier, for a time I didn't listen too closely.

Until the Dutchess spoke up. "You offer, then, a nearly instantaneous, totally secure means of transferring vital documents or other valuable objects between fixed locations. A facility invaluable to the very persons and agencies who could afford it. And it could *not* be tapped. Is this correct?"

Del nodded. "Yes'm. That's implicit in the defining equations; given a pair of matching singularities, we couldn't hook in a third one even if we wanted to."

Royce Geardon began to argue why not, which was like a dog debating what was wrong with the electric can opener; it didn't put one bite in his food dish.

Once again I began to lose my concentration, but then an idea popped up. I cut in: "We can't hook up three at once; that would probably violate Conservation of Reality or something. But singularities don't have to stay connected in the *same* pairings."

Del frowned; I said, "What ties any two together are control and telemetry: to match those two ends, fine-tune the timing, and hit Go. And like any phone or fax or vidfone line, these can be *switched*." Not as easily as a phone hookup, I made clear; in the early stages at least, we'd need to tune for each transmission. And the bandwidth involved was on the order of a cable TV feed, not mere voice. "But if one link performs, so will a network."

"What are the advantages?" Interested now, Royce Geardon squinted in obvious intensity.

Well, for one thing, say you had singularity transport to eight outlying points, you could get by with just one terminal at your central home office. Two at the outside. I said so.

Geardon nodded. "Yes. Yes, I see that."

Leigh Ortison, the pale man, spoke. "If no one else wants to ask the big one, I will. Can this thing be a people mover?"

Del spread his hands. "We have absolutely no idea."

"The hell you don't." Bellisle. "The papers didn't spell it out in so many words, but it doesn't take a genius to guess; they tried it at the Seattle site and it killed the subject."

"Wrong," I said. "Wrong twice. That device was only a mock-up, and the man died of an ice pick to the spinal cord."

I'd put Bellisle off balance so I kept going. "What effect a singularity device might have on living organisms is something we don't know yet. Once we build one, we'll find out. Starting with mice, most likely, and working up from there."

"And how long does it take to work up to people?"

"You haven't been listening, Mr. Bellisle," said Susan Kay Allert. "You saw Mitch's sketch. Upsize that to man-sized—say, seven feet long by two across—and the power requirement and overall cost go up by a factor of almost forty-six."

I stared. I'd been thinking of this mild, pastel little woman as someone whose math stopped at her checkbook.

And she didn't even have a hand calc out. Reevaluation time.

Hagen Bellisle looked defensive. "All right. I guess that's what I was asking. Thank you." The secret smile on Vanden Huik's face was gone almost too soon to notice.

Possibly for added cover she pulled a small commmphone from her purse and told the chauffeur he could make free with the car for an hour or so. "I almost forgot," she said, hanging up. "And the poor boy does hate to come knocking to use the biffy."

We went a few more rounds, sparring gingerly. The sketches we'd shown around were intentionally vague in several major respects. Del's idea: no sharpie was going to learn enough from them to enable someone else's research team to run with the ball.

Paranoid? Not really, not in the business world.

Geardon cleared his throat. "All right; I think we've learned all we can absorb for one day, enough to decide to go in or stay out." He looked around. "All right; show of hands. I'm in, with backing to carry fifty-one percent. Who's with me?"

"Not so fast, Royce." The old woman's voice came mellow enough; maybe it was her pacing that carried the edge. "I don't recall anyone granting your group an automatic majority holding, and certainly *I'm* not willing to do so. What is your—"

He cut her off. "That's my primary condition, Lise; it's not negotiable. Shall we continue?"

The Dutchess shook her head. "Not 'til I know who's pulling your strings. I've seen you operate; you'd negotiate sulfur mining with Satan himself, squatting in a kettle of it." Her eyes narrowed. "Just whose shilling did you take, old trickster? Who is it you're fronting for?"

Ortison gasped, then giggled. "The King's shilling, they used to call it. He's into Federal money—for a bit over half his group's share they can control *that*, which in turn . . ."

Right. Uncle buys twenty-six percent and runs the show.
Thus controlling all uses and applications.

The hell you say. I stood up. "This meeting is adjourned.
The *present* owners of all rights to the singularity process
need to convene." Jeez, gang, don't raise any quibbles!

As if we didn't have enough confusion, Alice came in.
"Mama? Isn't it time I started making dinner?"

Everybody spoke at once, no two on the same channel.
Royce Geardon denied nothing, just insisted we couldn't
prove it. Ortison said if the government was in, he was out.
Bellisle took it the other way: "You people are a pack of
subversives; I'm having no part of you." Lacking wheels,
there he stood with his ultimatum hanging out. Alice asked
did we want dinner on time or not? Susan Kay said they
would discuss it in the kitchen but not just now so go wait
there. Vanden Huik nodded decisively; apparently she'd
made up her mind about something.

Del Allert and I looked at each other. We didn't even
shrug; the situation implied the movement so why bother?

On Royce Geardon the pose of saintly patience fit like
mail order shoes at the wrong address. "Think carefully,
friends. I bring substantial backing to this enterprise; you
must consider our mutual circumstances on rational
grounds. I assure you . . ."

His pause gave Alice, who hadn't gone to the kitchen
after all, a chance to speak. "Do we *have* to give him dinner
here? He isn't good, Mama; let's don't."

We all saw how she looked at Geardon. He reached for
poise and didn't even come close. "Get that stupid moron
out of here!"

Face taut, Del stopped his own lunge barely in time to
grab Susan Kay who wasn't holding back anything at all.
Teeth bared, fingers clawed, she strained against his grip;
deep in her throat came a strange high "*Rr-rr-rr*" like one cat
warning an intruding other. Her nails weren't all that long,
maybe, but they could have marked Geardon up pretty
well.

Holding firm, Del bent to his mother's ear and whispered; after a long moment she shuddered and let him ease her into a chair. He spoke; face wooden, only his voice showed how close the call still was. "The phone's over there, Geardon. Call a cab, get your ass out of here. You can wait on the porch."

He turned on Bellisle. "You, too. Hanging around with us subversives could contaminate your FBI file. Don't worry; Geardon's good for fifty-one percent of the fare."

Across the room, standing beside the phone he hadn't touched yet, the older man spoke up again. "All right. You can eject me, if you're that foolish, but you can't exclude the United States government if they want in. You'll see; they—"

"Put a potato in it, Royce." And with all the tension in that room, Annelise Vanden Huik managed to sound bored.

Standing blank-faced, Geardon wasn't home free yet. With an intent look, Alice marched over to confront him, her face less than six inches below his own. "I'm not a moron, I was sick. Before I was born." Her voice was earnest but lacked anger. She turned to come away but after one step wheeled back. "So there," she said, very softly, and went to the kitchen.

Finally, Geardon could make his call.

The next half hour wasn't the most comfortable I've ever lived. Knowing the two men had to be chilling, out there in the brisk wind, somehow I felt guilty even though I'd had practically nothing to do with the blowup and they had it coming anyway.

The taxi finally did show, and only a couple of minutes later Annelise's limo returned. To sit in isolated grandeur; she offered the driver no communication. Nor he to her.

Dinner was what we used to call a clearance casserole; I'm not sure how many items it contained, each in small quantity, but I'll bet it uncluttered the fridge and freezer a lot. The funny thing is how good such an impromptu mix can turn out.

By unspoken agreement, during the meal no one talked business. Over coffee, though—and now I could indulge—a clearing of Vanden Huik's throat signaled the meeting to order.

"Now the payday high rollers are out, let's get down to some serious poker. Since you are still with us, Mr. Ortison, I assume you're interested in continuing?"

"That's right, ma'am." Looking like a man who'd sat through a hideously embarrassing family fight, Leigh Ortison spoke deferentially. "What basis of operation do you have in mind?"

Instead of answering, she spoke to Susan Kay. "How large a share do you and your group," kindly including me in her nod, "propose to keep for yourselves? That is, what percent do Mr. Ortison and I buy with our financial sponsorship?"

Without hesitation Mrs. Allert said, "Financial benefit and decision control aren't the same. On the money end, I feel my family's contribution is worth a twenty-five percent interest. Mr. Banning brings vital data and some preliminary financing; I've guaranteed him and his associates a total of eight. Leaving sixty-seven for whoever funds the major development."

"I see. All right with you, Leigh?"

"Yes. How do you want our own split? Halves?"

"If we operate through one of my foreign subsidiaries, to keep us clear of Royce Geardon's bureaucratic cronies, I'd prefer holding thirty-seven. Will thirty do you?"

A nod. "I won't have time for all that jockeying, anyway."

"Very well." Annelise looked and sounded cheerful; with the room emptied of antagonism, she'd dropped her Dutchess role completely. "Now what was that other part, Mrs. Allert?"

"Simply that what we *do* with the devices, once they're up and running—who we sell to, and for what purpose— that's where I and mine must have a major voice."

Her expression said take it or leave it. Not belligerently, though; in obvious suspense, she waited. Until Annelise said, "I'm assuming you don't mean to be arbitrary—that you do intend to discuss matters, heed advice, and so forth." On the old face, her impish grin surprised me. "I have no intention of seeing the device used for nefarious ends. I wouldn't sell it to terrorists, for instance. Especially those in high office."

Not too much later, we had ourselves a deal.

CHAPTER THIRTY

Lacking a national language the Swiss make do with German, French, Italian, and Romansch. Geneva speaks French; Annelise's subsidiary in that city is named Vanden Huik Suisse.

With finances more or less in hand, she put our entire program into the hands of VHS—which does not make VCRs; I asked. Her own hands, yes; nonetheless, in fine Swiss gloves they screened us from Big Uncle. When a working area was leased from VH Labs, one of Lise's domestic corporate masks, governmental oversight amounted to routine approval by a minor agency.

It seemed the long way around, though, to get the lot of us up to a rainsoaked stretch of rolling tundra, bounded by the Pacific Ocean on one side and the Arctic on the other.

Not that things happened all that fast. Early on, I insisted that the ghost of Detweiler's interest in the device be laid to rest. "You don't know George. He'd sue our ass off."

On his contracts with Coogan I spelled out what little I knew. Lise nodded. "I will call him." But not on Susan Kay's phone; from the stretch buggy came a leather-cased videophone terminal. The chauffeur hooked it in, with the

Allerts' TV as a monitor, so we could all sit out of camera range and watch.

I hadn't known George possessed a vidfone; it had to be a new thing. But Lise had checked the appropriate directory, and when he answered he came on-screen looking every bit his own firmly packed self. "George Detweiler." Which was true.

"My name is Annelise Vanden Huik."

Detweiler's automatic scowl lightened. "Sure, I've heard of you. What do you—I mean, to what do I owe the pleasure?"

"Pleasure? Well, one hopes so. To the point, then: you have funded research on a device represented to you by a Dr. Pedicord, and hold certain agreements pertaining thereto."

"How—? Hey, what the hell's it to *you?*"

At our end not a ruffle showed. "To me, the hell, as you so charmingly put it is that neither of those men held title to what they sold. The true ownership is vested in a consortium which I have the honor to head."

George's eyes were small to begin with; narrowed, the result wasn't at all pretty. "You'll have a time proving any of that."

"Please, Mr. Detweiler. You have been unfairly treated, I realize. But before you escalate misunderstanding into fruitless conflict, I recommend that you hear me."

She was back to Dutchess mode, her Power Delivery.

And it worked; George fidgeted. "I'm listening."

"The specifications you obtained were stolen by Pedicord from his employer, Bernard Allert, the actual inventor. You—"

"It was the other way around! Coogan told me . . ."

"Now you just hold on!" Susan Kay moved into the camera's view. "I don't know who this Coogan person is, but my husband, Bernard Allert, discovered singularity transfer. Pedicord worked for him until Bernard caught him doping and fired him. Social Security records can prove who paid who, and we have Bernard's original papers, dated well before he ever met Pedicord. So you see, Mr. Detweiler, you've been sold stolen goods."

"Yeah? I'm just out of luck? That's what you're saying? Well, let me tell you something. . . ."

Stopping for breath was his mistake; Annelise said, "You are not yet done listening. If you are wise, I mean to say." And a two-count later, "Your position may retain a certain nuisance value; on that premise I am prepared to make you an offer."

Offer. The magic word. "Let's hear it."

George had trouble making up his mind. He could settle for half his actual documented losses, paid now, or for a three percent interest in the undertaking. (Ortison glared; aside, Lise said, "From my share, Leigh," and the glare ebbed.) In return for full quittance of any further claim, plus copies of all relevant structural and experimental data from Range A.

And who decided what was relevant? Just pack the whole suitcase, George; we'll sort it out as we go along.

Finally he said, "Oh, what the hell. I didn't get where I am by not taking chances; I'll go with the three percent."

While they dotted the *i*'s and so forth, I went to the john, coming back just as Annelise switched off. Giving me an almost accusing look she said, "How could you endure working for that man? Whining and creeping . . ." She shook her head. "I'm surprised he chose the risk."

Remembering something, I said, "I'm not. He's already taken a tax write-off; if you repaid him he'd have to return a lot of it to the IRS. This way it's all gravy."

I shrugged. "Anyway, now we're shut of him."

"Not entirely," said Leigh Ortison. "Detweiler insisted on placing a representative on the project to look after his interests. Someone who has experience with the equipment."

"Does George sign that paycheck, or is it our baby?"

"I don't pay anyone I can't fire," said Annelise.

Ortison chuckled. "And still she kept a veto option; if she doesn't like Detweiler's man she can ask for a replacement."

Hmm. "Actually, I don't think George has too many choices."

* * *

"So sleep in tomorrow," I said. "Don't go to work until noon." Dauna didn't answer right away; I took that as a yes. We'd made the most of my first night home until I was fresh out of most. By morning, though, resurrection should transpire.

They say we're supposed to get over these adolescent urgencies as we grow older. They are full of it.

Next morning after she was off to the magazine I spent some depressing time calling to decline perfectly good jobs I'd've loved to take under other circumstances. "Well you see I'll be out of town for a while," and I recommended a colleague who'd do the same for me. At least I hoped he would; you never knew.

Once I had cut myself off thoroughly from my usual sources of income, it was time for the tough part. I called Detweiler Industries and asked for Lee Malcolm, who was supposed to deliver the Range A data. He or she was home sick; I asked who played backstop and was put on hold without my consent, listening to better music than you usually get from the On Hold Network, until a familiar voice said, "Yes? Mr. Detweiler?"

"Not hardly." And waited to see if recognition were mutual.

Nope. "Who's calling this station?" said Larry Des Palmos.

I told him. And then, what my business was.

So I drove up to the former Range A and took custody of the stack of paper Detweiler owed Vanden Huik. Maybe it was all there and maybe not; I didn't figure it for vital either way.

Des Palmos was out; I signed for the material with a thin young woman who looked overworked and underpaid. Thanking her, I hefted the bundle and thought I was out free.

Then the door opened and here came Larry. We did greetings, and he said, "How come it's you, picking the stuff up? I didn't know you had an in with the new management."

"Each day bringeth its own learning, saith the Buddha. Or maybe the old guy in the karate movies. Nice to see you, Larry." Disengaging the handshake I started to sidle past.

Nope. "You'll be seeing more of me," he said, "if you're on the development team. I'm Detweiler's bird dog for the job."

I paused. "He trusts you that much?"

Des Palmos looked sheepish. "He has a handle on me."

"A handle has two ends." And on that cryptic note, I left.

When I got home, my marching orders from Annelise Vanden Huik were on the answering machine.

Within the month I was plodding my soggy way across lumpy tundra, against wind-driven rain that broke the speed limit.

Calling back, I hadn't reached Annelise. At her main office a young fellow told me I could leave a message, so I did.

Susan Kay was more informative. "She's gone north, to oversee the construction site. Mr. Ortison's in New York. But I doubt he could tell you much. He did send a liaison man along, a Dr. Aguinaldo. Tall chap, didn't say a lot. Seems to know a little something about singularity equipment, though."

Right; all we needed was some new expert out of left field. "Is Del with them?" Yes, he was, heading up the new team and ordering materials as needed. Construction was being handled by Morris-Karter, a midwest firm, under Lise's general supervision.

Annelise had told my answering machine some of this; the added details were welcome. Such as where the job was. I thanked Susan Kay, hung up, and began following instructions.

*　*　*

By the time Dauna got home I had ordered up, by phone, most of what Lise had recommended. Such as climate-worthy clothing. And had fired off the Range A papers, Express rate, to a designated mail drop up in Anchorage. I hadn't called Alaska West Air yet because I had in mind a slight change of plan.

I waited until a suitable moment, considerably later in the day, to ask Dauna, "Hey, you ever been out the Chain?"

She pushed the sheet back and raised up on one elbow to look at me directly. "The what?"

"Aleutians. The island chain west of—"

"I know where they are. No, I haven't. Why? Have you?"

Once, yes, during my Army days. But not very far. "We put in at Dutch Harbor on Unalaska, saw the remains of some War-Two construction across the bay." And the ruins of the airfield at the east end of Umnak, overlooking that stark, forbidding cliff.

"Where the Dutchess is setting up," I said now, "is farther out, past Adak. Some flat rock her daddy took a big long lease on, way back when. To raise foxes, I think. Or maybe sheep."

"Ugh," she said. "I've already met sheep. When I was a child. They have nasty habits and they smell bad."

"Forget the sheep. Do you want to come out and have a squint at the second incarnation of the singularity device?"

The tilt of her brows said I was crazy. "You can get away with that?"

"I can try."

"Then why not?"

Lise's on-site phone went through an Anchorage number to a very extended extension. I began, "I have us a chronicler. To keep a project journal, and get our story together for the press, when and if." I laid it on as thick as I dared. . . .

I doubt she intended me to hear her muffled laugh. "Bring anyone you want, Mitch. At your own expense; the travel budget has used up all its slack."

"Yeah. Well, how about pay and quarters and such?"

"I see no difficulty."

"Fine. We'll be there on the schedule you gave me."

So my first-class ticket on Alaska West Air blossomed into two coach seats. A couple of weeks after that talk, Dauna and I sat at the old Anchorage airport near Campbell Point, waiting for our connection and wondering what form it might take.

Who would have expected a charter VTOL? I'd never ridden anything that took off and landed straight up and down—and wasn't sure I wanted to.

But its presence said our destination held no airstrip. And when you gotta go . . .

Even if where you gotta go is a rock you never heard of.

Kanaga Island's only major topographic feature is a rounded peak rising about forty-four hundred feet near its northeast tip; less ambitious hills, such as those at the bulge where the island's otherwise skinny outline bends northward, don't appear on your average map. Covered solely by tundra grass and ubiquitous lichens, plus snow in season, this island lies between Adak to the east and Tanaga on the west. Temperatures chilly, humidity excessive, overall climate violently sidewise. Or to put it more graphically, the wind will take your head off.

On the south side, facing the Pacific, lies a bay big enough to interest the map trade. It gets considerable drainage when the snow melts. Now, in late spring, that melt had begun.

Most of it appeared in the bay as a brownish stain spreading from the foot of a wide, shallow valley. Above the cliffs, rising from tidal flats cluttered with jagged boulders, no river or stream was visible; water ran unseen along the narrow bottom of a ravine roofed by centuries' growth of lichen to form the present, gentler surface contours.

I didn't learn all that until later; the VTOL that brought us from Anchorage felt its way down through violent, shifting winds and thick patches of fog to a roughly semicircular plateau between the valley below and a natural amphitheater of rising ground behind, with the landing pad near the plateau's center.

As we touched down I saw people in hooded parkas emerging from the largest building, a concrete block with fewer windows than I liked. Walking, I could see, was a real chore. Not for long: a few yards out sat a jeeplike vehicle with huge dune buggy tires, hitched to a small flatbed trailer. Everybody climbed in or on, and in a moment the lot headed our way.

Dauna and I collected our carryons and prepared to deplane. "Watch it out there," the pilot warned. "That wind can grab you." From my visit to Umnak I already knew the problem, but thanked him anyway and tied my parka hood's laces snugly at the chin, checking to see that Dauna followed suit.

Then, with good-byes to Haney, our cheerful pilot, we stepped outside and on down. Even warned, the wind almost got us. For one thing, once we got off the blacktop pad, I hadn't remembered the mud being quite so slippery.

I didn't recognize anyone on the approaching rig. When it came near enough for anyone to be heard over the wind, a man pointed back toward the larger building and yelled, "Check in there, first."

I waved acknowledgment; with the wind facing me, no point in trying to be heard. Eyes squinted against the rain-laden blast, we plodded on. Reaching the building took considerably longer than the distance looked; footing varied between mud, water-soaked lichen, and remaining patches of hard-packed snow. At least the wind didn't shift abruptly and dump us facedown in the mud, a North Pacific foible I'd forgotten to warn Dauna about. And in daylight, I didn't even lose track of the building.

I didn't see any foxes, though. Or sheep.

I opened a door letting us in to the storm porch. Its inner doors didn't budge until the outer ones were firmly shut. An airlock of sorts, protection against gusts of cold air.

Going on inside, we met a stocky, bulky-clad woman

carrying a clipboard. "The Banning party, from Seattle?" As she smiled, broad face under very short muddy-blond hair, we admitted we were. "I'm Lennox Farnham. Construction chief, Morris-Karter. Come on in; Lise—Miz Vanden Huik—she's in our Admin office."

We followed. The Admin layout was big. Bare-walled and unpainted; cluttered, too. Several desks, two large drafting screens with all the control options: mouse, stick, or keyboard. Computer terminals, cartons all over the place, some unopened. A few people sorting through things or sitting at workstations. Harsh fluorescent lighting complementing the small, high windows. In one corner the inevitable coffee table.

Not rising, Annelise behind one of two larger desks waved us in. "You'll pardon me; this climate . . ." Yes, if she had any tendency toward arthritis, the place would bring it out. "Get some coffee. You too, Lennie."

The four of us exchanged greetings, Dauna clarifying her identity to Lennie Farnham, provisioned ourselves with coffee, and sat to talk. Major construction was pretty well wrapped; Lennie's crew would stay for the heavy lifting on the singularity device itself. A bit different from Coogan's operation—where by virtue of the Stork's peculiar needs, builders and techs were two separate groups. Except of course for Larry Des Palmos . . .

Who hadn't flown up yet, to serve as proxy eyes for George Detweiler. In another day or two, Lise said. I was in no hurry.

Del was in his lab, she said, reworking computer mock-ups of the device. "He'll want to see you right away, but get settled in first. Your other baggage should be in your quarters."

So a tall young fellow was assigned to show us where to go. On our way out we stopped at a small room where he took our pictures for project badges. Red tape is where you find it.

Outside was no better than before. As we moved out of the building's wind-shadow I saw a smaller structure, also con-

crete, behind and to one side. The wind carried a deep
throbbing sound: power plants. There should, I thought,
be an enclosed walkway between these two interdependent
units. Maybe later.

The rest of the settlement looked to be quarters and a
mess hall. A far cry from the Quonset and Pacific hut ruins
of Fort Glenn, by the crumbling weed-grown airstrip on
Umnak. Only a few feet above the tundra bulged shallow,
domed rectangles, skylighted along their outer edges. At
each end a storm porch rose, but the quarters themselves
were dug in at least six feet.

In terms of weather, the design made sense. Jim Conley,
our guide, led us down Building G's stairs to a sketchily
furnished lounge area from which a central corridor ran the
length of the place. About halfway along it he stopped to
indicate two doors, one on either side. "Take your picks.
Here's the keys. If you need anything else, call me at Orientation."

He walked back the way we'd come, leaving Dauna and
me staring at the two keys. G-11 and G-12, they were.

G-12 faced south; wanting all the daylight we could get,
that's the one we chose. They used to call them efficiency
apartments—everything in one room except the john.

The bed was too small. Adding the one from G-11 would
jam the place completely. Consulting the Xeroxed phone
list I called Orientation and reached Jim Conley. A double
room? He'd check.

Annelise called back. "Mitch, you didn't specify a roo-
mie."

She was right. "Well, it's okay, isn't it?"

"Certainly. We have VIP billets. I'll send Jim again."

So after a quick snack at the mess hall in lieu of lunch
which was overdue anyway, we wound up in A-6, least
posh of the VIP setups, thus least apt to be preempted by
bigger fish, later. It had a separate bedroom, a kitchenette,
and a dining nook. The walls had real colors, not the Navy
grey in building G.

Our skylights even faced south. For the time being, Dauna and I were in clover.

Having endured a long and tiring trip, we took an hour or so of R-and-R between unpacking and reporting back to the real world. The bathtub wasn't really long enough, but we made do.

Dauna's hair would take a time drying, so I went on ahead to the main building which they called, simply enough, Operations.

Ops, for short.

Annelise looked busy when I peeked in; I went on past and found Del Allert's big lab. I'd thought Admin cluttered, but compared to Del's setup, Lise and Lennie were Neat Freaks.

He looked around as I came in. "Hi! Look what I've got."

This was the first I'd seen of holographic displays for 3-D design work; it impressed me and I said so. In a three-foot cube appeared colored lines, gridplanes and what have you, focused around the dull yellow shape of our agreed transmission capsule, the cylinder capped at either end by hemispheres. Force lines, gradations of brilliance, and color shifts all indicated variations of field strengths and the like; of course I didn't know, yet, how Del had all those variables coded. By keyboard he could call up circuit parameter values for any point, designated by a blinking cursor dot in the display, on an auxiliary monitor.

"Terrific, Del. But don't these things cost like crazy?" From what I knew of our budget, this little jewel could take a mammoth bite off it.

"It's on loan." He grinned like—well, he *was* a kid with a new toy. "Annelise pried it loose from another company she has shares in. It's a big help."

I noticed something. Around each end of the capsule, where the hemispheres met the cylindrical portion, the visual telltales indicated a disproportionate buildup of— well, of *something*. I pointed. "What's that, anyway?"

His face went serious. "I don't know. It looks like some kind of stress peak, almost a discontinuity. And it shouldn't; that's a perfectly smooth transition. Nothing changes."

"Something must."

He stood back. "You want to play with it?"

I shook my head. "Later, maybe. When I have time to learn my way around this critter. Just now, though . . ."

I turned to a regular flat-screen terminal, the kind I was used to. Several grades above anything I'd ever worked with, but the drill couldn't be that much different. "Is this set up to work our configuration? I thought I'd try a cross section."

"Sure." So I booted up, and sat down to play.

The mock-up came on; I fiddled parameters until I had the feel, varying field gradients around the capsule, trying to equalize whatever imbalance produced those stress rings. But there they stayed; I couldn't taper my potential gradients enough to soften their effect without dropping out of operating range.

After an hour or so I hung it up. "Hey. We got coffee in here?" The facilities were present but he hadn't bothered using them; I didn't feel much like setting up from scratch, either. So we went down the hall and barged in on Lise and Lennie.

They were sitting back too, having a break. Apparently some kind of meeting had just dispersed; only Haney the VTOL pilot had stuck around Admin. He was saying, ". . . as soon as he's ready. Otherwise we're all loaded." He saw me and said, "Getting settled in okay?" I allowed as how I was, and he replied, "Out here the key to survival is being too dumb to go crazy." Setting down his empty cup, the man gave us a smile and walked out.

"Mr. Haney has flown these routes, I understand, for over fifteen years," said Annelise; her tone made the statement an explanation. Then, "I'm sorry you missed Dr. Aguinaldo; he's off to Anchorage for a few days." Flying out with Haney, I guessed.

Aguinaldo, though. Ortison's man, yes. Choosing a cup and pouring it full, I asked, "How is he? Any help, I mean? What are his qualifications, anyway?"

Del said, "He knew Dr. Pedicord after the man left us and before he turned up in Seattle. He—Aguinaldo, I mean—brought some preliminary specs and drawings on a later version of Dad's device. There's a copy in here somewhere." And from halfway down a stack of paper he handed me a packet.

I leafed through; yes, some changes from Allert's specs—but none of the Stork's pyrotechnic additions. Definitely Pedicord's scribbling, sloppy in places, as if done by a very tired hand. Or a drug-impaired one.

Then I noticed something; down in one corner, each sheet was dated. The trouble was, all the dates fell during the time Olin Pedicord was held captive by Eddie Machell.

CHAPTER THIRTY-ONE

I didn't say anything yet; I could wait. Aguinaldo, though, didn't return right away, and meanwhile construction of the device itself moved more quickly than I'd expected.

Range A's accelerators had been buried deep and safe before I ever saw the place; the smaller one, downtown, was enclosed in a shielded area closed to peons like me. Our particle-pooper here, only recently laid to rest, was built to more compact proportions. Most of its perimeter lay under the interface blockhouse, an add-on at the rear of Operations.

I tried to ignore the harsh fact that the interface was getting built almost faster than Del and I could design it. We had to get rid of those stress rings, and maybe our current transmission chamber configurations wouldn't do it. Everything else was wrapping up fast; I felt like the guy who forgot to bring the beer to the company picnic.

Early in our second week there, weather cut our supply line. Not unusual, out on the Chain, but Dauna and I both found winds in three figures a little unreal to cope with. To keep from getting blown off downwind, let alone try to move, you need to crouch way down and preferably have something to hold on to. And facing the wind straight on, breathing is a learning experience.

What I'm saying is, climate can get to be a problem.

First trip after the storm passed, Haney delivered Larry Des Palmos. The good news was, Nancy Ohara arrived too, with Larry hovering around her like a mother hen. Through the smallish welcoming crowd Dauna went straight to her, but Annelise steered me to another new arrival, a tall guy at Larry's other side. "Dr. Esteban Aguinaldo, Mitchell Banning," said the Dutchess.

"How do you do." No question mark. The man spoke slowly and deliberately, voice and face equally grave; his handshake was no rush job, either.

A bit of a sphinx, this one, and not at all what I'd been halfway expecting. Rather good-looking in an over-forties way: notably dark complexion, long straight nose ending with flared nostrils, lips somewhat full, ears tight against the skull, black hair smooth above a low, pronounced widow's peak—very Dracula.

I said I hoped he'd had a nice flight which in this climate was ridiculous; before I could think how to ask my major question he moved aside, with a distinctive languid swagger, to join another conversation.

I found myself stuck with Des Palmos. Larry had a smug look on his face and I couldn't imagine why; polite enough, though, asking how the job was going and how could he help, and all.

So I told him about the anomalous stress concentration

rings on the capsule simulations. Dauna and Nancy had come over; Ohara said, "All around the edges, at the ends? Larry—that's where the Catcher Two capsules showed damage."

"After Pedicord blew it all up?" he said.

Pedicord, hell! Des Palmos had blown it himself, abruptly cutting power when the thing was all the way wound up. By main force I sat on my protest and said to Nancy, "Capsules, you said. The one downtown, too?"

Yes—but for both units, only after Pedicord's one attempt at real transmission. And on the larger, fake installation, no such damage. "We thought," Nancy Ohara said now, "that the wild feedback, potentials arcing across and so on, caused the cracks and melted areas." She had a cute frown. "But none of it explained the distribution, confined to rings around each end."

"The surface does make a sharp bend there," Larry commented. "And bends concentrate any kind of field stress."

But my capsules had no abrupt changes; each hemisphere met the cylinder smoothly. I'd been all through that aspect with Del, and this time was no different. "Well, let's go put it on-screen," somebody said, and I got a kick out of the oohs and aahs when Nancy and Des Palmos spotted the holo layout. Dauna had seen it before, but she still liked to watch.

By now I'd learned enough to show off a few tricks, but when I tried some of the modifications I'd simulated on the flat screen, I couldn't get the fields to shape up right. So I was glad when Del came in; after introductions I said, "Here, you show 'em what we're up against."

As he put the familiar frustrating configurations through their paces, I looked over to the corner and saw that somebody had made coffee. It smelled fresh. When I went to pour a cup, Larry Des Palmos was right behind me. He waited until we were both fixed up, mine with cream and his not, then said, "How do you like Don Quixote? Isn't he a pip, though?"

I doubt my try at a poker face fooled him any. I waited,

and finally said, "He doesn't talk much, if that's what you mean. Ms. Vanden Huik seems to think he knows what he's doing."

He snickered. "Question is, does she know what *she's* doing? Or maybe whom. It might be fun finding out, don't you think?"

Had I ever really liked this smart aleck? I hoped not. I could get him fired and I knew it, but where was the satis-faction in having someone else do my hit for me?

I gave him the look. "If you're screwing around *this* time, Larry, any at all . . ." I would have his ass, was what. On toast.

But I didn't say that part. Instead, "George won't like it much." A little misdirection couldn't hurt.

Didn't help, either; he said, "George won't have a prob-lem."

He seemed utterly confident; stumped, I probably looked as blank as I felt. The joyous yell from Nancy Ohara got me out of the stalemate.

"Curvature!" she repeated as I went over there fast. The holo didn't tell me much; what did was the final string of numbers she had up on the monitor. Not right away, though.

Sometimes all it takes is a fresh viewpoint; on-screen was a list of numerical values for selected properties of the capsule's lengthwise cross section, all around its perimeter. Most of them I'd worked through before with no points scored; they tended to vary smoothly if at all.

The new one, there at the bottom, was different. Curva-ture. It showed utter discontinuity: constant for the semi-circle at each end cap, then a flat zero for the straight line along the cylinder. The surface itself made no abrupt change but this one parameter sure did. And what had eluded Del and me all this time, Nancy spotted in about five minutes.

When we were done hugging and jumping up and down, I went to the holo controls. First I shrank the capsule lengthwise, eliminating the cylinder altogether to leave only a sphere. No surprise, now that we had the clue; all the stress concentrations smoothed out to a homogeneous field distribution.

But for our uses, a sphere wasn't the best shape. So while Del and Nancy chattered away happily, Larry putting his oar in but making no headway, I stretched that sphere sidewise into a prolate spheroid, like they boot around in rugby. The forces concentrated somewhat at each end, where curvature was greatest—but gradients were gentle. No stress peaks.

Still not ideal; packages are apt to be wider than deep. So I flattened my football to an ellipsoid, no two axes the same, a nice oval cake of soap. Field distribution stayed smooth, varying gradually throughout. This, we could live with.

Del took over. "Let me figure a size here, to match the power usage we've specified." Because surface-to-volume ratios change like crazy when you fiddle with the shape of something.

I left him to it. Turning to Nancy Ohara I said, "There has to be some champagne around here somewhere. Let's round up Dauna and build us a party, soon as Del wraps up."

"Dauna's right here," Dauna said from behind me.

It grew to more than the four of us. Before we even got parka'd up to brave the weather, Annelise took over; we wound up in her place on her booze. Lennie Farnham came along; this was her show, too. Larry Des Palmos got in because I couldn't think how to ditch him, and Dr. Aguinaldo showed up on the way to Lise's digs and stuck to her like a barnacle. And somewhere along the line, Haney the philosophical pilot joined our group.

What the hell, there was plenty for all. I wasn't sure how many rooms the suite had, but the three I saw would be adequate for most people. Not lushly furnished, but as tasteful as you can get, starting with on-site project construction.

And the drink did flow. In some variety: I'd said champagne so that's what I stuck to, but except for Annelise herself, Dauna was the only one sharing that choice. Del stayed with juices and such. So, I noticed, did Nancy, as they talked it up pretty well between them. While Des Palmos and the tall Hispanic enigma sported big glasses of ice cubes pickled in sour mash.

Those two were getting on like Sears and Roebuck; in my nasty suspicious way I wondered why. For now, it didn't seem I was going to find out.

Tomorrow got awfully soon; Dauna and I ducked out early.

Chamber and capsule construction got moving the next day; now we had the king bug out, the little ones came easier. Mechanics, for instance: the simplest way to get our oval cake of soap in and out of a chamber of the same shape and not much larger on the inside. Well, part of the chamber's bottom and front slid out like a drawer, field circuits and all, the movable segment's connectors engaging only at the In position.

The capsule itself, centered in place by insulating struts specially fabricated by Leigh Ortison's labs to match the dielectric constant of air, opened on hinges; the top half swung up to one side, standing perpendicular.

Closed, it was watertight; its supports registered its loaded weight and relayed that datum to the far end, where water was vented into the other capsule to match the exchange mass. After the transfer swap, the initiating end could drain the water by remote button, too. I don't remember who came up with that solution; Del and I, who had flypapered our thinking into far more complicated schemes, felt properly skunked.

For now, the Alpha and Beta terminals sat at either end of the interface blockhouse, about sixty feet apart. If this link proved out, though, the Dutchess had bigger plans. Bigger with regard to distance and capsule size, both. Constrained more by powerhouse capacity than by the budget we settled for ellipsoids with inside diameters of two feet lengthwise, one and a half across, and one foot vertically.

Roughly the same volume in an eighteen-inch sphere would have been a lot simpler to design and build, but this way we wasted less space on inserts to give some flat bottom area. And people-sized capsules wouldn't be spherical, so we might as well work out the hard parts of the design early. Or so we saw it.

It took a few days to get our components out from Lise's specialized suppliers; a week or so later we were ready to test.

In all that time you'd think I'd have a chance to pin down Dr. Esteban Aguinaldo. I didn't, though. The morning after the party he rode back to Anchorage with Haney; any time he came out, his stay was brief. And during those visits, either I was busy or he was holed up in conference, purpose unspecified.

When he turned up the day before we planned to test, I did catch him once, heading into a meeting with Lennie Farnham's people. I grabbed his arm. "One moment, doctor." He blinked; I said, "If you knew Dr. Pedicord before he went to Seattle, howcome the specs you brought here are dated after he got there?"

He pulled the arm free; slowly and without inflection he said, "There is some mistake, some mix-up. Someone showed you other copies, not the ones I submitted." Without another word he went strutting into the meeting room and closed the door firmly.

His disclaimer *had* to be total horse apples. The trouble was, he sounded so sure of himself. Much as the puzzle nagged at me, for the time being I had to leave it on hold.

After all the razzmatazz at Range A—safety booth, seeing into the chamber room only via mirrors, whining ionization coronae and ersatz earthquake—Lise's setup at Ops seemed very tame indeed. The panel controlling both terminals sat right alongside Chamber Alpha, handily near the doors to Operations.

Here we all were, middle of a Tuesday morning, nearly twenty of us including a few of Farnham's top aides and several of Lise's; some I had names for if I stopped to think about it, but for the most part I knew only those I actually dealt with.

I didn't know who'd brought in the extra chairs, but there were plenty to go around. Not all were being used; as Del sat to the console several of us stood near, watching: Annelise, Lennox Farnham, Nancy, Larry Des Palmos, Aguinaldo—and me. Left to right, in that order.

Del had the accelerator already on line; now he brought up the exciter stages, building the convergent fields to operating strength. Here we had no ionization glow, no crackling in the air. A deep hum, yes: power building, but safely out of sight where it belonged, not arcing spectacularly around the premises.

At both ends of the room the chamber drawers were out and their capsules open. On a stand beside Chamber Alpha sat two objects: a red brick and a small tin pail, the latter holding just enough sand to match the brick's mass. On this first attempt we weren't using the water ballast system; the idea was to test one thing at a time.

When the meter readings satisfied Del he said, "Okay, you can load 'er now." Annelise put the brick into Alpha's capsule, closed it and slid the drawer firmly home; at the other end Lennie entrusted the pail of sand to Beta. When both rejoined us, Del looked back and grinned. "Here goes the payroll."

Slowly he advanced the lever energizing the final stage. Movement beside me came as a surprise; Aguinaldo said, "But you haven't—Olin always . . ." He stopped abruptly, wincing, and I saw Larry edge away slightly. Had he stepped on the man's foot?

"Olin always what?" I said. "How would you know?"

"We corresponded." I'd seen no envelopes bearing his name in the project mail bin. "And before—when he demonstrated alpha particle transfer, I saw how he . . ." His voice trailed off.

There was something wrong here, something he wasn't saying, but now the heavy guns went into action. The place vibrated—not with any hinkydink deliberate imbalance but the song of raw power doing its job. It wasn't frightening, just impressive.

Then Del's lever reached its stop and he hit the Go button. Everything bucked. Just a little and only once, but I didn't need to see the capsules opened to know we'd done it.

I did stay and watch, though. The drawers were slid out, the lids raised, and there it was: pail of sand here, brick at the far terminal. No question, no flimflam; I'd seen these chambers built, and what we saw was what we had. Transfer.

Finally and at last I'd seen a singularity device *work*, completely and unequivocally. After the false alarms and disillusionments at Range A, I had a little trouble absorbing the fact. While all around me, everybody went orbital.

Well, nearly everybody. One look, and Larry Des Palmos cut a beeline toward Ops proper. Aguinaldo started after him, but I grabbed a shoulder and swung him back around. "All right, mystery man. You had specs you shouldn't have, you know things you shouldn't know. Just where the hell are you coming from?"

His eyes widened; for a moment I almost had the answer. But he pulled free. "Not this time!" Whatever that meant. Then he was off, hotfooting it into Ops as Des Palmos had done.

I waited until Del powered down before following them, and arrived to see both men, far down the hall, coming out of the side office where Larry had a desk. Aguinaldo was agitated; I heard him say, "Then who *did* you call?"

Zipping up his parka, the smaller man only shook his head and kept walking. Aguinaldo got his own hooded coat from the rack near the main doors, and they left. If they noticed me at all, they didn't let on.

Anything Aguinaldo wanted to know, so did I. After checking the number of Larry's extension I went to Lise's office, sat at her terminal, and brought the outside calls record on-screen. Right; Larry's phone had just spent four minutes forty-two seconds cozied up to a stateside number.

I thought it looked familiar and I was right; Lise's personal directory had it listed. Detweiler Industries.

Well, Larry *was* George's representative, and certainly the Executive President deserved to hear this news.

Out of curiosity I pulled up a listing of calls made to that number. Before Larry's arrival there was one; since then, at least two a day. Busy little bird dog, our Larry.

Maybe there was something to it and maybe not. None of the calls were tagged as being recorded at this end, so for the moment I wasn't likely to find out.

When I told Dauna, she couldn't figure it out either.

Lunch was a blast, though; the celebration filled two long cafeteria tables and Annelise brought champagne. Not a lot, but enough for a couple of glasses all around. It sent us back to work in a fine mood: relaxed, but fired up and alert.

Lennie had set her best materials engineer to analyzing samples from the brick, the sand, and the pail; he reported absolutely no change from his earlier tests, of which this was the first I'd heard. So, basic success demonstrated, we upped our sights. For the first run I'd assured simultaneous triggering by simply making the control leads the same length to each chamber. Now it was time to try my fancy stuff.

To simulate distance I threw a fixed delay network into Beta's Go circuit. To match it with a variable net in the Alpha leads and make sure I had it right, I sent my test pulses out and back over the same route. Round-trip time difference showed on the 'scope; all I had to do was tune the two pips to coincide.

The automatic water ballast system worked, too, once we fixed a leaky coupling in the feed line.

We'd only begun, but the Dutchess had seen enough to hit her own Go button. She already had orders on tap for materials and construction of two new, distant chamber terminals; now she kept the phone warm, authorizing execution of plans. Del and I marked up our specs and materials lists with all the last-minute changes we'd put in, and these she faxed to the chosen sites.

"We'll need someone from here to supervise the tricky parts," she said next morning, "and especially for activation. More than one, probably." Her gaze lingered on Del and me; well, I didn't have much stuff to pack.

For the present, though, back to more cut-and-try. Del and Nancy and I were the team now. Dauna sat in, too; Technical is not her native tongue but she does add a certain spark. Des Palmos hung around until Annelise, maybe fed up with his nicking away at Del, trying to undercut Nancy's obvious preference for the younger man, preempted Larry for desk conference duty. Good.

Aguinaldo looked in twice, staying only long enough to annoy me with the reminder that I still had no answers out of him.

We were checking on possible problem areas. Water ballast had its limits; a high-density transmit mass could weigh considerably more than a capsuleful of water. So to the weight detector we added an alarm circuit; over its limit it vetoed the water and alerted the operator to load in proper return ballast. Or say both ends wish to send, and you need a mass difference but who wants it wet? For that, punch the alarm on manually.

No matter what, we were going to run into awkward operating situations. We'd just have to anticipate what we could and smooth the rest out later.

We swapped pairs of identical weights ranging from ten grams to ten kilos, then a series with slightly unequal masses. It all worked out the way Del and I had figured: over and above standby load, power drain ran linear with mass for exchange of equal weights, and by the square for the amount of any mismatch.

It's nice when the rig itself admits you had it right.

Maybe success caught us unprepared; when the new intercom squawked, shortly before noon the next day, the four of us had run out of agenda and were more or less down to playing games. Two identically set chronometers read the same after one underwent transfer. A lighted candle placed in Chamber Alpha still burned at Beta. In a glass of water a seltzer tablet fizzed its way from one capsule to t'other. A spinning top hadn't fallen over when we retrieved it. We were using up a lot of power, but that's what it was there for.

Del Allert grinned. "What we need is a hamster."

We didn't have one, though. And that's when the intercom came on. "Vanden Huik calling conference. Now."

"Sit down and I'll update." She had steam up; the others at the table held theirs: Farnham serious, Aguinaldo detached as he stuffed papers into his briefcase, Larry displaying the sulks. Lise continued. "Royce Geardon's back and Uncle Fed has him; they're trying to tie us up." She shook her head. "How he got onto us out here, I have no idea. At this point I'm waiting on some legal advice; meanwhile I urge your attention to the feasibility of sending living organisms through the device."

Del Allert muttered, "I *said* we need a hamster."

I don't think Annelise heard him. She said, "More immediately, we are expecting a VIP visit and some of you aren't going to like it. I refer to Mr. George Detweiler, who seems to be very much out of sorts for some reason."

She seemed to be looking at me so I said, "Hell, the man's not speaking to me; what more could I ask?"

As Aguinaldo's face lost all expression, Des Palmos went smug. "He's just pissed because his sister ran off to Canada with somebody. Vancouver, I think."

Oh? I said, "Any names mentioned?"

"Val somebody, is all I heard." Which didn't answer my unasked question, but who said *I* had to know?

Annelise said, "Detweiler's stuck in Anchorage, anyway. Arrived there last night. And there's a storm coming, a big one; it should strike here quite soon. Everything this side of Kodiak is grounded or heading for cover." And had better be.

Except for a couple of minor items, that was it. We broke for lunch; going to and from the cafeteria it was evident that the gusting, erratic winds were building fast. Aguinaldo spotted Haney over by the VTOL and went over to argue with him about something, but Haney put him to work helping secure the aircraft with stakes and guy lines. Down at the foot of the valley, surf rose to cover the boulder-strewn strip of sand and hammer at the cliffs that bracketed the bay. And as the fog thickened, gaining body, visibility lessened by the minute.

With Lise's urging in mind, Del and I didn't go straight back to Ops. Instead we began canvassing the quarters buildings, in search of something to stand in for the hamster we didn't have. So far I hadn't seen any pets around but you never knew.

Of course finding isn't keeping. The man in C-5 hadn't the slightest interest in the glory that could accrue to his parakeet as the first life-form ever to move from point Alpha to point Beta without traversing the distance between. "That little guy isn't no guinea pig! Hey, he talks and all. C'mon, Socrates, tell 'em your limerick. . . ."

I recognized the young man from Racine, but Socrates never got him past the first line.

The dog at E-2 was too big for the capsule. The assistant chef in D-12 couldn't make up her mind; squishing along beside her as she headed for work at the cafeteria, we tried to persuade her that Fluffy the cat could be as big a name as Washoe the chimp.

We got so intent about it that at first we didn't recognize the pulsing whine, close overhead and moving crosswind.

Until, through a thinner patch of fog, we glimpsed the plane.

It wheeled out, low over the bay, then back toward shore, out of our sight below the cliffs. We couldn't see or hear the impact itself, but the splash went up one helluva way.

CHAPTER THIRTY-TWO

We weren't the only ones watching. I don't know how, but by the time Del and I made it down to shore, Haney and Lennie Farnham had the tundra jeep free of its flatbed and jouncing downhill. They pulled up alongside us to stare at the light turboprop amphibian, wings tilted alarmingly and one adroop, grating on surf-covered rocks only a few yards offshore.

Haney jumped down and began pulling wire cable free of the winch. Then he shook his head. "Too heavy. Find me something," and Farnham handed him a coil of lighter rope. He tied one end around his waist and the other to the winch cable, grabbed hold at that knot, and slid down the bank. Then, in water that raged and tumbled, spuming up enough to hide him from view, Haney fought his way to the stranded plane.

Two men emerged to meet him, one bulky in a padded jacket and the other smaller. Then they all hung onto each other while Lennie and the winch pulled them out.

Up the bank and over the edge. The big man was Detweiler; who else? The other one Haney addressed as MacNeer. As George and I recognized each other, I remembered we weren't speaking. So I didn't.

* * *

I didn't move to get in the jeep, either; five in those seats was enough of a crowd. Del did, Detweiler greeting him more or less civilly. Lennie, done rewinding the cable and rope on the winch, gave me a querying look; I waved her on and started walking. So I had a clear objective view of how she screwed up.

They were arguing about something, George in front alongside Farnham while the others shared the back. The wind was up to medium-fierce; coming from behind, it helped me move uphill and carried even the engine noise ahead. Detweiler kept gesturing at the central dip, toward the valley's other side. The grade was easier there; I suppose he thought they could make better time.

Farnham didn't give in right away; she stayed on course nearly two-thirds of the way up. But when she did start across, it was still where at either side the solid ground dropped away steeply beneath deceptive lichen buildup. Slanting uphill, all four wheels pulling traction, I guess the front tires chewed away enough cover that a rear wheel broke through what was left.

I saw the jeep take a sharp tilt and stop cold, its left rear corner sunk to the frame while the right front wheel spun unhampered by any ground contact. I didn't envy whoever had to unstick it and didn't stop to commiserate. I just kept walking.

Until I noticed Del was following; then I waited for him.

Up at Ops we went in and reported to Annelise together. The passenger's identity didn't faze her; oddly, she wanted to know about the plane. All I could tell her was that the twin turboprop amphib looked like a smallish descendant of the old-time Navy PBY by way of a Republic Seabee. Only with sleeker lines.

Hearing the inimitable Detweiler charm coming loudly from down the hall, I ducked out of Lise's office with Del right behind me, heading for his lab. "What happened?" I asked him. "With the jeep, I mean."

Del shrugged. "The man's a juggernaut. Never set foot

here before, knows nothing about the place, but started telling Farnham what to do and yelled her into doing it." He paused. "That surprised me. I didn't think Lennie pushed easily."

"She doesn't." I thought about it. "Getting down alive through this weather, George had adrenaline coming out his ears."

"And Lennie didn't." Then, as if it followed, "I still don't like that man."

"Conformist!" We laughed; I said, "I think Dauna's back at quarters; I'd better go tell her who's arrived."

He showed no signs of shucking his parka. "I'm going to have another try at enshrining Fluffy in the annals of science."

We went out a side entrance, into growing storm and approaching dark, and split up near the cafeteria.

In A-6 I found Dauna, bathrobed, smiling as she pecked at her laptop's keyboard. "Hi. This place *is* surreal. I'm taking a rest on the project itself to set my scene. Weather effects, mood music up. Lighting, that incredible sidewise flash of sun across the tundra, only seconds of it, yesterday morning. Mist, fog, muted sounds, muted colors."

I grinned at her. "Except sometimes louder."

"The wind, yes. I noticed."

"And other things. We have a new development." I told her.

"Howard Hughes junior? It's a wonder he didn't fly the plane himself."

"Owner probably had too much sense to let him. Insurance will cover the plane, I expect. The storm won't spare it."

We made dinner in the kitchenette. Later I said, "I'd better get back to Ops, see if Del had any luck with Fluffy." And explained that part, too. So a few minutes later, well bundled up and crouched against cold, slashing rain, we plodded through blackness to the lights of Operations.

* * *

The side entrance was closest but the path had lumps in it; we brought a certain amount of mud inside with us, to the corridor junction just behind Lise's Admin office. We turned that way to find ourselves a few feet behind George Detweiler and Larry Des Palmos, the latter pointing toward the front entrance. Where, opening the inner door on his way out, I spotted the tall figure of Dr. Aguinaldo.

"Coogan!" Detweiler let out a real roar. And breaking into a lumbering run, "I'll tear your lying head off!"

What the hell? Taking two fast steps I jerked Larry around to face me. "Aguinaldo's the Stork? How can—?"

"The what?"

I'd gone one jump past his savvy. "He's Coogan? How do you know? And how did Detweiler find out?" And while we're at it, how many Mitch Bannings does it take to change a light bulb?

"I told him. Spotted Coogan on the plane coming out; I'd worked longer and closer with him than you ever did." He winked. "Remember I said Detweiler had a handle on me? Conspiracy to defraud: when I blew my guts that time at Range A, the bastard taped me in his pocket. He had me on a leash until the statute runs out. So I traded him Coogan for it. Pretty slick, huh?"

The pimpy grin did it. "Slicker'n a fresh cow pie, Larry. And twice as shitty."

Sprinting for the front doors I yelled back to Dauna, "Roust up some more people. Detweiler's out to kill him!"

At the outer doors I flipped switches until the outside floods came on. Stepping out, my eyes went shut against the wind, but a few steps away from Ops and I was squinting down the valley. The khaki tundra dimmed what light reached that far, and the rain didn't help, but I did spot movement. And the farther downhill I got, the better I could make it out. Holding to an easy trot, I headed toward it.

Them, rather: a tall figure making great dancing strides while behind came a burlier one, legs churning but not closing the distance. The Stork had gone too far downslope; he could be cornered there. Now he turned to head across the valley—but before he reached the treacherous middle he swung to make an arc around and above a sagging area.

Detweiler bellowed; I didn't need the words to catch his drift. Triumph sounded as he plunged straight across to head Coogan off. His course took him into the long shadow cast by the stuck jeep. It didn't bring him back out, though.

All that came from there was a godawful scream.

My first fear, that he'd fallen through to drown in the torrent below, vanished when he kept on yelling. So I slowed, picking my way to a point shortly below the jeep's position. Here the surface had spring to it but felt reasonably strong. I crouched and cupped my hands alongside my eyes, shutting out side illumination to get a glimpse of Detweiler.

All I saw was head and shoulders, the arms stretched flat to either side; the rest of him would be hanging free below, over a clear drop to the rush of spring melt at the ravine's bottom.

He didn't see me; hoping he could hear I yelled, "Detweiler! Shut up and save your strength. I'll try and get a rope to you." Back at the jeep I released the winch brake and began pulling line from its reel. Following the rope came stiffer, heavier cable. Detweiler was behind the jeep and at an angle; the cable made a sharp bend at the heavy bumper. No time to feed it under the jeep; I laid it next to the front tire and hoped its curve would ease the second bend. With a turn of line around one hand I started downhill, pausing at intervals to pull off more cable.

Soon as I could I got off to one side, to firmer ground. When I came even with George's position I could see his face; eyes wide and bulging, mouth gaping as he panted, not even closing it to swallow. He saw me then—not who I was, just somebody there—and gasped, "Give me the rope! Give me—"

"I can't come in there; we'd both go down. I'm going to cross lower down, then head back up and pull the rope tight on you. Don't grab it! The brake's off; you'd just go through."

He tried to argue but I didn't answer; maybe ten feet downhill of him I started across the thin part. Not walking; I lay flat and crawled. On solid ground again, I said, "Okay, now I pull. Just tip your hand up and let the line go under, so we get it in solid under that arm."

For a wonder, he followed orders. Uphill to the limit of my rope I pulled it taut under his other arm, then took my free end over to make a sliding loop around the upper length.

"All right, Detweiler! Now I draw this up to a snug loop. Keep your arms the way they are until the winch has you." I tugged and hauled, until finally the line came taut.

Back at the jeep I started the engine and engaged the winch. At first it pulled fine, but when the slack was gone it bucked once and the cable popped through under the wheel to grate on its supporting strut. The safety clutch smoked, and I heard pings as the strut's sharp edge sawed wire strands. I put the winch brake on, killed the engine, and climbed out again.

Even Arctic pants soak through eventually; cold water seeped along my legs and backside. The parka resisted better, but at wrists and neck the wind drove in wet cold. And after all the crawling and scrambling, my relatively inactive stay in the jeep chilled the sweat I'd worked up. Trying to think what to do next, I couldn't stop shivering.

Halfheartedly I pulled at the cable, but Detweiler was stuck like a champagne cork. Also, he outweighed me a bundle.

By now I saw others out there. But they weren't looking into this patch of shadow and the wind cut across sound. Also, enough manpower to pull George out would break through right along with him.

The situation was bloody hopeless.

* * *

Fifteen minutes later he was out. All it took was tying a new rope at the middle of the cable from Detweiler up to the jeep and taking the loose end over to solid tundra. Then I hailed the first person who came near enough, MacNeer who needed George alive to pay for his busted airplane, and we pulled.

The trick was vectors: pulling sidewise at the middle of a taut line gives you great leverage along its length. Mac and I churned our way maybe twelve feet, the rope stretching a little but the wire cable not at all, and got Detweiler's waistline to the surface. Now he could grab the rope and do some work on his own account. We let him.

As the bullseye lantern came along with Haney behind it, Detweiler stood and squinted a frown at me. "Shit. I was afraid it was you, but I hoped not." Some days are like that, I thought but didn't say. "I swore I'd never speak to you again."

"Sure. When I was thirteen I said the same thing about jerking off. Every day."

He did his best not to laugh. It wasn't good enough.

On the way up, still more out of breath than not, he said, "Vanden Huik said it was you insisted they clear a deal for my interest." When I didn't answer, because he hadn't asked anything, he went on. "Did you? Why?"

I shrugged, but through the parka he probably couldn't notice. "Why not?" What the hell, though: "You had something coming, was all."

"Yeah. Yeah, I did. So hearing that from her, I figured you'd made us even. Now I owe you. I don't like owing you."

No point in saying he'd owed me since prep. "Just live and let live with Coogan, and we're clear." And why the hell should he? "You already did a tax loss on most of his take, to IRS; now you have a prepaid share on top of it. Quit while you're ahead."

"All right then; the bastard's in free."

Except, back at Ops we found that Aguinaldo wasn't in at all. Not in any building on the entire project.

I couldn't seem to stop shivering; Dauna vetoed any idea of my joining the search party. Back in A-6 we shared a hot tub and hot toddies before going to bed early. Over a snack a bit later she called Admin. "No sign at all?" Then, hanging up, "It's not good. They've had to give up."

It took me longer than usual to get to sleep.

Under any ID or none at all, when the Stork did turn up he wasn't popular with those who'd spent several wet and miserable night hours in search of him. Come morning he climbed down from the VTOL where no one had thought to look; having slept well with doors secured and heater on low, he made a wary entrance into the cafeteria. At a table some distance from the door, George Detweiler glared but made no move.

Sitting with Dauna and Nancy, I rose quickly to meet the man of many names, and walked him to the chowline. "Fill your tray, Emil; then we'll talk." He looked nervous, and I didn't mind at all. Why *not* let him sweat a little?

Heading back to the table we met Annelise, not a frequent patron here. She didn't say much, just came along and sat, paying Aguinaldo more attention than he probably liked. We all let him eat, though, before starting any inquisition. I guess I stared; even knowing who he was, I couldn't relate this face to the versions I remembered.

When his tray was empty I said, "Terrific disguise." Part of it I could guess: surgery to straighten and flare the nose, pin the ears in close, change salient contours. And his new hairpiece was top of the line; even at close range it passed. Still, though, "The complexion looks too real for makeup."

"Side effect of a drug; its intended one is harmless to me."

And the acting: voice and posture and gestures. "You had me fooled. But what the hell are you doing here? And why?" After all, he'd left with quite a bundle. And before he could answer, "Where's Tixo? Did you just dump the little guy?"

Not at all; back on the Amazon, Tixo now headed his

tribe. "Both of them, the old chief's sons, were driven out, exiled. In their tribal superstitions, twins are a very evil omen. But when I took him back alone . . ." The Stork spread his hands.

He ran onto bad luck, though, Emil did. Local politicos, as voracious as himself and holding better cards, sniffed out his loot and tied most of it up on fabricated charges; he got away about two jumps ahead of a warrant. "I may recoup legally someday. But the process will be long and costly. Meanwhile . . ." He got wind of the latest singularity venture through an old acquaintance considering a scam on Leigh Ortison. "So I invested in a new identity. While healing, I studied enough of Olin's real work to qualify as special consultant to Mr. Ortison."

He leaned forward. "And I am performing, dear boy. My reports to my employer are exemplary; I earn my salary. And damn all, I need it! So I would appreciate . . ."

"It's out of my hands, uh—Doctor. Des Palmos pegged you and passed word to Detweiler; I can't shut *his* mouth."

"I can," said the Dutchess. "Now, Mr. Whatever your name is, perhaps you can tell me why I should."

It could have been an interesting conversation and probably was, but having run out of coffee, Dauna and Nancy and I had no excuse to hang around. We went into Ops just in time to meet Del Allert coming out of the blockhouse and whooping like a banshee. Draped over one arm, the cat Fluffy just looked bored.

Not that we didn't believe, you understand; we wanted to see, was all. So Del put Fluffy into the Beta capsule because now of course the proper water ballast had moved to the nearer end, and once the field stresses eased down he lifted the pompous little furry guy out of Alpha. That's when the four of us boiled all the way over. And with new cause to celebrate, Nancy and Del got heavy-duty kissy quite shamelessly before a live studio audience. Well, I can't say I hadn't suspected, a little.

A call to the cafeteria gave us word that Lise was gone

from there. Nancy didn't ask about Aguinaldo; reaching the Dutchess's own suite, she rattled off our news. Then, "Yes; all right. The Admin office, in two hours."

Nancy hung up. "She says don't get drunk yet."

We didn't. Over in A-6, Nancy and even Del joined us in toasting Fluffy's dauntless pioneering spirit, each of them nursing a small glass of chablis as our hero licked a shaggy grey forepaw. But that was as far as it went; when the time came we went into Admin considerably soberer than some judges.

The usual gang of suspects was there ahead of us, all being quiet as Annelise began. "Royce Geardon wanted to tie us hand and foot to a major government contingency contract, an exclusive. I may say, the sky isn't exactly the limit."

Dauna has all the intuition in our family. "Little Joe wants to shoot the moon!"

So Lise spilled it; in tough for reelection, our revered president needed to take the public's mind off his record. He talked moon a lot, but the only proposal for getting back up there required space stations orbiting Earth *and* moon, using modified shuttles for the two outer jumps. It looked cheaper than the old Saturn-Vs we'd lost the capacity to build anyway, but multiply fuel-mass ratios by three legs and the Apollo system began to look almost cost-efficient. "But," she said, "if, once a moon base were built, supplies and personnel could move via singularity transfer, he feels he can sell it on the Hill."

So Big Uncle wanted us body, soul, and tired ass, until he found out whether we could do the job. If we could it paid great but we stayed tied; if not they paid research costs at pay scales of their own choosing.

"And what," asked Dauna, "if the fish aren't biting?"

"Injunctions. Such as prohibiting any research on live specimens. Royce is dealing from a full deck of court orders."

"He's a little late with that," said Del.

"True. I asked for a delay until Monday to answer, and your success with the cat has put me in position to move decisively."

She smiled like the tiger in the limerick. "I was already negotiating with several interested parties, limiting the scope to nonliving subjects." Secure transfer between bank vaults, a shipping network for the diamond syndicate; Brinks might be losing a lot of business. The list grew. . . .

"This past two hours, however, I've been closing an option deal for human-sized Allert terminals."

"But we haven't tested on humans," Del put in. "Before we can build adequate gear, Geardon could shut the door on us."

"He could if we did it here," said Annelise. "Hanging out of the fax machine behind me is an overseas contract. Our clients there assure me permission for the research, and I'm having the patents done elsewhere, too. The U.S. has to honor them, and we bypass any chance of Patent Office hanky-panky here."

I'm getting old; I remember when we could trust the gummint.

"So now you tell 'em go fly it?" Big George finally stuck his oar in.

"By no means," she said. "We're definitely interested in the moon project."

"Then why not just take it in the first place?"

As Aguinaldo, the Stork could look every bit as pained as Elihu Coogan ever had. "Because now Ms. Vanden Huik can also pursue other marketing channels. As, indeed, she has done. Even in these times the administration must accept the validity of contracts finalized before it essays to prohibit them."

Well, he'd waited a long time to tell George off.

Annelise stood. "So we have our priorities. First, adapting our chamber and capsule designs, and the supporting hardware, to the scale of human transport. And secondly, to identify and resolve any problem areas that may arise on an Earth-moon link. We . . ."

"Power," said Del Allert. "The accelerator's good for well over a magnitude above what we've been drawing, but those Diesel generators in the powerhouse won't get it halfway there."

"Could they bring a minifusion converter on line?"

"They *and* the accelerator, you mean. Well, yes, but—" The "but" part was where in hell could she get one of *those* experimental breakthrough models. By now, though, he knew her well enough not to ask. We both did.

On the way out I found myself walking alongside Detweiler. My mean streak cut in. "Where's your pal Larry?"

"Counting his severance pay and waiting to fly out when the weather clears." George frowned. "I hate a fink."

By the end of the afternoon Del and I could see that scaling up the design was going to be more work than we'd thought. Nothing tricky, though. For best efficiency, minimum power requirement, the proportions needed changing. Tentatively we set our new ellipsoid's dimensions at seven feet by three by two. Upping the volume by a factor of fourteen and the power load by nearly thirty-four. A real bundle, even if you didn't know how much we were already pulling with the smaller capsules.

And that was the easy end. The hard part, which hit me a little before noon the next day, was that a point on the moon is by no means stationary with respect to a point on Earth.

Or vice versa. So the time delay on the trigger signals wasn't going to stay constant. Well, consider: day-around access meant satellite relay, sometimes more than one leg. Keeping track would be a nightmare; even synchronous comsats "hunt" a bit, from their nominal positions. All told, we could wind up with some pretty nasty timing discrepancies.

Annelise had a party going, including a lot of people I didn't really know. One I did know was our Dr. Aguinaldo who was staking out some inside track, acting almost like a co-host.

That was none of my business; I tried not to waste any time. "Lise? Talk a minute, maybe? Somewhere quiet?"

"My study." Inside a smaller room, this one somehow conveying a more personal touch, we sat. "What's on your mind?"

"We may not be able to do this moon thing." I tried explaining why. "Compensating for unpredictable variations after the fact. If we miss, a bad surge could blow the whole works." As Des Palmos had done with Catcher Two at Range A. "Unless we can work out a safeguard, I can't recommend trying that link."

The Dutchess gave me her prime stare. "You'll manage. Dr. Aguinaldo regards your abilities highly."

"How about his?" My business or not, I was asking. "What's he doing here? Do you have any idea who he really is?"

"He told me, yes. I've hired him away from Ortison. Mitch, the man is a strategic and tactical genius."

"Not to mention his expertise as a con man."

"Well, of course. But if ever he does try to con me, maybe I need the practice. And he does have a unique charm."

She must have read my mind, then. "I've had two marriages—call it two and a half. I don't buy any longer; I only rent."

What can you say? I headed back to the blockhouse.

Time discrepancy sucked juice; bad enough, it could be like a dead short. If it did that, you wouldn't want to be in a transfer capsule; it could wind up holding your ashes.

Synchronism got touchier with distance. I graphed that by adding bigger delays in my test networks. The increase function was by no means high-order. But out to the moon . . .

Del was still game. "All right, we can sic the computer onto statistical analysis. If that doesn't produce, send by multiple paths into an averaging circuit at the far end. We . . ."

"Right." If a complex solution existed, Del would find it. But I had a dim baseless hunch that maybe the answer was simpler. It kept me up all night and was well worth the fatigue.

"All I was trying to do," I said when it was my turn to speak after the banquet, "was calibrate the adverse effect of trigger impulse time lag. And then it struck me that one thing never changed. The transfer itself was always simultaneous because otherwise it couldn't occur at all."

So after I'd had a little sleep, early that blustery Kanaga morning, I went over and told Del how it might work. "We add an auxiliary link, a minichamber and capsule at each end. Time it the best we can but build to handle any overload we could possibly get. And at the instant *that* pair swaps, each end fires a local pulse to trigger the big ones. Automatic sync."

I didn't have to spell that out to this audience; they already knew it. After all, that's how the VIP crowd got there.

And bypassing the three-shuttle grind that brought us out to oversee the installation and train a team to set up the big freight container chambers, that's how Del and I came home.

You can eat a lot more in one-sixth gee than you can digest comfortably back here.